THE S

ANTON TCHEKOV

Edited, with an introduction, by

ROBERT N. LINSCOTT

THE

MODERN LIBRARY

NEW YORK

Random House IS THE PUBLISHER OF

THE MODERN LIBRARY

BENNETT A. CERF · DONALD S. KLOPFER · ROBERT K. HAAS

Manufactured in the United States of America

Printed by Parkway Printing Company   Bound by H. Wolff

THE publishers take pleasure in acknowledging their indebtedness to The Macmillan Company for permission to use the following copyrighted stories: "A Day in the Country," "Kashtanka," "An Inadvertence," "The Doctor," and "A Woman's Kingdom" translated by Constance Garnett, and to Charles Scribner's Sons for their copyrighted story "Dreams" translated by Marian Fell.

CONTENTS

ANTON TCHEKOV

1860–1904

"THE aim of fiction," said Anton Tchekov, in one of his letters, "is absolute and honest truth." In the success with which he achieved this aim, Tchekov is supreme among short story writers. He never deludes his readers with a trick ending, preferring rather to get his effects by revealing new aspects of life in seemingly commonplace situations; unsuspected shades of character in ordinary individuals. He understands his people so completely that every gesture they make is in character and adds to our knowledge of them. As a result, he sets them before the reader with the utmost economy of words, without interposing description or moralizing, and in such a way that we accept their actions as inevitable.

Born at Taganrog, Russia, the son of a poverty-ridden shop-keeper, the grandson of a serf, Tchekov first took up writing in order to support himself while studying to be a doctor, a career which he gradually abandoned as he found fiction and the drama more congenial. He had a healthy ability to take life on its own terms. His gaiety was not crushed by the poverty of his early years, nor by his long, losing struggle with tuberculosis. Success did not corrupt him. Always he fought against stupidity, cruelty, blind conservatism; fought in the shadow of an incurable disease without losing his zest for life; without growing harsh or bitter. Although remaining aloof from politics, he had an acutely practical social conscience. While others talked, he acted. Before the days of the Trans-Siberian Railroad, he journeyed alone all across Asia to Saghalien to investigate conditions in the penal settlement. When Gorki was denied admission to the Russian Academy, he resigned his much-coveted membership in protest. When peasants were dying of the cholera, he laid aside his writing to work among them as a doctor. This same profound integrity is evident in his writing.

The number and excellence of Tchekov's maturer stories precludes a completely satisfying collection within the bounds of a single volume, particularly as some of the best, notably "The Duel," are almost of novel length. Thanks are due to The Macmillan Company for permitting the inclusion of five copyrighted stories—"An Inadvertence," "Kashtanka," "A Day in the Country," "The Doctor," and "A Woman's Kingdom," from their collected edition of Tchekov's works translated by Constance Garnett, and to Charles Scribner's Sons for the right to reprint the copyrighted story, "Dreams," from *Stories of Russian Life* translated by Marian Fell.

ROBERT LINSCOTT.

BOSTON, MASS.
September, 1931

A DAY IN THE COUNTRY

BETWEEN eight and nine o'clock in the morning.

A dark leaden-coloured mass is creeping over the sky towards the sun. Red zigzags of lightning gleam here and there across it. There is a sound of far-away rumbling. A warm wind frolics over the grass, bends the trees, and stirs up the dust. In a minute there will be a spurt of May rain and a real storm will begin.

Fyokla, a little beggar-girl of six, is running through the village, looking for Terenty the cobbler. The white-haired, barefoot child is pale. Her eyes are wide-open, her lips are trembling.

"Uncle, where is Terenty?" she asks every one she meets. No one answers. They are all preoccupied with the approaching storm and take refuge in their huts. At last she meets Silanty Silitch, the sacristan, Terenty's bosom friend. He is coming along, staggering from the wind.

"Uncle, where is Terenty?"

"At the kitchen-gardens," answers Silanty.

The beggar-girl runs behind the huts to the kitchen-gardens and there finds Terenty; the tall old man with a thin, pock-marked face, very long legs, and bare feet, dressed in a woman's tattered jacket, is standing near the vegetable plots, looking with drowsy, drunken eyes at the dark storm-cloud. On his long crane-like legs he sways in the wind like a starling-cote.

"Uncle Terenty!" the white-headed beggar-girl addresses him. "Uncle, darling!"

Terenty bends down to Fyokla, and his grim, drunken face is overspread with a smile, such as come into people's faces when they look at something little, foolish, and absurd, but warmly loved.

"Ah! servant of God, Fyokla," he says, lisping tenderly, "where have you come from?"

"Uncle Terenty," says Fyokla, with a sob, tugging at the lapel of the cobbler's coat. "Brother Danilka has had an accident! Come along!"

"What sort of accident? Ough, what thunder! Holy, holy, holy. . . . What sort of accident?"

"In the count's copse Danilka stuck his hand into a hole in a tree, and he can't get it out. Come along, uncle, do be kind and pull his hand out!"

"How was it he put his hand in? What for?"

"He wanted to get a cuckoo's egg out of the hole for me."

"The day has hardly begun and already you are in trouble. . . ." Terenty shook his head and spat deliberately. "Well, what am I to do with you now? I must come . . . I must, may the wolf gobble you up, you naughty children! Come, little orphan!"

Terenty comes out of the kitchen-garden and, lifting high his long legs, begins striding down the village street. He walks quickly without stopping or looking from side to side, as though he were shoved from behind or afraid of pursuit. Fyokla can hardly keep up with him.

They come out of the village and turn along the dusty road towards the count's copse that lies dark blue in the distance. It is about a mile and a half away. The clouds have by now covered the sun, and soon afterwards there is not a speck of blue left in the sky. It grows dark.

"Holy, holy, holy . . ." whispers Fyokla, hurrying after Terenty. The first rain-drops, big and heavy, lie, dark dots on the dusty road. A big drop falls on Fyokla's cheek and glides like a tear down her chin.

"The rain has begun," mutters the cobbler, kicking up the dust with his bare, bony feet. "That's fine, Fyokla, old girl. The grass and the trees are fed by the rain, as we are by bread. And as for the thunder, don't you be frightened, little orphan. Why should it kill a little thing like you?"

As soon as the rain begins, the wind drops. The only sound is the patter of rain dropping like fine shot on the young rye and the parched road.

"We shall get soaked, Fyokla," mutters Terenty. "There won't be a dry spot left on us. . . . Ho-ho, my girl! It's run down my neck! But don't be frightened, silly. . . . The grass will be dry again, the earth will be dry again, and we shall be dry again. There is the same sun for us all."

A flash of lightning, some fourteen feet long, gleams above their heads. There is a loud peal of thunder, and it seems to Fyokla that something big, heavy, and round is rolling over the sky and tearing it open, exactly over her head.

"Holy, holy, holy . . ." says Terenty, crossing himself. "Don't be afraid, little orphan! It is not from spite that it thunders."

Terenty's and Fyokla's feet are covered with lumps of heavy, wet clay. It is slippery and difficult to walk, but Terenty strides on more and more rapidly. The weak little beggar-girl is breathless and ready to drop.

But at last they go into the count's copse. The washed trees, stirred by a gust of wind, drop a perfect waterfall upon them. Terenty stumbles over stumps and begins to slacken his pace.

"Whereabouts is Danilka?" he asks. "Lead me to him."

Fyokla leads him into a thicket, and, after going a quarter of a mile, points to Danilka. Her brother, a little fellow of eight, with hair as red as ochre and a pale sickly face, stands leaning against a tree, and, with his head on one side, looking sideways at the sky. In one hand he holds his shabby old cap, the other is hidden in an old lime tree. The boy is gazing at the stormy sky, and apparently not thinking of his trouble. Hearing footsteps and seeing the cobbler he gives a sickly smile and says:

"A terrible lot of thunder, Terenty. . . . I've never heard so much thunder in all my life."

"And where is your hand?"

"In the hole. . . Pull it out, please, Terenty!"

The wood had broken at the edge of the hole and jammed Danilka's hand: he could push it farther in, but could not pull it out. Terenty snaps off the broken piece, and the boy's hand, red and crushed, is released.

"It's terrible how it's thundering," the boy says again, rubbing his hand. "What makes it thunder, Terenty?"

"One cloud runs against the other," answers the cobbler. The party come out of the copse, and walk along the edge of it towards the darkened road. The thunder gradually abates, and its rumbling is heard far away beyond the village.

"The ducks flew by here the other day, Terenty," says Danilka, still rubbing his hand. "They must be nesting in the Gniliya Zaimishtcha marshes. . . . Fyokla, would you like me to show you a nightingale's nest?"

"Don't touch it, you might disturb them," says Terenty, wringing the water out of his cap. "The nightingale is a singing-bird, without sin. He has had a voice given him in his throat, to praise God and gladden the heart of man. It's a sin to disturb him."

"What about the sparrow?"

"The sparrow doesn't matter, he's a bad, spiteful bird. He is like a pickpocket in his ways. He doesn't like man to be happy. When Christ was crucified it was the sparrow brought nails to the Jews, and called 'alive! alive!'"

A bright patch of blue appears in the sky.

"Look!" says Terenty. "An ant-heap burst open by the rain! They've been flooded, the rogues!"

They bent over the ant-heap. The downpour has damaged it; the insects are scurrying to and fro in the mud, agitated, and busily trying to carry away their drowned companions.

"You needn't be in such a taking, you won't die of it!" says Terenty, grinning. "As soon as the sun warms you,

you'll come to your senses again. . . . It's a lesson to you, you stupids. You won't settle on low ground another time."

They go on.

"And here are some bees," cries Danilka, pointing to the branch of a young oak tree.

The drenched and chilled bees are huddled together on the branch. There are so many of them that neither bark nor leaf can be seen. Many of them are settled on one another.

"That's a swarm of bees," Terenty informs them. "They were flying looking for a home, and when the rain came down upon them they settled. If a swarm is flying, you need only sprinkle water on them to make them settle. Now if, say, you wanted to take the swarm, you would bend the branch with them into a sack and shake it, and they all fall in."

Little Fyokla suddenly frowns and rubs her neck vigorously. Her brother looks at her neck, and sees a big swelling on it.

"Hey-hey!" laughs the cobbler. "Do you know where you got that from, Fyokla, old girl? There are Spanish flies on some tree in the wood. The rain has trickled off them, and a drop has fallen on your neck—that's what has made the swelling."

The sun appears from behind the clouds and floods the wood, the fields, and the three friends with its warm light. The dark menacing cloud has gone far away and taken the storm with it. The air is warm and fragrant. There is a scent of bird-cherry, meadowsweet, and lilies-of-the-valley.

"That herb is given when your nose bleeds," says Terenty, pointing to a woolly-looking flower. "It does good."

They hear a whistle and a rumble, but not such a rumble as the storm-clouds carried away. A goods train races by before the eyes of Terenty, Danilka, and Fyokla. The engine, panting and puffing out black smoke, drags more than twenty vans after it. Its power is tremendous. The children are interested to know how an engine, not alive and without the help of horses, can move and drag such weights, and Terenty undertakes to explain it to them:

"It's all the steam's doing, children. . . . The steam does the work. . . . You see, it shoves under that thing near the wheels, and it . . . you see . . . it works. . . ."

They cross the railway line, and, going down from the embankment, walk towards the river. They walk not with any object, but just at random, and talk all the way. . . . Danilka asks questions, Terenty answers them. . . .

Terenty answers all his questions, and there is no secret in Nature which baffles him. He knows everything. Thus, for example, he knows the names of all the wild flowers, animals, and stones. He knows what herbs cure diseases, he has no difficulty in telling the age of a horse or a cow. Looking at the sunset, at the moon, or the birds, he can tell what sort of weather it will be next day. And indeed, it is not only Terenty who is so wise. Silanty Silitch, the innkeeper, the market-gardener, the shepherd, and all the villagers, generally speaking, know as much as he does. These people have learned not from books, but in the fields, in the wood, on the river bank. Their teachers have been the birds themselves, when they sang to them, the sun when it left a glow of crimson behind it at setting, the very trees, and wild herbs.

Danilka looks at Terenty and greedily drinks in every word. In spring, before one is weary of the warmth and the monotonous green of the fields, when everything is fresh and full of fragrance, who would not want to hear about the golden may-beetles, about the cranes, about the gurgling streams, and the corn mounting into ear?

The two of them, the cobbler and the orphan, walk about the fields, talk unceasingly, and are not weary. They could wander about the world endlessly. They walk, and in their talk of the beauty of the earth do not notice the frail little beggar-girl tripping after them. She is breathless and moves with a lagging step. There are tears in her eyes; she would be glad to stop these inexhaustible wanderers, but to whom and where can she go? She has no home or people of her own; whether she likes it or not, she must walk and listen to their talk.

Towards midday, all three sit down on the river bank. Danilka takes out of his bag a piece of bread, soaked and reduced to a mash, and they begin to eat. Terenty says a prayer when he has eaten the bread, then stretches himself on the sandy bank and falls asleep. While he is asleep, the boy gazes at the water, pondering. He has many different things to think of. He has just seen the storm, the bees, the ants, the train. Now, before his eyes, fishes are whisking about. Some are two inches long and more, others are no bigger than one's nail. A viper, with its head held high, is swimming from one bank to the other.

Only towards the evening our wanderers return to the village. The children go for the night to a deserted barn, where the corn of the commune used to be kept, while Terenty, leaving them, goes to the tavern. The children lie huddled together on the straw, dozing.

The boy does not sleep. He gazes into the darkness, and it seems to him that he is seeing all that he has seen in the day: the storm-clouds, the bright sunshine, the birds, the fish, lanky Terenty. The number of his impressions, together with exhaustion and hunger, are too much for him; he is as hot as though he were on fire, and tosses from side to side. He longs to tell someone all that is haunting him now in the darkness and agitating his soul, but there is no one to tell. Fyokla is too little and could not understand.

"I'll tell Terenty to-morrow," thinks the boy.

The children fall asleep thinking of the homeless cobbler, and, in the night, Terenty comes to them, makes the sign of the Cross over them, and puts bread under their heads. And no one sees his love. It is seen only by the moon which floats in the sky and peeps caressingly through the holes in the wall of the deserted barn.

OLD AGE

State-Councillor Uzelkov, architect, arrived in his native town, where he had been summoned to restore the cemetery church. He was born in the town, he had grown up and been married there, and yet when he got out of the train he hardly recognised it. Everything was changed. For instance, eighteen years ago, when he left the town to settle in Petersburg, where the railway station is now boys used to hunt for marmots: now as you come into the High Street there is a four storied "Hôtel Vienna," with apartments, where there was of old an ugly grey fence. But not the fence or the houses, or anything had changed so much as the people. Questioning the hall-porter, Uzelkov discovered that more than half of the people he remembered were dead or paupers or forgotten.

"Do you remember Uzelkov?" he asked the porter. "Uzelkov, the architect, who divorced his wife. . . . He had a house in Sviribev Street. . . . Surely you remember."

"No, I don't remember anyone of the name."

"Why, it's impossible not to remember. It was an exciting case. All the cabmen knew, even. Try to remember. His divorce was managed by the attorney, Shapkin, the swindler . . . the notorious sharper, the man who was thrashed at the club. . . ."

"You mean Ivan Nikolaich?"

"Yes. . . . Is he alive? dead?"

"Thank heaven, his honour's alive. His honour's a notary now, with an office. Well-to-do. Two houses in Kirpichny Street. Just lately married his daughter off."

Uzelkov strode from one corner of the room to another.

An idea flashed into his mind. From boredom, he decided to see Shapkin. It was afternoon when he left the hotel and quietly walked to Kirpichny Street. He found Shapkin in his office and hardly recognised him. From the well-built, alert attorney with a quick, impudent, perpetually tipsy expression, Shapkin had become a modest, grey-haired shrunken old man.

"You don't recognise me . . . You have forgotten . . ." Uzelkov began. "I'm your old client, Uzelkov."

"Uzelkov? Which Uzelkov? Ah!"

Remembrance came to Shapkin: he recognised him and was confused. Began exclamations, questions, recollections.

"Never expected . . . never thought . . ." chuckled Shapkin. "What will you have? Would you like champagne? Perhaps you'd like oysters. My dear man, what a lot of money I got out of you in the old days—so much that I can't think what I ought to stand you."

"Please don't trouble," said Uzelkov. "I haven't time. I must go to the cemetery and examine the church. I have a commission."

"Splendid. We'll have something to eat and a drink and go together. I've got some splendid horses! I'll take you there and introduce you to the churchwarden. . . . I'll fix up everything. . . . But what's the matter, my dearest man? You're not avoiding me, not afraid? Please sit nearer. There's nothing to be afraid of now. . . . Long ago, I really was pretty sharp, a bit of a rogue . . . but now I'm quieter than water, humbler than grass. I've grown old; got a family. There are children. . . . Time to die!"

The friends had something to eat and drink, and went in a coach and pair to the cemetery.

"Yes, it was a good time," Shapkin was reminiscent, sitting in the sledge. "I remember, but I simply can't believe it. Do you remember how you divorced your wife? It's almost twenty years ago, and you've probably forgotten everything, but I remember it as though I conducted the petition yesterday. My God, how rotten I was! Then I was a smart, casuistical devil, full of sharp practice and devilry . . . and I used to run into some shady affairs, particularly when there was a good fee, as in your case, for instance. What was it you paid me then? Five—six hundred. Enough to upset anybody! By the time you left for Petersburg you'd left the whole affair completely in my hands. 'Do what you like!' And your former wife, Sofya Mikhailovna, though she did come from a merchant family, was proud and selfish. To bribe her to take the guilt on herself was difficult—extremely difficult. I used to come to her for a business talk, and when she saw me, she would say to her maid: 'Masha, surely I told you I wasn't at home to scoundrels.' I tried one way, then another . . . wrote letters to her, tried to meet her accidentally—no good. I had to work through a third person. For a long time I had trouble with her, and she only yielded when you agreed to give her ten thousand. She succumbed. . . . She began to weep, spat in my face, but she yielded and took the guilt on herself."

"If I remember it was fifteen, not ten thousand she took from me," said Uzlekov.

"Yes, of course . . . fifteen, my mistake." Shapkin was disconcerted. "Anyway it's all past and done with now. Why shouldn't I confess, frankly? Ten I gave to her, and the remaining five I bargained out of you for my own share. I deceived both of you. . . . It's all past, why be ashamed of it? And who else was there to take from, Boris Petrovich, if not from you? I ask you. . . . You were rich and well-to-do. You married in caprice: you were divorced in caprice. You were making a fortune. I remember you got twenty thousand out of a single contract. Whom was I to tap, if not you? And I must confess, I was tortured by envy. If you got hold of a nice lot of money, people would take off their hats to you: but the same people would beat me for shillings and smack my face in the club. But why recall it? It's time to forget."

"Tell me, please, how did Sofya Mikhailovna live afterwards?"

"With her ten thousand? *On ne peut plus* badly. . . . God knows whether it was frenzy or pride and conscience that tortured her, because she had sold herself for money—or perhaps she loved you; but, she took to drink, you know. She received the money and began to gad about with officers in troikas. . . . Drunkenness, philandering, debauchery. . . . She would come into a tavern with an officer, and instead of port or a light wine, she would drink the strongest cognac to drive her into a frenzy."

"Yes, she was eccentric. I suffered enough with her. She would take offence at some trifle and then get nervous. . . . And what happened afterwards?"

"A week passed, a fortnight. . . . I was sitting at home writing. Suddenly, the door opened and she comes in. 'Take your cursed money,' she said and threw the parcel in my face. . . . She could not resist it. . . . Five hundred were missing. She had only got rid of five hundred."

"And what did you do with the money?"

"It's all past and done with. What's the good of concealing it? . . . I certainly took it. What are you staring at me like that for? Wait for the sequel. It's a complete novel, the sickness of a soul! Two months passed by. One night I came home drunk, in a wicked mood. . . . I turned on the light and saw Sofya Mikhailovna sitting on my sofa, drunk too, wandering a bit, with something savage in her face as if she had just escaped from the mad-house. 'Give me my money back,' she said. 'I've changed my mind. If I'm going to the dogs, I want to go madly, passionately. Make haste, you scoundrel, give me the money.' How indecent it was!"

"And you . . . did you give it her?"

"I remember. . . . I gave her ten rubles."

"Oh . . . is it possible?" Uzelkov frowned. "If you couldn't do it yourself, or you didn't want to, you could have written to me. . . . And I didn't know . . . I didn't know."

"My dear man, why should I write, when she wrote herself afterwards when she was in hospital?"

"I was so taken up with the new marriage that I paid no attention to letters. . . . But you were an outsider; you had no antagonism to Sofya Mikhailovna. . . . Why didn't you help her?"

"We can't judge by our present standards, Boris Petrovich. Now we think in this way; but then we thought quite differently. . . . Now I might perhaps give her a thousand rubles; but then even ten rubles . . . she didn't get them for nothing. It's a terrible story. It's time to forget. . . . But here you are!"

The sledge stopped at the churchyard gate. Uzelkov and Shapkin got out of the sledge, went through the gate and walked along a long, broad avenue. The bare cherry trees, the acacias, the grey crosses and monuments sparkled with hoar-frost. In each flake of snow the bright sunny day was reflected. There was the smell you find in all cemeteries of incense and fresh-dug earth.

"You have a beautiful cemetery," said Uzelkov. "It's almost an orchard."

"Yes, but it's a pity the thieves steal the monuments. Look, there, behind that cast-iron memorial, on the right, Sofya Mikhailovna is buried. Would you like to see?"

The friends turned to the right, stepping in deep snow towards the cast-iron memorial.

"Down here," said Shapkin, pointing to a little stone of white marble. "Some subaltern or other put up the monument on her grave."

Uzelkov slowly took off his hat and showed his bald pate to the snow. Eyeing him, Shapkin also took off his hat, and another baldness shone beneath the sun. The silence round about was like the tomb, as though the air were dead, too. The friends looked at the stone, silent, thinking.

"She is asleep!" Shapkin broke the silence. "And she cares

very little that she took the guilt upon herself and drank cognac. Confess, Boris Petrovich!"

"What?" asked Uzelkov, sternly.

"That, however loathsome the past may be, it's better than this." And Shapkin pointed to his grey hairs.

"In the old days I did not even think of death. . . . If I'd met her, I would have circumvented her, but now . . . well, now!"

Sadness took hold of Uzelkov. Suddenly he wanted to cry, passionately, as he once desired to love. . . . And he felt that these tears would be exquisite, refreshing. Moisture came out of his eyes and a lump rose in his throat, but . . . Shapkin was standing by his side, and Uzelkov felt ashamed of his weakness before a witness. He turned back quickly and walked towards the church.

Two hours later, having arranged with the churchwarden and examined the church, he seized the opportunity while Shapkin was talking away to the priest, and ran to shed a tear. He walked to the stone surreptitiously, with stealthy steps, looking round all the time. The little white monument stared at him absently, so sadly and innocently, as though a girl and not a wanton *divorcée* were beneath.

"If I could weep, could weep!" thought Uzelkov.

But the moment for weeping had been lost. Though the old man managed to make his eyes shine, and tried to bring himself to the right pitch, the tears did not flow and the lump did not rise in his throat. . . . After waiting for about ten minutes, Uzelkov waved his arm and went to look for Shapkin.

KASHTANKA

I

MISBEHAVIOUR

A YOUNG dog, a reddish mongrel, between a dachshund and a "yard-dog," very like a fox in face, was running up and down the pavement looking uneasily from side to side. From time to time she stopped and, whining and lifting first one chilled paw and then another, tried to make up her mind how it could have happened that she was lost.

She remembered very well how she had passed the day, and how, in the end, she had found herself on this unfamiliar pavement.

The day had begun by her master Luka Alexandritch's putting on his hat, taking something wooden under his arm wrapped up in a red handkerchief, and calling: "Kashtanka, come along!"

Hearing her name the mongrel had come out from under the work-table, where she slept on the shavings, stretched herself voluptuously and run after her master. The people Luka Alexandritch worked for lived a very long way off, so that, before he could get to any one of them, the carpenter had several times to step into a tavern to fortify himself. Kashtanka remembered that on the way she had behaved extremely improperly. In her delight that she was being taken for a walk she jumped about, dashed barking after the trams, ran into yards, and chased other dogs. The carpenter was continually losing sight of her, stopping, and angrily shouting at her. Once he had even, with an expression of fury in his face, taken her fox-like ear in his fist, smacked her, and said emphatically: "Pla-a-ague take you, you pest!"

After having left the work where it had been bespoken, Luka Alexandritch went into his sister's and there had something to eat and drink; from his sister's he had gone to see a bookbinder he knew; from the bookbinder's to a tavern, from the tavern to another crony's, and so on. In short, by the time Kashtanka found herself on the unfamiliar pavement, it was getting dusk, and the carpenter was as drunk as a cobbler. He was waving his arms and, breathing heavily, muttered:

"In sin my mother bore me! Ah, sins, sins! Here now we are walking along the street and looking at the street lamps, but when we die, we shall burn in a fiery Gehenna. . . ."

Or he fell into a good-natured tone, called Kashtanka to him, and said to her: "You, Kashtanka, are an insect of a creature, and nothing else. Beside a man, you are much the same as a joiner beside a cabinet-maker. . . ."

While he talked to her in that way, there was suddenly a burst of music. Kashtanka looked round and saw that a regiment of soldiers was coming straight towards her. Unable to endure the music, which unhinged her nerves, she turned round and round and wailed. To her great surprise, the carpenter, instead of being frightened, whining and barking, gave a broad grin, drew himself up to attention, and saluted with all his five fingers. Seeing that her master did not protest, Kashtanka whined louder than ever, and dashed across the road to the opposite pavement.

When she recovered herself, the band was not playing and the regiment was no longer there. She ran across the road to the spot where she had left her master, but alas, the carpenter was no longer there. She dashed forward, then back again and ran across the road once more, but the carpenter seemed to have vanished into the earth. Kashtanka began sniffing the pavement, hoping to find her master by the scent of his tracks, but some wretch had been that way just before in new rubber goloshes, and now all delicate scents were mixed with an acute stench of india-rubber, so that it was impossible to make out anything.

Kashtanka ran up and down and did not find her master, and meanwhile it had got dark. The street lamps were lighted on both sides of the road, and lights appeared in the windows. Big, fluffy snowflakes were falling and painting white the pavement, the horses' backs and the cabmen's caps, and the darker the evening grew the whiter were all these objects. Unknown customers kept walking incessantly to and fro, obstructing her field of vision and shoving against her with their feet. (All mankind Kashtanka divided into two uneven parts: masters and customers; between them there was an essential difference: the first had the right to beat her, and the second she had the right to nip by the calves of their legs.) These customers were hurrying off somewhere and paid no attention to her.

When it got quite dark, Kashtanka was overcome by despair and horror. She huddled up in an entrance and began whining piteously. The long day's journeying with Luka Alexandritch had exhausted her, her ears and her paws were freezing, and, what was more, she was terribly hungry. Only twice in the whole day had she tasted a morsel: she had eaten a little paste at the bookbinder's, and in one of the taverns she had found a sausage skin on the floor, near the counter—that was all. If she had been a human being she would have certainly thought: "No, it is impossible to live like this! I must shoot myself!"

II

A MYSTERIOUS STRANGER

But she thought of nothing, she simply whined. When her head and back were entirely plastered over with the soft feathery snow, and she had sunk into a painful doze of exhaustion, all at once the door of the entrance clicked, creaked, and struck her on the side. She jumped up. A man belonging to the class of customers came out. As Kashtanka whined and got under his feet, he could not help noticing her. He bent down to her and asked:

"Doggy, where do you come from? Have I hurt you? Oh, poor thing, poor thing. . . . Come, don't be cross, don't be cross. . . I am sorry."

Kashtanka looked at the stranger through the snow-flakes that hung on her eyelashes. and saw before her a short, fat little man, with a plump. shaven face wearing a top hat and a fur coat that swung open.

"What are you whining for?" he went on, knocking the snow off her back with his fingers. "Where is your master? I suppose you are lost? Ah, poor doggy! What are we going to do now?"

Catching in the stranger's voice a warm, cordial note, Kashtanka licked his hand, and whined still more pitifully.

"Oh, you nice funny thing!" said the stranger. "A regular fox! Well, there's nothing for it, you must come along with me! Perhaps you will be of use for something. . . . Well!"

He clicked with his lips, and made a sign to Kashtanka with his hand, which could only mean one thing: "Come along!" Kashtanka went.

Not more than half an hour later she was sitting on the floor in a big, light room, and, leaning her head against her side, was looking with tenderness and curiosity at the stranger who was sitting at the table, dining. He ate and threw pieces to her. . . . At first he gave her bread and the green rind of cheese, then a piece of meat, half a pie and chicken bones, while through hunger she ate so quickly that she had not time to distinguish the taste, and the more she ate the more acute was the feeling of hunger.

"Your master don't feed you properly," said the stranger, seeing with what ferocious greediness she swallowed the morsels without munching them. "And how thin you are! Nothing but skin and bones. . . ."

Kashtanka ate a great deal and yet did not satisfy her hunger, but was simply stupefied with eating. After dinner she lay down in the middle of the room, stretched her legs and, conscious of an agreeable weariness all over her body, wagged her tail. While her new master, lounging in an easy-chair, smoked a cigar, she wagged her tail and considered the question, whether it was better at the stranger's or at the carpenter's. The stranger's surroundings were poor and ugly; besides the easy-chairs, the sofa, the lamps and the rugs, there was nothing, and the room seemed empty. At the carpenter's the whole place was stuffed full of things: he had a table, a bench, a heap of shavings, planes, chisels, saws, a cage with a goldfinch, a basin. . . . The stranger's room smelt of nothing, while there was always a thick fog in the carpenter's room, and a glorious smell of glue, varnish, and shavings. On the other hand, the stranger had one great superiority—he gave her a great deal to eat and, to do him full justice, when Kashtanka sat facing the table and looking wistfully at him, he did not once hit or kick her, and did not once shout: "Go away, damned brute!"

When he had finished his cigar her new master went out, and a minute later came back holding a little mattress in his hands.

"Hey, you dog, come here!" he said, laying the mattress in the corner near the dog. "Lie down here, go to sleep!"

Then he put out the lamp and went away. Kashtanka lay down on the mattress and shut her eyes; the sound of a bark rose from the street, and she would have liked to answer it, but all at once she was overcome with unexpected melancholy. She thought of Luka Alexandritch, of his son Fedyushka, and her snug little place under the bench. . . . She remembered on the long winter evenings, when the carpenter was planing or reading the paper aloud, Fedyushka usually played with her. . . . He used to pull her from under the bench by her hind legs, and play such tricks with her, that she saw green before her eyes, and ached in every joint. He would make her walk on her hind legs, use her as a bell, that is, shake her violently by the tail so that she squealed and barked, and give her tobacco to sniff. . . . The following trick was particularly agonising: Fedyushka would tie a piece of meat to a thread and give it to Kashtanka, and then, when she had swallowed it he would, with a loud laugh, pull it back again from her stomach, and the more lurid were her memories the more loudly and miserably Kashtanka whined.

But soon exhaustion and warmth prevailed over melancholy. She began to fall asleep. Dogs ran by in her imagination: among them a shaggy old poodle, whom she had seen that day in the street with a white patch on his eye and tufts of wool by his nose. Fedyushka ran after the poodle with a chisel in his hand, then all at once he too was covered with shaggy wool, and began merrily barking beside Kashtanka. Kashtanka and he good-naturedly sniffed each other's noses and merrily ran down the street. . . .

III

NEW AND VERY AGREEABLE ACQUAINTANCES

When Kashtanka woke up it was already light, and a sound rose from the street, such as only comes in the daytime. There was not a soul in the room. Kashtanka stretched, yawned and, cross and ill-humoured, walked about the room. She sniffed the corners and the furniture, looked into the passage and found nothing of interest there. Besides the door that led into the passage there was another door. After thinking a little Kashtanka scratched on it with both paws, opened it, and went into the adjoining room. Here on the bed, covered with a rug, a customer, in whom she recognised the stranger of yesterday, lay asleep.

"Rrrrr . . ." she growled, but recollecting yesterday's dinner, wagged her tail, and began sniffing.

She sniffed the stranger's clothes and boots and thought they smelt of horses. In the bedroom was another door, also closed. Kashtanka scratched at the door, leaned her chest against it, opened it, and was instantly aware of a strange and very suspicious smell. Foreseeing an unpleasant encounter, growling and looking about her, Kashtanka walked into a little room with a dirty wall-paper and drew back in alarm. She saw something surprising and terrible. A grey gander came straight towards her, hissing, with its neck bowed down to the floor and its wings outspread. Not far from him, on a little mattress, lay a white tom-cat; seeing Kashtanka, he jumped up, arched his back, wagged his tail with his hair standing on end and he, too, hissed at her. The dog was frightened in earnest, but not caring to betray her alarm, began barking loudly and dashed at the cat. . . . The cat arched his back more than ever, mewed and gave Kashtanka a smack on the head with his paw. Kashtanka jumped back, squatted on all four paws, and craning her nose towards the cat, went off into loud, shrill barks; meanwhile the gander came up behind and gave her a painful peck in the back. Kashtanka leapt up and dashed at the gander.

"What's this?" They heard a loud angry voice, and the stranger came into the room in his dressing-gown, with a cigar between his teeth. "What's the meaning of this? To your places!"

He went up to the cat, flicked him on his arched back, and said:

"Fyodor Timofeyitch, what's the meaning of this? Have you got up a fight? Ah, you old rascal! Lie down!"

And turning to the gander he shouted: "Ivan Ivanitch, go home!"

The cat obediently lay down on his mattress and closed his eyes. Judging from the expression of his face and whiskers, he was displeased with himself for having lost his temper and got into a fight. Kashtanka began whining resentfully, while the gander craned his neck and began saying something rapidly, excitedly, distinctly, but quite unintelligibly.

"All right, all right," said his master, yawning. "You must live in peace and friendship." He stroked Kashtanka and went on: "And you, red-hair, don't be frightened. . . . They are capital company, they won't annoy you. Stay, what are we to call you? You can't go on without a name, my dear."

The stranger thought a moment and said: "I tell you what . . . you shall be Auntie. . . . Do you understand? Auntie!"

And repeating the word "Auntie" several times he went out. Kashtanka sat down and began watching. The cat sat motionless on his little mattress, and pretended to be asleep. The gander, craning his neck and stamping, went on talking rapidly and excitedly about something. Apparently it was a very clever gander; after every long tirade, he always stepped back with an air of wonder and made a show of being highly delighted with his own speech. . . . Listening to him and answering "R-r-r-r," Kashtanka fell to sniffing the corners. In one of the corners she found a little trough in which she saw some soaked peas and a sop of rye crusts. She tried the peas: they were not nice; she tried the sopped bread and began eating it. The gander was not at all offended that the strange dog was eating his food, but, on the contrary, talked even more excitedly, and to show his confidence went to the trough and ate a few peas himself.

IV

MARVELS ON A HURDLE

A little while afterwards the stranger came in again, and brought a strange thing with him like a hurdle, or like the figure II. On the crosspiece on the top of this roughly made wooden frame hung a bell, and a pistol was also tied to it; there were strings from the tongue of the bell, and the trigger of the pistol. The stranger put the frame in the middle of the room, spent a long time tying and untying something, then looked at the gander and said: "Ivan Ivanitch, if you please!"

The gander went up to him and stood in an expectant attitude.

"Now then," said the stranger, "let us begin at the very beginning. First of all, bow and make a curtsey! Look sharp!"

Ivan Ivanitch craned his neck, nodded in all directions, and scraped with his foot.

"Right. Bravo. . . . Now die!"

The gander lay on his back and stuck his legs in the air. After performing a few more similar, unimportant tricks, the stranger suddenly clutched at his head, and assuming an expression of horror, shouted: "Help! Fire! We are burning!"

Ivan Ivanitch ran to the frame, took the string in his beak, and set the bell ringing.

The stranger was very much pleased. He stroked the gander's neck and said:

"Bravo, Ivan Ivanitch! Now pretend that you are a jeweller selling gold and diamonds. Imagine now that you go to your shop and find thieves there. What would you do in that case?"

The gander took the other string in his beak and pulled it, and at once a deafening report was heard. Kashtanka was highly delighted with the bell ringing, and the shot threw her into so much ecstasy that she ran round the frame barking.

"Auntie, lie down!" cried the stranger; "be quiet!"

Ivan Ivanitch's task was not ended with the shooting. For a whole hour afterwards the stranger drove the gander round him on a cord, cracking a whip, and the gander had to jump over barriers and through hoops; he had to rear, that is, sit on his tail and wave his legs in the air. Kashtanka could not take her eyes off Ivanitch, wriggled with delight, and several times fell to running after him with shrill barks. After exhausting the gander and himself, the stranger wiped the sweat from his brow and cried:

"Marya, fetch Havronya Ivanovna here!"

A minute later there was the sound of grunting. . . . Kashtanka growled, assumed a very valiant air, and to be on the safe side, went nearer to the stranger. The door opened, an old woman looked in, and, saying something, led in a black and very ugly sow. Paying no attention to Kashtanka's growls, the sow lifted up her little hoof and grunted good-humouredly. Apparently it was very agreeable to her to see her master, the cat, and Ivan Ivanitch. When she went up to the cat and gave him a light tap on the stomach with her hoof, and then made some remark to the gander, a great deal of good-nature was expressed in her movements, and the quivering of her tail. Kashtanka realised at once that to growl and bark at such a character was useless.

The master took away the frame and cried: "Fyodor Timofeyitch, if you please!"

The cat stretched lazily, and reluctantly, as though performing a duty, went up to the sow.

"Come, let us begin with the Egyptian pyramid," began the master.

He spent a long time explaining something, then gave the word of command, "One . . two . . three!" At the word "three" Ivan Ivanitch flapped his wings and jumped on to the sow's back. . . . When, balancing himself with his wings and his neck, he got a firm foothold on the bristly back, Fyodor Timofeyitch listlessly and lazily, with manifest disdain, and with an air of scorning his art and not caring a pin for it, climbed on to the sow's back, then reluctantly mounted on to the gander, and stood on his hind legs. The result was what the stranger called the Egyptian pyramid. Kashtanka yapped with delight, but at that moment the old cat yawned and, losing his balance, rolled off the gander. Ivan Ivanitch lurched and fell off too. The stranger shouted, waved his hands, and began explaining something again. After spending an hour over the pyramid their indefatigable master proceeded to teach Ivan Ivanitch to ride on the cat, then began to teach the cat to smoke, and so on.

The lesson ended in the stranger's wiping the sweat off his brow and going away. Fyodor Timofeyitch gave a disdainful sniff, lay down on his mattress, and closed his eyes; Ivan Ivanitch went to the trough, and the pig was taken away by the old woman. Thanks to the number of her new impressions, Kashtanka hardly noticed how the day passed, and in the evening she was installed with her mattress in the room with the dirty wall-paper, and spent the night in the society of Fyodor Timofeyitch and the gander.

V

TALENT! TALENT!

A month passed.

Kashtanka had grown used to having a nice dinner every evening, and being called Auntie. She had grown used to the stranger too, and to her new companions. Life was comfortable and easy.

Every day began in the same way. As a rule, Ivan Ivanitch was the first to wake up, and at once went up to Auntie or to the cat, twisting his neck, and beginning to talk excitedly and persuasively, but, as before, unintelligibly. Sometimes he would crane up his head in the air and utter a long monologue. At first Kashtanka thought he talked so much because he was very clever, but after a little time had passed, she lost all her respect for him; when he went up to her with his long speeches she no longer wagged her tail, but treated him as a tiresome chatterbox, who would not let anyone sleep and, without the slightest ceremony, answered him with "R-r-r-r!"

Fyodor Timofeyitch was a gentleman of a very different

sort. When he woke he did not utter a sound, did not stir, and did not even open his eyes. He would have been glad not to wake, for, as was evident, he was not greatly in love with life. Nothing interested him, he showed an apathetic and nonchalant attitude to everything, he disdained everything and, even while eating his delicious dinner, sniffed contemptuously.

When she woke Kashtanka began walking about the room and sniffing the corners. She and the cat were the only ones allowed to go all over the flat; the gander had not the right to cross the threshold of the room with the dirty wall-paper, and Havronya Ivanovna lived somewhere in a little outhouse in the yard and made her appearance only during the lessons. Their master got up late, and immediately after drinking his tea began teaching them their tricks. Every day the frame, the whip, and the hoop were brought in, and every day almost the same performance took place. The lesson lasted three or four hours, so that sometimes Fyodor Timofeyitch was so tired that he staggered about like a drunken man, and Ivan Ivanitch opened his beak and breathed heavily, while their master became red in the face and could not mop the sweat from his brow fast enough.

The lesson and the dinner made the day very interesting, but the evenings were tedious. As a rule, their master went off somewhere in the evening and took the cat and the gander with him. Left alone, Auntie lay down on her little mattress and began to feel sad. . . .

Melancholy crept on her imperceptibly and took possession of her by degrees, as darkness does of a room. It began with the dog's losing every inclination to bark, to eat, to run about the rooms, and even to look at things; then vague figures, half dogs, half human beings, with countenances attractive, pleasant, but incomprehensible, would appear in her imagination; when they came Auntie wagged her tail, and it seemed to her that she had somewhere, at some time, seen them and loved them. . . . And as she dropped asleep, she always felt that those figures smelt of glue, shavings, and varnish.

When she had grown quite used to her new life, and from a thin, long mongrel, had changed into a sleek, well-groomed dog, her master looked at her one day before the lesson and said:

"It's high time, Auntie, to get to business. You have kicked up your heels in idleness long enough. I want to make an artiste of you. . . . Do you want to be an artiste?"

And he began teaching her various accomplishments. At the first lesson he taught her to stand and walk on her hind legs, which she liked extremely. At the second lesson she had to jump on her hind legs and catch some sugar, which her teacher held high above her head. After that, in the following lessons she danced, ran tied to a cord, howled to music, rang the bell, and fired the pistol, and in a month could successfully replace Fyodor Timofeyitch in the "Egyptian Pyramid." She learned very eagerly and was pleased with her own success; running with her tongue out on the cord, leaping through the hoop, and riding on old Fyodor Timofeyitch, gave her the greatest enjoyment. She accompanied every successful trick with a shrill, delighted bark, while her teacher wondered, was also delighted, and rubbed his hands.

"It's talent! It's talent!" he said. "Unquestionable talent! You will certainly be successful!"

And Auntie grew so used to the word talent, that every time her master pronounced it, she jumped up as if it had been her name.

VI

AN UNEASY NIGHT

Auntie had a doggy dream that a porter ran after her with a broom, and she woke up in a fright.

It was quite dark and very stuffy in the room. The fleas

were biting. Auntie had never been afraid of darkness before, but now, for some reason, she felt frightened and inclined to bark.

Her master heaved a loud sigh in the next room, then soon afterwards the sow grunted in her sty, and then all was still again. When one thinks about eating one's heart grows lighter, and Auntie began thinking how that day she had stolen the leg of chicken from Fyodor Timofeyitch, and had hidden it in the drawing-room, between the cupboard and the wall, where there were a great many spiders' webs and a great deal of dust. Would it not be as well to go now and look whether the chicken leg were still there or not? It was very possible that her master had found it and eaten it. But she must not go out of the room before morning, that was the rule. Auntie shut her eyes to go to sleep as quickly as possible, for she knew by experience that the sooner you go to sleep the sooner the morning comes. But all at once there was a strange scream not far from her which made her start and jump up on all four legs. It was Ivan Ivanitch, and his cry was not babbling and persuasive as usual, but a wild, shrill, unnatural scream, like the squeak of a door opening. Unable to distinguish anything in the darkness, and not understanding what was wrong, Auntie felt still more frightened and growled: "R-r-r-r. . . ."

Some time passed, as long as it takes to eat a good bone; the scream was not repeated. Little by little Auntie's uneasiness passed off and she began to doze. She dreamed of two big black dogs with tufts of last year's coat left on their haunches and sides; they were eating out of a big basin some swill, from which there came a white steam and a most appetising smell; from time to time they looked round at Auntie, showed their teeth and growled: "We are not going to give you any!" But a peasant in a fur-coat ran out of the house and drove them away with a whip; then Auntie went up to the basin and began eating, but as soon as the peasant went out of the gate, the two black dogs rushed at her growling, and all at once there was again a shrill scream.

"K-gee! K-gee-gee!" cried Ivan Ivanitch.

Auntie woke, jumped up and, without leaving her mattress, went off into a yelping bark. It seemed to her that it was not Ivan Ivanitch that was screaming but someone else, and for some reason the sow again grunted in her sty.

Then there was the sound of shuffling slippers, and the master came into the room in his dressing-gown with a candle in his hand. The flickering light danced over the dirty wall-paper and the ceiling, and chased away the darkness. Auntie saw that there was no stranger in the room. Ivan Ivanitch was sitting on the floor and was not asleep. His wings were spread out and his beak was open, and altogether he looked as though he were very tired and thirsty. Old Fyodor Timofeyitch was not asleep either. He, too, must have been awakened by the scream.

"Ivan Ivanitch, what's the matter with you?" the master asked the gander. "Why are you screaming? Are you ill?"

The gander did not answer. The master touched him on the neck, stroked his back, and said: "You are a queer chap. You don't sleep yourself, and you don't let other people. . . ."

When the master went out, carrying the candle with him, there was darkness again. Auntie felt frightened. The gander did not scream, but again she fancied that there was some stranger in the room. What was most dreadful was that this stranger could not be bitten, as he was unseen and had no shape. And for some reason she thought that something very bad would certainly happen that night. Fyodor Timofeyitch was uneasy too. Auntie could hear him shifting on his mattress, yawning and shaking his head.

Somewhere in the street there was a knocking at a gate and the sow grunted in her sty. Auntie began to whine, stretched out her front-paws and laid her head down upon them. She fancied that in the knocking at the gate, in the grunting of the sow, who was for some reason awake, in the darkness and the stillness, there was something as miserable and dreadful as in Ivan Ivanitch's scream. Everything was in agitation and anxiety, but why? Who was the stranger who could not be seen? Then two dim flashes of green gleamed for a minute near Auntie. It was Fyodor Timofeyitch, for the first time of their whole acquaintance coming up to her. What did he want? Auntie licked his paw, and not asking why he had come, howled softly and on various notes.

"K-gee!" cried Ivan Ivanitch, "K-g-ee!"

The door opened again and the master came in with a candle.

The gander was sitting in the same attitude as before, with his beak open, and his wings spread out, his eyes were closed.

"Ivan Ivanitch!" his master called him.

The gander did not stir. His master sat down before him on the floor, looked at him in silence for a minute, and said:

"Ivan Ivanitch, what is it? Are you dying? Oh, I remember now, I remember!" he cried out, and clutched at his head. "I know why it is! It's because the horse stepped on you to-day! My God! My God!"

Auntie did not understand what her master was saying, but she saw from his face that he, too, was expecting something dreadful. She stretched out her head towards the dark window, where it seemed to her some stranger was looking in, and howled.

"He is dying, Auntie!" said her master, and wrung his hands. "Yes, yes, he is dying! Death has come into your room. What are we to do?"

Pale and agitated, the master went back into his room, sighing and shaking his head. Auntie was afraid to remain in the darkness, and followed her master into his bedroom. He sat down on the bed and repeated several times: "My God, what's to be done?"

Auntie walked about round his feet, and not understanding why she was wretched and why they were all so uneasy, and trying to understand, watched every movement he made.

Fyodor Timofeyitch, who rarely left his little mattress, came into the master's bedroom too, and began rubbing himself against his feet. He shook his head as though he wanted to shake painful thoughts out of it, and kept peeping suspiciously under the bed.

The master took a saucer, poured some water from his wash-stand into it, and went to the gander again.

"Drink, Ivan Ivanitch!" he said tenderly, setting the saucer before him: "drink, darling."

But Ivan Ivanitch did not stir and did not open his eyes. His master bent his head down to the saucer and dipped his beak into the water, but the gander did not drink, he spread his wings wider than ever, and his head remained lying in the saucer.

"No, there's nothing to be done now," sighed his master. "It's all over. Ivan Ivanitch is gone!"

And shining drops, such as one sees on the window-pane when it rains, trickled down his cheeks. Not understanding what was the matter, Auntie and Fyodor Timofeyitch snuggled up to him and looked with horror at the gander.

"Poor Ivan Ivanitch!" said the master, sighing mournfully. "And I was dreaming I would take you in the spring into the country, and would walk with you on the green grass. Dear creature, my good comrade, you are no more! How shall I do without you now?"

It seemed to Auntie that the same thing would happen to her, that is, that she too, there was no knowing why, would close her eyes, stretch out her paws, open her mouth, and everyone would look at her with horror. Apparently the same reflections were passing through the brain of Fyodor Timofeyitch. Never before had the old cat been so morose and gloomy.

It began to get light, and the unseen stranger who had so frightened Auntie was no longer in the room. When it was quite daylight, the porter came in, took the gander, and carried him away. And soon afterwards the old woman came in and took away the trough.

Auntie went into the drawing-room and looked behind the cupboard: her master had not eaten the chicken bone, it was lying in its place among the dust and spiders' webs. But Auntie felt sad and dreary and wanted to cry. She did not even sniff at the bone, but went under the sofa, sat down there, and began softly whining in a thin voice.

VII

AN UNSUCCESSFUL DÉBUT

One fine evening the master came into the room with the dirty wall-paper, and, rubbing his hands, said:

"Well. . . ."

He meant to say something more, but went away without saying it. Auntie, who during her lessons had thoroughly studied his face and intonations, divined that he was agitated, anxious and, she fancied, angry. Soon afterwards he came back and said:

"To-day I shall take with me Auntie and Fyodor Timofeyitch. To-day, Auntie, you will take the place of poor Ivan Ivanitch in the 'Egyptian Pyramid.' Goodness knows how it will be! Nothing is ready, nothing has been thoroughly studied, there have been few rehearsals! We shall be disgraced, we shall come to grief!"

Then he went out again, and a minute later, came back in his fur-coat and top hat. Going up to the cat he took him by the fore-paws and put him inside the front of his coat, while Fyodor Timofeyitch appeared completely unconcerned, and did not even trouble to open his eyes. To him it was apparently a matter of absolute indifference whether he remained lying down, or were lifted up by his paws, whether he rested on his mattress or under his master's fur-coat. . . .

"Come along, Auntie," said her master.

Wagging her tail, and understanding nothing, Auntie followed him. A minute later she was sitting in a sledge by her master's feet and heard him, shrinking with cold and anxiety, mutter to himself:

"We shall be disgraced! We shall come to grief!"

The sledge stopped at a big strange-looking house, like a soup-ladle turned upside down. The long entrance to this house, with its three glass doors, was lighted up with a dozen brilliant lamps. The doors opened with a resounding noise and, like jaws, swallowed up the people who were moving to and fro at the entrance. There were a great many people, horses, too, often ran up to the entrance, but no dogs were to be seen.

The master took Auntie in his arms and thrust her in his coat, where Fyodor Timofeyitch already was. It was dark and stuffy there, but warm. For an instant two green sparks flashed at her; it was the cat, who opened his eyes on being disturbed by his neighbour's cold rough paws. Auntie licked his ear, and, trying to settle herself as comfortably as possible, moved uneasily, crushed him under her cold paws, and casually poked her head out from under the coat, but at once growled angrily, and tucked it in again. It seemed to her that she had seen a huge, badly lighted room, full of monsters; from behind screens and gratings, which stretched on both sides of the room, horrible faces looked out: faces of horses with horns, with long ears, and one fat, huge countenance with a tail instead of a nose, and two long gnawed bones sticking out of his mouth.

The cat mewed huskily under Auntie's paws, but at that moment the coat was flung open, the master said, "Hop!" and Fyodor Timofeyitch and Auntie jumped to the floor. They were now in a little room with grey plank walls; there was no other furniture in it but a little table with a looking-glass on it, a stool, and some rags hung about the corners, and instead of a lamp or candles, there was a bright fan-shaped light attached to a little pipe fixed in the wall. Fyodor Timofeyitch licked his coat which had been ruffled by Auntie, went under the stool, and lay down. Their master, still agitated and rubbing his hands, began undressing. . . . He undressed as he usually did at home when he was preparing to get under the rug, that is, took off everything but his underlinen, then he sat down on the stool, and, looking in the looking-glass, began playing the most surprising tricks with himself. . . . First of all he put on his head a wig, with a parting and with two tufts of hair standing up like horns, then he smeared his face thickly with something white, and over the white colour painted his eyebrows, his moustaches, and red on his cheeks. His antics did not end with that. After smearing his face and neck, he began putting himself into an extraordinary and incongruous costume, such as Auntie had never seen before, either in houses or in the street. Imagine very full trousers, made of chintz covered with big flowers, such as is used in working-class houses for curtains and covering furniture, trousers which buttoned up just under his armpits. One trouser leg was made of brown chintz, the other of bright yellow. Almost lost in these, he then put on a short chintz jacket, with a big scalloped collar, and a gold star on the back, stockings of different colours, and green slippers.

Everything seemed going round before Auntie's eyes and in her soul. The white-faced, sack-like figure smelt like her master, its voice, too, was the familiar master's voice, but there were moments when Auntie was tortured by doubts, and then she was ready to run away from the parti-coloured figure and to bark. The new place, the fan-shaped light, the smell, the transformation that had taken place in her master—all this aroused in her a vague dread and a foreboding that she would certainly meet with some horror such as the big face with the tail instead of a nose. And then, somewhere through the wall, some hateful band was playing, and from time to time she heard an incomprehensible roar. Only one thing reassured her—that was the imperturbability of Fyodor Timofeyitch. He dozed with the utmost tranquillity under the stool, and did not open his eyes even when it was moved.

A man in a dress coat and a white waistcoat peeped into the little room and said:

"Miss Arabella has just gone on. After her—you."

Their master made no answer. He drew a small box from under the table, sat down, and waited. From his lips and his hands it could be seen that he was agitated, and Auntie could hear how his breathing came in gasps.

"Monsieur George, come on!" someone shouted behind the door. Their master got up and crossed himself three times, then took the cat from under the stool and put him in the box.

"Come, Auntie," he said softly.

Auntie, who could make nothing out of it, went up to his hands, he kissed her on the head, and put her beside Fyodor Timofeyitch. Then followed darkness. . . . Auntie trampled on the cat, scratched at the walls of the box, and was so frightened that she could not utter a sound, while the box swayed and quivered, as though it were on the waves. . . .

"Here we are again!" her master shouted aloud: "here we are again!"

Auntie felt that after that shout the box struck against something hard and left off swaying. There was a loud deep roar, someone was being slapped, and that someone, probably the monster with the tail instead of a nose, roared and laughed so loud that the locks of the box trembled. In response to the roar, there came a shrill, squeaky laugh from her master, such as he never laughed at home.

"Ha!" he shouted, trying to shout above the roar. "Honoured friends! I have only just come from the station! My granny's kicked the bucket and left me a fortune! There is something very heavy in the box, it must be gold, ha! ha! I bet there's a million here! We'll open it and look. . . ."

The lock of the box clicked. The bright light dazzled Auntie's eyes, she jumped out of the box, and, deafened by the roar, ran quickly round her master, and broke into a shrill bark.

"Ha!" exclaimed her master. "Uncle Fyodor Timofeyitch! Beloved Aunt. dear relations! The devil take you!"

He fell on his stomach on the sand, seized the cat and Auntie, and fell to embracing them. While he held Auntie tight in his arms, she glanced round into the world into which fate had brought her and, impressed by its immensity, was for a minute dumfounded with amazement and delight, then jumped out of her master's arms, and to express the intensity of her emotions, whirled round and round on one spot like a top. This new world was big and full of bright light; wherever she looked, on all sides, from floor to ceiling there were faces, faces, faces, and nothing else.

"Auntie, I beg you to sit down!" shouted her master. Remembering what that meant, Auntie jumped on to a chair, and sat down. She looked at her master. His eyes looked at her gravely and kindly as always, but his face, especially his mouth and teeth, were made grotesque by a broad immovable grin. He laughed, skipped about, twitched his shoulders, and made a show of being very merry in the presence of the thousands of faces. Auntie believed in his merriment, all at once felt all over her that those thousands of faces were looking at her, lifted up her fox-like head, and howled joyously.

"You sit there, Auntie," her master said to her, "while Uncle and I will dance the Kamarinsky."

Fyodor Timofeyitch stood looking about him indifferently, waiting to be made to do something silly. He danced listlessly, carelessly, sullenly, and one could see from his movements, his tail and his ears, that he had a profound contempt for the crowd, the bright light, his master and himself. When he had performed his allotted task, he gave a yawn and sat down.

"Now, Auntie!" said her master, "we'll have first a song, and then a dance, shall we?"

He took a pipe out of his pocket, and began playing.

Auntie, who could not endure music, began moving uneasily in her chair and howled. A roar of applause rose from all sides. Her master bowed, and when all was still again, went on playing. . . . Just as he took one very high note, someone high up among the audience uttered a loud exclamation:

"Auntie!" cried a child's voice, "why, it's Kashtanka!"

"Kashtanka it is!" declared a cracked drunken tenor. "Kashtanka! Strike me dead, Fedyushka, it is Kashtanka. Kashtanka! here!"

Someone in the gallery gave a whistle, and two voices, one a boy's and one a man's, called loudly: "Kashtanka! Kashtanka!"

Auntie started, and looked where the shouting came from. Two faces, one hairy, drunken and grinning, the other chubby, rosy-cheeked and frightened-looking, dazed her eyes as the bright light had dazed them before. . . . She remembered, fell off the chair, struggled on the sand, then jumped up, and with a delighted yap dashed towards those faces. There was a deafening roar, interspersed with whistles and a shrill childish shout: "Kashtanka! Kashtanka!"

Auntie leaped over the barrier, then across someone's shoulders. She found herself in a box: to get into the next tier she had to leap over a high wall. Auntie jumped, but did not jump high enough, and slipped back down the wall. Then she was passed from hand to hand, licked hands and faces, kept mounting higher and higher, and at last got into the gallery. . . .

Half an hour afterwards, Kashtanka was in the street, following the people who smelt of glue and varnish. Luka Alexandritch staggered and instinctively, taught by experience, tried to keep as far from the gutter as possible.

"In sin my mother bore me," he muttered. "And you, Kashtanka, are a thing of little understanding. Beside a man, you are like a joiner beside a cabinetmaker."

Fedyushka walked beside him, wearing his father's cap.

Kashtanka looked at their backs, and it seemed to her that she had been following them for ages, and was glad that there had not been a break for a minute in her life.

She remembered the little room with dirty wall-paper, the gander, Fyodor Timofeyitch, the delicious dinners, the lessons, the circus, but all that seemed to her now like a long, tangled oppressive dream.

ENEMIES

About ten o'clock of a dark September evening the Zemstvo doctor Kirilov's only son, six-year-old Andrey, died of diphtheria. As the doctor's wife dropped on to her knees before the dead child's cot and the first paroxysm of despair took hold of her, the bell rang sharply in the hall.

When the diphtheria came all the servants were sent away from the house, that very morning. Kirilov himself went to the door, just as he was, in his shirt-sleeves with his waistcoat unbuttoned, without wiping his wet face or hands, which had been burnt with carbolic acid. It was dark in the hall, and of the person who entered could be distinguished only his middle height, a white scarf and a big, extraordinarily pale face, so pale that it seemed as though its appearance made the hall brighter. . . .

"Is the doctor in?" the visitor asked abruptly.

"I'm at home," answered Kirilov. "What do you want?"

"Oh, you're the doctor? I'm so glad!" The visitor was overjoyed and began to seek for the doctor's hand in the darkness. He found it and squeezed it hard in his own. "I'm very . . . very glad! We were introduced. . . . I am Aboguin . . . had the pleasure of meeting you this summer at Mr. Gnouchev's. I am very glad to have found you at home. . . . For God's sake, don't say you won't come with me immediately. . . . My wife has been taken dangerously ill . . . I have the carriage with me. . . ."

From the visitor's voice and movements it was evident that he had been in a state of violent agitation. Exactly as though he had been frightened by a fire or a mad dog, he could hardly restrain his hurried breathing, and he spoke quickly in a trembling voice. In his speech there sounded a note of real sincerity, of childish fright. Like all men who are frightened and dazed, he spoke in short, abrupt phrases and uttered many superfluous, quite unnecessary, words.

"I was afraid I shouldn't find you at home," he continued. "While I was coming to you I suffered terribly. . . . Dress yourself and let us go, for God's sake. . . . It happened like this, Papchinsky came to me—Alexander Siemionovich, you know him. . . . We were chatting. . . . Then we sat down to tea. Suddenly my wife cries out, presses her hands to her heart, and falls back in her chair. We carried her off to her bed and . . . and I rubbed her forehead with sal-volatile, and splashed her with water. . . . She lies like a corpse. . . . I'm afraid that her heart's failed. . . . Let us go. . . . Her father too died of heart-failure."

Kirilov listened in silence as though he did not understand the Russian language.

When Aboguin once more mentioned Papchinsky and his wife's father, and once more began to seek for the doctor's hand in the darkness, the doctor shook his head and said, drawling each word listlessly:

"Excuse me, but I can't go. . . . Five minutes ago my . . . son died."

"Is that true?" Aboguin whispered, stepping back. "My God, what an awful moment to come! It's a terribly fated day . . . terribly! What a coincidence . . . and it might have been on purpose!"

Aboguin took hold of the door handle and dropped his head in meditation. Evidently he was hesitating, not knowing whether to go away, or to ask the doctor once more.

"Listen," he said eagerly, seizing Kirilov by the sleeve. "I fully understand your state! God knows I'm ashamed to try to hold your attention at such a moment, but what can I do? Think yourself—who can I go to? There isn't another doctor here besides you. For heaven's sake come. I'm not asking for myself. It's not I that's ill!"

Silence began. Kirilov turned his back to Aboguin, stood still for a while and slowly went out of the hall into the drawing-room. To judge by his uncertain, machine-like movement, and by the attentiveness with which he arranged the hanging shade on the unlighted lamp in the drawing-room and consulted a thick book which lay on the table—at such a moment he had neither purpose nor desire, nor did he think of anything, and probably had already forgotten that there was a stranger standing in his hall. The gloom and the quiet of the drawing-room apparently increased his insanity. As he went from the drawing-room to his study he raised his right foot higher than he need, felt with his hands for the door-posts, and then one felt a certain perplexity in his whole figure, as though he had entered a strange house by chance, or for the first time in his life had got drunk, and now was giving himself up in bewilderment to the new sensation. A wide line of light stretched across the bookshelves on one wall of the study; this light, together with the heavy stifling smell of carbolic acid and ether came from the door ajar that led from the study into the bedroom. . . . The doctor sank into a chair before the table; for a while he looked drowsily at the shining books, then rose, and went into the bedroom.

Here, in the bedroom dead quiet reigned. Everything, down to the last trifle, spoke eloquently of the tempest undergone, of weariness, and everything rested. The candle which stood among a close crowd of phials, boxes and jars on the stool and the big lamp on the chest of drawers brightly lit the room. On the bed, by the window, the boy lay open-eyed, with a look of wonder on his face. He did not move, but it seemed that his open eyes became darker and darker every second and sank into his skull. Having laid her hands on his body and hid her face in the folds of the bed-clothes, the mother now was on her knees before the bed. Like the boy she did not move, but how much living movement was felt in the coil of her body and in her hands! She was pressing close to the bed with her whole being, with eager vehemence, as though she were afraid to violate the quiet and comfortable pose which she had found at last for her weary body. Blankets, cloths, basins, splashes on the floor, brushes and spoons scattered everywhere, a white bottle of lime-water, the stifling heavy air itself—everything died away, and as it were plunged into quietude.

The doctor stopped by his wife, thrust his hands into his trouser pockets and bending his head on one side looked fixedly at his son. His face showed indifference; only the drops which glistened on his beard revealed that he had been lately weeping.

The repulsive terror of which we think when we speak of death was absent from the bed-room. In the pervading dumbness, in the mother's pose, in the indifference of the doctor's face was something attractive that touched the heart, the subtle and elusive beauty of human grief, which it will take men long to understand and describe, and only music, it seems, is able to express. Beauty too was felt in the stern stillness. Kirilov and his wife were silent and did not weep, as though they confessed all the poetry of their condition. As once the season of their youth passed away, so now in this boy their right to bear children had passed away, alas! for ever to eternity. The doctor is forty-four years old, already grey and looks like an old man; his faded sick wife is thirty-five. Andrey was not merely the only son but the last.

In contrast to his wife the doctor's nature belonged to those which feel the necessity of movement when their soul is in pain. After standing by his wife for about five minutes, he passed from the bed-room lifting his right foot too high, into a little room half filled with a big broad divan. From there he went to the kitchen. After wandering about the fire-place and the cook's bed, he stooped through a little door and came into the hall.

Here he saw the white scarf and the pale face again.

"At last," sighed Aboguin, seizing the door-handle. "Let us go, please."

The doctor shuddered, glanced at him and remembered.

"Listen. I've told you already that I can't go," he said, livening. "What a strange idea!"

"Doctor, I'm made of flesh and blood, too. I fully understand your condition. I sympathise with you," Aboguin said in an imploring voice, putting his hand to his scarf. "But I am not asking for myself. My wife is dying. If you had heard her cry, if you'd seen her face, you would understand my insistence! My God—and I thought that you'd gone to dress yourself. The time is precious, Doctor! Let us go, I beg of you."

"I can't come," Kirilov said after a pause, and stepped into his drawing-room.

Aboguin followed him and seized him by the sleeve.

"You're in sorrow. I understand. But I'm not asking you to cure a toothache, or to give expert evidence,—but to save a human life." He went on imploring like a beggar. "This life is more than any personal grief. I ask you for courage, for a brave deed—in the name of humanity."

"Humanity cuts both ways," Kirilov said irritably. "In the name of the same humanity I ask you not to take me away. My God, what a strange idea! I can hardly stand on my feet and you frighten me with humanity. I'm not fit for anything now. I won't go for anything. With whom shall I leave my wife? No, no. . . ."

Kirilov flung out his open hands and drew back.

"And . . . and don't ask me," he continued, disturbed. "I'm sorry. . . . Under the Laws, Volume XIII., I'm obliged to go and you have the right to drag me by the neck. . . . Well, drag me, but . . . I'm not fit. . . . I'm not even able to speak. Excuse me."

"It's quite unfair to speak to me in that tone, Doctor," said Aboguin, again taking the doctor by the sleeve. "The thirteenth volume be damned! I have no right to do violence to your will. If you want to, come; if you don't, then God be with you; but it's not to your will that I apply, but to your feelings. A young woman is dying! You say your son died just now. Who could understand my terror better than you?"

Aboguin's voice trembled with agitation. His tremor and his tone were much more convincing than his words. Aboguin was sincere, but it is remarkable that every phrase he used came out stilted, soulless, inopportunely florid, and as it were insulted the atmosphere of the doctor's house and the woman who was dying. He felt it himself, and in his fear of being misunderstood he exerted himself to the utmost to make his voice soft and tender so as to convince by the sincerity of his tone at least, if not by his words. As a rule, however deep and beautiful the words they affect only the unconcerned. They cannot always satisfy those who are happy or distressed because the highest expression of happiness or distress is most often silence. Lovers understand each other best when they are silent, and a fervent passionate speech at the graveside affects only outsiders. To the widow and children it seems cold and trivial.

Kirilov stood still and was silent. When Aboguin uttered some more words on the higher vocation of a doctor, and self-sacrifice, the doctor sternly asked:

"Is it far?"

"Thirteen or fourteen versts. I've got good horses, Doctor. I give you my word of honour that I'll take you there and back in an hour. Only an hour."

The last words impressed the doctor more strongly than the references to humanity or the doctor's vocation. He thought for a while and said with a sigh:

"Well, let us go!"

He went off quickly, with a step that was not sure, to his study and soon after returned in a long coat. Aboguin, delighted, danced impatiently round him, helped him on with his overcoat, and accompanied him out of the house.

Outside it was dark, but brighter than in the hall. Now in the darkness the tall stooping figure of the doctor was clearly visible with the long, narrow beard and the aquiline nose. Besides his pale face Aboguin's big face could now be seen and a little student cap which hardly covered the crown of his head. The scarf showed white only in front, but behind it was hid under his long hair.

"Believe me, I'm able to appreciate your magnanimity," murmured Aboguin, as he helped the doctor to a seat in the carriage. "We'll whirl away. Luke, dear man, drive as fast as you can, do!"

The coachman drove quickly. First appeared a row of bare buildings, which stood along the hospital yard. It was dark everywhere, save that at the end of the yard a bright light from someone's window broke through the garden fence, and three windows in the upper story of the separate house seemed to be paler than the air. Then the carriage drove into dense obscurity where you could smell mushroom damp, and hear the whisper of the trees. The noise of the wheels awoke the rooks who began to stir in the leaves and raised a doleful, bewildered cry as if they knew that the doctor's son was dead and Aboguin's wife ill. Then began to appear separate trees, a shrub. Sternly gleamed the pond. where big black shadows slept. The carriage rolled along over an even plain. Now the cry of the rooks was but faintly heard far away behind. Soon it became completely still.

Almost all the way Kirilov and Aboguin were silent; save that once Aboguin sighed profoundly and murmured:

"It's terrible pain. One never loves his nearest so much as when there is the risk of losing them."

And when the carriage was quietly passing through the river, Kirilov gave a sudden start, as though the dashing of the water frightened him, and he began to move impatiently.

"Let me go," he said in anguish. "I'll come to you later.

I only want to send the attendant to my wife. She is all alone."

Aboguin was silent. The carriage, swaying and rattling against the stones, drove over the sandy bank and went on. Kirilov began to toss about in anguish, and glanced around. Behind the road was visible in the scant light of the stars and the willows that fringed the bank disappearing into the darkness. To the right the plain stretched smooth and boundless as heaven. On it in the distance here and there dim lights were burning, probably on the turf-pits. To the left, parallel with the road stretched a little hill, tufted with tiny shrubs, and on the hill a big half-moon stood motionless, red, slightly veiled with a mist, and surrounded with fine clouds which seemed to be gazing upon it from every side, and guarding it, lest it should disappear.

In all nature one felt something hopeless and sick. Like a fallen woman who sits alone in a dark room trying not to think of her past, the earth languished with reminiscence of spring and summer and waited in apathy for ineluctable winter. Wherever one's glance turned nature showed everywhere like a dark, cold, bottomless pit, whence neither Kirilov nor Aboguin nor the red half-moon could escape. . . .

The nearer the carriage approached the destination the more impatient did Aboguin become. He moved about, jumped up and stared over the driver's shoulder in front of him. And when at last the carriage drew up at the foot of the grand staircase, nicely covered with a striped linen awning and he looked up at the lighted windows of the first floor one could hear his breath trembling.

"If anything happens . . . I shan't survive it," he said, entering the hall with the doctor and slowly rubbing his hands in his agitation. "But I can't hear any noise. That means it's all right so far," he added, listening to the stillness.

No voices or steps were heard in the hall. For all the bright illumination the whole house seemed asleep. Now the doctor and Aboguin who had been in darkness up till now could examine each other. The doctor was tall, with a stoop, slovenly dressed, and his face was plain. There was something unpleasantly sharp, ungracious, and severe in his thick negro lips, his aquiline nose and his faded, indifferent look. His tangled hair, his sunken temples, the early grey in his long thin beard, that showed his shining chin, his pale grey complexion and the slipshod awkwardness of his manners—the hardness of it all suggested to the mind bad times undergone, an unjust lot and weariness of life and men. To look at the hard figure of the man, you could not believe that he had a wife and could weep over his child. Aboguin revealed something different. He was robust, solid and fair-haired, with a big head and large, yet soft, features, exquisitely dressed in the latest fashion. In his carriage, his tight-buttoned coat and his mane of hair you felt something noble and leonine. He walked with his head straight and his chest prominent, he spoke in a pleasant baritone, and in his manner of removing his scarf or arranging his hair there appeared a subtle, almost feminine, elegance. Even his pallor and childish fear as he glanced upwards to the staircase while taking off his coat, did not disturb his carriage or take from the satisfaction, the health and aplomb which his figure breathed.

"There's no one about, nothing I can hear," he said, walking upstairs. "No commotion. May God be good!"

He accompanied the doctor through the hall to a large salon, where a big piano showed dark and a lustre hung in a white cover. Thence they both passed into a small and beautiful drawing-room, very cosy, filled with a pleasant, rosy half-darkness.

"Please sit here a moment, Doctor," said Aboguin, "I . . . I won't be a second. I'll just have a look and tell them."

Kirilov was left alone. The luxury of the drawing-room, the pleasant half-darkness, even his presence in a stranger's unfamiliar house evidently did not move him. He sat in a chair looking at his hands burnt with carbolic acid. He had no more than a glimpse of the bright red lampshade, the 'cello case, and when he looked sideways across the room to where the clock was ticking, he noticed a stuffed wolf, as solid and satisfied as Aboguin himself.

It was still. . . . Somewhere far away in the other rooms someone uttered a loud "Ah!" A glass door, probably a cupboard door, rang, and again everything was still. After five minutes had passed, Kirilov did not look at his hands any more. He raised his eyes to the door through which Aboguin had disappeared.

Aboguin was standing on the threshold, but not the same man as went out. The expression of satisfaction and subtle elegance had disappeared from him. His face and hands, the attitude of his body were distorted with a disgusting expression either of horror or of tormenting physical pain. His nose, lips, moustache, all his features were moving and as it were trying to tear themselves away from his face, but the eyes were as though laughing from pain.

Aboguin took a long heavy step into the middle of the room, stooped, moaned, and shook his fists.

"Deceived!" he cried, emphasising the syllable *cei*. "She deceived me! She's gone! She fell ill and sent me for the doctor only to run away with this fool Papchinsky. My God!"

Aboguin stepped heavily towards the doctor, thrust his white soft fists before his face, and went on wailing, shaking his fists the while.

"She's gone off! She's deceived me! But why this lie? My God, my God! Why this dirty, foul trick, this devilish, serpent's game? What have I done to her? She's gone off."

Tears gushed from his eyes. He turned on his heel and began to pace the drawing-room. Now in his short jacket and his fashionable narrow trousers in which his legs seemed too thin for his body, he was extraordinarily like a lion. Curiosity kindled in the doctor's impassive face. He rose and eyed Aboguin.

"Well, where's the patient?"

"The patient, the patient," cried Aboguin, laughing, weeping, and still shaking his fists. "She's not ill, but accursed. Vile—dastardly. The Devil himself couldn't have planned a fouler trick. She sent me so that she could run away with a fool, an utter clown, an Alphonse! My God, far better she should have died. I'll not bear it. I shall not bear it."

The doctor stood up straight. His eyes began to blink, filled with tears; his thin beard began to move with his jaw right and left.

"What's this?" he asked, looking curiously about. "My child's dead. My wife in anguish, alone in all the house. . . . I can hardly stand on my feet, I haven't slept for three nights . . . and I'm made to play in a vulgar comedy, to play the part of a stage property! I don't . . . I don't understand it!"

Aboguin opened one fist, flung a crumpled note on the floor and trod on it, as upon an insect he wished to crush.

"And I didn't see . . . didn't understand," he said through his set teeth, brandishing one fist round his head, with an expression as though someone had trod on a corn. "I didn't notice how he came to see us every day. I didn't notice that he came in a carriage to-day! What was the carriage for? And I didn't see! Innocent!"

"I don't . . . I don't understand," the doctor murmured. "What's it all mean? It's jeering at a man, laughing at a man's suffering! That's impossible. . . . I've never seen it in my life before!"

With the dull bewilderment of a man who has just begun to understand that someone has bitterly offended him, the doctor shrugged his shoulders, waved his hands and not knowing what to say or do, dropped exhausted into a chair.

"Well, she didn't love me any more. She loved another man. Very well. But why the deceit, why this foul treachery?" Aboguin spoke with tears in his voice. "Why, why? What have I done to you? Listen, Doctor," he said passionately approaching Kirilov. "You were the unwilling witness of my misfortune, and I am not going to hide the truth from you. I swear I loved this woman. I loved her with devotion, like a slave. I sacrificed everything for her. I broke with my family, I gave up the service and my music. I forgave her things I could not have forgiven my mother and sister . . . I never once gave her an angry look . . . I never gave her any cause. Why this lie, then? I do not demand love, but why this abominable deceit? If you don't love any more then speak out honestly, above all when you know what I feel about this matter. . . ."

With tears in his eyes and trembling in all his bones, Aboguin was pouring out his soul to the doctor. He spoke passionately, pressing both hands to his heart. He revealed all the family secrets without hesitation, as though he were glad that these secrets were being torn from his heart. Had he spoken thus for an hour or two and poured out all his soul, he would surely have been easier.

Who can say whether, had the doctor listened and given him friendly sympathy, he would not, as so often happens, have been reconciled to his grief unprotesting, without turning to unprofitable follies? But it happened otherwise. While Aboguin was speaking the offended doctor changed countenance visibly. The indifference and amazement in his face gradually gave way to an expression of bitter outrage, indignation, and anger. His features became still sharper, harder, and more forbidding. When Aboguin put before his eyes the photograph of his young wife, with a pretty, but dry, inexpressive face like a nun's, and asked if it were possible to look at that face and grant that it could express a lie, the doctor suddenly started away, with flashing eyes, and said, coarsely forging out each several word:

"Why do you tell me all this? I do not want to hear! I don't want to," he cried and banged his fist upon the table. "I don't want your trivial vulgar secrets—to Hell with them. You dare not tell me such trivialities. Or do you think I have not yet been insulted enough! That I'm a lackey to whom you can give the last insult? Yes?"

Aboguin drew back from Kirilov and stared at him in surprise.

"Why did you bring me here?" the doctor went on, shaking his beard. "You marry out of high spirits, get angry out of high spirits, and make a melodrama—but where do I come in? What have I got to do with your romances? Leave me alone! Get on with your noble grabbing, parade your humane ideas, play"—the doctor gave a side-glance at the 'cello-case—"the double-bass and the trombone, stuff yourselves like capons, but don't dare to jeer at a real man! If you can't respect him, then you can at least spare him your attentions."

"What does all this mean?" Aboguin asked, blushing.

"It means that it's vile and foul to play with a man! I'm a doctor. You consider doctors and all men who work and don't reek of scent and harlotry, your footmen, your *mauvais tons*. Very well, but no one gave you the right to turn a man who suffers into a property."

"How dare you say that?" Aboguin asked quietly. Again his face began to twist about, this time in visible anger.

"How dare *you* bring me here to listen to trivial rubbish, when you know that I'm in sorrow?" the doctor cried and banged his fists on the table once more. "Who gave you the right to jeer at another's grief?"

"You're mad," cried Aboguin. "You're ungenerous. I too am deeply unhappy and . . . and . . ."

"Unhappy"—the doctor gave a sneering laugh—"don't touch the word, it's got nothing to do with you. Wasters who can't get money on a bill call themselves unhappy too. A capon's unhappy, oppressed with all its superfluous fat. You worthless lot!"

"Sir, you're forgetting yourself," Aboguin gave a piercing scream. "For words like those, people are beaten. Do you understand?"

Aboguin thrust his hand into his side pocket, took out a pocket-book, found two notes and flung them on the table.

"There's your fee," he said, and his nostrils trembled. "You're paid."

"You dare not offer me money," said the doctor, and brushed the notes from the table to the floor. "You don't settle an insult with money."

Aboguin and the doctor stood face to face, heaping each other with undeserved insults. Never in their lives, even in a frenzy, had they said so much that was unjust and cruel and absurd. In both the selfishness of the unhappy is violently manifest. Unhappy men are selfish, wicked, unjust, and less able to understand each other than fools. Unhappiness does not unite people, but separates them; and just where one would imagine that people should be united by the community of grief, there is more injustice and cruelty done than among the comparatively contented.

"Send me home, please," the doctor cried, out of breath.

Aboguin rang the bell violently. Nobody came. He rang once more; then flung the bell angrily to the floor. It struck dully on the carpet and gave out a mournful sound like a death-moan. The footman appeared.

"Where have you been hiding, damn you?" The master sprang upon him with clenched fists. "Where have you been just now? Go away and tell them to send the carriage round for this gentleman, and get the brougham ready for me. Wait," he called out as the footman turned to go. "Not a single traitor remains to-morrow. Pack off all of you! I will engage new ones. . . . Rabble!"

While they waited Aboguin and the doctor were silent. Already the expression of satisfaction and the subtle elegance had returned to the former. He paced the drawing-room, shook his head elegantly and evidently was planning something. His anger was not yet cool, but he tried to make as if he did not notice his enemy. . . . The doctor stood with one hand on the edge of the table, looking at Aboguin with that deep, rather cynical, ugly contempt with which only grief and an unjust lot can look, when they see satiety and elegance before them.

A little later, when the doctor took his seat in the carriage and drove away, his eyes still glanced contemptuously. It was dark. much darker than an hour ago. The red half-moon had now disappeared behind the little hill, and the clouds which watched it lay in dark spots round the stars. The brougham with the red lamps began to rattle on the road and passed the doctor. It was Aboguin on his way to protest, to commit all manner of folly.

All the way the doctor thought not of his wife or Andrey, but only of Aboguin and those who lived in the house he just left. His thoughts were unjust, inhuman, and cruel. He passed sentence on Aboguin, his wife, Papchinsky, and all those who live in rosy semi-darkness and smell of scent. All the way he hated them, and his heart ached with his contempt for them. The conviction he formed about them would last his life long.

Time will pass and Kirilov's sorrow, but this conviction, unjust and unworthy of the human heart, will not pass, but will remain in the doctor's mind until the grave.

ON THE WAY

In the room which the innkeeper, the Cossack Semión Tchistoplui, called "The Traveller,"—meaning thereby, "reserved exclusively for travellers,"—at a big, unpainted table, sat a tall and broad-shouldered man of about forty years of age. With his elbows on the table and his head resting on his hands, he slept. A fragment of a tallow candle, stuck in a pomade jar, illumined his fair hair, his thick, broad nose, his sunburnt cheeks, and the beetling brows that hung over his closed eyes. . . . Taken one by one, all his features—his nose, his cheeks, his eyebrows—were as rude and heavy as the furniture in "The Traveller"; taken together they produced an effect of singular harmony and beauty. Such, indeed, is often the character of the Russian face: the bigger, the sharper the individual features, the softer and more benevolent the whole. The sleeper was dressed as one of good class, in a threadbare jacket bound with new wide braid, a plush waistcoat, and loose black trousers, vanishing in big boots.

On a bench which stretched the whole way round the room slept a girl some eight years of age. She lay upon a foxskin overcoat, and wore a brown dress and long black stockings. Her face was pale, her hair fair, her shoulders narrow, her body slight and frail; but her nose ended in just such an ugly lump as the man's. She slept soundly, and did not seem to feel that the crescent comb which had fallen from her hair was cutting into her cheek.

"The Traveller" had a holiday air. The atmosphere smelt of newly-washed floors; there were no rags on the line which stretched diagonally across the room; and in the ikon corner, casting a red reflection upon the image of St. George the Victory-Bringer, burned a lamp. With a severe and cautious gradation from the divine to the earthly, there stretched from each side of the image a row of gaudily-painted pictures. In the dim light thrown from the lamp and candle-end these pictures seemed to form a continuous belt covered with black patches; but when the tiled stove, wishing to sing in accord with the weather, drew in the blast with a howl, and the logs, as if angered, burst into ruddy flames and roared with rage, rosy patches quivered along the walls; and above the head of the sleeping man might be seen first the faces of seraphim, then the Shah Nasr Edin, and finally a greasy, sunburnt boy, with staring eyes, whispering something into the ear of a girl with a singularly blunt and indifferent face.

The storm howled outside. Something wild and angry, but deeply miserable, whirled round the inn with the fury of a beast, and strove to burst its way in. It banged against the doors, it beat on the windows and roof, it tore the walls, it threatened, it implored, it quieted down, and then with the joyous howl of triumphant treachery it rushed up the stove pipe; but here the logs burst into flame, and the fire, like a chained hound, rose up in rage to meet its enemy. There was a sobbing, a hissing, and an angry roar. In all this might be distinguished both irritated weariness and unsatisfied hate, and the angered impotence of one accustomed to victory.

Enchanted by the wild, inhuman music, "The Traveller" seemed numbed into immobility for ever. But the door creaked on its hinges, and into the inn came the potboy in a new calico shirt. He walked with a limp, twitched his sleepy eyes, snuffed the candle with his fingers, and went out. The bells of the village church of Rogatchi, three hundred yards away, began to strike twelve. It was midnight. The storm played with the sounds as with snowflakes, it chased them to infinite distances, it cut some short and stretched some into long undulating notes; and it smothered others altogether in the universal tumult. But suddenly a chime resounded so loudly through the room that it might have been rung under the window. The girl on the foxskin overcoat started and raised her head. For a moment she gazed vacantly at the black window, then turned her eyes upon Nasr Edin, on whose face the firelight gleamed, and finally looked at the sleeping man.

"Papa!" she cried.

But her father did not move. The girl peevishly twitched her eyebrows, and lay down again with her legs bent under her. A loud yawn sounded outside the door. Again the hinges squeaked, and indistinct voices were heard. Someone entered, shook the snow from his coat, and stamped his feet heavily.

"Who is it?" drawled a female voice.

"Mademoiselle Ilováisky," answered a bass.

Again the door creaked. The storm tore into the cabin and howled. Someone, no doubt the limping boy, went to the door of "The Traveller," coughed respectfully, and raised the latch.

"Come in, please," said the female voice. "It is all quite clean, honey!"

The door flew open. On the threshold appeared a bearded muzhik, dressed in a coachman's caftan, covered with snow from head to foot. He stooped under the weight of a heavy portmanteau. Behind him entered a little female figure, not half his height, faceless and handless, rolled into a shapeless bundle, and covered also with snow. Both coachman and bundle smelt of damp. The candle-flame trembled.

"What nonsense!" cried the bundle angrily. "Of course we can go on! It is only twelve versts more, chiefly wood There is no fear of our losing the way."

"Lose our way or not, it's all the same . . . the horses won't go an inch farther," answered the coachman. "Lord bless you, miss. . . . As if I had done it on purpose!"

"Heavens knows where you've landed me! . . . Hush! there's someone asleep. You may go!"

The coachman shook the caked snow from his shoulders, set down the portmanteau, snuffled, and went out. And the little girl, watching, saw two tiny hands creeping out of the middle of the bundle, stretching upward, and undoing the network of shawls, handkerchiefs, and scarfs. First on the floor fell a heavy shawl, then a hood, and after it a white knitted muffler. Having freed its head, the bundle removed its cloak, and shrivelled suddenly into half its former size. Now it appeared in a long, grey ulster, with immense buttons and yawning pockets. From one pocket it drew a paper parcel. From the other came a bunch of keys, which the bundle put down so incautiously that the sleeping man started and opened his eyes. For a moment he looked around him vacantly, as if not realising where he was, then shook his head, walked to the corner of the room, and sat down. The bundle took off its ulster, again reduced itself by half, drew off its shoes, and also sat down.

It no longer resembled a bundle. It was a woman, a tiny, fragile, brunette of some twenty years of age, thin as a serpent, with a long pale face, and curly hair. Her nose was long and sharp, her chin long and sharp, her eyelashes long; and thanks to a general sharpness the expression of her face was stinging. Dressed in a tight-fitting black gown, with lace on the neck and sleeves, with sharp elbows and long, rosy fingers, she called to mind portraits of English ladies of the middle of the century. The serious, self-centred expression of her face served only to increase the resemblance.

The brunette looked around the room, glanced sidelong at the man and girl, and, shrugging her shoulders, went over and sat at the window. The dark windows trembled in the damp west wind. Outside great flakes of snow, flashing white, darted against the glass, clung to it for a second, and were whirled away by the storm. The wild music grew louder.

There was a long silence. At last the little girl rose suddenly, and, angrily ringing out every word, exclaimed:

"Lord! Lord! How unhappy I am! The most miserable being in the world!"

The man rose, and with a guilty air, ill-suited to his gigantic stature and long beard, went to the bench.

"You're not sleeping, dearie? What do you want?" He spoke in the voice of a man who is excusing himself.

"I don't want anything! My shoulder hurts! You are a wicked man, father, and God will punish you! Wait! You'll see how he'll punish you!"

"I know it's painful, darling . . . but what can I do?" He spoke in the tone employed by husbands when they make excuses to their angry wives. "If your shoulder hurts it is the long journey that is guilty. To-morrow it will be over, then we shall rest, and the pain will stop. . . ."

"To-morrow! To-morrow! . . . Every day you say to-morrow! We shall go on for another twenty days!"

"Listen, friend, I give you my word of honour that this is the last day. I never tell you untruths. If the storm delayed us, that is not my fault."

"I can bear it no longer! I cannot! I cannot!"

Sasha pulled in her leg sharply, and filled the room with a disagreeable whining cry. Her father waved his arm, and looked absent-mindedly at the brunette. The brunette shrugged her shoulders, and walked irresolutely towards Sasha.

"Tell me, dear," she said, "why are you crying? It is very nasty to have a sore shoulder . . . but what can be done?"

"The fact is, mademoiselle," said the man apologetically, "we have had no sleep for two nights, and drove here in a villainous cart. No wonder she is ill and unhappy. A drunken driver . . . the luggage stolen . . . all the time in a snow-storm . . . but what's the good of crying? . . . I, too, am tired out with sleeping in a sitting position, so tired that I feel almost drunk. Listen, Sasha . . . even as they are things are bad enough . . . yet you must cry!"

He turned his head away, waved his arm, and sat down.

"Of course, you mustn't cry!" said the brunette. "Only babies cry. If you are ill, dearie, you must undress and go to sleep. . . . Come, let me undress you!"

With the girl undressed and comforted, silence again took possession of the room. The brunette sat at the window, and looked questioningly at the wall, the ikon, and the stove. Apparently things around seemed very strange to her, the room, the girl with her fat nose and boy's short nightgown, and the girl's father. That strange man sat in the corner, looking vacantly about him like a drunken man, and rubbing his face with his hands. He kept silence, blinked his eyes; and judging from his guilty figure no one would expect that he would be the first to break the silence. Yet it was he who began. He smoothed his trousers, coughed, laughed, and said:

"A comedy, I swear to God! . . . I look around, and can't believe my eyes. Why did destiny bring us to this accursed inn? What did she mean to express by it? But life sometimes makes such a *salto mortale,* that you look and can't believe your eyes. Are you going far, miss?"

"Not very far," answered the brunette. "I was going from home, about twenty versts away, to a farm of ours where my father and brother are staying. I am Mademoiselle Ilováisky, and the farm is Ilováisk. It is twelve versts from this. What disagreeable weather!"

"It could hardly be worse."

The lame potboy entered the room, and stuck a fresh candle end in the pomade jar.

"Get the samovar!" said the man.

"Nobody drinks tea at this hour," grinned the boy. "It is a sin before Mass."

"Don't you mind . . . it is not you that'll burn in hell, but we. . . ."

While they drank their tea the conversation continued. Mdlle. Ilováisky learned that the stranger's name was Grigóri Petróvitch Likharyóff, that he was a brother of Likharyóff, the Marshal of the Nobility in the neighbouring district, that he had himself once been a landed proprietor, but had gone through everything. And in turn Likharyóff learned that his companion was Márya Mikháilovna Ilováisky, that her father had a large estate, and that all the management fell upon her shoulders, as both father and brother were improvident, looked at life through their fingers, and thought of little but greyhounds. . . .

"My father and brother are quite alone on the farm," said Mdlle. Ilováisky, moving her fingers (she had a habit in conversation of moving her fingers before her stinging face, and after every phrase, licking her lips with a pointed tongue); "they are the most helpless creatures on the face of the earth, and can't lift a finger to help themselves. My father is muddleheaded, and my brother every evening tired off his feet. Imagine! . . . who is to get them food after the Fast? Mother is dead, and our servants cannot lay a cloth without my supervision. They will be without proper food, while I spend all night here. It is very funny!"

Mdlle. Ilováisky shrugged her shoulders, sipped her tea, and said:

"There are certain holidays which have a peculiar smell. Easter, Trinity, and Christmas each has its own smell. Even atheists love these holidays. My brother, for instance, says there is no God, but at Easter he is the first to run off to the morning service."

Likharyóff lifted his eyes, turned them on his companion and laughed.

"They say that there is no God," continued Mdlle. Ilováisky, also laughing, "but why then, be so good as to tell me, do all celebrated writers, scholars, and clever men generally, believe at the close of their lives?"

"The man who in youth has not learnt to believe does not believe in old age, be he a thousand times a writer."

Judged by his cough, Likharyóff had a bass voice, but now either from fear of speaking too loud, or from a needless bashfulness, he spoke in a tenor. After a moment's silence, he sighed and continued:

"This is how I understand it. Faith is a quality of the soul. It is the same as talent . . . it is congenital. As far as I can judge from my own case, from those whom I have met in life, from all that I see around me, this congenital faith is inherent in all Russians to an astonishing degree. . . . May I have another cup? . . . Russian life presents itself as a continuous series of faiths and infatuations, but unbelief or negation it has not—if I may so express it—even smelt. That a Russian does not believe in God is merely a way of saying that he believes in something else."

Likharyóff took from Mdlle. Ilováisky another cup of tea, gulped down half of it at once, and continued:

"Let me tell you about myself. In my soul Nature planted exceptional capacity for belief. Half my life have I lived an atheist and a Nihilist, yet never was there a single moment when I did not believe. Natural gifts display themselves generally in early childhood, and my capacity for faith showed itself at a time when I could walk upright underneath the table. My mother used to make us children eat a lot, and when she gave us our meals, she had a habit of saying, 'Eat, children; there's nothing on earth like soup!' I believed this; I ate soup ten times a day, swallowed it like a shark to the point of vomiting and disgust. My nurse used to tell me fairy tales, and I believed in ghosts, in fairies, in wood-demons, in every kind of monster. I remember well! I used to steal corrosive sublimate from father's room, sprinkle it on gingerbread, and leave it in the attic, so that the ghosts might eat it and die. But when I learned to read and to understand what I read, my beliefs got beyond description. I even ran away to America, I joined a gang of robbers, I tried to enter a monastery, I hired boys to torture me for Christ's sake. When I ran away to America I did not go alone, but took with me just such another fool, and I was glad when we froze nearly to death, and when I was flogged. When I ran away to join the robbers, I returned every time with a broken skin. Most untranquil childhood! But when I was sent to school, and learned that the earth goes round the sun, and that white light so far from being white is composed of seven primary colours, my head went round entirely. At home everything seemed hideous, my mother, in the name of Elijah, denying lightning conductors, my father indifferent to the truths I preached. My new enlightenment inspired me! Like a madman I rushed about the house; I preached my truths to the stable boys, I was driven to despair by ignorance, I flamed with hatred against all who saw in white light only white. . . . But this is nonsense. . . . Serious, so to speak, manly infatuations began with me only at college. . . . Have you completed a university course?"

"At Novotcherkask—in the Don Institute."

"But that is not a university course. You can hardly know what this science is. All sciences, whatever they may be, have only one and the same passport, without which they are meaningless—an aspiration to truth! Every one of them—even your wretched pharmacology—has its end, not in profit, not in convenience and advantage to life, but in truth. It is astonishing! When you begin the study of any science you are captivated from the first. I tell you, there is nothing more seductive and gracious, nothing so seizes and overwhelms the human soul, as the beginning of a science. In the first five or six lectures you are exalted by the very brightest hopes—you seem already the master of eternal truth. . . . Well, I gave myself to science passionately, as to a woman loved. I was its slave, and, except it, would recognise no other sun. Day and night, night and day, without unbending my back, I studied. I learnt off formulas by heart; I ruined myself on books; I wept when I saw with my own eyes others exploiting science for personal aims. . . . But I got over my infatuation soon. The fact is, every science has a beginning, but it has no end—it is like a recurring decimal. Zoology discovered thirty-five thousand species of insects; chemistry counts sixty elementary substances. If, as time goes by, you add to these figures ten ciphers, you will be just as far from the end as now, for all contemporary scientific research consists in the multiplication of figures. . . This I began to understand when I myself discovered the thirty-five-thousand-and-first species, and gained no satisfaction. But I had no disillusion to outlive, for a new faith immediately appeared. I thrust myself into Nihilism with its proclamations, its hideous deeds, its tricks of all sorts. I went down to the people; I served as factory-hand; I greased the axles of railway carriages; I turned myself into a bargee. It was while thus wandering all over the face of Russia that I first saw Russian life. I became an impassioned admirer of that life. I loved the Russian people to distraction; I loved and trusted in its God, in its language, in its creations. . . . And so on eternally. . . . In my time I have been a Slavophile, and bored Aksakoff with my letters; and an Ukrainophile, and an archæologist, and a collector of specimens of popular creative art. . . . I have been carried away by ideas, by men, by events, by places. . . . I have been carried away unceasingly. . . . Five years ago I embodied as the negation of property; my latest faith was non-resistance to evil."

Sasha sighed gustily and moved. Likharyóff rose and went over to her.

"Will you have some tea, darling?" he asked tenderly.

"Drink it yourself!" answered Sasha.

"You have lived a varied life," said Márya Mikháilovna. "You have something to remember."

"Yes, yes; it is all very genial when you sit at the tea-table and gossip with a good companion; but you do not ask me what has all this gaiety cost me. With what have I paid for the diversity of my life? You must remember, in the first place, that I did not believe like a German Doctor of Philosophy. I did not live as a hermit, but my every faith bent me as a bow, and tore my body to pieces. Judge for yourself! Once I was as rich as my brother: now I am a beggar. Into this whirlpool of infatuation I cast my own estate, the property of my wife. the money of many others. I am forty-two to-day, with old age staring me in the face. and I am homeless as a dog that has lost his master by night. In my whole life I have never known repose. My soul was in constant torment; I suffered even from my hopes. . . . I have worn myself out with heavy unregulated work; I have suffered deprivation; five times I have been in prison. I have wandered through Archangel and Tobolsk . . . the very memory sickens me. I lived, but in the vortex never felt the process of life. Will you believe it, I never noticed how my wife loved me—when my children were born. What more can I tell you? To all who loved me I brought misfortune. . . . My mother has mourned for me now fifteen years, and my own brothers, who through me have been made to blush, who have been made to bend their backs, whose hearts have been sickened, whose money has been wasted, have grown at last to hate me like poison."

Likharyóff rose and again sat down.

"If I were only unhappy I should be thankful to God," he continued, looking at Mdlle. Ilováisky. "But my personal unhappiness fades away when I remember how often in my infatuations I was ridiculous, far from the truth, unjust, cruel, dangerous! How often with my whole soul have I hated and despised those whom I ought to have loved, and loved whom I ought to have hated! To-day, I believe; I fall down on my face and worship: to-morrow, like a coward, I flee from the gods and friends of yesterday, and silently swallow some scoundrel! God alone knows how many times I have wept with shame for my infatuations! Never in my life have I consciously lied or committed a wrong, yet my conscience is unclean! I cannot even boast that my hands are unstained with blood, for before my own eyes my wife faded to death—worn out by my improvidence. My own wife! . . . Listen; there are now in fashion two opposing opinions of woman. One class measures her skull to prove that she is lower than man, to determine her defects, to justify their own animality. The other would employ all their strength in lifting woman to their own level—that is to say, force her to learn by heart thirty-five thousand species of insects, to talk and write the same nonsense as they themselves talk and write."

Likharyóff's face darkened.

"But I tell you that woman always was and always will be the slave of man!" he said in a bass voice, thumping his fist upon the table. "She is wax—tender, plastic wax—from which man can mould what he will. Lord in heaven! Yet out of some trumpery infatuation for manhood she cuts her hair, forsakes her family, dies in a foreign land. . . . Of all the ideas to which she sacrifices herself not one is feminine! . . . Devoted, unthinking slave! Skulls I have never measured; but this I say from bitter, grievous experience: The proudest, the most independent women—once I had succeeded in communicating to them my inspiration, came after me, unreasoning, asking no questions, obeying my every wish. Of a nun I made a Nihilist, who, as I afterwards learned, killed a gendarme. My wife never forsook me in all my wanderings, and like a weathercock changed her faith as I changed my infatuations."

With excitement Likharyóff jumped up, and walked up and down the room.

"Noble, exalted slavery!" he exclaimed, gesticulating. "In this, in this alone, is hidden the true significance of woman's life. . . . Out of all the vile nonsense which accumulated in my head during my relations with women, one thing, as water from a filter, has come out pure, and that is neither ideas, nor philosophy, nor clever phrases, but this extraordinary submissiveness to fate, this uncommon benevolence, this all-merciful kindness."

Likharyóff clenched his fists, concentrated his eyes upon a single point, and, as if tasting every word, filtered through his clenched teeth:

"This magnanimous endurance, faith to the grave, the poetry of the heart. It is in this . . . yes, it is in this that the meaning of life is found, in this unmurmuring martyrdom, in the tears that soften stone, in the infinite all-forgiving love, which sweeps into the chaos of life in lightness and warmth. . . ."

Márya Mikháilovna rose slowly, took a step towards Likharyóff, and set her eyes piercingly upon his face. By the tears which sparkled on his eyelashes, by the trembling, passionate voice, by the flushed cheeks, she saw at a glance that women were not the accidental theme of his conversation. No, they were the object of his new infatuation, or, as he had put it, of his new belief. For the first time in her life she saw before her a man in the ecstacy of a burning, prophetic faith. Gesticulating—rolling his eyes, he seemed insane and ecstatical; but in the fire of his eyes, in the torrent of his words, in all the movements of his gigantic body, she saw only such beauty, that, herself not knowing what she did, she stood silently before him as if rooted to the ground, and looked with rapture into his face.

"Take my mother, for example!" he said, with an imploring look, stretching out his arms to her. "I poisoned her life, I disgraced in her eyes the race of Likharyóff, I brought her only such evil as is brought by the bitterest foe, and . . . what? My brothers give her odd kopecks for wafers and collections, and she, violating her religious feeling, hoards up those kopecks, and sends them secretly to me! Such deeds as this educate and ennoble the soul more than all your theories, subtle phrases, thirty-five thousand species! . . . But I might give you a thousand instances! Take your own case! Outside storm and darkness, yet through storm and darkness and cold, you drive, fearless, to your father and brother, that their holidays may be warmed by your caresses, although they, it may well be, have forgotten your existence. But wait! The day will come when you will learn to love a man, and you will go after him to the North Pole. . . . You would go!"

"Yes . . . if I loved him."

"You see!" rejoiced Likharyóff, stamping his feet. "Oh, God, how happy I am to have met you here! . . . Such has always been my good fortune . . . everywhere I meet with kind acquaintances. Not a day passes that I do not meet some man for whom I would give my own soul! In this world there are many more good people than evil! Already you and I have spoken frankly and out of the heart, as if we had known one another a thousand years. It is possible for a man to live his own life, to keep silent for ten years, to be reticent with his own wife and friends, and then some day suddenly he meets a cadet in a railway carriage, and reveals to him his whole soul. . . . You . . . I have the honour to see you for the first time, but I have confessed myself as I never did before. Why?"

Likharyóff rubbed his hands and smiled gaily. Then he walked up and down the room and talked again of women. The church bell chimed for the morning service.

"Heavens!" wept Sasha. "He won't let me sleep with his talk!"

"*Akh*, yes!" stammered Likharyóff. "Forgive me, darling. Sleep, sleep. . . . In addition to her, I have two boys," he whispered. "They live with their uncle, but she cannot bear to be a day without her father. . . . Suffers, grumbles, but sticks to me as a fly to honey. . . . But I have been talking nonsense, mademoiselle, and have prevented you also from sleeping. Shall I make your bed?"

Without waiting for an answer, he shook out the wet cloak, and stretched it on the bench with the fur on top, picked up the scattered mufflers and shawls, and rolled the ulster into a pillow—all this silently, with an expression of servile adoration, as though he were dealing not with women's rags, but with fragments of holy vessels. His whole figure seemed to express guilt and confusion, as if in the presence of such a tiny being he were ashamed of his height and strength. . . .

When Mdlle. Ilováisky had lain down he extinguished the candle, and sat on a stool near the stove. . . .

"Yes," he whispered, smoking a thick cigarette, and puffing the smoke into the stove. "Nature has set in every Russian an enquiring mind, a tendency to speculation, and extraordinary capacity for belief; but all these are broken into dust against our improvidence, indolence, and fantastic triviality. . . ."

Márya Mikháilovna looked in astonishment into the darkness, but she could see only the red spot on the ikon, and the quivering glare from the stove on Likharyóff's face. The darkness, the clang of the church bells, the roar of the storm, the limping boy, peevish Sasha and unhappy Likharyóff—all these mingled, fused in one great impression, and the whole of God's world seemed to her fantastic, full of mystery and magical forces. The words of Likharyóff resounded in her ears, and human life seemed to her a lovely, poetical fairy-tale, to which there was no end.

The great impression grew and grew, until it absorbed all consciousness and was transformed into a sweet sleep. Mdlle. Ilováisky slept. But in sleep she continued to see the lamp, and the thick nose with the red light dancing upon it. She was awakened by a cry.

"Papa, dear," tenderly implored a child's voice. "Let us go back to uncle's! There is a Christmas tree. Stepa and Kolya are there!"

"What can I do, darling?" reasoned a soft, male bass. "Try and understand me. . . ."

And to the child's crying was added the man's. The cry of this double misery breaking through the howl of the storm, touched upon the ears of the girl with such soft, human music, that she could not withstand the emotion, and wept also. And she listened as the great black shadow walked across the room, lifted up the fallen shawl and wrapped it round her feet.

Awakened again by a strange roar, she sprang up and looked around her. Through the windows, covered half-way up in snow, gleamed the blue dawn. The room itself was full of a grey twilight, through which she could see the stove, the sleeping girl, and Nasr Edin. The lamp and stove had both gone out. Through the wide-opened door of the room could be seen the public hall of the inn with its tables and benches. A man with a blunt, gipsy face and staring eyes stood in the middle of the room in a pool of melted snow, and held up a stick with a red star on the top. Around him was a throng of boys, immovable as statues, and covered with snow. The light of the star, piercing through its red paper covering, flushed their wet faces. The crowd roared in discord, and out of their roar Mdlle. Ilovásky understood only one quatrain:—

"Hey, boy, bold and fearless,
Take a knife sharp and shiny,
Come, kill and kill the Jew,
The sorrowing son . . ."

At the counter stood Likharyóff, looking with emotion at the singers, and tramping his feet in time. Seeing Márya Mikháilovna he smiled broadly, and entered the room. She also smiled.

"Congratulations!" he said. "I see you have slept well."

Mdlle. Ilováisky looked at him silently, and continued to smile.

After last night's conversation he seemed to her no longer tall and broad-shouldered, but a little man. A big steamer seems small to those who have crossed the ocean.

"It is time for me to go," she said. "I must get ready. Tell me, where are you going to?"

"I? First to Klinushka station, thence to Siergievo, and from Siergievo a drive of forty versts to the coal-mines of a certain General Shashkovsky. My brothers have got me a place as manager. . . . I will dig coal."

"Allow me . . . I know these mines. Shashkovsky is my uncle. But . . . why are you going there?" asked Márya Mikháilovna in surprise.

"As manager. I am to manage the mines."

"I don't understand." She shrugged her shoulders. "You say you are going to these mines. Do you know what that means? Do you know that it is all bare steppe, that there is not a soul near . . . that the tedium is such that you could not live there a single day? The coal is bad, nobody buys it, and my uncle is a maniac, a despot, a bankrupt. . . . He will not even pay your salary."

"It is the same," said Likharyóff indifferently. "Even for the mines, thanks!"

Mdlle. Ilováisky again shrugged her shoulders, and walked up and down the room in agitation.

"I cannot understand, I cannot understand," she said, moving her fingers before her face. "This is inconceivable . . . it is madness Surely you must realise that this . . . it is worse than exile. It is a grave for a living man. Akh, heavens!" she said passionately, approaching Likharyóff and moving her fingers before his smiling face. Her upper lip trembled and her stinging face grew pale. "Imagine it . . . a bare steppe . . . and solitude. Not a soul to say a word to . . . and you . . . infatuated with women! Mines and women!"

Mdlle. Ilováisky seemed ashamed of her warmth, and, turning away from Likharyóff, went over to the window.

"No . . . no . . . you cannot go there!" she said, rubbing her finger down the window-pane.

Not only through her head, but through her whole body ran a feeling that here behind her stood an unhappy, forsaken, perishing man. But he, as if unconscious of his misery, as if he had not wept the night before, looked at her and smiled good-humouredly. It would have been better if he had continued to cry. For a few minutes in agitation she walked up and down the room, and then stopped in the corner and began to think. Likharyóff said something, but she did not hear him. Turning her back to him, she took a credit note from her purse, smoothed it in her hand, and then, looking at him, blushed and thrust it into her pocket.

Outside the inn resounded the coachman's voice. Silently, with a severe, concentrated expression, Mdlle. Ilováisky began to put on her wraps. Likharyóff rolled her up in them, and chattered gaily. But every word caused her intolerable pain. It is not pleasant to listen to the jests of the wretched or dying.

When the transformation of a living woman into a formless bundle was complete, Mdlle. Ilováisky looked for the last time around "The Traveller," stood silent a moment, and then went out slowly. Likharyóff escorted her.

Outside, God alone knows why, the storm still raged. Great clouds of big, soft snowflakes restlessly whirled over the ground, finding no abiding place. Horses, sledge, trees, the bull tethered to the post—all were white, and seemed made of down.

"Well, God bless you!" stammered Likharyóff, as he helped Márya Mikháilovna into the sledge. "Don't think ill of me!"

Mdlle. Ilováisky said nothing. When the sledge started and began to circle round a great snowdrift, she looked at Likharyóff as if she wished to say something. Likharyóff ran up to the sledge, but she said not a word, and only gazed at him through her long eyelashes to which the snowflakes already clung.

Whether it be that his sensitive mind read this glance aright, or whether, as it may have been, that his imagination led him astray, it suddenly struck him that but a little more and this girl would have forgiven him his age, his failures, his misfortunes, and followed him, neither questioning nor reasoning, to the ends of the earth. For a long time he stood as if rooted to the spot, and gazed at the track left by the sledge-runners. The snowflakes settled swiftly on his hair, his beard, his shoulders. But soon the traces of the sledge-runners vanished, and he, covered with snow, began to resemble a white boulder, his eyes all the time continuing to search for something through the clouds of snow.

VANKA

NINE-YEAR-OLD Vanka Jukov, who has been apprentice to the shoemaker Aliakhine for three months, did not go to bed the night before Christmas. He waited till the master and mistress and the assistants had gone out to an early church-service, to procure from his employer's cupboard a small phial of ink and a penholder with a rusty nib; then, spreading a crumpled sheet of paper in front of him, began to write.

Before, however, deciding to make the first letter, he looked furtively at the door and at the window, glanced several times at the sombre ikon, on either side of which stretched shelves full of lasts, and heaved a heart-rending sigh. The sheet of paper was spread on a bench, and he himself was on his knees in front of it.

"Dear Grandfather Constantin Makaritch," he wrote, "I am writing you a letter. I wish you a Happy Christmas and all God's holy best. I have no father or mamenka, you are all I have."

Vanka gave a look towards the window in which shone the reflection of his candle, and vividly pictured to himself his grandfather, Constantin Makaritch, who was night-watchman at Messrs. Jivarevev. He was a small, lean, unusually lively and active old man of sixty-five, always smiling and blear-eyed. All day he slept in the servant's kitchen or trifled with the cooks. At night, enveloped in an ample sheep-skin coat, he strayed round the domain, tapping with his cudgel. Behind him, each hanging its head, walk the old bitch Kashtanka, and Viune, so named because of his black coat and long body, and his resemblance to a loach. Viune is an unusually civil and friendly dog, looking as kindly at a stranger as at his masters, but he is not to be trusted. Beneath his deference and humbleness is hid the most inquisitorial maliciousness. No one better than he knows how to sneak up and take a bite at a leg, to slip into the larder or steal a moujik's chicken. More than once they have nearly broken his hindlegs, twice he has been hung up, every week he is nearly flogged to death, but he recovers from it all.

At this moment, for certain, his grandfather is standing at the gate, blinking his eyes at the bright red windows of the village church, stamping his feet in their high-felt boots, and jesting with the people in the yard; his cudgel will be hanging from his belt, he will be hugging himself with cold, giving a little dry, old man's cough, and at times pinching a servant girl or a cook.

"Won't we take some snuff?" he asks, holding out his snuff-box to the women. The women take a pinch of snuff, and sneeze.

The old man goes into indescribable ecstasies, breaks into loud laughter, and cries:

"Off with it, it will freeze to your nose!"

He gives his snuff also to the dogs. Kashtanka sneezes, twitches her nose, and very offended walks away. Viune deferentially refuses to sniff, and wags his tail. It is glorious weather, not a breath of wind, clear, and frosty; it is a dark night, but the whole village, its white roofs, and streaks of smoke from the chimneys, the trees silvered with hoar-frost, and the snowdrifts, you can see it all. The sky scintillates with bright twinkling stars, and the Milky Way stands out so clearly that it looks as if it had been polished and rubbed over with snow for the holidays. . . .

Vanka sighs, dips his pen in the ink, and continues to write:

"Last night I got a thrashing, the patron dragged me by my hair into the yard, belaboured me with a shoemaker's stirrup, because, while I was rocking their brat in its cradle,

I unfortunately fell asleep. And during the week, my mistress told me to clean a herring, and I began by its tail, so she took the herring and thrust its phiz into my face. The assistants tease me, send me to the tavern for vodka, make me steal the patron's cucumbers, and the patron beats me with whatever is handy. Food there is none; in the morning it's bread, at dinner 'gruel,' and in the evening again bread, as for tea or sour-cabbage soup, the patrons themselves guzzle that. They make me sleep in the vestibule, and when their brat cries I don't sleep at all, but have to rock the cradle. Dear Grandpapa, for Heaven's sake take me away from here, home to our village, I can't bear this any more. . . . I bow to the ground to you, and will pray to God for ever and ever, take me from here or I shall die. . . ."

The corners of Vanka's mouth went down, he rubbed his eyes with his dirty fist, and sobbed.

"I'll grate your tobacco for you," he continued, "I pray to God for you, and if there is anything wrong, then flog me like the grey goat. And if you really think I shan't find work, then I'll ask the manager, for Christ's sake, to let me clean the boots, or I'll go instead of Fedia as underherdsman. Dear Grandpapa, I can't bear this any more, it'll kill me. . . . I wanted to run away to our village, but I have no boots, and I was afraid of the frost. And when I grow up I'll look after you, no one shall harm you, and when you die I'll pray for the repose of your soul, just like I do for mamma Pelagea.

"As for Moscow, it is a large town, there are all gentlemen's houses, lots of horses, no sheep, and the dogs are not vicious. The children don't come round at Christmas with a star, no one is allowed to sing in the choir, and once I saw in a shop window hooks on a line and fishing rods, all for sale, and for every kind of fish, awfully convenient. And there was one hook which would catch a sheat-fish weighing a pound. And there are shops with guns, like the master's, and I am sure they must cost 100 roubles each. And in the meat-shops there are woodcocks, partridges, and hares, but who shot them or where they come from the shopman won't say.

"Dear Grandpapa, and when the masters give a Christmas tree take a golden walnut and hide it in my green box. Ask the young lady, Olga Ignatievna, for it, say it's for Vanka."

Vanka sighed convulsively, and again stared at the window. He remembered that his grandfather always went through the forest to the Christmas tree, and took his grandson with him. What happy times! The frost crackled, his grandfather crackled, and as they both did Vanka did the same. Then before cutting down the Christmas tree his grandfather smoked his pipe, took a long pinch of snuff, and made fun of poor frozen little Vanka. . . . The young fir trees, wrapt in hoar-frost, stand motionless and wait; which of them will die? Suddenly a hare springing from somewhere darts over the snowdrift. . . . His grandfather could not help shouting:

"Catch it, catch it, catch it! Ah, short-tailed devil!"

When the tree was down, his grandfather dragged it to the master's house, and there they set about decorating it. The young lady, Olga Ignatievna, Vanka's great friend, busied herself most about it. When little Vanka's mother, Pelagea, was still alive, and was servant-woman in the house, Olga Ignatievna used to stuff him with sugar-candy, and, having nothing to do, taught him to read, write, count up to one hundred, and even to dance the quadrille. When Pelagea died, they placed the orphan Vanka in the kitchen with his grandfather, and from the kitchen he was sent to Moscow, to Aliakhine, the shoemaker.

"Come quick, dear grandpapa," continued Vanka, "I beseech you for Christ's sake take me from here. Have pity on a poor orphan, for here they all beat me, and I am frightfully hungry, and so bored that I can't tell you, I cry all the time. The other day the patron hit me on the head with a last; I fell to the ground, and only just returned to life. My life is a disaster, worse than any dog's. . . . I send greetings to Aliona, to one-eyed Egor, and the coachman, and don't let anyone have my harmonium. I remain, your grandson, Ivan Jukov, dear grandpapa, do come."

Vanka folded his sheet of paper in four, and put it into an envelope, purchased the night before for a kopeck. He thought a little, dipped the pen into the ink, and wrote the address:

"The village, to my grandfather." He then scratched his head, thought again, and added: "Constantin Makaritch." Pleased at having been able to write without disturbance, he put on his cap, and, omitting his sheep-skin coat, ran out in his shirt-sleeves into the street.

The shopman at the poulterer's, from whom he had inquired the night before, had told him that letters were to be put into post-boxes, and from thence they were conveyed over the whole earth in mail troikas by drunken post-boys and to the sound of bells. Vanka ran to the first post-box and slipped his precious letter into the slit.

An hour afterwards, lulled by hope, he was sleeping soundly. In his dreams he saw a stove, by the stove sat his grandfather with his legs dangling down, barefooted, and reading a letter to the cooks. . . . Around the stove walks Viune wagging his tail. . . .

LA CIGALE

I

To Olga Ivanovna's wedding came all her friends and acquaintances.

"Look at him! Isn't it true there is something in him?" she said to them, nodding towards her husband, as if to justify her marriage to this simple, commonplace, in no way remarkable man.

The bridegroom, Osip Stepanych Dymov, was a doctor, with the rank of Titular Councillor. He worked at two hospitals; in one as supernumerary ordinator; as dissector in the other. At one, from nine in the morning till midday, he received out-patients and worked in the wards; and, finished with this, he took a tram to the second hospital, and dissected bodies. His private practice was small, worth some five hundred rubles a year. That was all. What more could be said of him? On the other hand, Olga Ivanovna, her friends and acquaintances, were by no means ordinary. All were noted for something, and fairly well known; they had names; they were celebrated, or if not celebrated yet, they inspired great hope for the future. A talented actor, clever, modest, a fine gentleman, a master of declamation, who taught Olga Ivanovna to recite; a good-humoured opera-singer who told Olga Ivanovna with a sigh that she was throwing herself away—if she gave up idling and took herself in hand, she would make a famous singer; a few artists, chief of them the genre-ist, animal-, and landscape-painter Riabovsky, handsome, fair-haired, twenty-five, successful at exhibitions who sold his last picture for five hundred rubles—he touched up Olga Ivanovna's *études,* and predicted a future for her; a violoncellist, whose instrument wept, who frankly said that of all the women he knew Olga Ivanovna alone could accompany; a man of letters, young, but already known for his short stories, sketches, and plays. Who else? Yes, Vasily Vasilych, country gentleman, dilettante illustrator and vignettist, with his love of the national epos and his passion for old Russian art—on paper, china, and smoked plates he turned out veritable masterpieces. In such society—artistic, free, and spoiled by fate; and (though delicate and modest) oblivious of doctors save when ill; to whom "Dymov" sounded as impersonal as "Tarasov" or "Sidorov"—in such society, the bridegroom seemed out-of-place, needless, and even insignificant, although he was really a very tall and very broad-shouldered man. His evening dress seemed made for some one else. His beard was like a shopman's. Though it is true that had he been a writer or artist, this beard would have reminded them of Zola.

The artist told Olga Ivanovna that with her flaxen hair and wedding dress she was a graceful cherry-tree covered with tender, white blossoms in spring.

"No, but listen!" replied Olga Ivanovna, seizing his hand. "How suddenly all this happened! Listen, listen! . . . I should tell you that Dymov and my father were at the same hospital. While my poor father was ill, Dymov watched day and night at his bedside. Such self-sacrifice! Listen, Riabovsky! . . . And you, writer, listen—this is very interesting! Come nearer! Such sacrifice of self, such sincere concern! I myself could not sleep at night, and sat at my father's bedside, and suddenly! . . . I captivated the poor young man! My Dymov was up to his neck in love! In truth, things happened strangely. Well, after my father's death we sometimes met in the street; he paid me occasional visits, and one fine evening suddenly—he proposed to me! . . . I cried all night, and myself fell in love with him. And now, you see, I am married. Don't you think there is something in him? Something strong, mighty, leonine! Just now his face is turned three-quarters from us and the light is bad, but when he turns round just look at his forehead! Riabovsky, what do you think of his forehead? Dymov, we are speaking of you." She turned to her husband. "Come here! Give your honest hand to Riabovsky. . . . That's right. Be friends!"

With a simple, kindly smile, Dymov gave his hand to the artist, and said—

"I'm delighted! There was a Riabovsky at college with me. Was he a relation of yours?"

II

Olga Ivanovna was twenty-two years old, Dymov thirty-one. After the marriage they lived well. Olga Ivanovna hung the drawing-room with drawings, her own and her friends', framed and unframed; and about the piano and furniture, arranged in pretty confusion Chinese parasols, easels, many-coloured draperies, poniards, busts, photographs. The dining-room she decked with the bright-coloured oleographs beloved by peasants, bast-shoes and sickles, and these, with the scythe and hay-rake in the corner, made a room in national style. To make her bedroom like a cave, she draped the ceiling and walls with dark cloth, hung a Venetian lantern over the bed, and set near the door a figure with a halberd. And every one agreed that the young couple had a charming flat.

Rising every day at eleven, Olga Ivanovna sat at the piano, or, if the sun shone, painted in oils. At one o'clock she drove to her dressmaker's. As neither she nor Dymov was rich, many ingenious shifts were resorted to to keep her in the new-looking dresses which made such an impression on all. Pieces of old dyed cloth; worthless patches of tulle, lace, plush, and silk, came back from the dressmaker miracles, not dresses but ravishing dreams. Done with the dressmaker, Olga Ivanovna drove to some actress friend to learn theatrical news and get tickets for first-nights or benefits; thence to an artist's studio or picture gallery, ending up with some other celebrity whom she invited to visit her, or simply gossiped to. And those whom she counted celebrities and great men received her as an equal, and told her in one voice that if she did not throw away her opportunities, her talents, taste, and intellect would yield something really great. She sang, played, painted, modelled, acted in amateur theatricals; and did everything well: if she merely made lanterns for illuminations, or dressed herself up, or tied some one's necktie, the result was invariably graceful, artistic, charming. But none of her talents outshone her skill in meeting and getting on terms of intimacy with men of note. Let a man get the least reputation, or even be talked about, and in a single day she had met him, established friendly relations, and invited him to her home. And each new acquaintance was a festival in himself. She worshipped the well-known, was proud of them, and dreamed of them all night. Her thirst was insatiable. The old celebrities departed and were forgotten, and new celebrities replaced them; and to these last she grew accustomed in time; they lost their charm, so that she sought for more.

She dined at home with her husband at five o'clock. She was in ecstasies over his simplicity, common sense, and good humour. She jumped up from her chair, embraced his head, and covered it with kisses.

"You are clever, a noble man, Dymov!" she exclaimed. "You have only one drawback You take no interest in art. You deny music and painting."

"I don't understand them," he answered kindly. "All my life I have studied only science and medicine. I have not time for art."

"But that is awful, Dymov!"

"Why awful? Your friends know nothing of science or medicine, yet you don't blame them for that. To each man his own! I don't understand landscapes or operas, but I look at the matter thus: if talented men devote their lives to such things, and clever men pay vast sums for them, that means they are useful. I don't understand them, but not to understand does not mean to deny."

"Give me your hand! Let me press your honest hand!"

After dinner Olga Ivanovna drove away to her friends; after that followed theatres or concerts. She returned after midnight. And so every day.

On Wednesdays she gave evening parties. There were no cards and no dancing. Hostess and guests devoted themselves to art. The actor recited, the singer sang, artists sketched in Olga Ivanovna's numberless albums; the hostess painted, modelled, accompanied, and sang. In the pauses between these recreations, they talked of books, the theatre, and art. No women were present, because Olga Ivanovna considered all women, except actresses and dressmakers, tiresome and contemptible. When the hall bell rang the hostess started, and exclaimed triumphantly, "It's he!" meaning thereby some newly met celebrity. Dymov kept out of sight, and few remembered his existence. But at half-past eleven the dining-room door flew open, and Dymov appeared with a kindly smile, rubbing his hands, and said—

"Come, gentlemen, to supper!"

Whereupon all thronged to the dining-room, and each time found awaiting them the same things: a dish of oysters, a joint of ham or veal, sardines, cheese, caviar, mushrooms, vodka, and two decanters of wine.

"My dear *maître d'hôtel!*" cried Olga Ivanovna, waving her hands ecstatically. "You are simply adorable! Gentlemen, look at his forehead! Dymov, show us your profile. Look at him, gentlemen: it is the face of a Bengal tiger with an expression as kind and good as a deer's. My sweetheart!"

And the guests ate steadily and looked at Dymov. But soon they forgot his presence, and returned to theatre, music, and art.

The young couple were happy. Their life, it seemed, flowed as smoothly as oil. But the third week of the honeymoon was crossed by a cloud. Dymov got erysipelas at the hospital, and his fine black hair was cut off. Olga Ivanovna sat with him and cried bitterly, but when he got better she bound a white handkerchief around his head and sketched him as a Bedouin. And both were happy. Three days after he had returned to hospital a second misfortune occurred.

"I am in bad luck, mama!" he said at dinner. "To-day I had four dissections, and I cut two fingers. I noticed it only just now."

Olga Ivanovna was frightened. But Dymov smiled, dismissed the accident as a trifle, and said that he cut himself often.

"I am carried away by my work, mama, and forget what I'm about."

Olga Ivanovna dreaded blood-poisoning, and at night prayed to God. But no consequences followed, and life, serene and happy, flowed without trouble or alarm. The present was all delight, and behind it came spring—spring already near, beaming and beckoning, with a thousand joys. Pleasures it promised without end. In April, May, and June a villa far from town, with walks, fishing, studies, nightingales. From June till autumn the artists' tour on the Volga, and in this tour, as member of the Artists' Association, Olga Ivanovna would take part. She had already ordered two expensive dresses of gingham, and laid in a stock of colours, brushes, canvas, and a new palette. Almost every day came Riabovsky to watch her progress in painting. When she showed him her work he thrust his hands deep in his pockets, compressed tightly his lips, grunted, and said—

"So! . . . This cloud of yours glares; the light is not right for evening. The foreground is somehow chewed up, and there is something, you understand. . . . And the cabin is somehow crushed . . . you should make that corner a little darker. But on the whole it's not bad. . . . I can praise it."

And the less intelligibly he spoke the better Olga Ivanovna understood.

III

After dinner, on the second day of Trinity week, Dymov bought some *hors d'œuvres* and sweets and took train for his villa in the country. Two whole weeks he had not seen his wife, and he longed to be with her again. During the journey and afterwards, as he searched for the villa in a big wood, he felt hungry and fatigued, and rejoiced at the thought of supping in freedom with his wife and having a sound sleep. So, looking at his parcel of caviar, cheese, and white-fish, he felt happy.

Before he found the villa the sun had begun to set. The old servant said that her mistress was not at home, but that she would soon return. The villa, a very ugly villa, with low ceilings, papered with writing-paper, and uneven, chinky floors, contained only three rooms. In one was a bed, in another canvas, brushes, dirty paper, and men's clothes and hats scattered on chairs and window-sills; and in the third Dymov found three strangers, two dark and bearded, the third—evidently an actor—clean-shaven and stout.

"What do you want?" asked the actor in a bass voice, looking at Dymov shyly. "You want Olga Ivanovna? Wait; she'll be back shortly."

Dymov sat down and waited. One of the dark men, looking at him drowsily and lazily, poured tea into his glass and asked—

"Would you like some tea?"

Dymov wanted both to eat and drink, but, fearing to spoil his appetite, he refused the tea. Soon afterwards came footsteps and a familiar laugh; the door flew open, and in came Olga Ivanovna wearing a big hat. On her arm hung a basket, and behind her, with a big parasol and a deck-chair, came merry, rosy-cheeked Riabovsky.

"Dymov!" cried Olga Ivanovna, radiant with joy. "Dymov!" she repeated, laying her head and both hands on his shoulder. "It is you? Why did you not come sooner? Why? Why?"

"I couldn't, mama! I am always busy, and when I end my work there's generally no train."

"How glad I am you've come! I dreamed of you all, all last night. *Akh*, if you knew how I love you—and how opportunely you've come! You are my saviour! To-morrow we have a most original wedding." She laughed and re-tied her husband's tie. "A young telegraphist at the station, a certain Chikeldeyev, is going to be married. A handsome boy, not at all stupid; in his face, you know, there's something strong, bearish. . . . He'd sit admirably as model for a Varangian. We are all interested in him, and promised to come to the wedding. . . . He is a poor man, solitary and shy, and it would be a sin to refuse. Imagine! . . . after church there'll be the wedding, then all go to the bride's house . . . you understand . . . the woods, the birds' songs, sun-spots on the grass, and we ourselves—variegated spots on a bright green background. . . . Most original, quite in the style of the French impressionists! But what am I to wear, Dymov? I have nothing here, literally nothing. . . . No dress, no flowers, no gloves! . . . You must save me. Your arrival means that fate is on my side. Here are the keys, sweetheart! take the train home and bring my rose-coloured dress from the wardrobe. You know it; it's the first you'll see. Then in the chest of drawers—the bottom right-hand drawer—you'll find two boxes. At the top there's only tulle and other rags, but underneath you'll find flowers. Bring all the flowers—carefully! I don't know . . . then I'll choose. . . . And buy me some gloves."

"All right," said Dymov. "I'll get them to-morrow!"

"How to-morrow?" asked Olga Ivanovna, looking at him with surprise. "You can't do it to-morrow. The first train leaves at nine, and the wedding is at eleven. No, dear; go to-night! If you can't get back yourself to-morrow send a messenger. The train is nearly due. Don't miss it, my soul!"

"All right!"

"*Akh,* how sorry I am to have to send you!" she said, and tears came into her eyes. "Why did I promise the telegraph clerk, like a fool!"

Dymov hastily gulped down a glass of tea, and, still smiling kindly, returned to the station. And the caviar, the cheese, and the white-fish were eaten by the actor and the two dark men.

IV

It was a still moonlight night of July. Olga Ivanovna stood on the deck of a Volga steamer and looked now at the river, now at its beautiful banks. Beside her stood Riabovsky, and affirmed that the black shadows on the water were not shadows but a dream; that this magic stream with its fantastic shimmer, this unfathomable sky, these mournful banks—which expressed but the vanity of life, and the existence of something higher, something eternal, something blessed—called to us to forget ourselves, to die, to fade into memories. The past was trivial and tedious, the future insignificant; and this magic night, this one night of life, would soon be past, would have hurried into eternity. Why, then, live?

And Olga Ivanovna listened, first to Riabovsky's voice, then to the midnight silence, and thought that she was immortal, and would never die. The river's turquoise hue, a hue she had never seen before, the sky, the banks, the black shadows, and the irresponsible joy which filled her heart, all whispered to her that she would become a great artist, that somewhere far away, beyond these distances, beyond the moonlight night, somewhere in infinite space there awaited success and glory, and the love of the world. When she looked earnestly into the distance, she saw crowds, lights; she heard solemn music and cries of rapture; she saw herself in a white dress surrounded by flowers cast at her from all sides. And she believed that here beside her, leaning on the bulwark, stood a really great man, a genius, the elected of God. He had already accomplished things beautiful, new, uncommon; what he would do when time had ripened his great talents would be greater immeasurably—that was written legibly in his face, his expressions, his relations to the world around. Of the shadows, the hues of nights, the moonlight, he spoke in language all his own, and unconsciously betrayed the power of his magic mastery over Nature. He was handsome and original; and his life, unhampered, free, alien to the trifles of the world, seemed the life of a bird.

"It is getting cold!" said Olga Ivanovna, shuddering.

Riabovsky wrapped her in his cloak and said mournfully—

"I feel myself in your power. I am a slave. Why are you so ravishing to-night?"

He looked at her steadily, and his eyes were so terrible that she feared to look at him.

"I love you madly . . ." he whispered, breathing against her cheek. "Say to me but one word, and I will not live . . . I will abandon my art. . . ." He stammered in his extreme agitation. "Love me, love. . . ."

"Don't speak in that way!" said Olga Ivanovna, closing her eyes. "It is terrible. And Dymov?"

"What is Dymov? Why Dymov? What have I to do with Dymov? The Volga, the moon, beauty, my love, my raptures . . . and no Dymov at all! . . . *Akh,* I know nothing. . . . I do not want the past; give me but one moment . . . one second!"

Olga Ivanovna's heart beat quickly. She tried to think of her husband; but her whole past, her marriage, Dymov, even the evening parties seemed to her trivial, contemptible, dull, needless, and remote. . . And, indeed, who was Dymov? Why Dymov? What had she to do with Dymov? Did he exist really in Nature; was he only a dream?

"He has had more happiness than he could expect, a simple and ordinary man," she thought, closing her eyes. "Let them condemn me, let them curse me; but I will take all and perish, take all and perish. . . . We must experience everything in life. . . . Lord, how painful and how good!"

"Well, what? What?" stammered the artist, embracing her. He kissed her hands greedily, while she strove to withdraw them. "You love me? Yes? O what a night! O night divine!"

"Yes, what a night!" she whispered, looking into his eyes which glittered with tears. Then she looked around her, clasped her arms about him, and kissed him firmly on the lips.

"We are near Kineshma," said a voice somewhere across the deck.

Heavy footfalls echoed behind them. A waiter passed from the buffet.

"Waiter!" cried Olga Ivanovna, laughing and crying in her joy. "Bring us some wine."

Pale with excitement, the artist sat on a bench, and stared at Olga Ivanovna with grateful, adoring eyes. But in a moment he shut these eyes, and said with a weary smile—

"I am tired."

And he leaned his head against the bulwark.

V

The second of September was warm and windless but dull. Since early morning a light mist had wandered across the Volga, and at nine o'clock it began to rain. There was no hope of a clear sky. At breakfast Riabovsky told Olga Ivanovna that painting was the most thankless and tedious of arts, that he was no artist, and that only fools thought him talented. Then, for no cause whatever, he seized a knife and cut to pieces his best study. After breakfast, in bad humour, he sat at a window and looked at the river, and found it without life—dull, dead, and cold. All around spoke of frowning autumn's approach. It seemed already that the green carpet on the banks, the diamond flashes from the water, the clear blue distances—all the vanity and parade of Nature had been taken from the Volga and packed in a box until the coming spring; and that the ravens flying over the river mocked it and cried, "Naked! Naked!" Riabovsky listened to their cry, and brooded on the exhaustion and loss of his talent: and he thought that all the world was conditional, relative, and stupid, and that he should not have tied himself up with this woman. In one word he was out of spirits and sulked.

On her bed behind the partition, pulling at her pretty hair, sat Olga Ivanovna; and pictured herself at home, first in the drawing-room, then in her bedroom, then in her husband's study; imagination bore her to theatres, to her dressmaker, to her friends. What was Dymov doing now? Did he think of her? The season had already begun; it was time to think of the evening parties. And Dymov? Dear Dymov! How kindly, with what infantile complaints, he begged her in his letters to come home! Every month he sent her seventy-five rubles, and when she wrote that she had borrowed a hundred from the artists he sent her also that hundred. The good, the generous man! Olga Ivanovna was tired of the tour; she suffered from tedium, and wished to escape as soon as possible from the muzhiks, from the river damp, from the feeling of physical uncleanliness caused by living in huts and wandering from village to village. Had Riabovsky not promised his brother artists to stay till the twentieth of September, they might have left at once. And how good it would be to leave!

"My God!" groaned Riabovsky. "Will the sun ever come out? I cannot paint a landscape without the sun!"

"But your study of a cloudy sky?" said Olga Ivanovna, coming from behind the partition. "You remember, the one with the trees in the foreground to the right, and the cows and geese at the left. You could finish that."

"What?" The artist frowned. "Finish it? Do you really think I'm so stupid that I don't know what to do?"

"What I do think is that you've changed to me!" sighed Olga Ivanovna.

"Yes; and that's all right."

Olga Ivanovna's face quivered; she went to the stove and began to cry.

"We only wanted tears to complete the picture! Do stop! I have a thousand reasons for crying, but I don't cry."

"A thousand reasons!" burst out Olga Ivanovna. "The chief reason is that you are tired of me. Yes!" She began to sob. "I will tell you the truth: you are ashamed of your love. You try to hide it, to prevent the others noticing, but that is useless, because they knew about it long ago."

"Olga, I ask only one thing," said the artist imploringly. He put his hand to his ear. "One thing only; do not torture me! I want nothing more from you!"

"Then swear to me that you love me still!"

"This is torture!" hissed Riabovsky through his teeth. He jumped up. "It will end in my throwing myself into the Volga, or going out of my mind. Leave me alone!"

"Then kill me! Kill me!" cried Olga Ivanovna. "Kill me!"

She again sobbed, and retired behind the partition. Raindrops pattered on the cabin roof. Riabovsky with his hands to his head walked from corner to corner; then with a determined face, as if he wanted to prove something, put on his cap, took his gun. and went out of the hut.

When he left, Olga Ivanovna lay on her bed and cried. At first she thought that it would be good to take poison, so that Riabovsky on his return would find her dead. But soon her thoughts bore her back to the drawing-room and to her husband's study; and she fancied herself sitting quietly beside Dymov, enjoying physical rest and cleanliness; and spending the evening listening to *Cavalleria Rusticana*. And a yearning for civilisation, for the sound of cities, for celebrities filled her heart. A peasant woman entered the hut, and lazily prepared the stove for dinner. There was a smell of soot, and the air turned blue from smoke. Then in came several artists in muddy top boots, their faces wet with rain; and they looked at the drawings, and consoled themselves by saying that even in bad weather the Volga had its especial charm. The cheap clock on the wall ticked away; half-frozen flies swarmed in the ikon-corner and buzzed; and cockroaches could be heard under the benches.

Riabovsky returned at sunset. He flung his cap on the table, and, pale, tired, and muddy, dropped on a bench and shut his eyes.

"I am tired," he said, and wrinkled his brows, trying to open his eyes.

To show him kindness, and prove that her anger had passed, Olga Ivanovna came up to him, kissed him silently, and drew a comb through his long, fair hair.

"What are you doing?" he asked, starting as if something cold had touched him. He opened his eyes. "What are you doing? Leave me alone, I beg of you!"

He repulsed her with both hands; and his face seemed to express repugnance and vexation. The peasant woman cautiously brought him a plate, and Olga Ivanovna noticed how she stuck her big fingers in the soup. And the dirty peasant woman with her pendent stomach, the soup which Riabovsky ate greedily, the hut, which she had loved at first for its plainness and artistic disorder, seemed to her unbearable. She felt a deep sense of offence, and said coldly—

"We must part for a time, otherwise we'll only quarrel seriously out of sheer tedium. I am tired of this. I am going to-day."

"Going, how? On the steamer?"

"To-day is Thursday—there is a steamer at half-past nine."

"Eh? Yes! . . . All right, go," said Riabovsky softly, using a towel for a table-napkin. "It's tiresome here for you, and there's nothing to do. Only a great egoist would try to keep you. Go . . . we will meet after the twentieth."

Olga Ivanovna, in good spirits, packed her clothes. Her cheeks burnt with pleasure. "Is it possible?" she asked herself. "Is it possible I shall soon paint in the drawing-room and sleep in a bedroom and dine off a tablecloth?" Her heart grew lighter, and her anger with the artist disappeared.

"I'll leave you the colours and brushes, Riabusha," she said. "You'll bring everything. . . . And, mind, don't idle when I am gone; don't sulk, but work. You are my boy, Riabusha!"

At ten o'clock Riabovsky kissed her good-bye in the hut, to avoid—as she saw—kissing her on the landing-stage in the presence of others. Soon afterwards the steamer arrived and took her away.

Two and a half days later she reached home. Still in her hat and waterproof cloak, panting with excitement, she went through the drawing-room into the dining-room. In his shirt-sleeves, with unbuttoned waistcoat, Dymov sat at the table and sharpened a knife; on a plate before him was a grouse. As Olga Ivanovna entered the house she resolved to hide the truth from her husband, and felt that she was clever and strong enough to succeed. But when she saw his broad, kindly, happy smile and his bright, joyful eyes, she felt that to deceive such a man would be base and impossible, as impossible as to slander, steal, or kill; and she made up her mind in a second to tell him the whole story. When he had kissed and embraced her she fell upon her knees and hid her face.

"What? What is it, mama?" he asked tenderly. "You got tired of it?"

She raised her face, red with shame, and looked at him guiltily and imploringly. But fear and shame forbade her to tell the truth.

"It is nothing," she said. "I only . . ."

"Sit down here!" he said, lifting her and seating her at

the table. "There we are! Eat the grouse! You are starving, of course, poor child!"

She breathed in greedily her native air and ate the grouse. And Dymov looked at her with rapture and smiled merrily.

VI

Apparently about the middle of winter Dymov first suspected his wife's unfaithfulness. He behaved as if his own conscience reproached him. He no longer looked her straight in the face; no longer smiled radiantly when she came in sight; and, to avoid being alone with her, often brought home to dinner, his colleague, Korostelev, a little short-haired man, with a crushed face, who showed his confusion in Olga Ivanovna's society by buttoning and unbuttoning his coat and pinching his right moustache. During dinner the doctors said that when the diaphragm rises abnormally high the heart sometimes beats irregularly, that neuritis had greatly increased, and they discussed Dymov's discovery made during dissection that a case of cancer of the pancreas had been wrongly diagnosed as "malignant anæmia." And it was plain that both men spoke only of medicine in order that Olga Ivanovna might be silent and tell no lies. After dinner, Korostelev sat at the piano, and Dymov sighed and said to him—

"*Akh,* brother! Well! Play me something mournful."

Whereupon, raising his shoulders and spreading his hands, Korostelev strummed a few chords and sang in tenor, "Show me but one spot where Russia's peasants do not groan!" and Dymov sighed again, rested his head on his hands, and seemed lost in thought.

Of late Olga Ivanovna had behaved recklessly. She awoke each morning in bad spirits, tortured by the thought that Riabovsky no longer loved her, that—thanks to the Lord, all the same!—all was over. But as she drank her coffee she reasoned that Riabovsky had stolen her from her husband,

and that now she belonged to neither. Then she remembered a friend's remark that Riabovsky was getting ready for the exhibition a striking picture, a mixture of landscape and *genre,* in the style of Polienov, and that this picture sent every one into raptures; this, she consoled herself, he had done under her influence. Thanks to her influence, indeed, he had on the whole changed for the better, and deprived of it, he would probably perish. She remembered that when last he visited her he came in a splashed cloth coat and a new tie and asked her languidly, "Am I good-looking?" And, in truth, elegant Riabovsky with his blue eyes and long curls was very good-looking—or, it may be, he merely seemed so and he had treated her with affection.

Having remembered and reasoned much, Olga Ivanovna dressed, and in deep agitation drove to Riabovsky's studio. He was in good humour, delighted with what was indeed a fine picture; he hopped, played the fool, and answered every serious question with a joke. Olga Ivanovna was jealous of the picture, and hated it, but for the sake of good manners, she stood before it five minutes, and, sighing as people sigh before holy things, said softly—

"Yes, you never painted like that before. Do you know, it almost frightens me."

And she began to implore him to love her, not to forsake her, to pity her—poor and unfortunate! She kissed his hand, cried, made him swear his love, and boasted that without her influence he would go off the track and perish utterly. Thus having spoilt his good humour, and humiliated herself, she would drive away to a dressmaker, or to some actress friend to ask for free tickets.

Once when she found Riabovsky out she left a note swearing that if he did not visit her at once she would take poison. And he, frightened, came and stayed to dinner. Ignoring her husband's presence, he spoke to her impudently; and she answered in the same tone. They felt chained to one another; they were despots and foes; and their anger hid from them their own rudeness, which even close-clipped Korostelev remarked. After dinner Riabovsky said good-bye hastily and went.

"Where are you going?" asked Olga Ivanovna. She stood in the hall, and looked at him with hatred.

Riabovsky frowned and blinked, and named a woman she knew, and it was plain that he enjoyed her jealousy, and wished to annoy her. Olga Ivanovna went to her bedroom and lay on her bed; from jealousy, anger, and a sense of humiliation and shame, she bit her pillow, and sobbed aloud. Dymov left Korostelev alone, came into the bedroom, and, confused and abstracted, said softly—

"Don't cry so loudly, mama! . . . What good is it? We must keep silence about this. . . People mustn't see. . . . You know yourself that what has happened is beyond recall."

Unable to appease the painful jealousy which made her temples throb, thinking, nevertheless, that what had happened was not beyond recall, she washed and powdered her face, and flew off to the woman friend. Finding no Riabovsky there she drove to another, then to a third. . . . At first she felt ashamed of these visits, but she soon reconciled herself; and one evening even called on every woman she knew and sought Riabovsky; and all of them understood her.

Of her husband she said to Riabovsky—

"This man tortures me with his magnanimity."

And this sentence so pleased her that, meeting artists who knew of her affair with Riabovsky, she repeated with an emphatic gesture—

"This man tortures me with his magnanimity."

In general, her life remained unchanged. She resumed her Wednesday-evening parties. The actor declaimed, the painters sketched, the violoncellist played, the singers sang; and invariably half an hour before midnight the dining-room door opened, and Dymov said with a smile—

"Come, gentlemen, supper is ready."

As before, Olga Ivanovna sought celebrities, found them, and, insatiable, sought for more. As before, she returned home late. But Dymov, no longer sleeping as of old, sat in his study and worked. He went to bed at three, and rose at eight.

Once as she stood before the pier-glass dressing for the theatre, Dymov, in evening dress and a white tie, came into the bedroom. He smiled kindly, with his old smile, and looked his wife joyfully in the face. His face shone.

"I have just defended my dissertation," he said. He sat down and stroked his leg.

"Your dissertation?" said Olga Ivanovna.

"Yes," he laughed. He stretched forward so as to see in the mirror the face of his wife, who continued to stand with her back to him and dress her hair. "Yes," he repeated. "Do you know what? I expect to be offered a privat-docentship in general pathology. That is something."

It was plain from his radiant face that had Olga Ivanovna shared his joy and triumph he would have forgiven and forgotten everything. But "privat-docentship" and "general pathology" had no meaning for her, and, what's more, she feared to be late for the theatre. She said nothing.

Dymov sat still for a few minutes, smiled guiltily, and left the room.

VII

This was an evil day.

Dymov's head ached badly; he ate no breakfast, and did not go to the hospital, but lay on the sofa in his study. At one o'clock Olga Ivanovna went to Riabovsky's, to show him her *Nature morte*, and ask why he had not come the day before. The *Nature morte* she herself did not take seriously; she had painted it only as an excuse to visit the artist.

She went to his apartment unannounced. As she took off her goloshes in the hall she heard hasty footsteps, and the rustle of a woman's dress; and as she hurried into the studio a brown skirt flashed for a moment before her and vanished behind a big picture, which together with its easel was hung with black calico. There was no doubt that a woman hid there. How often had Olga Ivanovna herself hidden behind that picture! Riabovsky, in confusion, stretched out both hands as if surprised at her visit, and said with a constrained smile—

"Ah, I am glad to see you. What is the news?"

Olga Ivanovna's eyes filled with tears. She was ashamed and angered, and would have given millions to be spared speaking before the strange woman, the rival, the liar, who hid behind the picture and tittered, no doubt, maliciously.

"I have brought a study . . ." she said in a thin, frightened voice. Her lips trembled. "*Nature morte.*"

"What? What? A study?"

The artist took the sketch, looked at it, and walked mechanically into another room. Olga Ivanovna followed submissively.

"*Nature morte* . . ." he stammered, seeking rhymes. "*Kurort* . . . *sort* . . . *porte* . . ."

From the studio came hasty footfalls and the rustle of a skirt. She had gone. Olga Ivanovna felt impelled to scream and strike the artist on the head; but tears blinded her, she was crushed by her shame, and felt as if she were not Olga Ivanovna the artist, but a little beetle.

"I am tired . . ." said Riabovsky languidly. He looked at the study, and shook his head as if to drive away sleep. "This is charming, of course, but . . . it is study to-day, and study to-morrow, and study last year, and study it will be again in a month. . . . How is it you don't get tired? If I were you, I should give up painting, and take up seriously music, or something else. . . . You are not an artist but a musician. You cannot imagine how tired I am. Let me order some tea. Eh?"

He left the room, and Olga Ivanovna heard him giving

an order. To avoid good-byes and explanations, still more to prevent herself sobbing, she went quickly into the hall, put on her goloshes, and went out. Once in the street she sighed faintly. She felt that she was for ever rid of Riabovsky and painting, and the heavy shame which had crushed her in the studio. All was over! She drove to her dressmaker. then to Barnay, who had arrived the day before, and from Barnay to a music shop, thinking all the time how she would write Riabovsky a cold, hard letter, full of her own worth; and that the spring and summer she would spend with Dymov in the Crimea, free herself for ever from the past, and begin life anew.

On her return, late as usual, she sat in her street clothes in the drawing-room, and prepared to write. Riabovsky had told her she was no artist; in revenge she would write that he had painted every year one and the same tiresome thing, that he had exhausted himself, and would never again produce original work. She would write also that he owed much to her beneficent influence; and that if he made mistakes it was only because her influence was paralysed by various ambiguous personages who hid behind his pictures.

"Mama!" cried Dymov from his study, without opening the door.

"What is it?"

"Mama, don't come in, but just come to the door. It is this. The day before yesterday I took diphtheria at the hospital, and now . . . I feel bad. Send at once for Korostelev."

Olga Ivanovna called her husband and men-friends by their surnames; she disliked his name Osip, which reminded her of Gogol's Osip, and the pun "*Osip okrip, a Arkhip osip.*" But this time she cried—

"Osip, that is impossible!"

"Send! I am ill," said Dymov from behind the door; and she heard him walking to the sofa and lying down. "Send!" came his hoarse voice.

"What can it be?" thought Olga Ivanovna, chilled with fear. "Why, this is dangerous!"

Without any aim she took a candle, and went into her room, and there, wondering what she should do, she saw herself unexpectedly in the glass. With her pale, terrified face, her high-sleeved jacket with the yellow gathers on the breast, her skirt with its strange stripes, she seemed to herself frightful and repulsive. And suddenly she felt sorry for Dymov, sorry for his infinite love, his young life, the forsaken bed on which he had not slept so long. And remembering his kindly, suppliant smile, she cried bitterly, and wrote Korostelev an imploring letter. It was two o'clock in the morning.

VIII

When at eight next morning Olga Ivanovna, heavy from sleeplessness, untidy, unattractive, and guilty-faced, came out of her bedroom, an unknown, black-bearded man, obviously a doctor, passed her in the hall. There was a smell of drugs. Outside Dymov's study stood Korostelev, twisting his left moustache with his right hand.

"Excuse me, I cannot let you in," he said, looking at her savagely. "You might catch the disease. And in any case, what's the use? He's raving."

"Is it really diphtheria?" whispered Olga Ivanovna.

"People who do foolish things ought to pay for them," muttered Korostelev, ignoring Olga Ivanovna's question. "Do you know how he got this diphtheria? On Tuesday he sucked through a tube the diphtheria laminæ from a boy's throat. And why? Stupid. . . . Like a fool!"

"Is it dangerous? Very?" asked she.

"Yes, it's a very bad form, they say. We must send for Schreck, we must . . ."

First came a little, red-haired, long-nosed man with a Jewish accent; then a tall, stooping, untidy man like a proto-deacon; lastly a young, very stout, red-faced man with spectacles.

All these doctors came to attend their sick colleague. Korostelev, having served his turn, remained in the house, wandering about like a shadow. The maid-servant was kept busy serving the doctors with tea, and running to the apothecary's, and no one tidied the rooms. All was still and sad.

Olga Ivanovna sat in her room, and reflected that God was punishing her for deceiving her husband. That silent, uncomplaining, inexplicable man—impersonified, it seemed, by kindness and mildness, weak from excessive goodness—lay on his sofa and suffered alone, uttering no groan. And if he did complain in his delirium, the doctors would guess that the diphtheria was not the only culprit. They would question Korostelev, who knew all, and not without cause looked viciously at his friend's wife as if she were chief and real offender, and disease only her accomplice. She no longer thought of the moonlight Volga night, the love avowal, the romance of life in the peasant's hut; she remembered only that from caprice and selfishness she had smeared herself from head to feet with something vile and sticky which no washing would wash away.

"*Akh,* how I lied to him!" she said, remembering her restless love of Riabovsky. "May it be accursed!"

At four o'clock she dined with Korostelev, who ate nothing, but drank red wine, and frowned. She too ate nothing. But she prayed silently, and vowed to God that if Dymov only recovered, she would love him again and be his faithful wife. Then, forgetting herself for a moment, she looked at Korostelev and thought: "How tiresome it is to be such a simple, undistinguished, obscure man, and to have such bad manners." It seemed to her that God would strike her dead for her cowardice in keeping away from her husband. And altogether she was oppressed by a dead melancholy, and a feeling that her life was ruined, and that nothing now would mend it.

After dinner, darkness. Olga Ivanovna went into the drawing-room, and found Korostelev asleep on a couch, his head resting on a silken cushion embroidered with gold. He snored loudly.

Alone the doctors, coming on and off duty, ignored the disorder. The strange man sleeping and snoring in the drawing-room, the studies on the walls, the wonderful decorations, the mistress's dishevelled hair and untidy dress—none of these awakened the least interest. One of the doctors laughed; and this laugh had such a timid sound that it was painful to hear.

When next Olga Ivanovna entered the drawing-room Korostelev was awake. He sat up and smoked.

"He has got diphtheria . . . in the nasal cavity," he said quietly. "Yes . . . and his heart is weak. . . . It is a bad business."

"Better send for Schreck," said Olga Ivanovna.

"He's been. It was he noticed that the diphtheria had got into the nose. Yes . . . but what is Schreck? In reality, Schreck is nothing. He is Schreck, I am Korostelev, and nothing more!"

Time stretched into eternity. Olga Ivanovna lay dressed on her unmade bed, and slumbered. She felt that the whole flat from roof to ceiling was filled with a giant block of iron, and that if the iron were only removed, all would be well again. But then she remembered that there was no iron, but only Dymov's illness.

"*Nature morte* . . ." she thought, again losing consciousness. "Sport, *kurort*. . . . And what about Schreck? Schreck, greck, vreck, kreck. Where are my friends now? Do they know of the sorrow that has overtaken us? O Lord, save . . . deliver us! Schreck, greck. . . ."

And again the iron. Time stretched into eternity, and the clock downstairs struck innumerable times. Now and then the bell was rung. Doctors came. . . . In came the servant with an empty glass on a salver, and said—

"Shall I make the bed, ma'am?"

And, receiving no answer, she went out. Again the clock

struck—dreams of rain on the Volga—and again some one arrived, this time, it seemed, a stranger. Olga Ivanovna started, and saw Korostelev.

"What time is it?" she asked.

"About three."

"Well, what?"

"Just that. I came to say that he's dying."

He sobbed, sat down on her bed, and wiped away his tears with his sleeve. At first Olga Ivanovna understood nothing; then she turned cold, and began to cross herself.

"He is dying," he repeated in a thin voice; and again he sobbed. "He is dying—because he sacrificed himself. What a loss to science!" He spoke bitterly. "This man, compared with the best of us, was a great man, an exceptional man! What gifts! What hopes he awakened in us all!" Korostelev wrung his hands. "Lord, my God, you will not find such a scholar if you search till judgment day! Oska Dymov, Oska Dymov, what have you done? My God!"

In despair he covered his face with his hands and shook his head.

"And what moral fortitude!" he continued, each second increasing in anger. "Good, pure, loving soul—not a man, but a crystal! How he served his science, how he's died for it. Worked—day and night—like an ox, sparing himself never; and he, the young scholar, the coming professor, was forced to seek a practice and spend his nights translating to pay for these . . . these dirty rags!"

Korostelev looked fiendishly at Olga Ivanovna, seized the sheet with both hands, and tore it as angrily as if it, and not she, were guilty.

"And he never spared himself . . . nor did others spare him. And for what purpose . . . why?"

"Yes, a man in a hundred!" came a deep voice from the dining-room.

Olga Ivanovna recalled her life with Dymov, from beginning to end, in all its details; and suddenly she realised that her husband was indeed an exceptional man, a rare—compared with all her other friends—a great man. And remembering how he was looked up to by her late father and by all his colleagues, she understood that there was indeed good reason to predict for him future fame. The walls, the ceiling, the lamp, the carpet winked at her derisively, as if saying, "You have let it slip by, slip by!" With a cry, she rushed out of the room, slipped past some unknown man in the dining-room, and rushed into her husband's study. Covered with a counterpane to the waist, Dymov lay, motionless, on the couch. His face had grown thin, and was a greyish-yellow never seen on the living; his black eyebrows and his kindly smile were all that remained of Dymov. She felt his chest, his forehead, his hands. His chest was still warm, his forehead and hands were icy. And his half-closed eyes looked not at Olga Ivanovna, but down at the counterpane.

"Dymov!" she cried loudly. "Dymov!"

She wished to explain to him that the past was but a mistake; that all was not yet lost; that life might yet be happy and beautiful; that he was a rare, an uncommon, a great man; that she would worship him from this day forth, and pray, and torture herself with holy dread. . . .

"Dymov!" she cried, tapping his shoulder, refusing to believe that he would never awaken. "Dymov! Dymov!"

But in the drawing-room Korostelev spoke to the maidservant.

"Don't ask silly questions! Go at once to the church watchman, and get the women's address. They will wash the body, and lay it out, and do all that's wanted."

GRIEF

"To Whom Shall I Tell My Grief?"

It is twilight. A thick wet snow is slowly twirling around the newly lighted street-lamps, and lying in soft thin layers on the roofs, the horses' backs, people's shoulders and hats. The cab-driver, Iona Potapov, is quite white, and looks like a phantom; he is bent double as far as a human body can bend double; he is seated on his box, and never makes a move. If a whole snowdrift fell on him, it seems as if he would not find it necessary to shake it off. His little horse is also quite white, and remains motionless; its immobility, its angularity, and its straight wooden-looking legs, even close by give it the appearance of a ginger-bread horse worth a kopeck. It is, no doubt, plunged in deep thought. If you were snatched from the plough, from your usual grey surroundings, and were thrown into this slough full of monstrous lights, unceasing noise and hurrying people, you too would find it difficult not to think.

Iona and his little horse have not moved from their place for a long while. They left their yard before dinner, and, up to now, not a "fare." The evening mist is descending over the town, the white lights of the lamps are replacing brighter rays, and the hubbub of the street is getting louder. "Cabby, for Viborg way!" suddenly hears Iona. "Cabby!"

Iona jumps, and through his snow-covered eyelashes, sees an officer in a greatcoat, with his hood over his head.

"Viborg way!" the officer repeats. "Are you asleep, eh? Viborg way!"

With a nod of assent Iona picks up the reins, in consequence of which layers of snow slip off the horse's back and neck. The officer seats himself in the sleigh, the cab-driver smacks his lips to encourage his horse, stretches out his neck like a swan, sits up, and, more from habit than necessity, brandishes his whip. The little horse also stretches his neck, bends his wooden-looking legs, and makes a move undecidedly.

"What are you doing, were-wolf!" is the exclamation Iona hears, from the dark mass moving to and fro as soon as they started.

"Where the devil are you going? To the r-r-right!"

"You do not know how to drive. Keep to the right!" calls the officer angrily.

A coachman from a private carriage swears at him; a passer-by, who has run across the road and rubbed his shoulder against the horse's nose, looks at him furiously as he sweeps the snow from his sleeve. Iona shifts about on his seat as if he were on needles, moves his elbows as if he were trying to keep his equilibrium, and gapes about like someone suffocating, and who does not understand why and wherefore he is there.

"What scoundrels they all are!" jokes the officer; "one would think they had all entered into an agreement to jostle you or fall under your horse."

Iona looks round at the officer, and moves his lips. He evidently wants to say something, but the only sound that issues is a snuffle.

"What?" asks the officer.

Iona twists his mouth into a smile, and with an effort says hoarsely:

"My son, barin, died this week."

"Hm! What did he die of?"

Iona turns with his whole body towards his fare, and says:

"And who knows! They say high fever. He was three days in hospital, and then died. . . . God's will be done."

"Turn round! The devil!" sounded from the darkness. "Have you popped off, old doggie, eh? Use your eyes!"

"Go on, go on," said the officer, "otherwise we shall not get there by to-morrow. Hurry a bit!"

The cab-driver again stretches his neck, sits up, and, with a bad grace, brandishes his whip. Several times again he turns to look at his fare, but the latter had closed his eyes, and apparently is not disposed to listen. Having deposited the officer in the Viborg, he stops by the tavern, doubles himself up on his seat, and again remains motionless, while the snow once more begins to cover him and his horse. An hour, and another. . . . Then, along the footpath, with a squeak of goloshes, and quarrelling, came three young men, two of them tall and lanky, the third one short and hump-backed.

"Cabby, to the Police Bridge!" in a cracked voice calls the hump-back. "The three of us for two griveniks!" (20 kopecks).

Iona picks up his reins, and smacks his lips. Two griveniks is not a fair price, but he does not mind if it is a rouble or five kopecks—to him it is all the same now, so long as they are wayfarers. The young men, jostling each other and using bad language, approach the sleigh, and all three at once try to get on to the seat; then begins a discussion which two shall sit and who shall be the one to stand. After wrangling, abusing each other, and much petulance, it was at last decided that the hump-back should stand, as he was the smallest.

"Now then, hurry up!" says the hump-back in a twanging voice, as he takes his place, and breathes in Iona's neck. "Old furry. Here, mate, what a cap you have got, there is not a worse one to be found in all Petersburg! . . ."

"Hi—hi,—hi—hi," giggles Iona. "Such a . . ."

"Now you, 'such a,' hurry up, are you going the whole way at this pace? Are you? . . . Do you want it in the neck?"

"My head feels like bursting," says one of the lanky ones. "Last night at the Donkmasovs, Vaska and I drank the whole of four bottles of cognac."

"I don't understand what you lie for," said the other lanky one angrily; "you lie like a brute."

"God strike me, it's the truth!"

"It's as much a truth as that a louse coughs!"

"Hi, hi," grins Iona, "what gay young gentlemen!"

"Pshaw, go to the devil!" indignantly says the hump-back. "Are you going to get on or not, you old pest? Is that the way to drive? Use the whip a bit! Go on, devil, go on, give it him well!"

Iona feels at his back the little man wriggling, and the tremble in his voice. He listens to the insults hurled at him, sees the people, and little by little the feeling of loneliness leaves him. The hump-back goes on swearing until he gets mixed up in some elaborate six-foot oath, or chokes with coughing. The lankies begin to talk about a certain Nadejda Petrovna. Iona looks round at them several times; he waits for a temporary silence, then, turning round again, he murmurs:

"My son—died this week."

"We must all die," sighed the hump-back, wiping his lips after an attack of coughing. "Now, hurry up, hurry up! Gentlemen, I really cannot go any farther like this! When will he get us there?"

"Well, just you stimulate him a little in the neck!"

"You old pest, do you hear, I'll bone your neck for you! If one treated the like of you with ceremony one would have to go on foot! Do you hear, old serpent Gorinytch! Or do you not care a spit?"

Iona hears rather than feels the blows they deal him.

"Hi, hi," he laughs. "They are gay young gentlemen, God bless 'em!"

"Cabby, are you married?" asks a lanky one.

"I? Hi, hi, gay young gentlemen! Now I have only a wife: the moist ground. . . . Hi, ho, ho . . . that is to say, the grave! My son has died, and I am alive. . . . A wonderful thing, death mistook the door . . . instead of coming to me, it went to my son. . . ."

Iona turns round to tell them how his son died, but at this

moment the hump-back, giving a little sigh, announces, "Thank God, they have at last reached their destination," and Iona watches them disappear through the dark entrance. Once more he is alone, and again surrounded by silence. . . . His grief, which had abated for a short while, returns and rends his heart with greater force. With an anxious and a hurried look, he searches among the crowds passing on either side of the street to find if there is just one person who will listen to him. But the crowds hurry by without noticing him or his trouble. Yet it is such an immense, illimitable grief. Should his heart break and the grief pour out, it would flow over the whole earth it seems, and yet, no one sees it. It has managed to conceal itself in such an insignificant shell that no one can see it even by day and with a light.

Iona sees a hall-porter with some sacking, and decides to talk to him.

"Friend, what sort of time is it?" he asks.

"Past nine. What are you standing here for? Move on."

Iona moves on a few steps, doubles himself up, and abandons himself to his grief. He sees it is useless to turn to people for help In less than five minutes he straightens himself, holds up his head as if he felt some sharp pain, and gives a tug at the reins: he can bear it no longer, "The stables," he thinks, and the little horse, as if he understood, starts off at a trot.

About an hour and a half later Iona is seated by a large dirty stove. Around the stove, on the floor, on the benches, people are snoring; the air is thick and suffocatingly hot. Iona looks at the sleepers, scratches himself, and regrets having returned so early.

"I have not even earned my fodder," he thinks. "That's what's my trouble. A man who knows his job, who has had enough to eat, and his horse too, can always sleep peacefully."

A young cab-driver in one of the corners half gets up, grunts sleepily, and stretches towards a bucket of water.

"Do you want a drink?" Iona asks him.

"Don't I want a drink!"

"That's so? Your good health! But listen, mate—you know, my son is dead. . . . Did you hear? This week, in hospital. . . . It's a long story."

Iona looks to see what effect his words have, but sees none—the young man has hidden his face, and is fast asleep again. The old man sighs, and scratches his head. Just as much as the young one wanted to drink, the old man wanted to talk. It will soon be a week since his son died, and he has not been able to speak about it properly to anyone. One must tell it slowly and carefully; how his son fell ill, how he suffered, what he said before he died, how he died. One must describe every detail of the funeral, and the journey to the hospital to fetch the defunct's clothes. His daughter Anissia remained in the village—one must talk about her too. Was it nothing he had to tell? Surely the listener would gasp and sigh, and sympathise with him? It is better, too, to talk to women; although they are stupid, two words are enough to make them sob.

"I'll go and look at my horse," thinks Iona; "there's always time to sleep. No fear of that!"

He puts on his coat, and goes to the stables to his horse; he thinks of the corn, the hay, the weather. When he is alone, he dare not think of his son; he could speak about him to anyone, but to think of him, and picture him to himself, is unbearably painful.

"Are you tucking in?" Iona asks his horse, looking at his bright eyes; "go on, tuck in, though we've not earned our corn, we can eat hay. Yes! I am too old to drive—my son could have, not I. He was a first-rate cab-driver. If only he had lived!"

Iona is silent for a moment, then continues:

"That's how it is, my old horse. There's no more Kuzma Ionitch. He has left us to live, and he went off pop. Now let's say, you had a foal, you were that foal's mother, and suddenly, let's say, that foal went and left you to live after him. It would be sad, wouldn't it?"

The little horse munches, listens, and breathes over his master's hand. . . .

Iona's feelings are too much for him, and he tells the little horse the whole story.

AN INADVERTENCE

Pyotr Petrovitch Strizhin, the nephew of Madame Ivanov, the colonel's widow,—the man whose new goloshes were stolen last year,—came home from a christening party at two o'clock in the morning. To avoid waking the household he took off his things in the lobby, made his way on tiptoe to his room, holding his breath, and began getting ready for bed without lighting a candle.

Strizhin leads a sober and regular life. He has a sanctimonious expression of face, he reads nothing but religious and edifying books, but at the christening party, in his delight that Lyubov Spiridonovna had passed through her confinement successfully, he had permitted himself to drink four glasses of vodka and a glass of wine, the taste of which suggested something midway between vinegar and castor oil. Spirituous liquors are like sea-water and glory: the more you imbibe of them the greater your thirst. And now as he undressed, Strizhin was aware of an overwhelming craving for drink.

"I believe Dashenka has some vodka in the cupboard in the right-hand corner," he thought. "If I drink one wine-glassful, she won't notice it."

After some hesitation, overcoming his fears, Strizhin went to the cupboard. Cautiously opening the door he felt in the right-hand corner for a bottle and poured out a wine-glassful, put the bottle back in its place, then, making the sign of the cross, drank it off. And immediately something like a miracle took place. Strizhin was flung back from the cupboard to the chest with fearful force like a bomb. There were flashes before his eyes, he felt as though he could not breathe, and all over his body he had a sensation as though he had fallen into a marsh full of leeches. It seemed to him as though, instead of vodka, he had swallowed dynamite, which blew up his body, the house, and the whole street. . . . His head, his arms, his legs—all seemed to be torn off and to be flying away somewhere to the devil, into space.

For some three minutes he lay on the chest, not moving and scarcely breathing, then he got up and asked himself:

"Where am I?"

The first thing of which he was clearly conscious on coming to himself was the pronounced smell of paraffin.

"Holy saints," he thought in horror, "it's paraffin I have drunk instead of vodka."

The thought that he had poisoned himself threw him into a cold shiver, then into a fever. That it was really poison that he had taken was proved not only by the smell in the room but also by the burning taste in his mouth, the flashes before his eyes, the ringing in his head, and the colicky pain in his stomach. Feeling the approach of death and not buoying himself up with false hopes, he wanted to say good-bye to those nearest to him, and made his way to Dashenka's bedroom (being a widower he had his sister-in-law called Dashenka, an old maid, living in the flat to keep house for him).

"Dashenka," he said in a tearful voice as he went into the bedroom, "dear Dashenka!"

Something grumbled in the darkness and uttered a deep sigh.

"Dashenka."

"Eh? What?" A woman's voice articulated rapidly. "Is that you, Pyotr Petrovitch? Are you back already? Well, what is it? What has the baby been christened? Who was godmother?"

"The godmother was Natalya Andreyevna Velikosvyetsky, and the godfather Pavel Ivanitch Bezsonnitsin. . . . I. . . . I believe, Dashenka, I am dying. And the baby has been christened Olimpiada, in honour of their kind patroness. . . . I . . . I have just drunk paraffin, Dashenka!"

"What next! You don't say they gave you paraffin there?"

"I must own I wanted to get a drink of vodka without asking you, and . . . and the Lord chastised me: by accident in the dark I took paraffin. . . . What am I to do?"

Dashenka, hearing that the cupboard had been opened without her permission, grew more wideawake. . . She quickly lighted a candle, jumped out of bed, and in her nightgown, a freckled, bony figure in curl-papers, padded with bare feet to the cupboard.

"Who told you you might?" she asked sternly, as she scrutinised the inside of the cupboard. "Was the vodka put there for you?"

"I . . . I haven't drunk vodka but paraffin, Dashenka . . ." muttered Strizhin, mopping the cold sweat on his brow.

"And what did you want to touch the paraffin for? That's nothing to do with you, is it? Is it put there for you? Or do you suppose paraffin costs nothing? Eh? Do you know what paraffin is now? Do you know?"

"Dear Dashenka," moaned Strizhin, "it's a question of life and death, and you talk about money!"

"He's drunk himself tipsy and now he pokes his nose into the cupboard!" cried Dashenka, angrily slamming the cupboard door. "Oh, the monsters, the tormentors! I'm a martyr, a miserable woman, no peace day or night! Vipers, basilisks, accursed Herods, may you suffer the same in the world to come! I am going to-morrow! I am a maiden lady and I won't allow you to stand before me in your underclothes! How dare you look at me when I am not dressed!"

And she went on and on. . . . Knowing that when Dashenka was enraged there was no moving her with prayers or vows or even by firing a cannon, Strizhin waved his hand in despair, dressed, and made up his mind to go to the doctor. But a doctor is only readily found when he is not wanted. After running through three streets and ringing five times at Dr. Tchepharyants's, and seven times at Dr. Bultyhin's, Strizhin raced off to a chemist's shop, thinking possibly the chemist could help him. There, after a long interval, a little dark and curly-headed chemist came out to him in his dressing gown, with drowsy eyes, and such a wise and serious face that it was positively terrifying.

"What do you want?" he asked in a tone in which only very wise and dignified chemists of Jewish persuasion can speak.

"For God's sake. . . . I entreat you . . ." said Strizhin breathlessly, "give me something. I have just accidentally drunk paraffin, I am dying!"

"I beg you not to excite yourself and to answer the questions I am about to put to you. The very fact that you are excited prevents me from understanding you. You have drunk paraffin. Yes?"

"Yes, paraffin! Please save me!"

The chemist went coolly and gravely to the desk, opened a book, became absorbed in reading it. After reading a couple of pages he shrugged one shoulder and then the other, made a contemptuous grimace and, after thinking for a minute, went into the adjoining room. The clock struck four, and when it pointed to ten minutes past the chemist came back with another book and again plunged into reading.

"H'm," he said as though puzzled, "the very fact that you feel unwell shows you ought to apply to a doctor, not a chemist."

"But I have been to the doctors already. I could not ring them up."

"H'm . . . you don't regard us chemists as human beings, and disturb our rest even at four o'clock at night, though every dog, every cat, can rest in peace. . . . You don't try to understand anything, and to your thinking we are not people and our nerves are like cords."

Strizhin listened to the chemist, heaved a sigh, and went home.

"So I am fated to die," he thought.

And in his mouth was a burning and a taste of paraffin, there were twinges in his stomach, and a sound of boom, boom, boom in his ears. Every moment it seemed to him that his end was near, that his heart was no longer beating.

Returning home he made haste to write: "Let no one be blamed for my death," then he said his prayers, lay down and pulled the bedclothes over his head. He lay awake till morning expecting death, and all the time he kept fancying how his grave would be covered with fresh green grass and how the birds would twitter over it. . . .

And in the morning he was sitting on his bed, saying with a smile to Dashenka:

"One who leads a steady and regular life, dear sister, is unaffected by any poison. Take me, for example. I have been on the verge of death. I was dying and in agony, yet now I am all right. There is only a burning in my mouth and a soreness in my throat, but I am all right all over, thank God. . . . And why? It's because of my regular life."

"No, it's because it's inferior paraffin!" sighed Dashenka, thinking of the household expenses and gazing into space. "The man at the shop could not have given me the best quality, but that at three farthings. I am a martyr, I am a miserable woman. You monsters! May you suffer the same, in the world to come, accursed Herods. . . ."

And she went on and on. . . .

THE BLACK MONK

I

ANDREY VASILYEVICH KOVRIN, *Magister*, had worn himself out, and unsettled his nerves. He made no effort to undergo regular treatment; but only incidentally, over a bottle of wine, spoke to his friend the doctor; and his friend the doctor advised him to spend all the spring and summer in the country. And in the nick of time came a long letter from Tanya Pesotzky, asking him to come and stay with her father at Borisovka. He decided to go.

But first (it was in April) he travelled to his own estate, to his native Kovrinka, and spent three weeks in solitude; and only when the fine weather came drove across the country to his former guardian and second parent, Pesotzky, the celebrated Russian horticulturist. From Kovrinka to Borisovka, the home of the Pesotzkys, was a distance of some seventy versts, and in the easy, springed calêche the drive along the roads, soft in springtime, promised real enjoyment.

The house at Borisovka was large, faced with a colonnade, and adorned with figures of lions with the plaster falling off. At the door stood a servant in livery. The old park, gloomy and severe, laid out in English fashion, stretched for nearly a verst from the house down to the river, and ended there in a steep clay bank covered with pines whose bare roots resembled shaggy paws. Below sparkled a deserted stream; overhead the snipe circled about with melancholy cries—all, in short, seemed to invite a visitor to sit down and write a ballad. But the gardens and orchards, which together with the seed-plots occupied some eighty acres, inspired very different feelings. Even in the worst of weather they were bright and joy-inspiring. Such wonderful roses, lilies, camellias, such tulips, such a host of flowering plants of every possible kind and colour, from staring white to sooty black,—such a wealth of blossoms Kovrin had never seen before. The spring was only beginning, and the greatest rarities were hidden under glass; but already enough bloomed in the alleys and beds to make up an empire of delicate shades. And most charming of all was it in the early hours of morning, when dewdrops glistened on every petal and leaf.

In childhood the decorative part of the garden, called contemptuously by Pesotzky "the rubbish," had produced on Kovrin a fabulous impression. What miracles of art, what studied monstrosities, what mockeries of nature! Espaliers of fruit trees, a pear tree shaped like a pyramidal poplar, globular oaks and lindens, apple-tree houses, arches, monograms, candelabra—even the date 1862 in plum trees, to commemorate the year in which Pesotzky first engaged in the art of gardening. There were stately, symmetrical trees, with trunks erect as those of palms, which after examination proved to be gooseberry or currant trees. But what most of all enlivened the garden and gave it its joyous tone was the constant movement of Pesotzky's gardeners. From early morning to late at night, by the trees, by the bushes, in the alleys, and on the beds swarmed men as busy as ants, with barrows, spades, and watering-pots.

Kovrin arrived at Borisovka at nine o'clock. He found Tanya and her father in great alarm. The clear starlight night foretold frost, and the head gardener, Ivan Karlych, had gone to town, so that there was no one who could be relied upon. At supper they spoke only of the impending frost; and it was decided that Tanya should not go to bed at all, but should inspect the gardens at one o'clock and see if all were in order, while Yegor Semionovich should rise at three o'clock, or even earlier.

Kovrin sat with Tanya all the evening and after midnight

accompanied her to the garden. The air already smelt strongly of burning. In the great orchard, called "the commercial," which every year brought Yegor Semionovich thousands of rubles profit, there already crept along the ground the thick, black, sour smoke which was to clothe the young leaves and save the plants. The trees were marshalled like chessmen in straight rows—like ranks of soldiers; and this pedantic regularity, together with the uniformity of height, made the garden seem monotonous and even tiresome. Kovrin and Tanya walked up and down the alleys, and watched the fires of dung, straw, and litter; but seldom met the workmen, who wandered in the smoke like shadows. Only the cherry and plum trees and a few apple trees were in blossom, but the whole garden was shrouded in smoke, and it was only when they reached the seed-plots that Kovrin was able to breathe.

"I remember when I was a child sneezing from the smoke," he said, shrugging his shoulders, "but to this day I cannot understand how smoke saves plants from the frost."

"Smoke is a good substitute when there are no clouds," answered Tanya.

"But what do you want the clouds for?"

"In dull and cloudy weather we have no morning frosts."

"Is that so?" said Kovrin.

He laughed and took Tanya by the hand. Her broad, very serious, chilled face; her thick, black eyebrows; the stiff collar on her jacket which prevented her from moving her head freely; her dress tucked up out of the dew; and her whole figure, erect and slight, pleased him.

"Heavens! how she has grown!" he said to himself. "When I was here last time, five years ago, you were quite a child. You were thin, long-legged, and untidy, and wore a short dress, and I used to tease you. What a change in five years!"

"Yes, five years!" sighed Tanya. "A lot of things have happened since then. Tell me, Andrei, honestly," she said, looking merrily into his face, "do you feel that you have got out of touch with us? But why do I ask? You are a man, you live your own interesting life, you . . . Some estrangement is natural. But whether that is so or not, Andriusha, I want you now to look on us as your own. We have a right to that."

"I do, already, Tanya."

"Your word of honour?"

"My word of honour."

"You were surprised that we had so many of your photographs. But surely you know how my father adores you, worships you. You are a scholar, and not an ordinary man; you have built up a brilliant career, and he is firmly convinced that you turned out a success because he educated you. I do not interfere with his delusion. Let him believe it!"

Already dawn. The sky paled, and the foliage and clouds of smoke began to show themselves more clearly. The nightingale sang, and from the fields came the cry of quails.

"It is time for bed!" said Tanya. "It is cold too." She took Kovrin by the hand. "Thanks, Andriusha, for coming We are cursed with most uninteresting acquaintances, and not many even of them. With us it is always garden, garden, garden, and nothing else. Trunks, timbers," she laughed, "pippins, rennets, budding, pruning, grafting. . . . All our life goes into the garden, we never even dream of anything but apples and pears. Of course this is all very good and useful, but sometimes I cannot help wishing for change. I remember when you used to come and pay us visits, and when you came home for the holidays, how the whole house grew fresher and brighter as if someone had taken the covers off the furniture. I was then a very little girl, but I understood. . . ."

Tanya spoke for a time, and spoke with feeling. Then suddenly it came into Kovrin's head that during the summer he might become attached to this little, weak, talkative being, that he might get carried away, fall in love—in their position what was more probable and natural? The thought pleased him, amused him, and as he bent down to the kind, troubled face, he hummed to himself Pushkin's couplet:

"Oniegin, I will not conceal
That I love Tatyana madly."

By the time they reached the house Yegor Semionovich had risen. Kovrin felt no desire to sleep; he entered into conversation with the old man, and returned with him to the garden. Yegor Semionovich was tall, broad-shouldered, and fat. He suffered from shortness of breath, yet walked so quickly that it was difficult to keep up with him. His expression was always troubled and hurried, and he seemed to be thinking that if he were a single second late everything would be destroyed.

"There, brother, is a mystery for you!" he began, stopping to recover breath. "On the surface of the ground, as you see, there is frost, but raise the thermometer a couple of yards on your stick, and it is quite warm. . . . Why is that?"

"I confess I don't know," said Kovrin, laughing.

"No! . . . You can't know everything. . . . The biggest brain cannot comprehend everything. You are still engaged with your philosophy?"

"Yes, . . I am studying psychology, and philosophy generally."

"And it doesn't bore you?"

"On the contrary, I couldn't live without it."

"Well, God grant . . ." began Yegor Semionovich, smoothing his big whiskers thoughtfully. "Well, God grant . . . I am very glad for your sake, brother, very glad. . . ."

Suddenly he began to listen, and making a terrible face, ran off the path and soon vanished among the trees in a cloud of smoke.

"Who tethered this horse to the tree?" rang out a despairing voice. "Which of you thieves and murderers dared to tether this horse to the apple tree? My God, my God! Ruined, ruined, spoiled, destroyed! The garden is ruined, the garden is destroyed! My God!"

When he returned to Kovrin his face bore an expression of injury and impotence.

"What on earth can you do with these accursed people?" he asked in a whining voice, wringing his hands. "Stepka brought a manure cart here last night and tethered the horse to an apple tree . . . tied the reins, the idiot, so tight, that the bark is rubbed off in three places. What can you do with men like this? I speak to him and he blinks his eyes and looks stupid. He ought to be hanged!"

When at last he calmed down, he embraced Kovrin and kissed him on the cheek.

"Well, God grant . . . God grant! . . ." he stammered. "I am very, very glad that you have come. I cannot say how glad. Thanks!"

Then, with the same anxious face, and walking with the same quick step, he went round the whole garden, showing his former ward the orangery, the hothouses, the sheds, and two beehives which he described as the miracle of the century.

As they walked about, the sun rose, lighting up the garden. It grew hot. When he thought of the long, bright day before him, Kovrin remembered that it was but the beginning of May, and that he had before him a whole summer of long, bright, and happy days; and suddenly through him pulsed the joyous, youthful feeling which he had felt when as a child he played in this same garden. And in turn, he embraced the old man and kissed him tenderly. Touched by remembrances, the pair went into the house and drank tea out of the old china cups, with cream and rich biscuits; and these trifles again reminded Kovrin of his childhood and youth. The splendid present and the awakening memories of the past mingled, and a feeling of intense happiness filled his heart.

He waited until Tanya awoke, and having drunk coffee with her, walked through the garden, and then went to his room and began to work. He read attentively, making notes; and only lifted his eyes from his books when he felt that he must look out of the window or at the fresh roses, still wet with dew, which stood in vases on his table. It seemed to him that every little vein in his body trembled and pulsated with joy.

II

But in the country Kovrin continued to live the same nervous and untranquil life as he had lived in town. He read much, wrote much, studied Italian; and when he went for walks, thought all the time of returning to work. He slept so little that he astonished the household; if by chance he slept in the daytime for half an hour, he could not sleep all the following night. Yet after these sleepless nights he felt active and gay.

He talked much, drank wine, and smoked expensive cigars. Often, nearly every day, young girls from the neighbouring country-houses drove over to Borisovka, played the piano with Tanya, and sang. Sometimes the visitor was a young man, also a neighbour, who played the violin well. Kovrin listened eagerly to their music and singing, but was exhausted by it, so exhausted sometimes that his eyes closed involuntarily, and his head drooped on his shoulder.

One evening after tea he sat upon the balcony, reading. In the drawing-room Tanya—a soprano, one of her friends—a contralto, and the young violinist studied the well-known serenade of Braga. Kovrin listened to the words, but though they were Russian, could not understand their meaning. At last, laying down his book and listening attentively, he understood. A girl with a disordered imagination heard by night in a garden some mysterious sounds, sounds so beautiful and strange that she was forced to recognise their harmony and holiness, which to us mortals are incomprehensible, and therefore flew back to heaven. Kovrin's eyelids drooped. He rose, and in exhaustion walked up and down the drawing-room, and then up and down the hall. When the music ceased, he took Tanya by the hand and went out with her to the balcony.

"All day—since early morning," he began, "my head has been taken up with a strange legend. I cannot remember whether I read it, or where I heard it, but the legend is very remarkable and not very coherent. I may begin by saying that it is not very clear. A thousand years ago a monk, robed in black, wandered in the wilderness—somewhere in Syria or Arabia. . . . Some miles away the fishermen saw another black monk moving slowly over the surface of the lake. The second monk was a mirage. Now put out of your mind all the laws of optics, which legend, of course, does not recognise, and listen. From the first mirage was produced another mirage, from the second, a third, so that the image of the Black Monk is eternally reflected from one stratum of the atmosphere to another. At one time it was seen in Africa, then in Spain, then in India, then in the Far North. At last it issued from the limits of the earth's atmosphere, but never came across conditions which would cause it to disappear. Maybe it is seen to-day in Mars or in the constellation of the Southern Cross. Now the whole point, the very essence of the legend, lies in the prediction that exactly a thousand years after the monk went into the wilderness, the mirage will again be cast into the atmosphere of the earth and show itself to the world of men. This term of a thousand years, it appears, is now expiring. . . . According to the legend we must expect the Black Monk to-day or to-morrow."

"It is a strange story," said Tanya, whom the legend did not please.

"But the most astonishing thing," laughed Kovrin, "is that I cannot remember how this legend came into my head. Did I read it? Did I hear it? Or can it be that I dreamed of the Black Monk? I cannot remember. But the legend interests me. All day long I thought of nothing else."

Releasing Tanya, who returned to her visitors, he went out of the house, and walked lost in thought beside the flower-beds. Already the sun was setting. The freshly watered flowers exhaled a damp, irritating smell. In the house the music had again begun, and from the distance the violin produced the effect of a human voice. Straining his memory in an attempt to recall where he had heard the legend, Kovrin walked slowly across the park, and then, not noticing where he went, to the river-bank.

By the path which ran down among the uncovered roots to the water's edge Kovrin descended, frightening the snipe, and disturbing two ducks. On the dark pine trees glowed the rays of the setting sun, but on the surface of the river darkness had already fallen. Kovrin crossed the stream. Before him now lay a broad field covered with young rye. Neither human dwelling nor human soul was visible in the distance; and it seemed that the path must lead to the unexplored, enigmatical region in the west where the sun had already set—where still, vast and majestic, flamed the afterglow.

"How open it is—how peaceful and free?" thought Kovrin, walking along the path. "It seems as if all the world is looking at me from a hiding-place and waiting for me to comprehend it."

A wave passed over the rye, and the light evening breeze blew softly on his uncovered head. Yet a minute more and the breeze blew again, this time more strongly, the rye rustled, and from behind came the dull murmur of the pines. Kovrin stopped in amazement. On the horizon, like a cyclone or waterspout, a great, black pillar rose up from earth to heaven. Its outlines were undefined: but from the first it might be seen that it was not standing still, but moving with inconceivable speed towards Kovrin; and the nearer it came the smaller and smaller it grew. Involuntarily Kovrin rushed aside and made a path for it. A monk in black clothing, with grey hair and black eyebrows, crossing his hands upon his chest, was borne past. His bare feet were above the ground. Having swept some twenty yards past Kovrin, he looked at him, nodded his head, and smiled kindly and at the same time slyly. His face was pale and thin. When he had passed by Kovrin he again began to grow, flew across the river, struck inaudibly against the clay bank and pine trees, and, passing through them, vanished like smoke.

"You see," stammered Kovrin, "after all, the legend was true!"

Making no attempt to explain this strange phenomenon; satisfied with the fact that he had so closely and so plainly seen not only the black clothing but even the face and eyes of the monk; agitated agreeably, he returned home.

In the park and in the garden visitors were walking quietly; in the house the music continued. So he alone had seen the Black Monk. He felt a strong desire to tell what he had seen to Tanya and Yegor Semionovich, but feared that they would regard it as an hallucination, and decided to keep his counsel. He laughed loudly, sang, danced a mazurka, and felt in the best of spirits; and the guests and Tanya noticed upon his face a peculiar expression of ecstasy and inspiration, and found him very interesting.

III

When supper was over and the visitors had gone, he went to his own room, and lay on the sofa. He wished to think of the monk. But in a few minutes Tanya entered.

"There, Andriusha, you can read father's articles . . ." she said. "They are splendid articles. He writes very well."

"Magnificent!" said Yegor Semionovich, coming in after her, with a forced smile. "Don't listen to her, please! . . . Or read them only if you want to go to sleep—they are a splendid soporific."

"In my opinion they are magnificent," said Tanya, deeply

convinced. "Read them, Andriusha, and persuade father to write more often. He could write a whole treatise on gardening."

Yegor Semionovich laughed, blushed, and stammered out the conventional phrases used by abashed authors. At last he gave in.

"If you must read them, read first these papers of Gauché's, and the Russian articles," he stammered, picking out the papers with trembling hands. "Otherwise you won't understand them. Before you read my replies you must know what I am replying to. But it won't interest you . . . stupid. And it's time for bed."

Tanya went out. Yegor Semionovich sat on the end of the sofa and sighed loudly.

"Akh, brother mine . . ." he began after a long silence. "So you see, my dear *Magister,* I write articles, and exhibit at shows, and get medals sometimes. . . . Pesotzky, they say, has apples as big as your head. . . . Pesotzky has made a fortune out of his gardens. . . . In one word:

" 'Rich and glorious is Kochubey.' "

"But I should like to ask you what is going to be the end of all this? The gardens—there is no question of that—are splendid, they are models. . . . Not gardens at all, in short, but a whole institution of high political importance, and a step towards a new era in Russian agriculture and Russian industry. . . . But for what purpose? What ultimate object?"

"That question is easily answered."

"I do not mean in that sense. What I want to know is what will happen with the garden when I die? As things are, it would not last without me a single month. The secret does not lie in the fact that the garden is big and the workers many, but in the fact that I love the work—you understand? I love it, perhaps, more than I love myself. Just look at me! I work from morning to night. I do everything with my own hands. All grafting, all pruning, all planting—everything is done by me. When I am helped I feel jealous, and get irritated to the point of rudeness. The whole secret is in love, in a sharp master's eye, in a master's hands, and in the feeling when I drive over to a friend and sit down for half an hour, that I have left my heart behind me and am not myself—all the time I am in dread that something has happened to the garden. Now suppose I die to-morrow, who will replace all this? Who will do the work? The head gardeners? The workmen? Why, the whole burden of my present worries is that my greatest enemy is not the hare or the beetle or the frost, but the hands of the stranger."

"But Tanya?" said Kovrin, laughing. "Surely she is not more dangerous than a hare? . . . She loves and understands the work."

"Yes, Tanya loves it and understands it. If after my death the garden should fall to her as mistress, then I could wish for nothing better. But suppose—which God forbid—she should marry!" Yegor Semionovich whispered and looked at Kovrin with frightened eyes. "That's the whole crux. She might marry, there would be children, and there would be no time to attend to the garden. That is bad enough. But what I fear most of all is that she may marry some spendthrift who is always in want of money, who will lease the garden to tradesmen, and the whole thing will go to the devil in the first year. In a business like this a woman is the scourge of God."

Yegor Semionovich sighed and was silent for a few minutes.

"Perhaps you may call it egoism. But I do not want Tanya to marry. I am afraid! You've seen that fop who comes along with a fiddle and makes a noise. I know Tanya would never marry him, yet I cannot bear the sight of him. . . . In short, brother, I am a character . . . and I know it."

Yegor Semionovich rose and walked excitedly up and down the room. It was plain that he had something very serious to say, but could not bring himself to the point.

"I love you too sincerely not to talk to you frankly," he said, thrusting his hands into his pockets. "In all delicate questions I say what I think, and dislike mystification. I tell you plainly, therefore, that you are the only man whom I should not be afraid of Tanya marrying. You are a clever man, you have a heart, and you would not see my life's work ruined. And what is more, I love you as my own son . . . and am proud of you. So if you and Tanya were to end . . . in a sort of romance . . . I should be very glad and very happy. I tell you this straight to your face, without shame, as becomes an honest man."

Kovrin smiled. Yegor Semionovich opened the door, and was leaving the room, but stopped suddenly on the threshold.

"And if you and Tanya had a son, I could make a horticulturist out of him," he added. "But that is an idle fancy. Good night!"

Left alone, Kovrin settled himself comfortably, and took up his host's articles. The first was entitled "Intermediate Culture," the second "A Few Words in Reply to the Remarks of Mr. Z. about the Treatment of the Soil of a New Garden," the third "More about Grafting." The others were similar in scope. But all breathed restlessness and sickly irritation. Even a paper with the peaceful title of "Russian Apple Trees" exhaled irritability. Yegor Semionovich began with the words "Audi alteram partem," and ended it with "Sapienti sat"; and between these learned quotations flowed a whole torrent of acid words directed against "the learned ignorance of our patent horticulturists who observe nature from their academic chairs," and against M. Gauché, "whose fame is founded on the admiration of the profane and *dilettanti*." And finally Kovrin came across an uncalled-for and quite insincere expression of regret that it is no longer legal to flog peasants who are caught stealing fruit and injuring trees.

"His is good work, wholesome and fascinating," thought Kovrin, "yet in these pamphlets we have nothing but bad temper and war to the knife. I suppose it is the same everywhere; in all careers men of ideas are nervous, and victims of this kind of exalted sensitiveness. I suppose it must be so."

He thought of Tanya, so delighted with her father's articles, and then of Yegor Semionovich. Tanya, small, pale, and slight, with her collar-bone showing, with her widely-opened, her dark and clever eyes, which it seemed were always searching for something. And Yegor Semionovich with his little, hurried steps. He thought again of Tanya, fond of talking, fond of argument, and always accompanying even the most insignificant phrases with mimicry and gesticulation. Nervous—she must be nervous in the highest degree.

Again Kovrin began to read, but he understood nothing, and threw down his books. The agreeable emotion with which he had danced the mazurka and listened to the music still held possession of him, and aroused a multitude of thoughts. It flashed upon him that if this strange, unnatural monk had been seen by him alone, he must be ill, ill to the point of suffering from hallucinations. The thought frightened him, but not for long.

He sat on the sofa, and held his head in his hands, curbing the inexplicable joy which filled his whole being; and then walked up and down the room for a minute, and returned to his work. But the thoughts which he read in books no longer satisfied him. He longed for something vast, infinite. astonishing. Toward morning he undressed and went unwillingly to bed; he felt that he had better rest. When at last he heard Yegor Semionovich going to his work in the garden, he rang, and ordered the servant to bring him some wine. He drank several glasses; his consciousness became dim, and he slept.

IV

Yegor Semionovich and Tanya often quarrelled and said disagreeable things to one another. This morning they had both been irritated, and Tanya burst out crying and went to her room, coming down neither to dinner nor to tea. At first Yegor Semionovich marched about, solemn and dignified, as if wishing to give everyone to understand that for him justice and order were the supreme interests in life. But he was unable to keep this up for long; his spirits fell, and he wandered about the park and sighed, "Akh, my God!" At dinner he ate nothing, and at last, tortured by his conscience, he knocked softly at the closed door, and called timidly:

"Tanya! Tanya!"

Through the door came a weak voice, tearful but determined.

"Leave me alone! . . . I implore you."

The misery of father and daughter reacted on the whole household, even on the labourers in the garden. Kovrin, as usual, was immersed in his own interesting work, but at last even he felt tired and uncomfortable. He determined to interfere, and disperse the cloud before evening. He knocked at Tanya's door, and was admitted.

"Come, come! What a shame!" he began jokingly; and then looked with surprise at her tear-stained and afflicted face covered with red spots. "Is it so serious, then? Well, well!"

"But if you knew how he tortured me!" she said, and a flood of tears gushed out of her big eyes. "He tormented me!" she continued, wringing her hands. "I never said a word to him. . . . I only said there was no need to keep unnecessary labourers, if . . . if we can get day workmen. . . . You know the men have done nothing for the whole week! . . I only said this, and he roared at me, and said a lot of things . . . most offensive . . . deeply insulting. And all for nothing."

"Never mind!" said Kovrin, straightening her hair. "You have had your scoldings and your cryings, and that is surely enough. You can't keep up this for ever . . . it is not right . . . all the more since you know he loves you infinitely."

"He has ruined my whole life," sobbed Tanya. "I never hear anything but insults and affronts. He regards me as superfluous in his own house. Let him! He will have cause! I shall leave here to-morrow, and study for a position as telegraphist. . . . Let him!" .

"Come, come. Stop crying, Tanya. It does you no good. . . . You are both irritable and impulsive, and both in the wrong. Come, and I will make peace!"

Kovrin spoke gently and persuasively, but Tanya continued to cry, twitching her shoulders and wringing her hands as if she had been overtaken by a real misfortune. Kovrin felt all the sorrier owing to the smallness of the cause of her sorrow. What a trifle it took to make this little creature unhappy for a whole day, or, as she had expressed it, for a whole life! And as he consoled Tanya, it occurred to him that except this girl and her father there was not one in the world who loved him as a kinsman; and had it not been for them, he, left fatherless and motherless in early childhood, must have lived his whole life without feeling one sincere caress, or tasting ever that simple, unreasoning love which we feel only for those akin to us by blood. And he felt that his tired, strained nerves, like magnets, responded to the nerves of this crying, shuddering girl. He felt, too, that he could never love a healthy, rosy-cheeked woman; but pale, weak, unhappy Tanya appealed to him.

He felt pleasure in looking at her hair and her shoulders; and he pressed her hand, and wiped away her tears. . . . At last she ceased crying. But she still continued to complain of her father, and of her insufferable life at home, imploring Kovrin to try to realise her position. Then by degrees she began to smile, and to sigh that God had cursed her with such a wicked temper; and in the end laughed aloud, called herself a fool, and ran out of the room.

A little later Kovrin went into the garden. Yegor Semionovich and Tanya, as if nothing had happened, were walking side by side up the alley, eating rye-bread and salt. Both were very hungry.

V

Pleased with his success as peacemaker, Kovrin went into the park. As he sat on a bench and mused, he heard the rattle of a carriage and a woman's laugh—visitors evidently again. Shadows fell in the garden, the sound of a violin, the music of a woman's voice reached him almost inaudibly; and this reminded him of the Black Monk. Whither, to what country, to what planet, had that optical absurdity flown?

Hardly had he called to mind the legend and painted in imagination the black apparition in the rye-field when from behind the pine trees opposite to him, walked inaudibly—without the faintest rustling—a man of middle height. His grey head was uncovered, he was dressed in black, and bare-footed like a beggar. On his pallid, corpse-like face stood out sharply a number of black spots. Nodding his head politely the stranger or beggar walked noiselessly to the bench and sat down, and Kovrin recognised the Black Monk. For a minute they looked at one another, Kovrin with astonishment, but the monk kindly and, as, before, with a sly expression on his face.

"But you are a mirage," said Kovrin. "Why are you here, and why do you sit in one place? That is not in accordance with the legend."

"It is all the same," replied the monk softly, turning his face toward Kovrin. "The legend, the mirage, I—all are products of your own excited imagination. I am a phantom."

"That is to say you don't exist?" asked Kovrin.

"Think as you like," replied the monk, smiling faintly. "I exist in your imagination, and as your imagination is a part of Nature, I must exist also in Nature."

"You have a clever, a distinguished face—it seems to me as if in reality you had lived more than a thousand years," said Kovrin. "I did not know that my imagination was capable of creating such a phenomenon. Why do you look at me with such rapture? Are you pleased with me?"

"Yes. For you are one of the few who can justly be named the elected of God. You serve eternal truth. Your thoughts, your intentions, your astonishing science, all your life bear the stamp of divinity, a heavenly impress; they are dedicated to the rational and the beautiful, and that is, to the Eternal."

"You say, to eternal truth. Then can eternal truth be accessible and necessary to men if there is no eternal life?"

"There is eternal life," said the monk.

"You believe in the immortality of men."

"Of course. For you, men, there awaits a great and a beautiful future. And the more the world has of men like you the nearer will this future be brought. Without you, ministers to the highest principles, living freely and consciously, humanity would be nothing; developing in the natural order it must wait the end of its earthly history. But you, by some thousands of years, hasten it into the kingdom of eternal truth—and in this is your high service. You embody in yourself the blessing of God which rested upon the people."

"And what is the object of eternal life?" asked Kovrin.

"The same as all life—enjoyment. True enjoyment is in knowledge, and eternal life presents innumerable, inexhaustible fountains of knowledge; it is in this sense it was said: 'In My Father's house are many mansions. . . .'"

"You cannot conceive what a joy it is to me to listen to you," said Kovrin, rubbing his hands with delight.

"I am glad."

"Yet I know that when you leave me I shall be tormented by doubt as to your reality. You are a phantom, a hallucination. But that means that I am physically diseased, that I am not in a normal state?"

"What if you are? That need not worry you. You are ill because you have overstrained your powers, because you have borne your health in sacrifice to one idea, and the time is near when you will sacrifice not merely it but your life also. What more could you desire? It is what all gifted and noble natures aspire to."

"But if I am physically diseased, how can I trust myself?"

"And how do you know that the men of genius whom all the world trusts have not also seen visions? Genius, they tell you now, is akin to insanity. Believe me, the healthy and the normal are but ordinary men—the herd. Fears as to a nervous age, over-exhaustion and degeneration can trouble seriously only those whose aims in life lie in the present—that is the herd."

"The Romans had as their ideal: *mens sana in corpore sano.*"

"All that the Greeks and Romans said is not true. Exaltations, aspirations, excitements, ecstasies—all those things which distinguish poets, prophets, martyrs to ideas from ordinary men are incompatible with the animal life, that is, with physical health. I repeat, if you wish to be healthy and normal go with the herd."

"How strange that you should repeat what I myself have so often thought!" said Kovrin. "It seems as if you had watched me and listened to my secret thoughts. But do not talk about me. What do you imply by the words: eternal truth?"

The monk made no answer. Kovrin looked at him, but could not make out his face. His features clouded and melted away; his head and arms disappeared; his body faded into the bench and into the twilight, and vanished utterly.

"The hallucination has gone," said Kovrin, laughing. "It is a pity."

He returned to the house lively and happy. What the Black Monk had said to him flattered, not his self-love, but his soul, his whole being. To be the elected, to minister to eternal truth, to stand in the ranks of those who hasten by thousands of years the making mankind worthy of the kingdom of Christ, to deliver humanity from thousands of years of struggle, sin, and suffering, to give to one idea everything, youth, strength, health, to die for the general welfare—what an exalted, what a glorious ideal! And when through his memory flowed his past life, a life pure and chaste and full of labour, when he remembered what he had learnt and what he had taught, he concluded that in the words of the monk there was no exaggeration.

Through the park, to meet him, came Tanya. She was wearing a different dress from that in which he had last seen her.

"You here?" she cried. "We were looking for you, looking . . . But what has happened?" she asked in surprise, looking into his glowing, enraptured face, and into his eyes, now full of tears. "How strange you are, Andriusha!"

"I am satisfied, Tanya," said Kovrin, laying his hand upon her shoulder. "I am more than satisfied; I am happy! Tanya, dear Tanya, you are inexpressibly dear to me. Tanya, I am so glad!"

He kissed both her hands warmly, and continued:

"I have just lived through the brightest, most wonderful, most unearthly moments. . . . But I cannot tell you all, for you would call me mad, or refuse to believe me. . . Let me speak of you! Tanya, I love you, and have long loved you. To have you near me, to meet you ten times a day, has become a necessity for me. I do not know how I shall live without you when I go home."

"No!" laughed Tanya. "You will forget us all in two days. We are little people, and you are a great man."

"Let us talk seriously," said he. "I will take you with me, Tanya! Yes? You will come? You will be mine?"

Tanya cried "What?" and tried to laugh again. But the laugh did not come, and, instead, red spots stood out on her cheeks. She breathed quickly, and walked on rapidly into the park.

"I did not think . . . I never thought of this . . . never thought," she said, pressing her hands together as if in despair.

But Kovrin hastened after her, and, with the same glowing, enraptured face, continued to speak.

"I wish for a love which will take possession of me altogether, and this love only you, Tanya, can give me. I am happy! How happy!"

She was overcome, bent, withered up, and seemed suddenly to have aged ten years. But Kovrin found her beautiful, and loudly expressed his ecstasy:

"How lovely she is!"

VI

When he learned from Kovrin that not only had a romance resulted, but that a wedding was to follow, Yegor Semionovich walked from corner to corner, and tried to conceal his agitation. His hands shook, his neck seemed swollen and purple; he ordered the horses to be put into his racing droshky, and drove away. Tanya, seeing how he whipped the horses and how he pushed his cap down over his ears, understood his mood, locked herself into her room, and cried all day.

In the orangery the peaches and plums were already ripe. The packing and despatch to Moscow of such a delicate load required much attention, trouble, and bustle. Owing to the heat of the summer every tree had to be watered; the process was costly in time and working-power; and many caterpillars appeared, which the workmen, and even Yegor Semionovich and Tanya, crushed with their fingers, to the great disgust of Kovrin. The autumn orders for fruit and trees had to be attended to, and a vast correspondence carried on. And at the very busiest time, when it seemed no one had a free moment, work began in the fields and deprived the garden of half its workers. Yegor Semionovich, very sunburnt, very irritated, and very worried, galloped about, now to the garden, now to the fields; and all the time shouted that they were tearing him to bits, and that he would put a bullet through his brain.

On top of all came the bustle over Tanya's trousseau, to which the Pesotzkys attributed infinite significance. With the eternal snipping of scissors, rattle of sewing-machines, smell of flat-irons, and the caprices of the nervous and touchy dressmaker, the whole house seemed to spin around. And, to make matters worse, visitors arrived every day, and these visitors had to be amused, fed, and lodged for the night. Yet work and worry passed unnoticed in a mist of joy. Tanya felt as if love and happiness had suddenly burst upon her, although ever since her fourteenth year she had been certain that Kovrin would marry nobody but herself. She was eternally in a state of astonishment, doubt, and disbelief in herself. At one moment she was seized by such great joy that she felt she must fly away to the clouds and pray to God; but a moment later she remembered that when August came she would have to leave the home of her childhood and forsake her father; and she was frightened by the thought—God knows whence it came—that she was trivial, insignificant, and unworthy of a great man like Kovrin. When such thoughts came she would run up to her room, lock herself in, and cry bitterly for hours. But when visitors were present, it broke in upon her that Kovrin was a singularly handsome man, that all the women loved him and envied her; and in these moments her heart was as full of rapture and pride as if she had conquered the whole world. When he dared to smile on any other woman she trembled with jealousy, went to her room, and again—tears. These new feelings possessed her altogether; she helped her father mechanically, noticing neither papers nor caterpillars, nor workmen, nor how swiftly time was passing by.

Yegor Semionovich was in much the same state of mind. He still worked from morning to night, flew about the gardens, and lost his temper; but all the while he was wrapped in a magic reverie. In his sturdy body contended two men, one the real Yegor Semionovich, who, when he listened to the gardener, Ivan Karlovich's report of some mistake or disorder, went mad with excitement, and tore his hair; and the other the unreal Yegor Semionovich—a half-intoxicated old man, who broke off an important conversation in the middle of a word, seized the gardener by the shoulder, and stammered:

"You may say what you like, but blood is thicker than water. His mother was an astonishing, a most noble, a most brilliant woman. It was a pleasure to see her good, pure, open, angel face. She painted beautifully, wrote poetry, spoke five foreign languages, and sang. . . . Poor thing, Heaven rest her soul, she died of consumption!"

The unreal Yegor Semionovich sighed, and after a moment's silence continued:

"When he was a boy growing up to manhood in my house he had just such an angel face, open and good. His looks, his movements, his words were as gentle and graceful as his mother's. And his intellect! It is not for nothing he has the degree of *Magister*. But you just wait, Ivan Karlovich; you'll see what he'll be in ten years' time. Why, he'll be out of sight!"

But here the real Yegor Semionovich remembered himself, seized his head and roared:

"Devils! Frost-bitten! Ruined, destroyed! The garden is ruined; the garden is destroyed!"

Kovrin worked with all his former ardour, and hardly noticed the bustle about him. Love only poured oil on the flames. After every meeting with Tanya, he returned to his rooms in rapture and happiness, and set to work with his books and manuscripts with the same passion with which he had kissed her and sworn his love. What the Black Monk had told him of his election by God, of eternal truth, and of the glorious future of humanity, gave to all his work a peculiar, unusual significance. Once or twice every week, either in the park or in the house, he met the monk, and talked with him for hours; but this did not frighten, but on the contrary delighted him, for he was now assured that such apparitions visit only the elect and exceptional who dedicate themselves to the ministry of ideas.

Assumption passed unobserved. Then came the wedding celebrated by the determined wish of Yegor Semionovich with what was called *éclat,* that is, with meaningless festivities which lasted for two days. Three thousand rubles were consumed in food and drink; but what with the vile music, the noisy toasts, the fussing servants, the clamour, and the closeness of the atmosphere, no one appreciated the expensive wines or the astonishing *hors d'œuvres* specially ordered from Moscow.

VII

One of the long winter nights. Kovrin lay in bed, reading a French novel. Poor Tanya, whose head every evening ached as the result of the unaccustomed life in town, had long been sleeping, muttering incoherent phrases in her dreams.

The clock struck three. Kovrin put out the candle and lay down, lay for a long time with closed eyes unable to sleep owing to the heat of the room and Tanya's continued muttering. At half-past four he again lighted the candle. The Black Monk was sitting in a chair beside his bed.

"Good night!" said the monk, and then, after a moment's silence, asked, "What are you thinking of now?"

"Of glory," answered Kovrin. "In a French novel which I have just been reading, the hero is a young man who does foolish things, and dies from a passion for glory. To me this passion is inconceivable."

"Because you are too clever. You look indifferently on fame as a toy which cannot interest you."

"That is true."

"Celebrity has no attraction for you. What flattery, joy, or instruction can a man draw from the knowledge that his name will be graven on a monument, when time will efface the inscription sooner or later? Yes, happily there are too many of you for brief human memory to remember all your names."

"Of course," said Kovrin. "And why remember them? . . . But let us talk of something else. Of happiness, for instance. What is this happiness?"

When the clock struck five he was sitting on the bed with his feet trailing on the carpet and his head turned to the monk, and saying:

"In ancient times a man became frightened at his happiness, so great it was, and to placate the gods laid before them in sacrifice his beloved ring. You have heard? Now I, like Polycrates, am a little frightened at my own happiness. From morning to night I experience only joy—joy absorbs me and stifles all other feelings. I do not know the meaning of grief, affliction, or weariness. I speak seriously, I am beginning to doubt."

"Why?" asked the monk in an astonished tone. "Then you think joy is a supernatural feeling? You think it is not the normal condition of things? No! The higher a man has climbed in mental and moral development the freer he is, the greater satisfaction he draws from life. Socrates, Diogenes, Marcus Aurelius knew joy and not sorrow. And the apostle said, 'rejoice exceedingly.' Rejoice and be happy!"

"And suddenly the gods will be angered," said Kovrin jokingly. "But it would hardly be to my taste if they were to steal my happiness and force me to shiver and starve."

Tanya awoke, and looked at her husband with amazement and terror. He spoke, he turned to the chair, he gesticulated, and laughed; his eyes glittered and his laughter sounded strange.

"Andriusha, whom are you speaking to?" she asked, seizing the hand which he had stretched out to the monk. "Andriusha, who is it?"

"Who?" answered Kovrin. "Why, the monk! . . . He is sitting there." He pointed to the Black Monk.

"There is no one there, . . . no one. Andriusha; you are ill."

Tanya embraced her husband, and, pressing against him as if to defend him against the apparition, covered his eyes with her hand.

"You are ill," she sobbed, trembling all over. "Forgive me, darling, but for a long time I have fancied you were unnerved in some way. . . . You are ill, . . . physically, Andriusha."

The shudder communicated itself to him. He looked once more at the chair, now empty, and suddenly felt weakness in his arms and legs. He began to dress.

"It is nothing, Tanya, nothing, . . ." he stammered, and still shuddered. "But I am a little unwell. . . . It is time to recognise it."

"I have noticed it for a long time. and father noticed it," she said, trying to restrain her sobs. "You have been speaking so funnily to yourself, and smiling so strangely, . . . and you do not sleep. O, my God, my God, save us!" she cried in terror. "But do not be afraid, Andriusha, do not fear, . . . for God's sake do not be afraid. . . ."

She also dressed. . . . It was only as he looked at her that Kovrin understood the danger of his position, and realised the meaning of the Black Monk and of their conversations. It became plain to him that he was mad.

Both, themselves not knowing why, dressed and went into the hall; she first, he after her. There they found Yegor Semionovich in his dressing-gown. He was staying with them, and had been awakened by Tanya's sobs.

"Do not be afraid, Andriusha," said Tanya, trembling as if in fever. "Do not be afraid . . . father, this will pass off . . . it will pass off."

Kovrin was so agitated that he could hardly speak. But

he tried to treat the matter as a joke. He turned to his father-in-law and attempted to say:

"Congratulate me . . . it seems I have gone out of my mind." But his lips only moved, and he smiled bitterly.

At nine o'clock they put on his overcoat and a fur cloak, wrapped him up in a shawl, and drove him to the doctor's. He began a course of treatment.

VIII

Again summer. By the doctor's orders Kovrin returned to the country. He had recovered his health, and no longer saw the Black Monk. It only remained for him to recruit his physical strength. He lived with his father-in-law, drank much milk, worked only two hours a day, never touched wine, and gave up smoking.

On the evening of the 19th June, before Elijah's day, a vesper service was held in the house. When the priest took the censer from the sexton, and the vast hall began to smell like a church, Kovrin felt tired. He went into the garden. Taking no notice of the gorgeous blossoms around him he walked up and down, sat for a while on a bench, and then walked through the park. He descended the sloping bank to the margin of the river, and stood still, looking questioningly at the water. The great pines, with their shaggy roots, which a year before had seen him so young, so joyous, so active, no longer whispered, but stood silent and motionless, as if not recognising him. . . . And, indeed, with his short-clipped hair, his feeble walk, and his changed face, so heavy and pale and changed since last year, he would hardly have been recognised anywhere.

He crossed the stream. In the field, last year covered with rye, lay rows of reaped oats. The sun had set, and on the horizon flamed a broad, red afterglow, foretelling stormy weather. All was quiet; and, gazing towards the point at which a year before he had first seen the Black Monk,

Kovrin stood twenty minutes watching the crimson fade. When he returned to the house, tired and unsatisfied, Yegor Semionovich and Tanya were sitting on the steps of the terrace, drinking tea. They were talking together, and, seeing Kovrin, stopped. But Kovrin knew by their faces that they had been speaking of him.

"It is time for you to have your milk," said Tanya to her husband.

"No, not yet," he answered, sitting down on the lowest step. "You drink it. I do not want it."

Tanya timidly exchanged glances with her father, and said in a guilty voice:

"You know very well that the milk does you good."

"Yes, any amount of good," laughed Kovrin. "I congratulate you, I have gained a pound in weight since last Friday." He pressed his hands to his head and said in a pained voice: "Why . . . why have you cured me? Bromide mixtures, idleness, warm baths, watching in trivial terror over every mouthful, every step . . . all this in the end will drive me to idiocy. I had gone out of my mind . . . I had the mania of greatness. . . . But for all that I was bright, active, and ever happy. . . . I was interesting and original. Now I have become rational and solid, just like the rest of the world. I am a mediocrity, and it is tiresome for me to live. . . . Oh, how cruelly . . . how cruelly you have treated me! I had hallucinations . . . but what harm did that cause to anyone? I ask you what harm?"

"God only knows what you mean!" sighed Yegor Semionovich. "It is stupid even to listen to you."

"Then you need not listen."

The presence of others, especially of Yegor Semionovich, now irritated Kovrin; he answered his father-in-law drily, coldly, even rudely, and could not look on him without contempt and hatred. And Yegor Semionovich felt confused, and coughed guiltily, although he could not see how he was in the wrong. Unable to understand the cause of such a sudden reversal of their former hearty relations, Tanya leaned against her father, and looked with alarm into his eyes. It was becoming plain to her that their relations every day grew worse and worse, that her father had aged greatly, and that her husband had become irritable, capricious, excitable, and uninteresting. She no longer laughed and sang, she ate nothing, and whole nights never slept, but lived under the weight of some impending terror, torturing herself so much that she lay insensible from dinner-time till evening. When the service was being held, it had seemed to her that her father was crying; and now as she sat on the terrace she made an effort not to think of it.

"How happy were Buddha and Mahomet and Shakespeare that their kind-hearted kinsmen and doctors did not cure them of ecstasy and inspiration!" said Kovrin. "If Mahomet had taken potassium bromide for his nerves, worked only two hours a day, and drunk milk, that astonishing man would have left as little behind him as his dog. Doctors and kind-hearted relatives only do their best to make humanity stupid, and the time will come when mediocrity will be considered genius, and humanity will perish. If you only had some idea," concluded Kovrin peevishly, "if you only had some idea how grateful I am!"

He felt strong irritation, and to prevent himself saying too much, rose and went into the house. It was a windless night, and into the window was borne the smell of tobacco plants and jalap. Through the windows of the great dark hall, on the floor and on the piano, fell the moonrays. Kovrin recalled the raptures of the summer before, when the air, as now, was full of the smell of jalap and the moonrays poured through the window. . . . To awaken the mood of last year he went to his own room, lighted a strong cigar, and ordered the servant to bring him wine. But now the cigar was bitter and distasteful, and the wine had lost its flavour of the year before. How much it means to get out of practice! From a single cigar, and two sips of wine, his head went round, and he was obliged to take bromide of potassium.

Before going to bed Tanya said to him:

"Listen. Father worships you, but you are annoyed with him about something, and that is killing him. Look at his face; he is growing old, not by days but by hours! I implore you, Andriusha, for the love of Christ, for the sake of your dead father, for the sake of my peace of mind—be kind to him again!"

"I cannot, and I do not want to."

"But why?" Tanya trembled all over. "Explain to me why!"

"Because I do not like him; that is all," answered Kovrin carelessly, shrugging his shoulders. "But better not talk of that: he is your father."

"I cannot, cannot understand," said Tanya. She pressed her hands to her forehead and fixed her eyes on one point. "Something terrible, something incomprehensible is going on in this house. You, Andriusha, have changed; you are no longer yourself. . . . You—a clever, an exceptional man—get irritated over trifles. . . . You are annoyed by such little things that at any other time you yourself would have refused to believe it. No . . . do not be angry, do not be angry," she continued, kissing his hands, and frightened by her own words. "You are clever, good, and noble. You will be just to father. He is so good."

"He is not good, but merely good-humoured. These vaudeville uncles—of your father's type—with well-fed, easy-going faces, are characters in their way, and once used to amuse me, whether in novels, in comedies, or in life. But they are now hateful to me. They are egoists to the marrow of their bones. . . . Most disgusting of all is their satiety, and this stomachic, purely bovine—or swinish—optimism."

Tanya sat on the bed, and laid her head on a pillow.

"This is torture!" she said; and from her voice it was plain that she was utterly weary and found it hard to speak.

"Since last winter not a moment of rest. . . . It is terrible, my God! I suffer . . ."

"Yes, of course! I am Herod, and you and your papa the massacred infants. Of course!"

His face seemed to Tanya ugly and disagreeable. The expression of hatred and contempt did not suit it. She even observed that something was lacking in his face: ever since his hair had been cut off, it seemed changed. She felt an almost irresistible desire to say something insulting, but restrained herself in time, and overcome with terror, went out of the bedroom.

IX

Kovrin received an independent chair. His inaugural address was fixed for the 2nd of December, and a notice to that effect was posted in the corridors of the University. But when the day came a telegram was received by the University authorities that he could not fulfill the engagement, owing to illness.

Blood came from his throat. He spat it up, and twice in one month it flowed in streams. He felt terribly weak, and fell into a somnolent condition. But this illness did not frighten him, for he knew that his dead mother had lived with the same complaint more than ten years. His doctors, too, declared that there was no danger, and advised him merely not to worry, to lead a regular life, and to talk less.

In January the lecture was postponed for the same reason, and in February it was too late to begin the course. It was postponed till the following year.

He no longer lived with Tanya, but with another woman, older than himself, who looked after him as if he were a child. His temper was calm and obedient; he submitted willingly, and when Varvara Nikolayevna—that was her name—made arrangements for taking him to the Crimea, he consented to go, although he felt that from the change no good would come.

They reached Sevastopol late one evening, and stopped there to rest, intending to drive to Yalta on the following day. Both were tired by the journey. Varvara Nikolayevna drank tea, and went to bed. But Kovrin remained up. An hour before leaving home for the railway station he had received a letter from Tanya, which he had not read; and the thought of this letter caused him unpleasant agitation. In the depths of his heart he knew that his marriage with Tanya had been a mistake. He was glad that he was finally parted from her; but the remembrance of this woman, who towards the last had seemed to turn into a walking, living mummy, in which all had died except the great, clever eyes, awakened in him only pity and vexation against himself. The writing on the envelope reminded him that two years before he had been guilty of cruelty and injustice, and that he had avenged on people in no way guilty his spiritual vacuity, his solitude, his disenchantment with life. . . . He remembered how he had once torn into fragments his dissertation and all the articles written by him since the time of his illness, and thrown them out of the window, how the fragments flew in the wind and rested on the trees and flowers; in every page he had seen strange and baseless pretensions, frivolous irritation, and a mania for greatness. And all this had produced upon him an impression that he had written a description of his own faults. Yet when the last copybook had been torn up and thrown out of the window, he felt bitterness and vexation, and went to his wife and spoke to her cruelly. Heavens, how he had ruined her life! He remembered how once, wishing to cause her pain, he had told her that her father had played in their romance an unusual rôle, and had even asked him to marry her; and Yegor Semionovich, happening to overhear him, had rushed into the room, so dumb with consternation that he could not utter a word, but only stamped his feet on one spot and bellowed strangely as if his tongue had been cut out. And Tanya, looking at her father, cried out in a heart-rending voice, and fell insensible on the floor. It was hideous.

The memory of all this returned to him at the sight of the well-known handwriting. He went out on to the balcony. It was warm and calm, and a salt smell came to him from the sea. The moonlight, and the lights around, were imaged on the surface of the wonderful bay—a surface of a hue impossible to name. It was a tender and soft combination of dark blue and green; in parts the water resembled copperas, and in parts, instead of water, liquid moonlight filled the bay. And all these combined in a harmony of hues which exhaled tranquillity and exaltation.

In the lower story of the inn, underneath the balcony, the windows were evidently open, for women's voices and laughter could plainly be heard. There must be an entertainment.

Kovrin made an effort over himself, unsealed the letter, and, returning to his room, began to read:

"My father has just died. For this I am indebted to you, for it was you who killed him. Our garden is being ruined; it is managed by strangers; what my poor father so dreaded is taking place. For this also I am indebted to you. I hate you with all my soul, and wish that you may perish soon! Ah, how I suffer! My heart burns with an intolerable pain! . . . May you be accursed! I took you for an exceptional man, for a genius; I loved you, and you proved a madman. . . ."

Kovrin could read no more; he tore up the letter and threw the pieces away. . . . He was overtaken by restlessness—almost by terror. . . . On the other side of the screen, slept Varvara Nikolayevna; he could hear her breathing. From the story beneath came the women's voices and laughter, but he felt that in the whole hotel there was not one living soul except himself. The fact that wretched. overwhelmed Tanya had cursed him in her letter, and wished him ill, caused him pain; and he looked fearfully at the door as if fearing to see again that unknown power which in two years had brought about so much ruin in his own life and in the lives of all who were dearest to him.

By experience he knew that when the nerves give way the best refuge lies in work. He used to sit at the table and concentrate his mind upon some definite thought. He took from his red portfolio a copybook containing the conspect of a small work of compilation which he intended to carry out during his stay in the Crimea, if he became tired of inactivity. . . . He sat at the table, and worked on this conspect, and it seemed to him that he was regaining his former peaceful, resigned, impersonal mood. His conspect led him to speculation on the vanity of the world. He thought of the great price which life demands for the most trivial and ordinary benefits which it gives to men. To reach a chair of philosophy under forty years of age; to be an ordinary professor; to expound commonplace thoughts—and those thoughts the thoughts of others—in feeble, tiresome, heavy language; in one word, to attain the position of a learned mediocrity, he had studied fifteen years, worked day and night, passed through a severe psychical disease, survived an unsuccessful marriage—been guilty of many follies and injustices which it was torture to remember. Kovrin now clearly realised that he was a mediocrity, and he was willingly reconciled to it, for he knew that every man must be satisfied with what he is.

The conspect calmed him, but the torn letter lay upon the floor and hindered the concentration of his thoughts. He rose, picked up the fragments, and threw them out of the window. But a light wind blew from the sea, and the papers fluttered back on to the window sill. Again he was overtaken by restlessness akin to terror, and it seemed to him that in the whole hotel except himself there was not one living soul. . . . He went on to the balcony. The bay, as if alive, stared up at him from its multitude of light- and dark-blue eyes, its eyes of turquoise and fire, and beckoned him. It was warm and stifling; how delightful, he thought, to bathe!

Suddenly beneath the balcony a violin was played, and two women's voices sang. All this was known to him. The song which they sang told of a young girl, diseased in imagination, who heard by night in a garden mysterious sounds, and found in them a harmony and a holiness incomprehensible to us mortals. . . . Kovrin held his breath, his heart ceased to beat, and the magical, ecstatic rapture which he had long forgotten trembled in his heart again.

A high, black pillar, like a cyclone or waterspout, appeared on the opposite coast. It swept with incredible swiftness across the bay towards the hotel; it became smaller and smaller, and Kovrin stepped aside to make room for it. . . . The monk, with uncovered grey head, with black eyebrows, barefooted, folding his arms upon his chest, swept past him, and stopped in the middle of the room.

"Why did you not believe me?" he asked in a tone of reproach, looking caressingly at Kovrin. "If you had believed me when I said you were a genius, these last two years would not have been passed so sadly and so barrenly."

Kovrin again believed that he was the elected of God and a genius; he vividly remembered all his former conversation with the Black Monk, and wished to reply. But the blood flowed from his throat on to his chest, and he, not knowing what to do, moved his hands about his chest till his cuffs were red with the blood. He wished to call Varvara Nikolayevna, who slept behind the screen, and making an effort to do so, cried:

"Tanya!"

He fell on the floor, and raising his hands, again cried:

"Tanya!"

He cried to Tanya, cried to the great garden with the miraculous flowers, cried to the park, to the pines with their shaggy roots, to the rye-field, cried to his marvellous science, to his youth, his daring, his joy, cried to the life which had been so beautiful. He saw on the floor before him a great pool of blood, and from weakness could not utter a single word. But an inexpressible, infinite joy filled his whole being. Beneath the balcony the serenade was being played, and the Black Monk whispered to him that he was a genius, and died only because his feeble, mortal body had lost its balance, and could no longer serve as the covering of genius.

When Varvara Nikolayevna awoke, and came from behind her screen. Kovrin was dead. But on his face was frozen an immovable smile of happiness.

THE KISS

On the evening of the twentieth of May, at eight o'clock, all six batteries of the N Artillery Brigade on their way to camp arrived at the village of Miestechky with the intention of spending the night.

The confusion was at its worst—some officers fussed about the guns, others in the church square arranged with the quartermaster—when from behind the church rode a civilian upon a most remarkable mount. The small, short-tailed bay with well-shaped neck progressed with a wobbly motion, all the time making dance-like movements with its legs as if some one were switching its hoofs. When he had drawn rein level with the officers the rider doffed his cap and said ceremoniously—

"His Excellency, General von Rabbek, whose house is close by, requests the honour of the officers' company at tea. . ."

The horse shook its head, danced, and wobbled to the rear; its rider again took off his cap, and, turning his strange steed, disappeared behind the church.

"The devil take it!" was the general exclamation as the officers dispersed to their quarters. "We can hardly keep our eyes open, yet along comes this von Rabbek with his tea! I know that tea!"

The officers of the six batteries had lively memories of a past invitation. During recent manœuvres they had been asked, together with their Cossack comrades, to tea at the house of a local country gentleman, an officer in retirement, by title a Count; and this hearty, hospitable Count overwhelmed them with attentions, fed them to satiety, poured vodka down their throats, and made them stay the night.

All this, of course, they enjoyed. The trouble was that the old soldier entertained his guests too well. He kept them up till daybreak while he poured forth tales of past adventures; he dragged them from room to room to point out valuable paintings, old engravings, and rare arms; he read them holograph letters from celebrated men. And the weary officers, bored to death, listened, gaped, yearned for their beds, and yawned cautiously in their sleeves, until at last when their host released them it was too late for sleep.

Was von Rabbek another old Count? It might easily be. But there was no neglecting his invitation. The officers washed and dressed, and set out for von Rabbek's house. At the church square they learnt that they must descend the hill to the river, and follow the bank till they reached the general's gardens, where they would find a path direct to the house. Or, if they chose to go up hill, they would reach the general's barns half a verst from Miestechky. It was this route they chose.

"But who is this von Rabbek?" asked one. "The man who commanded the N Cavalry Division at Plevna?"

"No, that was not von Rabbek, but simply Rabbe—without the von."

"What glorious weather!"

At the first barn they came to, two roads diverged; one ran straight forward and faded in the dusk; the other turning to the right led to the general's house. As the officers drew near they talked less loudly. To right and left stretched rows of red-roofed brick barns, in aspect heavy and morose as the barracks of provincial towns. In front gleamed the lighted windows of von Rabbek's house.

"A good omen, gentlemen!" cried a young officer. "Our setter runs in advance. There is game ahead!"

On the face of Lieutenant Lobytko, the tall stout officer referred to, there was not one trace of hair though he was twenty-five years old. He was famed among comrades for the instinct which told him of the presence of women in the neighbourhood. On hearing his comrade's remark, he turned his head and said—

"Yes. There are women there. My instinct tells me."

A handsome, well-preserved man of sixty, in mufti, came to the hall door to greet his guests. It was von Rabbek. As he pressed their hands, he explained that though he was delighted to see them, he must beg pardon for not asking them to spend the night; as guests he already had his two sisters, their children, his brother, and several neighbours—in fact, he had not one spare room. And though he shook their hands and apologised and smiled, it was plain that he was not half as glad to see them as was last year's Count, and that he had invited them merely because good manners demanded it. The officers climbing the soft-carpeted steps and listening to their host understood this perfectly well; and realised that they carried into the house an atmosphere of intrusion and alarm. Would any man—they asked themselves—who had gathered his two sisters and their children, his brother and his neighbours, to celebrate, no doubt, some family festival, find pleasure in the invasion of nineteen officers whom he had never seen before?

A tall, elderly lady, with a good figure, and a long face with black eyebrows, who resembled closely the ex-Empress Eugenie, greeted them at the drawing-room door. Smiling courteously and with dignity, she affirmed that she was delighted to see the officers, and only regretted that she could not ask them to stay the night. But the courteous, dignified smile disappeared when she turned away, and it was quite plain that she had seen many officers in her day, that they caused not the slightest interest, and that she had invited them merely because an invitation was dictated by good breeding and by her position in the world.

In a big dining-room seated at a big table sat ten men and women, drinking tea. Behind them, veiled in cigar-smoke, stood several young men, among them one, red-whiskered and extremely thin, who spoke English loudly with a lisp. Through an open door the officers saw into a brightly lighted room with blue wall-paper.

"You are too many to introduce singly, gentlemen!" said the general loudly, with affected joviality. "Make one another's acquaintance, please—without formalities!"

The visitors, some with serious, even severe faces, some smiling constrainedly, all with a feeling of awkwardness, bowed, and took their seats at the table. Most awkward of all felt Staff-Captain Riabovich, a short, round-shouldered, spectacled officer, whiskered like a lynx. While his brother officers looked serious or smiled constrainedly, his face, his lynx whiskers, and his spectacles seemed to explain: "I am the most timid, modest, undistinguished officer in the whole brigade." For some time after he took his seat at the table he could not fix his attention on any single thing. Faces, dresses, the cut-glass cognac bottles, the steaming tumblers, the moulded cornices—all merged in a single, overwhelming sentiment which caused him intense fright and made him wish to hide his head. Like an inexperienced lecturer he saw everything before him, but could distinguish nothing, and was in fact the victim of what men of science diagnose as "psychical blindness."

But slowly conquering his diffidence, Riabovich began to distinguish and observe. As became a man both timid and unsocial, he remarked first of all the amazing temerity of his new friends. Von Rabbek, his wife, two elderly ladies, a girl in lilac, and the red-whiskered youth who, it appeared, was a young von Rabbek, sat down among the officers as unconcernedly as if they had held rehearsals, and at once plunged into various heated arguments in which they soon involved their guests. That artillerists have a much better time than cavalrymen or infantrymen was proved conclusively by the lilac girl, while von Rabbek and the elderly ladies affirmed the converse. The conversation became desultory. Riabovich listened to the lilac girl fiercely debating themes she knew nothing about and took no interest in, and watched the insincere smiles which appeared on and disappeared from her face.

While the von Rabbek family with amazing strategy inveigled their guests into the dispute, they kept their eyes on every glass and mouth. Had every one tea, was it sweet enough, why didn't one eat biscuits, was another fond of cognac? And the longer Riabovich listened and looked, the more pleased he was with this disingenuous, disciplined family.

After tea the guests repaired to the drawing-room. Instinct had not cheated Lobytko. The room was packed with young women and girls, and ere a minute had passed the setter-lieutenant stood beside a very young, fair-haired girl in black, and, bending down as if resting on an invisible sword, shrugged his shoulders coquettishly. He was uttering, no doubt, most unentertaining nonsense, for the fair girl looked indulgently at his sated face, and exclaimed indifferently, "Indeed!" And this indifferent "Indeed!" might have quickly convinced the setter that he was on a wrong scent.

Music began. As the notes of a mournful valse throbbed out of the open window, through the heads of all flashed the feeling that outside that window it was spring-time, a night of May. The air was odorous of young poplar leaves, of roses and lilacs—and the valse and the spring were sincere. Riabovich, with valse and cognac mingling tipsily in his head, gazed at the window with a smile; then began to follow the movements of the women; and it seemed that the smell of roses, poplars, and lilacs came not from the gardens outside, but from the women's faces and dresses.

They began to dance. Young von Rabbek valsed twice round the room with a very thin girl; and Lobytko, slipping on the parqueted floor, went up to the girl in lilac, and was granted a dance. But Riabovich stood near the door with the wall-flowers, and looked silently on. Amazed at the daring of men who in sight of a crowd could take unknown women by the waist, he tried in vain to picture himself doing the same. A time had been when he envied his comrades their courage and dash, suffered from painful heart-searchings, and was hurt by the knowledge that he was timid, round-shouldered, and undistinguished, that he had lynx whiskers, and that his waist was much too long. But with years he had grown reconciled to his own insignificance, and now looking at the dancers and loud talkers, he felt no envy, but only mournful emotions.

At the first quadrille von Rabbek junior approached and invited two non-dancing officers to a game of billiards. The three left the room; and Riabovich who stood idle, and felt impelled to join in the general movement, followed. They passed the dining-room, traversed a narrow glazed corridor, and a room where three sleepy footmen jumped from a sofa with a start; and after walking, it seemed, through a whole houseful of rooms, entered a small billiard-room.

Von Rabbek and the two officers began their game. Riabovich, whose only game was cards, stood near the table and looked indifferently on, as the players, with unbuttoned coats, wielded their cues, moved about, joked, and shouted obscure technical terms. Riabovich was ignored, save when one of the players jostled him or caught his cue, and turning towards him said briefly, "Pardon!" so that before the game was over he was thoroughly bored, and impressed by a sense of his superfluity, resolved to return to the drawing-room, and turned away.

It was on the way back that his adventure took place. Before he had gone far he saw that he had missed the way. He remembered distinctly the room with the three sleepy footmen; and after passing through five or six rooms entirely vacant, he saw his mistake. Retracing his steps, he turned to the left, and found himself in an almost dark room which he had not seen before; and after hesitating a minute, he boldly opened the first door he saw, and found himself in complete darkness. Through a chink of the door in front peered a bright light; from afar throbbed the dulled music of a mournful mazurka. Here, as in the drawing-room, the windows were open wide, and the smell of poplars, lilacs, and roses flooded the air.

Riabovich paused in irresolution. For a moment all was still. Then came the sound of hasty footsteps; then, without any warning of what was to come, a dress rustled, a woman's breathless voice whispered "At last!" and two soft, scented, unmistakably womanly arms met round his neck, a warm cheek impinged on his, and he received a sounding kiss. But hardly had the kiss echoed through the silence when the unknown shrieked loudly, and fled away—as it seemed to Riabovich—in disgust. Riabovich himself nearly screamed, and rushed headlong towards the bright beam in the door-chink.

As he entered the drawing-room his heart beat violently, and his hands trembled so perceptibly that he clasped them behind his back. His first emotion was shame, as if every one in the room already knew that he had just been embraced and kissed. He retired into his shell, and looked fearfully around. But finding that hosts and guests were calmly dancing or talking, he regained courage, and surrendered himself to sensations experienced for the first time in life. The unexampled had happened. His neck, fresh from the embrace of two soft, scented arms, seemed anointed with oil; near his left moustache, where the kiss had fallen, trembled a slight, delightful chill, as from peppermint drops; and from head to foot he was soaked in new and extraordinary sensations, which continued to grow and grow.

He felt that he must dance. talk, run into the garden, laugh unrestrainedly. He forgot altogether that he was round-shouldered, undistinguished. lynx-whiskered, that he had an "indefinite exterior"—a description from the lips of a woman he had happened to overhear. As Madame von Rabbek passed him he smiled so broadly and graciously that she came up and looked at him questioningly.

"What a charming house you have!" he said, straightening his spectacles.

And Madame von Rabbek smiled back, said that the house still belonged to her father, and asked were his parents alive, how long he had been in the Army, and why he was so thin. After hearing his answers she departed. But though the conversation was over, he continued to smile benevolently, and think what charming people were his new acquaintances.

At supper Riabovich ate and drank mechanically what was put before him, heard not a word of the conversation, and devoted all his powers to the unraveling of his mysterious, romantic adventure. What was the explanation? It was plain that one of the girls, he reasoned, had arranged a meeting in the dark room, and after waiting some time in vain had, in her nervous tension, mistaken Riabovich for her hero. The mistake was likely enough, for on entering the dark room Riabovich had stopped irresolutely as if he, too, were waiting for some one. So far the mystery was explained.

"But which of them was it?" he asked, searching the women's faces. She certainly was young, for old women do not indulge in such romances. Secondly, she was not a servant. That was proved unmistakably by the rustle of her dress, the scent, the voice . . .

When at first he looked at the girl in lilac she pleased him; she had pretty shoulders and arms, a clever face, a charming voice. Riabovich piously prayed that it was she. But, smiling insincerely, she wrinkled her long nose, and that at once gave her an elderly air. So Riabovich turned his eyes on the blonde in black. The blonde was younger, simpler, sincerer; she had charming kiss-curls, and drank from her tumbler with inexpressible grace. Riabovich hoped it was she—but soon he noticed that her face was flat, and bent his eyes on her neighbour.

"It is a hopeless puzzle," he reflected. "If you take the

arms and shoulders of the lilac girl, add the blonde's curls, and the eyes of the girl on Lobytko's left, then——"

He composed a portrait of all these charms, and had a clear vision of the girl who had kissed him. But she was nowhere to be seen.

Supper over, the visitors, sated and tipsy, bade their entertainers good-bye. Both host and hostess again apologised for not asking them to spend the night.

"I am very glad, very glad, gentlemen!" said the general, and this time seemed to speak sincerely, no doubt because speeding the parting guest is a kindlier office than welcoming him unwelcomed. "I am very glad indeed! I hope you will visit me on your way back. Without ceremony, please! Which way will you go? Up the hill? No, go down the hill and through the garden. That way is shorter."

The officers took his advice. After the noise and glaring illumination within doors, the garden seemed dark and still. Until they reached the wicket-gate all kept silence. Merry, half tipsy, and content, as they were, the night's obscurity and stillness inspired pensive thoughts. Through their brains, as through Riabovich's, sped probably the same question: "Will the time ever come when I, like von Rabbek, shall have a big house, a family, a garden, the chance of being gracious—even insincerely—to others, of making them sated, tipsy, and content?"

But once the garden lay behind them, all spoke at once, and burst into causeless laughter. The path they followed led straight to the river, and then ran beside it, winding around bushes, ravines, and over-hanging willow-trees. The track was barely visible; the other bank was lost entirely in gloom. Sometimes the black water imaged stars, and this was the only indication of the river's speed. From beyond it sighed a drowsy snipe, and beside them in a bush, heedless of the crowd, a nightingale chanted loudly. The officers gathered in a group, and swayed the bush, but the nightingale continued his song.

"I like his cheek!" they echoed admiringly. "He doesn't care a kopeck! The old rogue!"

Near their journey's end the path turned up the hill, and joined the road not far from the church enclosure; and there the officers, breathless from climbing, sat on the grass and smoked. Across the river gleamed a dull red light, and for want of a subject they argued the problem, whether it was a bonfire, a window-light, or something else. Riabovich looked also at the light, and felt that it smiled and winked at him as if it knew about the kiss.

On reaching home, he undressed without delay, and lay upon his bed. He shared the cabin with Lobytko and a Lieutenant Merzliakov, a staid, silent little man, by repute highly cultivated, who took with him everywhere *The Messenger of Europe,* and read it eternally. Lobytko undressed, tramped impatiently from corner to corner, and sent his servant for beer. Merzliakov lay down, balanced the candle on his pillow, and hid his head behind *The Messenger of Europe.*

"Where is she now?" muttered Riabovich, looking at the soot-blacked ceiling.

His neck still seemed anointed with oil, near his mouth still trembled the speck of peppermint chill. Through his brain twinkled successively the shoulders and arms of the lilac girl, the kiss-curls and honest eyes of the girl in black, the waists, dresses, brooches. But though he tried his best to fix these vagrant images, they glimmered, winked, and dissolved; and as they faded finally into the vast black curtain which hangs before the closed eyes of all men, he began to hear hurried footsteps, the rustle of petticoats, the sound of a kiss. A strong, causeless joy possessed him. But as he surrendered himself to this joy, Lobytko's servant returned with the news that no beer was obtainable. The lieutenant resumed his impatient march up and down the room.

"The fellow's an idiot," he exclaimed, stopping first near

Riabovich and then near Merzliakov. "Only the worst numbskull and blockhead can't get beer! *Canaille!*"

"Every one knows there's no beer here," said Merzliakov, without lifting his eyes from *The Messenger of Europe.*

"You believe that!" exclaimed Lobytko. "Lord in heaven, drop me on the moon, and in five minutes I'll find both beer and women! I will find them myself! Call me a rascal if I don't!"

He dressed slowly, silently lighted a cigarette, and went out.

"Rabbek, Grabbek, Labbek," he muttered, stopping in the hall. "I won't go alone, devil take me! Riabovich, come for a walk! What?"

As he got no answer, he returned, undressed slowly, and lay down. Merzliakov sighed, dropped *The Messenger of Europe,* and put out the light. "Well?" muttered Lobytko, puffing his cigarette in the dark.

Riabovich pulled the bed-clothes up to his chin, curled himself into a roll, and strained his imagination to join the twinkling images into one coherent whole. But the vision fled him. He soon fell asleep, and his last impression was that he had been caressed and gladdened, that into his life had crept something strange, and indeed ridiculous, but uncommonly good and radiant. And this thought did not forsake him even in his dreams.

When he awoke the feeling of anointment and peppermint chill were gone. But joy, as on the night before, filled every vein. He looked entranced at the window-panes gilded by the rising sun, and listened to the noises outside. Some one spoke loudly under the very window. It was Lebedetzky, commander of his battery, who had just overtaken the brigade. He was talking to the sergeant-major, loudly, owing to lack of practice in soft speech.

"And what next?" he roared.

"During yesterday's shoeing, your honour, *Golubtchik* was pricked. The *feldscher* ordered clay and vinegar. And last night, your honour, mechanic Artemieff was drunk, and the lieutenant ordered him to be put on the limber of the reserve gun-carriage."

The sergeant-major added that Karpov had forgotten the tent-pegs and the new lanyards for the friction-tubes, and that the officers had spent the evening at General von Rabbek's. But here at the window appeared Lebedetzky's red-bearded face. He blinked his short-sighted eyes at the drowsy men in bed, and greeted them.

"Is everything all right?"

"The saddle wheeler galled his withers with the new yoke," answered Lobytko.

The commander sighed, mused a moment, and shouted—

"I am thinking of calling on Alexandra Yegorovna. I want to see her. Good-bye! I will catch you up before night."

Fifteen minutes later the brigade resumed its march. As he passed von Rabbek's barns Riabovich turned his head and looked at the house. The Venetian blinds were down; evidently all still slept. And among them slept she—she who had kissed him but a few hours before. He tried to visualise her asleep. He projected the bedroom window opened wide with green branches peering in, the freshness of the morning air, the smell of poplars, lilacs, and roses, the bed, a chair, the dress which rustled last night, a pair of tiny slippers, a ticking watch on the table—all these came to him clearly with every detail. But the features, the kind, sleepy smile—all, in short, that was essential and characteristic—fled his imagination as quicksilver flees the hand. When he had covered half a verst he again turned back. The yellow church, the house, gardens, and river were bathed in light. Imagining an azure sky, the green-banked river specked with silver sunshine flakes was inexpressibly fair; and, looking at Miestechky for the last time, Riabovich felt sad, as if parting for ever with something very near and dear.

By the road before him stretched familiar, uninteresting scenes; to the right and left, fields of young rye and buckwheat with hopping rooks; in front, dust and the napes of human necks; behind, the same dust and faces. Ahead of the column marched four soldiers with swords—that was the advance guard. Next came the bandsmen. Advance guard and bandsmen, like mutes in a funeral procession, ignored the regulation intervals and marched too far ahead. Riabovich, with the first gun of Battery No. 5, could see four batteries ahead.

To a layman, the long, lumbering march of an artillery brigade is novel, interesting, inexplicable. It is hard to understand why a single gun needs so many men; why so many, such strangely harnessed horses are needed to drag it. But to Riabovich, a master of all these things, it was profoundly dull. He had learned years ago why a solid sergeant-major rides beside the officer in front of each battery, why the sergeant-major is called the *unosni,* and why the drivers of leaders and wheelers ride behind him. Riabovich knew why the near horses are called saddle-horses, and why the off horses are called led-horses—and all of this was interesting beyond words. On one of the wheelers rode a soldier still covered with yesterday's dust, and with a cumbersome, ridiculous guard on his right leg. But Riabovich, knowing the use of this leg-guard, found it in no way ridiculous. The drivers, mechanically and with occasional cries, flourished their whips. The guns in themselves were impressive. The limbers were packed with tarpaulin-covered sacks of oats; and the guns themselves, hung around with tea-pots and satchels, looked like harmless animals, guarded for some obscure reason by men and horses. In the lee of the gun tramped six gunners, swinging their arms; and behind each gun came more *unosniye,* leaders, wheelers; and yet more guns, each as ugly and uninspiring as the one in front. And as every one of the six batteries in the brigade had four guns, the procession stretched along the road at least half a verst. It ended with a wagon train, with which, its head bent in thought, walked the donkey Magar, brought from Turkey by a battery commander.

Dead to his surroundings, Riabovich marched onward, looking at the napes ahead or at the faces behind. Had it not been for last night's event, he would have been half asleep. But now he was absorbed in novel, entrancing thoughts. When the brigade set out that morning he had tried to argue that the kiss had no significance save as a trivial though mysterious adventure; that it was without real import; and that to think of it seriously was to behave himself absurdly. But logic soon flew away and surrendered him to his vivid imaginings. At times he saw himself in von Rabbek's dining-room, *tête-à-tête* with a composite being, formed of the girl in lilac and the blonde in black. At times he closed his eyes, and pictured himself with a different, this time quite an unknown, girl of cloudy feature; he spoke to her, caressed her, bent over her shoulder; he imagined war and parting . . . then reunion, the first supper together, children. . . .

"To the brakes!" rang the command as they topped the brow of each hill.

Riabovich also cried "To the brakes!" and each time dread that the cry would break the magic spell, and recall him to realities.

They passed a big country house. Riabovich looked across the fence into the garden, and saw a long path, straight as a ruler, carpeted with yellow sand, and shaded by young birches. In an ecstasy of enchantment, he pictured little feminine feet treading the yellow sand; and, in a flash, imagination restored the woman who had kissed him, the woman he had visualised after supper the night before. The image settled in his brain and never afterwards forsook him.

The spell reigned until midday, when a loud command came from the rear of the column.

"Attention! Eyes right! Officers!"

In a *calèche* drawn by a pair of white horses appeared the

general of brigade. He stopped at the second battery, and called out something which no one understood. Up galloped several officers, among them Riabovich.

"Well, how goes it?" The general blinked his red eyes, and continued, "Are there any sick?"

Hearing the answer, the little skinny general mused a moment, turned to an officer, and said—

"The driver of your third-gun wheeler has taken off his leg-guard and hung it on the limber. *Canaille!* Punish him!"

Then raising his eyes to Riabovich, he added—

"And in your battery, I think, the harness is too loose."

Having made several other equally tiresome remarks, he looked at Lobytko, and laughed.

"Why do you look so downcast, Lieutenant Lobytko? You are sighing for Madame Lopukhov, eh? Gentlemen, he is pining for Madame Lopukhov!"

Madame Lopukhov was a tall, stout lady, long past forty. Being partial to big women, regardless of age, the general ascribed the same taste to his subordinates. The officers smiled respectfully; and the general, pleased that he had said something caustic and laughable, touched the coachman's back and saluted. The *calèche* whirled away.

"All this, though it seems to me impossible and unearthly, is in reality very commonplace," thought Riabovich, watching the clouds of dust raised by the general's carriage. "It is an everyday event, and within every one's experience. . . . This old general, for instance, must have loved in his day; he is married now, and has children. Captain Wachter is also married, and his wife loves him, though he has an ugly red neck and no waist. . . . Salmanoff is coarse, and a typical Tartar, but he has had a romance ending in marriage. . . . I, like the rest, must go through it all sooner or later."

And the thought that he was an ordinary man, and that his life was ordinary, rejoiced and consoled him. He boldly visualised *her* and his happiness, and let his imagination run mad.

Towards evening the brigade ended its march. While the other officers sprawled in their tents, Riabovich, Merzliakov, and Lobytko sat around a packing-case and supped. Merzliakov ate slowly, and, resting *The Messenger of Europe* on his knees, read on steadily. Lobytko, chattering without cease, poured beer into his glass. But Riabovich, whose head was dizzy from uninterrupted day-dreams, ate in silence. When he had drunk three glasses he felt tipsy and weak; and an overmastering impulse forced him to relate his adventure to his comrades.

"A most extraordinary thing happened to me at von Rabbek's," he began, doing his best to speak in an indifferent, ironical tone. "I was on my way, you understand, from the billiard-room . . ."

And he attempted to give a very detailed history of the kiss. But in a minute he had told the whole story. In that minute he had exhausted every detail; and it seemed to him terrible that the story required such a short time. It ought, he felt, to have lasted all the night. As he finished, Lobytko, who as a liar himself believed in no one, laughed incredulously. Merzliakov frowned. and, with his eyes still glued to *The Messenger of Europe,* said indifferently—

"God knows who it was! She threw herself on your neck, you say, and didn't cry out! Some lunatic, I expect!"

"It must have been a lunatic," agreed Riabovich.

"I, too, have had adventures of that kind," began Lobytko, making a frightful face. "I was on my way to Kovno. I travelled second class. The carriage was packed, and I couldn't sleep So I gave the guard a ruble, and he took my bag, and put me in a *coupé.* I lay down, and pulled my rug over me. It was pitch dark, you understand. Suddenly I felt some one tapping my shoulder and breathing in my face. I stretched out my hand and felt an elbow. Then I opened my eyes. Imagine! A woman! Coal-black eyes, lips red as good coral, nostrils breathing passion, breasts—buffers!"

"Draw it mild!" interrupted Merzliakov in his quiet voice. "I can believe about the breasts, but if it was pitch dark how could you see the lips?"

By laughing at Merzliakov's lack of understanding, Lobytko tried to shuffle out of the dilemma. The story annoyed Riabovich. He rose from the box, lay on his bed, and swore that he would never again take any one into his confidence.

Life in camp passed without event. The days flew by, each like the one before. But on every one of these days Riabovich felt, thought, and acted as a man in love. When at daybreak his servant brought him cold water, and poured it over his head, it flashed at once into his half-awakened brain that something good and warm and caressing had crept into his life.

At night when his comrades talked of love and of women, he drew in his chair, and his face was the face of an old soldier who talks of battles in which he has taken part. And when the rowdy officers, led by setter Lobytko, made Don Juanesque raids upon the neighbouring "suburb," Riabovich, though he accompanied them, was morose and conscience-struck, and mentally asked *her* forgiveness. In free hours and sleepless nights, when his brain was obsessed by memories of childhood, of his father, his mother, of everything akin and dear, he remembered always Miestechky, the dancing horse, von Rabbek, von Rabbek's wife, so like the ex-Empress Eugenie, the dark room, the chink in the door.

On the thirty-first of August he left camp. this time not with the whole brigade but with only two batteries. As an exile returning to his native land, he was agitated and enthralled by day-dreams. He longed passionately for the queer-looking horse, the church, the insincere von Rabbeks, the dark room; and that internal voice which cheats so often the love-lorn whispered an assurance that he should see *her* again. But doubt tortured him. How should he meet her?

What must he say? Would she have forgotten the kiss? If it came to the worst—he consoled himself—if he never saw her again, he might walk once more through the dark room, and remember. . . .

Towards evening the white barns and well-known church rose on the horizon. Riabovich's heart beat wildly. He ignored the remark of an officer who rode by, he forgot the whole world, and he gazed greedily at the river glimmering afar, at the green roofs, at the dove-cote, over which fluttered birds, dyed golden by the setting sun.

As he rode towards the church, and heard again the quartermaster's raucous voice, he expected every second a horseman to appear from behind the fence and invite the officers to tea. . . . But the quartermaster ended his harangue, the officers hastened to the village, and no horseman appeared.

"When Rabbek hears from the peasants that we are back he will send for us," thought Riabovich. And so assured was he of this, that when he entered the hut he failed to understand why his comrades had lighted a candle, and why the servants were preparing the samovar.

A painful agitation oppressed him. He lay on his bed. A moment later he rose to look for the horseman. But no horseman was in sight. Again he lay down; again he rose; and this time, impelled by restlessness, went into the street, and walked towards the church. The square was dark and deserted. On the hill stood three silent soldiers. When they saw Riabovich they started and saluted, and he, returning their salute, began to descend the well-remembered path.

Beyond the stream, in a sky stained with purple, the moon slowly rose. Two chattering peasant women walked in a kitchen garden and pulled cabbage leaves; behind them their log cabins stood out black against the sky. The river bank was as it had been in May; the bushes were the same; things differed only in that the nightingale no longer sang, that it smelt no longer of poplars and young grass.

When he reached von Rabbek's garden Riabovich peered

through the wicket-gate. Silence and darkness reigned. Save only the white birch trunks and patches of pathway, the whole garden merged in a black, impenetrable shade. Riabovich listened greedily, and gazed intent. For a quarter of an hour he loitered; then hearing no sound, and seeing no light, he walked wearily towards home.

He went down to the river. In front rose the general's bathing box; and white towels hung on the rail of the bridge. He climbed on to the bridge and stood still: then, for no reason whatever, touched a towel. It was clammy and cold. He looked down at the river which sped past swiftly, murmuring almost inaudibly against the bathing-box piles. Near the left bank glowed the moon's ruddy reflection, overrun by ripples which stretched it, tore it in two, and, it seemed, would sweep it away as twigs and shavings are swept.

"How stupid! How stupid!" thought Riabovich, watching the hurrying ripples. "How stupid everything is!"

Now that hope was dead, the history of the kiss, his impatience, his ardour, his vague aspirations and disillusion appeared in a clear light. It no longer seemed strange that the general's horseman had not come, and that he would never again see *her* who had kissed him by accident instead of another. On the contrary, he felt, it would be strange if he did ever see her again. . . .

The water flew past him, whither and why no one knew. It had flown past in May: it had sped a stream into a great river: a river, into the sea; it had floated on high in mist and fallen again in rain; it might be, the water of May was again speeding past under Riabovich's eyes. For what purpose? Why?

And the whole world—life itself seemed to Riabovich an inscrutable, aimless mystification. . . Raising his eyes from the stream and gazing at the sky, he recalled how Fate in the shape of an unknown woman had once caressed him; he recalled his summer fantasies and images—and his whole life seemed to him unnaturally thin and colourless and wretched. . . .

When he reached the cabin his comrades had disappeared. His servant informed him that all had set out to visit "General Fonrabbkin," who had sent a horseman to bring them. . . For a moment Riabovich's heart thrilled with joy. But that joy he extinguished. He cast himself upon his bed, and wroth with his evil fate, as if he wished to spite it, ignored the invitation.

IN EXILE

Old Simeon, whose nickname was Brains, and a young Tartar, whose name nobody knew, were sitting on the bank of the river by a wood-fire. The other three ferrymen were in the hut. Simeon who was an old man of about sixty, skinny and toothless, but broad-shouldered and healthy, was drunk. He would long ago have gone to bed, but he had a bottle in his pocket and was afraid of his comrades asking him for vodka. The Tartar was ill and miserable, and, pulling his rags about him, he went on talking about the good things in the province of Simbirsk, and what a beautiful and clever wife he had left at home. He was not more than twenty-five, and now, by the light of the wood-fire, with his pale, sorrowful, sickly face, he looked a mere boy.

"Of course, it is not a paradise here," said Brains, "you see, water, the bare bushes by the river, clay everywhere—nothing else. . . . It is long past Easter and there is still ice on the water and this morning there was snow. . . ."

"Bad! Bad!" said the Tartar with a frightened look.

A few yards away flowed the dark, cold river, muttering, dashing against the holes in the clayey banks as it tore along to the distant sea. By the bank they were sitting on, loomed a great barge, which the ferrymen call a *karbass*. Far away and away, flashing out, flaring up, were fires crawling like snakes—last year's grass being burned. And behind the water again was darkness. Little banks of ice could be heard knocking against the barge. . . . It was very damp and cold. . . .

The Tartar glanced at the sky. There were as many stars as at home, and the darkness was the same, but something was missing. At home in the Simbirsk province the stars and the sky were altogether different.

"Bad! Bad!" he repeated.

"You will get used to it," said Brains with a laugh. "You are young yet and foolish; the milk is hardly dry on your lips, and in your folly you imagine that there is no one unhappier than you, but there will come a time when you will say: God give every one such a life! Just look at me. In a week's time the floods will be gone, and we will fix the ferry here, and all of you will go away into Siberia and I shall stay here, going to and fro I have been living thus for the last two-and-twenty years, but, thank God, I want nothing. God give everybody such a life."

The Tartar threw some branches onto the fire, crawled near to it and said:

"My father is sick. When he dies, my mother and my wife have promised to come here."

"What do you want your mother and your wife for?" asked Brains. "Just foolishness, my friend. It's the devil tempting you, plague take him. Don't listen to the Evil One. Don't give way to him When he talks to you about women you should answer him sharply: 'I don't want them!' When he talks of freedom, you should stick to it and say: 'I don't want it. I want nothing! No father, no mother, no wife, no freedom, no home, no love! I want nothing.' Plague take 'em all."

Brains took a swig at his bottle and went on:

"My brother, I am not an ordinary peasant. I don't come from the servile masses. I am the son of a deacon, and when I was a free man at Rursk, I used to wear a frock coat, and now I have brought myself to such a point that I can sleep naked on the ground and eat grass. God give such a life to everybody. I want nothing. I am afraid of nobody and I think there is no man richer or freer than I. When they sent me here from Russia I set my teeth at once and said: 'I want nothing!' The devil whispers to me about my wife and my kindred, and about freedom and I say to him: 'I want nothing!' I stuck to it, and, you see, I live happily and have nothing to grumble at. If a man gives the devil the least opportunity and listens to him just once, then he is lost and has no hope of salvation: he will be over ears in the mire and will never get out. Not only peasants the like of you are lost, but the nobly born and the educated also. About fifteen years ago a certain nobleman was sent here from Russia. He had had some trouble with his brothers and had made a forgery in a will. People said he was a prince or a baron, but perhaps he was only a high official—who knows? Well, he came here and at once bought a house and land in Moukhzyink. 'I want to live by my own work,' said he, 'in the sweat of my brow, because I am no longer a nobleman but an exile.' 'Why,' said I. 'God help you, for that is good.' He was a young man then, ardent and eager; he used to mow and go fishing, and he would ride sixty miles on horseback. Only one thing was wrong; from the very beginning he was always driving to the post-office at Guyrin. He used to sit in my boat and sigh: 'Ah! Simeon, it is a long time since they sent me any money from home.' 'You are better without money, Vassili Sergnevich,' said I. 'What's the good of it? You just throw away the past, as though it had never happened, as though it were only a dream, and start life afresh. Don't listen to the devil, I said, 'he won't do you any good, and he will only tighten the noose. You want money now, but in a little while you will want something else, and then more and more. If,' said I, 'you want to be happy you must want nothing. Exactly. . . . If,' I said, 'fate has been hard on you and me, it is no good asking her for charity and falling at her feet. We must ignore her and laugh at her.' That's what I said to him. . . . Two years later I ferried him over and he rubbed his hands and laughed. 'I'm going,' said he, 'to Guyrin to meet my wife. She has taken pity on me, she said, and she is coming here. She is very kind and good.' And he gave a gasp of joy. Then one day he came with his wife, a beautiful young lady with a little girl in her arms and a lot of luggage. And Vassili Andreich kept turning and looking at her and could not look at her or praise her enough. 'Yes, Simeon, my friend, even in Siberia people live.' Well, thought I, all right, you won't be content. And from that time on, mark you, he used to go to Guyrin every week to find out if money had been sent from Russia. A terrible lot of money was wasted. 'She stays here,' said he, 'for my sake, and her youth and beauty wither away here in Siberia. She shares my bitter lot with me,' said he, 'and I must give her all the pleasure I can for it. . . .' To make his wife happier he took up with the officials and any kind of rubbish. And they couldn't have company without giving food and drink, and they must have a piano and a fluffy little dog on the sofa—bad cess to it. . . . Luxury, in a word, all kinds of tricks. My lady did not stay with him long How could she? Clay, water, cold, no vegetables, no fruit; uneducated people and drunkards, with no manners, and she was a pretty pampered young lady from the metropolis. . . . Of course she got bored. And her husband was no longer a gentleman, but an exile—quite a different matter. Three years later, I remember, on the eve of the Assumption, I heard shouts from the other bank. I went over in the ferry and saw my lady, all wrapped up, with a young gentleman, a government official, in a troika. . . . I ferried them across, they got into the carriage and disappeared, and I saw no more of them. Toward the morning Vassili Andreich came racing up in a coach and pair. 'Has my wife been across, Simeon, with a gentleman in spectacles?' 'She has,' said I, 'but you might as well look for the wind in the fields.' He raced after them and kept it up for five days and nights. When he came back he jumped on to the ferry and began to knock his head against the side and to cry aloud. 'You see,' said I, 'there you are.' And I laughed and reminded him: 'Even in Siberia people live.' But he went on beating his head harder than ever. . . . Then he got the desire for freedom. His wife had gone to Russia and he longed to go there to see her and take her away from her lover. And he began to go to the post-office every day, and then to the authorities of the town. He was always sending applications or personally handing them to the authorities, asking to have his term remitted and to be allowed to go, and he told me that he had spent over two hundred roubles on telegrams. He sold his land and mortgaged his house to the money-lenders. His hair went grey, he grew round-shouldered, and his face got yellow and consumptive-looking. He used to cough whenever he spoke and tears used to come to his eyes. He spent eight years on his applications, and at last he became happy again and lively: he had thought of a new dodge. His daughter, you see, had grown up. He doted on her and could never take his eyes off her. And, indeed, she was very pretty, dark and clever. Every Sunday he used to go to church with her at Guyrin. They would stand side by side on the ferry, and she would smile and he would devour her with his eyes. 'Yes, Simeon,' he would say. 'Even in Siberia people live. Even in Siberia there is happiness. Look what a fine daughter I have. You wouldn't find one like her in a thousand miles' journey.' 'She's a nice girl,' said I. 'Oh, yes.' . . . And I thought to myself: 'You wait. . . . She is young. Young blood will have its way; she wants to live and what life is there here?' And she began to pine away. . . . Wasting, wasting away, she withered away, fell ill and had to keep to her bed. . . . Consumption. That's Siberian happiness, plague take it; that's Siberian life. . . . He rushed all over the place after the doctors and dragged them home with him. If he heard of a doctor or a quack three hundred miles off he would rush off after him. He spent a terrific amount of money on doctors and I think it would have been much better spent on drink. All the same she had to die. No help for it. Then it was all up with him. He thought of hanging himself, and of trying to escape to Russia. That would be the end of him. He would try to escape: he would be caught, tried, penal servitude, flogging."

"Good! Good!" muttered the Tartar with a shiver.

"What is good?" asked Brains.

"Wife and daughter. What does penal servitude and suffering matter? He saw his wife and his daughter. You say one should want nothing. But nothing—is evil! His wife spent three years with him. God gave him that. Nothing is evil, and three years is good. Why don't you understand that?"

Trembling and stammering as he groped for Russian words, of which he knew only a few, the Tartar began to say: "God forbid he should fall ill among strangers, and die and be buried in the cold sodden earth, and then, if the wife could come to him if only for one day or even for one hour, he would gladly endure any torture for such happiness, and would even thank God. Better one day of happiness than nothing."

Then once more he said what a beautiful clever wife he had left at home, and with his head in his hands he began to cry and assured Simeon that he was innocent, and had been falsely accused. His two brothers and his uncle had stolen some horses from a peasant and beat the old man nearly to death, and the community never looked into the matter at all, and judgment was passed by which all three brothers were exiled to Siberia, while his uncle, a rich man, remained at home.

"You will get used to it," said Simeon.

The Tartar relapsed into silence and stared into the fire with his eyes red from weeping; he looked perplexed and frightened, as if he could not understand why he was in the cold and the darkness, among strangers, and not in the province of Simbirsk. Brains lay down near the fire, smiled at something, and began to say in an undertone:

"But what a joy she must be to your father," he muttered after a pause. "He loves her and she is a comfort to him, eh? But, my man, don't tell me. He is a strict, harsh old man. And girls don't want strictness; they want kisses and laughter, scents and pomade. Yes. . . . Ah! What a life!" Simeon swore heavily. "No more vodka! That means bedtime. What? I'm going, my man."

Left alone, the Tartar threw more branches on the fire, lay down, and, looking into the blaze, began to think of his native village and of his wife; if she could come if only for a month, or even a day, and, then, if she liked, go back again! Better a month or even a day, than nothing. But even if his wife kept her promise and came, how could he provide for her? Where was she to live?

"If there is nothing to eat how are we to live?" asked the Tartar aloud.

For working at the oars day and night he was paid two kopecks a day; the passengers gave tips, but the ferrymen shared them out and gave nothing to the Tartar, and only laughed at him. And he was poor, cold, hungry, and fearful. . . . With his whole body aching and shivering he thought it would be good to go into the hut and sleep; but there was nothing to cover himself with, and it was colder there than on the bank. He had nothing to cover himself with there, but he could make up a fire. . . .

In a week's time, when the floods had subsided and the ferry would be fixed up, all the ferrymen except Simeon would not be wanted any longer and the Tartar would have to go from village to village, begging and looking for work. His wife was only seventeen; beautiful, soft, and shy. . . . Could she go unveiled begging through the villages? No. The idea of it was horrible.

It was already dawn. The barges, the bushy willows above the water, the swirling flood began to take shape, and up above in a clayey cliff a hut thatched with straw, and above that the straggling houses of the village, where the cocks had begun to crow.

The ginger-coloured clay cliff, the barge, the river, the strange wild people, hunger, cold, illness—perhaps all these things did not really exist. Perhaps, thought the Tartar, it was only a dream. He felt that he must be asleep, and he heard his own snoring. . . . Certainly he was at home in the Simbirsk province; he had but to call his wife and she would answer; and his mother was in the next room. . . . But what awful dreams there are! Why? The Tartar smiled and opened his eyes. What river was that? The Volga?

It was snowing.

"Hi! Ferry!" some one shouted on the other bank. *"Karba-a-ass!"*

The Tartar awoke and went to fetch his mates to row over to the other side. Hurrying into their sheepskins, swearing sleepily in hoarse voices, and shivering from the cold, the four men appeared on the bank. After their sleep, the river from which there came a piercing blast, seemed to them horrible and disgusting. They stepped slowly into the barge. . . . The Tartar and the three ferrymen took the long, broad-bladed oars, which in the dim light looked like a crab's claw, and Simeon flung himself with his belly against the tiller. And on the other side the voice kept on shouting, and a revolver was fired twice, for the man probably thought the ferrymen were asleep or gone to the village inn.

"All right. Plenty of time!" said Brains in the tone of one who was convinced that there is no need for hurry in this world—and indeed there is no reason for it.

The heavy, clumsy barge left the bank and heaved through the willows, and by the willows slowly receding it was possible to tell that the barge was moving. The ferrymen plied the oars with a slow measured stroke; Brains hung over the tiller with his stomach pressed against it and swung from side to side. In the dim light they looked like men sitting on some antediluvian animal with long limbs, swimming out to a cold dismal nightmare country.

They got clear of the willows and swung out into mid-stream. The thud of the oars and the splash could be heard on the other bank and shouts came: "Quicker! Quicker!" After another ten minutes the barge bumped heavily against the landing-stage.

"And it is still snowing, snowing all the time," Simeon murmured, wiping the snow off his face. "God knows where it comes from!"

On the other side a tall, lean old man was waiting in a short fox-fur coat and a white astrachan hat. He was standing some distance from his horses and did not move; he had a stern concentrated expression as if he were trying to remember something and were furious with his recalcitrant memory. When Simeon went up to him and took off his hat with a smile he said:

"I'm in a hurry to get to Anastasievka. My daughter is worse again and they tell me there's a new doctor at Anastasievka."

The coach was clamped onto the barge and they rowed back. All the while as they rowed the man, whom Simeon called Vassili Andreich, stood motionless, pressing his thick lips tight and staring in front of him. When the driver craved leave to smoke in his presence, he answered nothing, as if he did not hear. And Simeon hung over the rudder and looked at him mockingly and said:

"Even in Siberia people live. L-i-v-e!"

On Brains's face was a triumphant expression as if he were proving something, as if pleased that things had happened just as he thought they would. The unhappy, helpless look of the man in the fox-fur coat seemed to give him great pleasure.

"The roads are now muddy, Vassili Andreich," he said, when the horses had been harnessed on the bank. "You'd better wait a couple of weeks, until it gets dryer. . . . If there were any point in going—but you know yourself that people are always on the move day and night and there's no point in it. Sure!"

Vassili Andreich said nothing, gave him a tip, took his seat in the coach and drove away.

"Look! He's gone galloping after the doctor!" said Simeon, shivering in the cold. "Yes. To look for a real doctor, trying to overtake the wind in the fields, and catch the devil by the tail, plague take him! What queer fish there are! God forgive me, a miserable sinner."

The Tartar went up to Brains, and, looking at him with mingled hatred and disgust, trembling, and mixing Tartar words up with his broken Russian, said:

"He good . . . good. And you . . . bad! You are bad! The gentleman is a good soul, very good, and you are a beast, you are bad! The gentleman is alive and you are dead. . . . God made man that he should be alive, that he should have happiness, sorrow. grief, and you want nothing, so you are not alive, but a stone! A stone wants nothing and so do you. . . . You are a stone—and God does not love you and the gentleman he does."

They all began to laugh: the Tartar furiously knit his brows, waved his hand, drew his rags round him and went to the fire. The ferrymen and Simeon went slowly to the hut.

"It's cold," said one of the ferrymen hoarsely, as he stretched himself on the straw with which the damp, clay floor was covered.

"Yes It's not warm," another agreed. . . . "It's a hard life."

All of them lay down. The wind blew the door open. The snow drifted into the hut. Nobody could bring himself to get up and shut the door; it was cold, but they put up with it.

"And I am happy," muttered Simeon as he fell asleep. "God give such a life to everybody."

"You certainly are the devil's own. Even the devil don't need to take you."

Sounds like the barking of a dog came from outside.

"Who is that? Who is there?"

"It's the Tartar crying."

"Oh! he's a queer fish."

"He'll get used to it!" said Simeon, and at once he fell asleep. Soon the others slept too and the door was left open.

A WORK OF ART

Holding under his arm an object wrapped in a newspaper, Sasha Smirnov, the only son of his mother, walked nervously into the office of Doctor Koshelkov.

"Well, my dear boy," exclaimed the doctor warmly, "how do you feel today? What's the good news?"

Sasha began to blink with his eyes, put his hand over his heart, and stammered nervously:

"My mother sends her regards and begs to thank you. . . . I am my mother's only son, and you have saved my life . . . and we both hardly know how to thank you."

"Come, come, my young friend, let us not speak of it," interrupted the doctor, literally melting with pleasure. "I have only done what anybody else in my place would have done."

"I am the only son of my mother. . . . We are poor people and consequently we are not in position to pay you for your trouble . . . and it makes it very embarrassing for us, Doctor, although both of us, mother and I, who am the only son of my mother, beg of you to accept from us, a token of our gratitude, this object which . . . is an object of rare worth, a wonderful masterpiece in antique bronze."

The doctor made a grimace.

"Why, my dear friend," he said, "it is entirely unnecessary. I don't need this in the least."

"Oh, no, no," stammered Sasha. "I beg you please accept it!"

He began to unwrap the bundle, continuing his entreaties in the meantime:

"If you do not accept this, you will offend both my mother and myself. . . . This is a very rare work of art . . . an antique bronze. It is a relic left by my dead father. We have been prizing it as a very dear remembrance. . . . My father used to buy up bronze antiques, selling them to lovers of old statuary. . . . And now we continue in the same business, my mother and myself."

Sasha undid the package and enthusiastically placed it on the table.

It was a low candelabrum of antique bronze, a work of real art representing a group: On a pedestal stood two figures of women clad in the costume of Mother Eve and in poses that I have neither the audacity nor the temperament to describe. These figures were smiling coquettishly and in general gave one the impression that, were it not for the fact that they were obliged to support the candle-stick, they would lean down from their pedestal and exhibit a performance which . . . my dear reader, I am even ashamed to think of it!

When the doctor espied the present, he slowly scratched his head, cleared his throat and blew his nose.

"Yes, indeed, a very pretty piece of work," he mumbled. . . . "But,—how shall I say it—not quite . . . I mean . . . rather unconventional . . . not a bit literary, is it? . . . You know . . . the devil knows. . . ."

"Why?"

"Beelzebub himself could not have conceived anything more ugly. Should I place such a phantasmagoria upon my table I would pollute my entire home!"

"Why, Doctor, what a strange conception you have of art!" cried Sasha in offended tones. "This is a real masterpiece. Just look at it! Such is its harmonious beauty that just to contemplate it fills the soul with ecstasy and makes the throat choke down a sob! When you see such loveliness you forget all earthly things. . . . Just look at it! What life, what motion, what expression!"

"I quite understand all this, my dear boy," interrupted the doctor. "But I am a married man. Little children run in and out of this room and ladies come here continually."

"Of course," said Sasha, "if you look at it through the eyes of the rabble, you see this noble masterpiece in an entirely different light. But you certainly are above all that, Doctor, and especially when your refusal to accept this gift will deeply offend both my mother and myself, who am the only son of my mother. . . . You have saved my life . . . and in return we give you our dearest possession and . . . my only regret is that we are unable to give you the mate to this candelabrum."

"Thanks, friend, many thanks. . . . Remember me to your mother and . . . But for God's sake! You can see for yourself, can't you? Little children run in and out of this room, and ladies come here continually. . . . However, leave it here! There's no arguing with you."

"Don't say another word!" exclaimed Sasha joyously. "Put the candelabrum right here, next to the vase. By Jove, but it's a pity that I haven't got the mate to give you. But it can't be helped, Well, good-bye, Doctor!"

After the departure of Sasha the doctor looked for a long time at the candelabrum and scratched his head.

"This is beautiful, all right," he thought. "It would be a pity to throw it away. . . . And yet I dare not keep it. . . . Hm! . . . Now who in the world is there to whom I can present or donate it?"

After long deliberation he hit upon a good friend of his, the lawyer Ukhov, to whom he was indebted for legal services.

"Fine!" chuckled the doctor. "Being a close friend of his, I cannot very well offer him money, and so I will give him this piece of indecency instead. . . . And he's just the man for it . . . single, and somewhat of a gay bird, too."

No sooner thought than done Dressing himself, the doctor took the candelabrum and went to the home of Ukhov.

"Good morning, old chap!" he said. "I have come here to thank you for your trouble. . . . You will not take money, and I will therefore repay you by presenting you with this exquisite masterpiece. . . . Now say for yourself, isn't it a dream?"

As soon as the lawyer caught sight of it he was exhilarated with its beauty.

"What a wonderful work of art!" he laughed uproariously. "Ye gods, what conceptions artists will get in their heads! What alluring charm! Where did you get this little dandy?"

But now his exhilaration had oozed away and he became frightened. Looking stealthily toward the door, he said:

"But, I can't accept it, old chap. You must take it right back."

"Why?" asked the doctor in alarm.

"Because . . . because . . . my mother often visits me, my clients come here . . . and besides, I would be disgraced even in the eyes of my servants."

"Don't say another word!" cried the doctor gesticulating wildly. "You simply have got to accept it! It would be rank ingratitude for you to refuse it! Such a masterpiece! What motion, what expression. . . . You will greatly offend me if you don't take it!"

"If only this were daubed over or covered with fig-leaves. . . ."

But the doctor refused to listen to him. Gesticulating even more wildly, he ran out of Ukhov's house in the thought that he was rid of the present.

When the doctor was gone the lawyer carefully examined the candelabrum, and then, just as the doctor had done, he began to wonder what in the world he could do with it

"O very beautiful object," he thought. "It is a pity to throw it away, and yet it is disgraceful to keep it. I had best present it to someone . . . I've got it! . . . This very evening I'm going to give it to the comedian Shoshkin. The rascal loves such things, and besides, this is his benefit night. . . ."

No sooner thought than done. That afternoon the well-packed candelabrum was brought to the comedian Shoshkin.

That whole evening the dressing-room of the comedian

Shoshkin was besieged by men who hastened to inspect the present. And during all the time the room re-echoed with hilarious laughter which most closely resembled the neighing of horses.

If any of the actresses approached the door and said, "May I enter?" the hoarse voice of Shoshkin was immediately heard to reply:

"Oh, no, no, my darling, you mustn't. I am not dressed!"

After the performance the comedian shrugged his shoulders, gesticulated with his hands and said:

"Now what in the world am I to do with this? I live in a private apartment! I am often visited by actresses! And this isn't a photograph that one could conceal in a drawer!"

"Why don't you sell it?" suggested the wig maker. "There is a certain old woman who buys up antique bronzes. . . . Her name is Smirnova. . . . You had better take a run over there; they'll show you the place all right, everybody knows her. . . ."

The comedian followed his advice. . . .

Two days later Koshelkov, his head supported on his hand, was sitting in his office concocting pills. Suddenly the door was opened and into the office rushed Sasha. He was smiling radiantly and his breast heaved with joy. . . . In his hands he held something wrapped in a newspaper.

"Doctor!" he cried breathlessly. "Imagine my joy! As luck would have it, I've just succeeded in getting the mate to your candelabrum! Mother is so happy! I am the only son of my mother. . . . You have saved my life."

And Sasha, quivering with thankfulness and rapture, placed a candelabrum before the doctor. The latter opened his mouth as if to say something, but uttered not a word. . . . His power of speech was gone. . . .

DREAMS

Two soldiers are escorting to the county town a vagrant who does not remember who he is. One of them is black-bearded and thick-set, with legs so uncommonly short that, seen from behind, they seem to begin much lower down than those of other men; the other is long, lank, spare, and straight as a stick, with a thick beard of a dark-reddish hue. The first waddles along, looking from side to side and sucking now a straw and now the sleeve of his coat. He slaps his thigh and hums to himself, and looks, on the whole, light-hearted and care-free. The other, with his lean face and narrow shoulders, is staid and important-looking; in build and in the expression of his whole person he resembles a priest of the Starover Faith or one of those warriors depicted on antique icons. "For his wisdom God has enlarged his brow," that is to say, he is bald, which still more enhances the resemblance. The first soldier is called Andrew Ptaka, the second Nikander Sapojnikoff.

The man they are escorting is not in the least like what every one imagines a tramp should be. He is small and sickly and feeble, with little, colourless, absolutely undefined features. His eyebrows are thin, his glance is humble and mild, and his whiskers have barely made their appearance though he is already past thirty. He steps timidly along, stooping, with his hands thrust into his sleeves. The collar of his threadbare, unpeasant-like little coat is turned right up to the brim of his cap, so that all that can venture to peep out at the world is his little red nose. When he speaks, it is in a high, obsequious little voice, and then he immediately coughs. It is hard, very hard to recognise in him a vagabond who is hiding his name. He looks more like some impoverished, God-forsaken son of a priest, or a clerk discharged for intemperance, or a merchant's son who has essayed his puny strength on the stage and is now returning to his home to play out the last act of the parable of the prodigal son. Perhaps, judging from the dull patience with which he battles with the clinging autumn mud, he is a fanatic; some youth trained for a monk who is wandering from one monastery to another all over Russia, doggedly seeking "a life of peace and freedom from sin," which he cannot find.

The wayfarers have been walking a long time, but for all their efforts they cannot get away from the same spot of ground. Before them lie ten yards of dark-brown, muddy road, behind them lies as much; beyond that, wherever they turn, rises a dense wall of white fog. They walk and walk, but the ground they walk on is always the same; the wall comes no nearer; the spot remains a spot. Now and then they catch glimpses of white, irregular cobblestones, a dip in the road, or an armful of hay dropped by some passing wagon; a large pool of muddy water gleams for a moment, or a shadow, vaguely outlined, suddenly and unexpectedly appears before them. The nearer they come to this, the smaller and darker it grows; they come nearer still, and before them rises a crooked mile-post with its numbers effaced, or a woebegone birch-tree, naked and wet, like a wayside beggar. The birch-tree is whispering something with the remains of its yellow foliage; one leaf breaks off and flutters sluggishly to the ground, and then again there come fog and mud and the brown grass by the roadside. Dim, evil tears hang on these blades—not the tears of quiet joy that the earth weeps when she meets and accompanies the summer sun, and with which at dawn she quenches the thirst of quail and rails and graceful, long-billed snipe! The feet of the travellers are caught by the thick, sticky mud; every step costs them an effort.

Andrew Ptaka is a trifle provoked. He is scrutinising the

vagrant and trying to understand how a live, sober man could forget his name.

"You belong to the Orthodox Church, don't you?" he asks.

"I do," answers the tramp briefly.

"H'm—have you been christened?"

"Of course I have; I'm not a Turk! I go to church and observe the fasts and don't eat flesh when it's forbidden to do so—"

"Well, then, what name shall I call you by?"

"Call me what you please, lad."

Ptaka shrugs his shoulders and slaps his thigh in extreme perplexity. The other soldier, Nikander, preserves a sedate silence. He is not so simple as Ptaka, and evidently knows very well reasons which might induce a member of the Orthodox Church to conceal his identity. His expressive face is stern and cold. He walks apart and disdains idle gossip with his companions. He seems to be endeavouring to show to every one and everything, even to the mist, how grave and sensible he is.

"The Lord only knows what to think about you!" pursues Ptaka. "Are you a peasant or not? Are you a gentleman or not? Or are you something between the two? I was rinsing out a sieve in a pond one day and caught a little monster as long as my finger here, with gills and a tail. Thinks I—it's a fish! Then I take another look at it—and I'll be blessed if it didn't have feet! It wasn't a fish and it wasn't a reptile—the devil only knows what it was! That's just what you are. What class do you belong to?"

"I am a peasant by birth," sighs the tramp. "My mother was a house serf. In looks I'm not a peasant, and that is because fate has willed it so, good man. My mother was a nurse in a gentleman's house and had every pleasure the heart could desire, and I, as her flesh and blood, belonged, in her lifetime, to the household. They petted me and spoiled me and beat me till they beat me from common to well-bred. I slept in a bed, had a real dinner every day, and wore trousers and low shoes like any little noble. Whatever my mother had to eat, I had. They gave her dresses and dressed me, too. Oh, we lived well! The candy and cake I ate in my childhood would buy a good horse now if I could sell them! My mother taught me to read and write, and from the time I was a baby instilled the fear of God into me and trained me so well that to this day I couldn't use an impolite, peasant word. I don't drink vodka, boy, and I dress cleanly and can make a respectable appearance in good society. God give her health if she is still alive; if she is dead, take her soul, O Lord, to rest in thy heavenly kingdom where the blessed find peace!"

The tramp uncovers his head, with its sparse bristles, casts his eyes upward, and makes the sign of the cross twice.

"Give her peace, O Lord, in green places!" he says in a drawling voice, more like an old woman's than a man's. "Keep thy slave Keenia in all thy ways, O Lord! If it had not been for my good mother I should have been a simple peasant now, not knowing a thing. As it is, lad, ask me what you please; I know everything: the Holy Scriptures, all godly things, all the prayers, and the Catechisms. I live according to the Scriptures; I do wrong to no one; I keep my body pure; I observe the fasts and eat as it is ordered. Some men find pleasure only in vodka and brawling, but when I have time I sit in a corner and read a book, and as I read I cry and cry—"

"Why do you cry?"

"Because the things they tell of are so pitiful. Sometimes you pay only five kopecks for a book and weep and wail over it to despair—"

"Is your father dead?" asks Ptaka.

"I don't know, lad. It's no use hiding a sin; I don't know who my father was. What I think is that I was an illegitimate son of my mother's. My mother lived all her life with the gentry and never would marry a common peasant."

"So she flew higher, up to his master!" laughs Ptaka.

"That is so. My mother was pious and godly, and of

course it is a sin, a great sin, to say so, but, nevertheless, maybe I have noble blood in my veins. Maybe I am a peasant in station only and am really a high-born gentleman."

The "high-born gentleman" utters all this in a soft, sickly sweet voice, wrinkling his narrow brows and emitting squeaky noises from his cold, red, little nose.

Ptaka listens to him, eyes him with astonishment, and still shrugs his shoulders.

After going four miles the soldiers and the tramp sit down on a little knoll to rest.

"Even a dog can remember his name," mutters Ptaka. "I am called Andrew and he is called Nikander; every man has his God-given name and no one could possibly forget it—not possibly!"

"Whose business is it of any one's to know who I am?" sighs the tramp, leaning his cheek on his hand. "And what good would it do me if they knew? If I were allowed to go wherever I liked I should be worse off than I am now. I know the law, my Christian friends—now I am a vagrant who does not remember his name, and the worst they could do to me would be to send me to eastern Siberia with thirty or forty lashes, but if I should tell them my real name and station I should be sent to hard labor again—I know!"

"You mean to say you have been a convict?"

"I have, my good friend. My head was shaved and I wore chains for four years."

"What for?"

"For murder, good man. When I was still a boy, about eighteen years old, my mother put arsenic into our master's glass by mistake instead of soda. There were a great many different little boxes in the storeroom and it was not hard to mistake them."

The tramp sighs, shakes his head, and continues:

"She was a godly woman, but who can say? The soul of another is a dark forest. Maybe she did it by mistake. Maybe it was because her master had attached another servant to himself and her heart could not forgive the insult. Perhaps she did put it in on purpose—God only knows! I was young then and couldn't understand everything. I remember now that our master did, in fact, take another mistress at that time and that my mother was deeply hurt. Our trial went on for two years after that. My mother was condemned to twenty years' penal servitude and I to seven on account of my youth."

"And what charge were you convicted on?"

"For being an accomplice. I handed our master the glass. It was always that way: my mother would prepare the soda and I would hand him the glass. But I am confessing all this before you, brothers, as before God. You won't tell any one—"

"No one will ever ask us," says Ptaka. "So that means you ran away from prison, does it?"

"Yes, I ran away, good friend. Fourteen of us escaped. God be with them! They ran away and took me along, too. Now judge for yourself, lad, and tell me honestly whether I have any reason for telling my name? I should be condemned to penal servitude again; and what sort of a convict am I? I am delicate and sickly; I like cleanliness in my food and in the places where I sleep. When I pray to God I like to have a little shrine lamp or a candle burning, and I don't like to have noises going on round me when I'm praying. When I prostrate myself I don't like to have the floor all filthy and spat over, and I prostrate myself forty times morning and night for my mother's salvation."

The tramp takes off his cap and crosses himself.

"But let them send me to eastern Siberia if they want to!" he cries. "I'm not afraid of that."

"What? Is that better?"

"It is an entirely different affair. At hard labour you are no better off than a crab in a basket. You are crowded and pushed and hustled; there's not a quiet corner to take breath; it's a hell on earth—the Mother of God forbid it! A ruffian you are, and a ruffian's treatment you receive—worse than any dog's. You get nothing to eat; there is nowhere to sleep and nowhere to say your prayers. In exile it's different. You first enroll yourself in the company, as every one else does. The government is compelled by law to give you your share of land. Yes, indeed! Land, they say, is cheap there, as cheap as snow. You can take all you want! They would give me land for farming, lad, and land for a garden, and land for a house. Then I would plough and sow, as other men do, raise cattle and bees and sheep and dogs—I'd get myself a Siberian cat to keep the rats and mice from eating my property, I'd build me a house, brothers, and buy icons; and, God willing, I'd marry and have children—"

The tramp is murmuring to himself now and has ceased looking at his listeners; he is gazing off somewhere to one side. Artless as his reveries are, he speaks with such sincerity and such heartfelt earnestness that it is hard not to believe what he says. The little mouth of the vagrant is twisted by a smile, and his whole face, his eyes, and his nose are numbed and paralysed by the foretaste of far-off happiness. The soldiers listen and regard him earnestly, not without compassion. They also believe what he says.

"I am not afraid of Siberia," the tramp murmurs on. "Siberia and Russia are the same thing. They have the same God there as here, and the same Czar, and they speak the language of Orthodox Christians, as I am speaking with you; only there is greater plenty, and the people are richer. Everything is better there. Take, for example, the rivers. They are a thousand times finer than ours. And fish! The fishing in them is simply beyond words! Fishing, brothers, is the greatest joy of my life. I don't ask for bread; only let me sit and hold a fishing-line! Indeed, that is true! I catch fish on a hook and line and in pots and with bow nets, and when the ice comes I use cast nets. I am not strong enough to fish with a cast net myself; so I have to hire a peasant for five kopecks to do that for me. Heavens, what fun it is! It's like seeing your own brother again to catch an eel or a mudfish! And you have to treat every fish differently, I can tell you. You use a minnow for one, and a worm for another, and a frog or a grasshopper for a third; you've got to know all that. Take, for example, the eel. The eel isn't a dainty fish; it will take even a newt. Pikes like earthworms—garfish, butterflies. There is no greater joy on earth than fishing for chubs in swift water. You bait your hook with a butterfly or a beetle, so that it will float on the surface; and you let your line run out some twenty or thirty yards without a sinker; then you stand in the water without your trousers and let the bait float down with the current till—tug! and there's a chub on the hook! Then you have to watch ever so closely for just the right moment to hook it or the confounded thing will go off with your bait. The moment it twitches the line you've got to pull; there isn't a second to lose! The number of fish I have caught in my life is a caution! When we were escaping and the other convicts were asleep in the forest, I couldn't sleep and would go off in search of a river. The rivers there are so wide and swift and steep-banked—it's a caution. And all along their shores lie dense forests. The trees are so high that it makes your head swim to look up to the top of them. According to prices here every one of those pine-trees is worth ten roubles—"

Under the confused stress of his imagination, the dream pictures of the past, and the sweet foretaste of happiness, the piteous little man stops speaking and only moves his lips as if whispering to himself. The feeble, beatific smile does not leave his face. The soldiers say nothing. Their heads have sunk forward onto their breasts and they are lost in meditation. In the autumn silence, when a chill, harsh fog from the earth settles on the soul and rises like a prison wall before one to testify to the narrow limits of man's freedom, ah! then it is sweet to dream of wide, swift rivers with bold, fertile banks, of dense forests, of boundless plains! Idly, peacefully, the fancy pictures to itself a man, a tiny speck, appearing on the steep, uninhabited bank of a river in the early morning, before the flush of dawn has faded from the sky. The summits of the everlasting pines rise piled high in terraces on either side of the stream and, muttering darkly, look sternly at that free man. Roots, great rocks, and thorny bushes obstruct his path, but he is strong of body and valiant of heart and fears neither the pines nor the rocks nor the solitude nor the rolling echoes that reiterate every footfall.

The imagination of the soldiers is painting for them pictures of a free life which they have never lived. Is it that they darkly recall images of things heard long ago? Or have these visions of a life of liberty come down to them with their flesh and blood as an inheritance from their remote, wild ancestors? God only knows!

The first to break the silence is Nikander, who until now has not let fall a word. Perhaps he is jealous of the vagrant's visionary happiness; perhaps he feels in his heart that dreams of bliss are incongruous amidst surroundings of grey mist and brown-black mud—at any rate, he looks sternly at the tramp and says:

"That is all very well, brother; that is all very fine, but you'll never reach that land of plenty! How could you? You would go thirty miles and then give up the ghost—a little half-dead creature like you! You've only walked four miles to-day and yet, look at you! You can't seem to get rested at all!"

The tramp turns slowly to Nikander and the blissful smile fades from his face. He looks with dismay at the grave countenance of the soldier as if he had been caught doing wrong and seems to have recollected something, for he nods his head. Silence falls once more. All three are busy with their own thoughts. The soldiers are trying to force their minds to grasp what perhaps God alone can conceive of: the terrible expanse that lies between them and that land of freedom. Images more clear, precise, and terrifying are crowding into the vagrant's head—courts of justice, dungeons for exiles and for convicts, prison barracks, weary halts along the road, the cold of winter, illness, the death of his companions—all rise vividly before him.

The tramp blinks, and little drops stand out upon his brow. He wipes his forehead with his sleeve, draws a deep breath as if he had just jumped out of a hot oven, wipes his forehead with the other sleeve, and glances fearfully behind him.

"It is quite true that you could never get there," Ptaka assents. "You're not a walker! Look at yourself—all skin and bone! It would kill you, brother."

"Of course it would kill him; he couldn't possibly do it," declares Nikander. "He'll be sent straight to the hospital, anyway, as it is. That's a fact!"

The nameless wanderer looks with terror at the stern, impassive faces of his evil-boding fellow travellers; then, lowering his eyes, he rapidly crosses himself without taking off his cap. He is trembling all over, his head is shaking, and he is beginning to writhe like a caterpillar that some one has stepped on.

"Come on! Time to go!" cries Nikander, rising. "We have rested long enough!"

Another minute and the travellers are plodding along the muddy road. The tramp is stooping more than before and has thrust his hands still deeper into the sleeves of his coat. Ptaka is silent.

A WOMAN'S KINGDOM

I

CHRISTMAS EVE

HERE was a thick roll of notes. It came from the bailiff at the forest villa; he wrote that he was sending fifteen hundred roubles, which he had been awarded as damages, having won an appeal. Anna Akimovna disliked and feared such words as "awarded damages" and "won the suit." She knew that it was impossible to do without the law, but for some reason, whenever Nazaritch, the manager of the factory, or the bailiff of her villa in the country, both of whom frequently went to law, used to win lawsuits of some sort for her benefit, she always felt uneasy and, as it were, ashamed. On this occasion, too, she felt uneasy and awkward, and wanted to put that fifteen hundred roubles further away that it might be out of her sight.

She thought with vexation that other girls of her age—she was in her twenty-sixth year—were now busy looking after their households, were weary and would sleep sound, and would wake up tomorrow morning in holiday mood; many of them had long been married and had children. Only she, for some reason, was compelled to sit like an old woman over these letters, to make notes upon them, to write answers, then to do nothing the whole evening till midnight, but wait till she was sleepy; and tomorrow they would all day long be coming with Christmas greetings and asking for favours; and the day after tomorrow there would certainly be some scandal at the factory—some one would be beaten or would die of drinking too much vodka, and she would be fretted by pangs of conscience; and after the holidays Nazaritch would turn off some twenty of the workpeople for absence from work, and all of the twenty would hang about at the front door, without their caps on, and she would be ashamed to go out to them, and they would be driven away like dogs. And all her acquaintances would say behind her back, and write to her in anonymous letters, that she was a millionaire and exploiter—that she was devouring other men's lives and sucking the blood of the workers.

Here there lay a heap of letters read through and laid aside already. They were all begging letters. They were from people who were hungry, drunken, dragged down by large families, sick, degraded, despised. . . . Anna Akimovna had already noted on each letter, three roubles to be paid to one, five to another; these letters would go the same day to the office, and next the distribution of assistance would take place, or, as the clerks used to say, the beasts would be fed.

They would distribute also in small sums four hundred and seventy roubles—the interest on a sum bequeathed by the late Akin Ivanovitch for the relief of the poor and needy. There would be a hideous crush. From the gates to the doors of the office there would stretch a long file of strange people with brutal faces, in rags, numb with cold, hungry and already drunk, in husky voices calling down blessings upon Anna Akimovna, their benefactress, and her parents: those at the back would press upon those in front, and those in front would abuse them with bad language. The clerk would get tired of the noise, the swearing, and the sing-song whining and blessing, would fly out and give some one a box on the ear to the delight of all. And her own people, the factory hands, who received nothing at Christmas but their wages, and had already spent every farthing of it, would stand in the middle of the yard, looking on and laughing—some enviously, others ironically.

"Merchants, and still more their wives, are fonder of

beggars than they are of their own workpeople," thought Anna Akimovna. "It's always so."

Her eyes fell upon the roll of money. It would be nice to distribute that hateful, useless money among the workpeople tomorrow, but it did not do to give the workpeople anything for nothing, or they would demand it again next time. And what would be the good of fifteen hundred roubles when there were eighteen hundred workmen in the factory besides their wives and children? Or she might, perhaps, pick out one of the writers of those begging letters—some luckless man who had long ago lost all hope of anything better, and give him the fifteen hundred. The money would come upon the poor creature like a thunder-clap, and perhaps for the first time in his life he would feel happy. This idea struck Anna Akimovna as original and amusing, and it fascinated her. She took one letter at random out of the pile and read it. Some petty official called Tchalikov had long been out of a situation, was ill, and living in Gushtchin's Buildings; his wife was in consumption, and he had five little girls. Anna Akimovna knew well the four-storied house, Gushtchin's Buildings, in which Tchalikov lived. Oh, it was a horrid, foul, unhealthy house!

"Well, I will give it to that Tchalikov," she decided. "I won't send it; I had better take it myself to prevent unnecessary talk. Yes," she reflected, as she put the fifteen hundred roubles in her pocket, "and I'll have a look at them, and perhaps I can do something for the little girls."

She felt light-hearted; she rang the bell and ordered the horses to be brought round.

When she got into the sledge it was past six o'clock in the evening. The windows in all the blocks of buildings were brightly lighted up, and that made the huge courtyard seem very dark: at the gates, and at the far end of the yard near the warehouses and the workpeople's barracks, electric lamps were gleaming.

Anna Akimovna disliked and feared those huge dark buildings, warehouses, and barracks where the workmen lived. She had only once been in the main building since her father's death. The high ceilings with iron girders; the multitude of huge, rapidly turning wheels, connecting straps and levers; the shrill hissing; the clank of steel; the rattle of the trolleys; the harsh puffing of steam; the faces—pale, crimson, or black with coal-dust; the shirts soaked with sweat; the gleam of steel, of copper, and of fire; the smell of oil and coal; and the draught, at times very hot and at times very cold—gave her an impression of hell. It seemed to her as though the wheels, the levers, and the hot hissing cylinders were trying to tear themselves away from their fastenings to crush the men, while the men, not hearing one another, ran about with anxious faces, and busied themselves about the machines, trying to stop their terrible movement. They showed Anna Akimovna something and respectfully explained it to her. She remembered how in the forge a piece of red-hot iron was pulled out of the furnace; and how an old man with a strap round his head, and another, a young man in a blue shirt with a chain on his breast, and an angry face, probably one of the foremen, struck the piece of iron with hammers; and how the golden sparks had been scattered in all directions; and how, a little afterwards, they had dragged out a huge piece of sheet-iron with a clang. The old man had stood erect and smiled, while the young man had wiped his face with his sleeve and explained something to her. And she remembered, too, how in another department an old man with one eye had been filing a piece of iron, and how the iron filings were scattered about; and how a red-haired man in black spectacles, with holes in his shirt, had been working at a lathe, making something out of a piece of steel: the lathe roared and hissed and squeaked, and Anna Akimovna felt sick at the sound, and it seemed as though they were boring into her ears. She looked, listened, did not understand, smiled graciously, and felt ashamed. To get hundreds of thousands of roubles from a business which one does not understand and cannot like—how strange it is!

And she had not once been in the workpeople's barracks. There, she was told, it was damp; there were bugs, debauchery, anarchy. It was an astonishing thing: a thousand roubles were spent annually on keeping the barracks in good order, yet, if she were to believe the anonymous letters, the condition of the workpeople was growing worse and worse every year.

"There was more order in my father's day," thought Anna Akimovna, as she drove out of the yard, "because he had been a workman himself. I know nothing about it and only do silly things."

She felt depressed again, and was no longer glad that she had come, and the thought of the lucky man upon whom fifteen hundred roubles would drop from heaven no longer struck her as original and amusing. To go to some Tchalikov or other, when at home a business worth a million was gradually going to pieces and being ruined, and the workpeople in the barracks were living worse than convicts, meant doing something silly and cheating her conscience. Along the highroad and across the fields near it, workpeople from the neighbouring cotton and paper factories were walking towards the lights of the town. There was the sound of talk and laughter in the frosty air. Anna Akimovna looked at the women and young people, and she suddenly felt a longing for a plain rough life among a crowd. She recalled vividly that far-away time when she used to be called Anyutka, when she was a little girl and used to lie under the same quilt with her mother, while a washerwoman who lodged with them used to wash clothes in the next room; while through the thin walls there came from the neighbouring flats sounds of laughter, swearing, children's crying, the accordion, and the whirr of carpenters' lathes and sewing-machines; while her father, Akim Ivanovitch, who was clever at almost every craft, would be soldering something near the stove, or drawing or planing, taking no notice whatever of the noise and stuffiness. And she longed to wash, to iron, to run to the shop and the tavern as she used to do every day when she lived with her mother. She ought to have been a work-girl and not the factory owner! Her big house with is chandeliers and pictures; her footman Mishenka, with his glossy moustache and swallow-tail coat; the devout and dignified Varvarushka, and smooth-tongued Agafyushka; and the young people of both sexes who came almost every day to ask her for money, and with whom she always for some reason felt guilty; and the clerks, the doctors, and the ladies who were charitable at her expense, who flattered her and secretly despised her for her humble origin—how wearisome and alien it all was to her!

Here was the railway crossing and the city gate; then came houses alternating with kitchen gardens; and at last the broad street where stood the renowned Gushtchin's Buildings. The street, usually quiet, was now on Christmas Eve full of life and movement. The eating-houses and beer-shops were noisy. If some one who did not belong to that quarter but lived in the centre of the town had driven through the street now, he would have noticed nothing but dirty, drunken, and abusive people; but Anna Akimovna, who had lived in those parts all her life, was constantly recognizing in the crowd her own father or mother or uncle. Her father was a soft fluid character, a little fantastical, frivolous, and irresponsible. He did not care for money, respectability or power; he used to say that a working man had no time to keep the holy-days and go to church; and if it had not been for his wife, he would probably never have gone to confession, taken the sacrament or kept the fasts. While her uncle, Ivan Ivanovitch, on the contrary, was like flint; in everything relating to religion, politics, and morality, he was harsh and relentless, and kept a strict watch, not only over himself, but also over all his servants and acquaintances. God forbid that one should go into his room without crossing oneself before the ikon! The luxurious mansion in which Anna Akimovna now lived he had always kept locked up, and only opened it on great holidays for important visitors, while he lived himself in the office, in a little room covered with ikons. He had learnings towards the Old Believers, and was continually entertaining priests and bishops of the old ritual, though he had been christened, and married, and had buried his wife in accordance with the Orthodox rites. He disliked Akim, his only brother and his heir, for his frivolity, which he called simpleness and folly, and for his indifference to religion. He treated him as an inferior, kept him in the position of a workman, paid him sixteen roubles a month. Akim addressed his brother with formal respect, and on the days of asking forgiveness, he and his wife and daughter bowed down to the ground before him. But three years before his death Ivan Ivanovitch had drawn closer to his brother, forgave his shortcomings, and ordered him to get a governess for Anyutka.

There was a dark, deep, evil-smelling archway under Gushtchin's Buildings; there was a sound of men coughing near the walls. Leaving the sledge in the street, Anna Akimovna went in at the gate and there inquired how to get to No. 46 to see a clerk called Tchalikov. She was directed to the furthest door on the right in the third story. And in the courtyard and near the outer door, and even on the stairs, there was still the same loathsome smell as under the archway. In Anna Akimovna's childhood, when her father was a simple workman, she used to live in a building like that, and afterwards, when their circumstances were different, she had often visited them in the character of a Lady Bountiful. The narrow stone staircase with its steep dirty steps, with landings at every story; the greasy swinging lanterns; the stench; the troughs, pots, and rags on the landings near the doors,—all this had been familiar to her long ago. . . . One door was open, and within could be seen Jewish tailors in caps, sewing. Anna Akimovna met people on the stairs, but it never entered her head that people might be rude to her.

She was no more afraid of peasants or workpeople, drunk or sober, than of her acquaintances of the educated class.

There was no entry at No. 46; the door opened straight into the kitchen. As a rule the dwellings of workmen and mechanics smell of varnish, tar, hides, smoke, according to the occupation of the tenant; the dwellings of persons of noble or official class who have come to poverty may be known by a peculiar rancid, sour smell. This disgusting smell enveloped Anna Akimovna on all sides, and as yet she was only on the threshold. A man in a black coat, no doubt Tchalikov himself, was sitting in a corner at the table with his back to the door, and with him were five little girls. The eldest, a broad-faced thin girl with a comb in her hair, looked about fifteen, while the youngest, a chubby child with hair that stood up like a hedge-hog, was not more than three. All the six were eating. Near the stove stood a very thin little woman with a yellow face, far gone in pregnancy. She was wearing a skirt and a white blouse, and had an oven fork in her hand.

"I did not expect you to be so disobedient, Liza," the man was saying reproachfully. "Fie, fie, for shame! Do you want papa to whip you—eh?"

Seeing an unknown lady in the doorway, the thin woman started, and put down the fork.

"Vassily Nikititch!" she cried, after a pause, in a hollow voice, as though she could not believe her eyes.

The man looked round and jumped up. He was a flat-chested, bony man with narrow shoulders and sunken temples. His eyes were small and hollow with dark rings round them, he had a wide mouth, and a long nose like a bird's beak—a little bit bent to the right. His beard was parted in the middle, his moustache was shaven, and this made him look more like a hired footman than a government clerk.

"Does Mr. Tchalikov live here?" asked Anna Akimovna.

"Yes, madam," Tchalikov answered severely, but immediately recognizing Anna Akimovna, he cried: "Anna Akimovna!" and all at once he gasped and clasped his hands as though in terrible alarm. "Benefactress!"

With a moan he ran to her, grunting inarticulately as though he were paralysed—there was cabbage on his beard and he smelt of vodka—pressed his forehead to her muff, and seemed as though he were in a swoon.

"Your hand, your holy hand!" he brought out breathlessly. "It's a dream, a glorious dream! Children, awaken me!"

He turned towards the table and said in a sobbing voice, shaking his fists:

"Providence has heard us! Our saviour, our angel, has come! We are saved! Children, down on your knees! on your knees!"

Madame Tchalikov and the little girls, except the youngest one, began for some reason rapidly clearing the table.

"You wrote that your wife was very ill," said Anna Akimovna, and she felt ashamed and annoyed. "I am not going to give them the fifteen hundred," she thought.

"Here she is, my wife," said Tchalikov in a thin feminine voice, as though his tears had gone to his head. "Here she is, unhappy creature! With one foot in the grave! But we do not complain, madam. Better death than such a life. Better die, unhappy woman!"

"Why is he playing these antics?" thought Anna Akimovna with annoyance. "One can see at once he is used to dealing with merchants."

"Speak to me like a human being," she said. "I don't care for farces."

"Yes, madam; five bereaved children round their mother's coffin with funeral candles—that's a farce? Eh?" said Tchalikov bitterly, and turned away.

"Hold your tongue," whispered his wife, and she pulled at his sleeve. "The place has not been tidied up, madam," she said, addressing Anna Akimovna; "please excuse it . . . you know what it is where there are children. A crowded hearth, but harmony."

"I am not going to give them the fifteen hundred," Anna Akimovna thought again.

And to escape as soon as possible from these people and from the sour smell, she brought out her purse and made up her mind to leave them twenty-five roubles, not more; but she suddenly felt ashamed that she had come so far and disturbed people for so little.

"If you give me paper and ink, I will write at once to a doctor who is a friend of mine to come and see you," she said, flushing red. "He is a very good doctor. And I will leave you some money for medicine."

Madame Tchalikov was hastening to wipe the table.

"It's messy here! What are you doing?" hissed Tchalikov, looking at her wrathfully. "Take her to the lodger's room! I make bold to ask you, madam, to step into the lodger's room," he said, addressing Anna Akimovna. "It's clean there."

"Osip Ilyitch told us not to go into his room!" said one of the little girls, sternly.

But they had already led Anna Akimovna out of the kitchen, through a narrow passage room between two bedsteads: it was evident from the arrangement of the beds that in one two slept lengthwise, and in the other three slept across the bed. In the lodger's room, that came next, it really was clean. A neat-looking bed with a red woollen quilt, a pillow in a white pillow-case, even a slipper for the watch, a table covered with a hempen cloth and on it, an ink-stand of milky-looking glass, pens, paper, photographs in frames—everything as it ought to be; and another table for rough work, on which lay tidily arranged a watchmaker's tools and watches taken to pieces. On the walls hung hammers, pliers, awls, chisels, nippers, and so on, and there were three hanging clocks which were ticking; one was a big clock with thick weights, such as one sees in eating-houses.

As she sat down to write the letter, Anna Akimovna saw

facing her on the table the photographs of her father and of herself. That surprised her.

"Who lives here with you?" she asked.

"Our lodger, madam, Pimenov. He works in your factory."

"Oh, I thought he must be a watchmaker."

"He repairs watches privately, in his leisure hours. He is an amateur."

After a brief silence during which nothing could be heard but the ticking of the clocks and the scratching of the pen on the paper. Tchalikov heaved a sigh and said ironically, with indignation:

"It's a true saying: gentle birth and a grade in the service won't put a coat on your back. A cockade in your cap and a noble title, but nothing to eat. To my thinking, if any one of humble class helps the poor he is much more of a gentleman than any Tchalikov who has sunk into poverty and vice."

To flatter Anna Akimovna, he uttered a few more disparaging phrases about his gentle birth, and it was evident that he was humbling himself because he considered himself superior to her. Meanwhile she had finished her letter and had sealed it up. The letter would be thrown away and the money would not be spent on medicine—that she knew, but she put twenty-five roubles on the table all the same, and after a moment's thought, added two more red notes. She saw the wasted, yellow hand of Madame Tchalikov, like the claw of a hen, dart out and clutch the money tight.

"You have graciously given this for medicine," said Tchalikov in a quivering voice, "but hold out a helping hand to me also . . . and the children!" he added with a sob. "My unhappy children! I am not afraid for myself; it is for my daughters I fear! It's the hydra of vice that I fear!"

Trying to open her purse, the catch of which had gone wrong, Anna Akimovna was confused and turned red. She felt ashamed that people should be standing before her, looking at her hands and waiting, and most likely at the bottom of their hearts laughing at her. At that instant some one came into the kitchen and stamped his feet, knocking the snow off.

"The lodger has come in," said Madame Tchalikov.

Anna Akimovna grew even more confused. She did not want any one from the factory to find her in this ridiculous position. As ill-luck would have it, the lodger came in at the very moment when, having broken the catch at last, she was giving Tchalikov some notes, and Tchalikov, grunting as though he were paralysed, was feeling about with his lips where he could kiss her. In the lodger she recognised the workman who had once clanked the sheet-iron before her in the forge, and had explained things to her. Evidently he had come in straight from the factory; his face looked dark and grimy, and on one cheek near his nose was a smudge of soot. His hands were perfectly black, and his unbelted shirt shone with oil and grease. He was a man of thirty, of medium height, with black hair and broad shoulders, and a look of great physical strength. At the first glance Anna Akimovna perceived that he must be a foreman, who must be receiving at least thirty-five roubles a month, and a stern, loud-voiced man who struck the workmen in the face; all this was evident from his manner of standing, from the attitude he involuntarily assumed at once on seeing a lady in his room, and most of all from the fact that he did not wear top-boots, that he had breast pockets, and a pointed, picturesquely clipped beard. Her father, Akim Ivanovitch, had been the brother of the factory owner, and yet he had been afraid of foremen like this lodger and had tried to win their favour.

"Excuse me for having come in here in your absence," said Anna Akimovna.

The workman looked at her in surprise, smiled in confusion and did not speak.

"You must speak a little louder, madam . . ." said Tchalikov softly. "When Mr. Pimenov comes home from the factory in the evenings he is a little hard of hearing."

But Anna Akimovna was by now relieved that there was nothing more for her to do here; she nodded to them and went rapidly out of the room. Pimenov went to see her out.

"Have you been long in our employment?" she asked in a loud voice, without turning to him.

"From nine years old. I entered the factory in your uncle's time."

"That's a long while! My uncle and my father knew all the workpeople, and I know hardly any of them. I had seen you before, but I did not know your name was Pimenov."

Anna Akimovna felt a desire to justify herself before him, to pretend that she had just given the money not seriously, but as a joke.

"Oh, this poverty," she sighed. "We give charity on holidays and working days, and still there is no sense in it. I believe it is useless to help such people as this Tchalikov."

"Of course it is useless," he agreed. "However much you give him, he will drink it all away. And now the husband and wife will be snatching it from one another and fighting all night," he added with a laugh.

"Yes, one must admit that our philanthropy is useless, boring, and absurd. But still, you must agree, one can't sit with one's hand in one's lap; one must do something. What's to be done with the Tchalikovs, for instance?"

She turned to Pimenov and stopped, expecting an answer from him; he, too, stopped and slowly, without speaking, shrugged his shoulders. Obviously he knew what to do with the Tchalikovs, but the treatment would have been so coarse and inhuman that he did not venture to put it into words. And the Tchalikovs were to him so utterly uninteresting and worthless, that a moment later he had forgotten them; looking into Anna Akimovna's eyes, he smiled with pleasure, and his face wore an expression as though he were dreaming about something very pleasant. Only, now standing close to him, Anna Akimovna saw from his face, and especially from his eyes, how exhausted and sleepy he was.

"Here, I ought to give him the fifteen hundred roubles!" she thought, but for some reason this idea seemed to her incongruous and insulting to Pimenov.

"I am sure you are aching all over after your work, and you come to the door with me," she said as they went down the stairs. "Go home."

But he did not catch her words. When they came out into the street, he ran on ahead, unfastened the cover of the sledge and helping Anna Akimovna in, said:

"I wish you a happy Christmas!"

II

CHRISTMAS MORNING

"They have left off ringing ever so long! It's dreadful; you won't be there before the service is over! Get up!"

"Two horses are racing, racing . . ." said Anna Akimovna, and she woke up; before her, candle in hand, stood her maid, red-haired Masha. "Well, what is it?"

"Service is over already," said Masha with despair. "I have called you three times! Sleep till evening for me, but you told me yourself to call you!"

Anna Akimovna raised herself on her elbow and glanced towards the window. It was still quite dark outside, and only the lower edge of the window-frame was white with snow. She could hear a low, mellow chime of bells; it was not the parish church, but somewhere further away. The watch on the little table showed three minutes past six.

"Very well, Masha. . . . In three minutes . . ." said Anna Akimovna in an imploring voice, and she snuggled under the bed-clothes.

She imagined the snow at the front door, the sledge, the dark sky, the crowd in the church, and the smell of juniper, and she felt dread at the thought; but all the same, she made up her mind that she would get up at once and go to early service. And while she was warm in bed and struggling with sleep—which seems, as though to spite one, particularly sweet when one ought to get up—and while she had visions of an immense garden on a mountain and then Gushtchin's Buildings, she was worried all the time by the thought that she ought to get up that very minute and go to church.

But when she got up it was quite light, and it turned out to be half-past nine. There had been a heavy fall of snow in the night; the trees were clothed in white, and the air was particularly light, transparent, and tender, so that when Anna Akimovna looked out of the window her first impulse was to draw a deep, deep breath. And when she had washed, a relic of far-away childish feelings—joy that today was Christmas—suddenly stirred within her; after that she felt light-hearted, free and pure in soul, as though her soul, too, had been washed or plunged in the white snow. Masha came in, dressed up and tightly laced, and wished her a happy Christmas; then she spent a long time combing her mistress's hair and helping her to dress. The fragrance and feeling of the new, gorgeous, splendid dress, its faint rustle, and the smell of fresh scent, excited Anna Akimovna.

"Well, it's Christmas," she said gaily to Masha. "Now we will try our fortunes."

"Last year, I was to marry an old man. It turned up three times the same."

"Well, God is merciful."

"Well, Anna Akimovna, what I think is, rather than neither one thing nor the other, I'd marry an old man," said Masha mournfully, and she heaved a sigh. "I am turned twenty; it's no joke."

Every one in the house knew that red-haired Masha was in love with Mishenka, the footman, and this genuine, passionate, hopeless love had already lasted three years.

"Come, don't talk nonsense," Anna Akimovna consoled her. "I am going on for thirty, but I am still meaning to marry a young man."

While his mistress was dressing, Mishenka, in a new swallow-tail and polished boots, walked about the hall and drawing-room and waited for her to come out, to wish her a happy Christmas. He had a peculiar walk, stepping softly and delicately; looking at his feet, his hands, and the bend of his head, it might be imagined that he was not simply walking, but learning to dance the first figure of a quadrille. In spite of his fine velvety moustache and handsome, rather flashy appearance, he was steady, prudent, and devout as an old man. He said his prayers, bowing down to the ground, and liked burning incense in his room. He respected people of wealth and rank and had a reverence for them; he despised poor people, and all who came to ask favours of any kind, with all the strength of his cleanly flunkey soul. Under his starched shirt he wore a flannel, winter and summer alike, being very careful of his health; his ears were plugged with cotton-wool.

When Anna Akimovna crossed the hall with Masha, he bent his head downwards a little and said in his agreeable, honeyed voice:

"I have the honour to congratulate you, Anna Akimovna, on the most solemn feast of the birth of our Lord."

Anna Akimovna gave him five roubles, while poor Masha was numb with ecstasy. His holiday get-up, his attitude, his voice, and what he said, impressed her by their beauty and elegance; as she followed her mistress she could think of nothing, could see nothing, she could only smile, first blissfully and then bitterly. The upper story of the house was called the best or visitors' half, while the name of the business part—old people's or simply women's part—was given to the rooms on the lower story where Aunt Tatyana Ivanovna kept house. In the upper part the gentry and educated visitors were entertained; in the lower story, simpler folk and the aunt's personal friends. Handsome, plump, and healthy, still young and fresh, and feeling she had on a magnificent dress which seemed to her to diffuse a sort of radiance all about her, Anna Akimovna went down to the lower story. Here she was met with reproaches for forgetting God now that she was so highly educated, for sleeping too late for the service, and for not coming downstairs to break the fast, and they all clasped their hands and exclaimed with perfect sincerity that she was lovely, wonderful; and she believed it, laughed, kissed them, gave one a rouble, another three or five according to their position. She liked being downstairs. Wherever one looked there were shrines, ikons, little lamps, portraits of ecclesiastical personages—the place smelt of monks; there was a rattle of knives in the kitchen, and already a smell of something savoury, exceedingly appetising, was pervading all the rooms. The yellow-painted floors shone, and from the doors narrow rugs with bright blue stripes ran like little paths to the ikon corner, and the sunshine was simply pouring in at the windows.

In the dining-room some old women, strangers, were sitting; in Varvarushka's room, too, there were old women, and with them a deaf and dumb girl, who seemed abashed about something and kept saying, "Bli, bli! . . ." Two skinny-looking little girls who had been brought out of the orphanage for Christmas came up to kiss Anna Akimovna's hand, and stood before her transfixed with admiration of her splendid dress; she noticed that one of the girls squinted, and in the midst of her light-hearted holiday mood she felt a sick pang at her heart at the thought that young men would despise the girl, and that she would never marry. In the cook Agafya's room, five huge peasants in new shirts were sitting round the samovar; these were not workmen from the factory, but relations of the cook. Seeing Anna Akimovna, all the peasants jumped up from their seats, and from regard for decorum, ceased munching, though their mouths were full. The cook Stepan, in a white cap, with a knife in his hand, came into the room and gave her his greetings; porters in high felt boots came in, and they, too, offered their greetings.

The water-carrier peeped in with icicles on his beard, but did not venture to come in.

Anna Akimovna walked through the rooms followed by her retinue—the aunt, Varvarushka, Nikandrovna, the sewing-maid Marfa Petrovna, and the downstairs Masha. Varvarushka—a tall, thin, slender woman, taller than any one in the house, dressed all in black, smelling of cypress and coffee—crossed herself in each room before the ikon, bowing down from the waist. And whenever one looked at her one was reminded that she had already prepared her shroud and that lottery tickets were hidden away by her in the same box.

"Anyutinka, be merciful at Christmas," she said, opening the door into the kitchen. "Forgive him, bless the man! Have done with it!"

The coachman Panteley, who had been dismissed for drunkenness in November, was on his knees in the middle of the kitchen. He was a good-natured man, but he used to be unruly when he was drunk, and could not go to sleep, but persisted in wandering about the buildings and shouting in a threatening voice, "I know all about it!" Now from his beefy and bloated face and from his bloodshot eyes it could be seen that he had been drinking continually from November till Christmas.

"Forgive me, Anna Akimovna," he brought out in a hoarse voice, striking his forehead on the floor and showing his bull-like neck.

"It was Auntie dismissed you; ask her."

"What about auntie?" said her aunt, walking into the kitchen, breathing heavily; she was very stout, and on her bosom one might have stood a tray of teacups and a samovar. "What about auntie now? You are mistress here, give your own orders; though these rascals might be all dead for all I care. Come, get up, you hog!" she shouted at Panteley, losing patience. "Get out of my sight! It's the last time I forgive you, but if you transgress again—don't ask for mercy!"

Then they went into the dining-room to coffee. But they

had hardly sat down, when the downstairs Masha rushed headlong in, saying with horror, "The singers!" And ran back again. They heard some one blowing his nose, a low bass cough, and footsteps that sounded like horses' iron-shod hoofs tramping about the entry near the hall. For half a minute all was hushed. . . . The singers burst out so suddenly and loudly that every one started. While they were singing, the priest from the almshouses with the deacon and the sexton arrived. Putting on the stole, the priest slowly said that when they were ringing for matins it was snowing and not cold, but that the frost was sharper towards morning, God bless it! and now there must be twenty degrees of frost.

"Many people maintain, though, that winter is healthier than summer," said the deacon; then immediately assumed an austere expression and chanted after the priest. "Thy Birth, O Christ our Lord. . . ."

Soon the priest from the workmen's hospital came with the deacon, then the Sisters from the hospital, children from the orphanage, and then singing could be heard almost uninterruptedly. They sang, had lunch, and went away.

About twenty men from the factory came to offer their Christmas greetings. They were only the foremen, mechanicians, and their assistants, the pattern-makers, the accountant, and so on—all of good appearance, in new black coats. They were all first-rate men, as it were picked men; each one knew his value—that is, knew that if he lost his berth today, people would be glad to take him on at another factory. Evidently they liked Auntie, as they behaved freely in her presence and even smoked, and when they had all trooped in to have something to eat, the accountant put his arm round her immense waist. They were free-and-easy, perhaps, partly also because Varvarushka, who under the old masters had wielded great power and had kept watch over the morals of the clerks, had now no authority whatever in the house; and perhaps because many of them still remembered the time when Auntie Tatyana Ivanovna, whose brothers kept a strict hand over her, had been dressed like a simple peasant woman like Agafya, and when Anna Akimovna used to run about the yard near the factory buildings and every one used to call her Anyutya.

The foremen ate, talked, and kept looking with amazement at Anna Akimovna, how she had grown up and how handsome she had become! But this elegant girl, educated by governesses and teachers, was a stranger to them; they could not understand her, and they instinctively kept closer to "Auntie," who called them by their names, continually pressed them to eat and drink, and, clinking glasses with them, had already drunk two wineglasses of rowanberry wine with them. Anna Akimovna was always afraid of their thinking her proud, an upstart, or a crow in peacock's feathers; and now while the foremen were crowding round the food, she did not leave the dining-room, but took part in the conversation. She asked Pimenov, her acquaintance of the previous day:

"Why have you so many clocks in your room?"

"I mend clocks," he answered. "I take the work up between times, on holidays, or when I can't sleep."

"So if my watch goes wrong I can bring it to you to be repaired?" Anna Akimovna asked, laughing.

"To be sure, I will do it with pleasure," said Pimenov, and there was an expression of tender devotion in his face, when, not herself knowing why, she unfastened her magnificent watch from its chain and handed it to him; he looked at it in silence and gave it back. "To be sure, I will do it with pleasure," he repeated. "I don't mend watches now. My eyes are weak, and the doctors have forbidden me to do fine work. But for you I can make an exception."

"Doctors talk nonsense," said the accountant. They all laughed. "Don't you believe them," he went on, flattered by the laughing; "last year a tooth flew out of a cylinder and hit old Kalmykov such a crack on the head that you could see his brains, and the doctor said he would die; but he is alive and working to this day, only he has taken to stammering since that mishap."

"Doctors do talk nonsense they do, but not so much," sighed Auntie. "Pyotr Andreyitch, poor dear, lost his sight. Just like you, he used to work day in day out at the factory near the hot furnace, and he went blind. The eyes don't like heat. But what are we talking about?" she said, rousing herself. "Come and have a drink. My best wishes for Christmas, my dears. I never drink with any one else, but I drink with you, sinful woman as I am. Please God!"

Anna Akimovna fancied that after yesterday Pimenov despised her as a philanthropist, but was fascinated by her as a woman. She looked at him and thought that he behaved very charmingly and was nicely dressed. It is true that the sleeves of his coat were not quite long enough, and the coat itself seemed short-waisted, and his trousers were not wide and fashionable, but his tie was tied carelessly and with taste and was not as gaudy as the others'. And he seemed to be a good-natured man, for he ate submissively whatever Auntie put on his plate. She remembered how black he had been the day before, and how sleepy, and the thought of it for some reason touched her.

When the men were preparing to go, Anna Akimovna put out her hand to Pimenov. She wanted to ask him to come in sometimes to see her, without ceremony, but she did not know how to—her tongue would not obey her; and that they might not think she was attracted by Pimenov, she shook hands with his companions, too.

Then the boys from the school of which she was a patroness came. They all had their heads closely cropped and all wore grey blouses of the same pattern. The teacher—a tall, beardless young man with patches of red on his face—was visibly agitated as he formed the boys into rows; the boys sang in tune, but with harsh, disagreeable voices. The manager of the factory, Nazaritch, a bald, sharp-eyed Old Believer, could never get on with the teachers, but the one who was now anxiously waving his hands he despised and hated, though he could not have said why. He behaved rudely and condescendingly to the young man, kept back his salary, meddled with the teaching, and had finally tried to dislodge him by appointing, a fortnight before Christmas, as porter to the school a drunken peasant, a distant relation of his wife's, who disobeyed the teacher and said rude things to him before the boys.

Anna Akimovna was aware of all this, but she could be of no help, for she was afraid of Nazaritch herself. Now she wanted at least to be very nice to the schoolmaster, to tell him she was very much pleased with him; but when after the singing he began apologising for something in great confusion, and Auntie began to address him familiarly as she drew him without ceremony to the table, she felt, for some reason, bored and awkward, and giving orders that the children should be given sweets, went upstairs.

"In reality there is something cruel in these Christmas customs," she said a little while afterwards, as it were to herself, looking out of window at the boys, who were flocking from the house to the gates and shivering with cold, putting their coats on as they ran. "At Christmas one wants to rest, to sit at home with one's own people, and the poor boys, the teacher, and the clerks and foremen, are obliged for some reason to go through the frost, then to offer their greetings, show their respect, be put to confusion . . ."

Mishenka, who was standing at the door of the drawing-room and overheard this, said:

"It has not come from us, and it will not end with us. Of course, I am not an educated man, Anna Akimovna, but I do understand that the poor must always respect the rich. It is well said, 'God marks the rogue.' In prisons, night refuges, and pot-houses you never see any but the poor, while decent people, you may notice, are always rich. It has been said of the rich, 'Deep calls to deep.' "

"You always express yourself so tediously and incomprehensibly," said Anna Akimovna, and she walked to the other end of the big drawing-room.

It was only just past eleven. The stillness of the big room, only broken by the singing that floated up from below, made her yawn. The bronzes, the albums, and the pictures on the walls, representing a ship at sea, cows in a meadow, and views of the Rhine, were so absolutely stale that her eyes simply glided over them without observing them. The holiday mood was already growing tedious. As before, Anna Akimovna felt that she was beautiful, good-natured, and wonderful, but now it seemed to her that that was of no use to any one; it seemed to her that she did not know for whom and for what she had put on this expensive dress, too, and, as always happened on all holidays, she began to be fretted by loneliness and the persistent thought that her beauty, her health, and her wealth, were a mere cheat, since she was not wanted, was of no use to any one, and nobody loved her. She walked through all the rooms, humming and looking out of windows; stopping in the drawing-room, she could not resist beginning to talk to Mishenka.

"I don't know what you think of yourself, Misha," she said, and heaved a sigh. "Really, God might punish you for it."

"What do you mean?"

"You know what I mean. Excuse my meddling in your affairs. But it seems you are spoiling your own life out of obstinacy. You'll admit that it is high time you got married, and she is an excellent and deserving girl. You will never find any one better. She's a beauty, clever, gentle, and devoted. . . . And her appearance! . . . If she belonged to our circle or a higher one, people would be falling in love with her for her red hair alone. See how beautifully her hair goes with her complexion. Oh, goodness! You don't understand anything, and don't know what you want," Anna Akimovna said bitterly, and tears came into her eyes. "Poor girl, I am so sorry for her! I know you want a wife with money, but I have told you already I will give Masha a dowry."

Mishenka could not picture his future spouse in his imagination except as a tall, plump, substantial, pious woman, stepping like a peacock, and, for some reason, with a long shawl over her shoulders; while Masha was thin, slender, tightly laced, and walked with little steps, and, worst of all, she was too fascinating and at times extremely attractive to Mishenka, and that, in his opinion, was incongruous with matrimony and only in keeping with loose behaviour. When Anna Akimovna had promised to give Masha a dowry, he had hesitated for a time; but once a poor student in a brown overcoat over his uniform, coming with a letter for Anna Akimovna, was fascinated by Masha, and could not resist embracing her near the hat-stand, and she had uttered a faint shriek; Mishenka, standing on the stairs above, had seen this, and from that time had begun to cherish a feeling of disgust for Masha. A poor student! Who knows, if she had been embraced by a rich student or an officer the consequences might have been different.

"Why don't you wish it?" Anna Akimovna asked. "What more do you want?"

Mishenka was silent and looked at the arm-chair fixedly, and raised his eyebrows.

"Do you love some one else?"

Silence. The red-haired Masha came in with letters and visiting cards on a tray. Guessing that they were talking about her, she blushed to tears.

"The postmen have come," she muttered. "And there is a clerk called Tchalikov waiting below. He says you told him to come to-day for something."

"What insolence!" said Anna Akimovna, moved to anger. "I gave him no orders. Tell him to take himself off; say I am not at home!"

A ring was heard. It was the priest from her parish. They were always shown into the aristocratic part of the house—

that is, upstairs. After the priests, Nazaritch, the manager of the factory, came to pay his visit, and then the factory doctor; then Mishenka announced the inspector of the elementary schools. Visitors kept arriving.

When there was a moment free, Anna Akimovna sat down in a deep arm-chair in the drawing-room, and shutting her eyes, thought that her loneliness was quite natural because she had not married and never would marry. . . . But that was not her fault. Fate itself had flung her out of the simple working-class surroundings in which, if she could trust her memory, she had felt so snug and at home, into these immense rooms, where she could never think what to do with herself, and could not understand why so many people kept passing before her eyes. What was happening now seemed to her trivial, useless, since it did not and could not give her happiness for one minute.

"If I could fall in love," she thought, stretching; the very thought of this sent a rush of warmth to her heart. "And if I could escape from the factory . . ." she mused, imagining how the weight of those factory buildings, barracks, and schools would roll off her conscience, roll off her mind. . . . Then she remembered her father, and thought if he had lived longer he would certainly have married her to a working man—to Pimenov, for instance. He would have told her to marry, and that would have been all about it. And it would have been a good thing; then the factory would have passed into capable hands.

She pictured his curly head, his bold profile, his delicate, ironical lips and the strength, the tremendous strength, in his shoulders, in his arms, in his chest, and the tenderness with which he had looked at her watch that day.

"Well," she said, "it would have been all right. . . . I would have married him."

"Anna Akimovna," said Mishenka, coming noiselessly into the drawing-room.

"How you frighten me!" she said, trembling all over. "What do you want?"

"Anna Akimovna," he said, laying his hand on his heart and raising his eyebrows, "you are my mistress and my benefactress, and no one but you can tell me what I ought to do about marriage, for you are as good as a mother to me. . . . But kindly forbid them to laugh and jeer at me downstairs. They won't let me pass without it."

"How do they jeer at you?"

"They call me Mashenka's Mishenka."

"Pooh, what nonsense!" cried Anna Akimovna indignantly. "How stupid you all are! What a stupid you are, Misha! How sick I am of you! I can't bear the sight of you."

III

DINNER

Just as the year before, the last to pay her visits were Krylin, an actual civil councillor, and Lysevitch, a well-known barrister. It was already dark when they arrived. Krylin, a man of sixty, with a wide mouth and with grey whiskers close to his ears, with a face like a lynx, was wearing a uniform with an Anna ribbon, and white trousers. He held Anna Akimovna's hand in both of his for a long while, looked intently in her face, moved his lips, and at last said, drawling upon one note:

"I used to respect your uncle . . . and your father, and enjoyed the privilege of their friendship. Now I feel it an agreeable duty, as you see, to present my Christmas wishes to their honoured heiress. . . In spite of my infirmities and the distance I have to come. . . . And I am very glad to see you in good health."

The lawyer Lysevitch, a tall, handsome fair man. with a slight sprinkling of grey on his temples and beard, was distinguished by exceptionally elegant manners; he walked with a swaying step, bowed as it were reluctantly, and shrugged his shoulders as he talked, and all this with an indolent grace, like a spoiled horse fresh from the stable. He was well fed, extremely healthy, and very well off; on one occasion he had won forty thousand roubles, but concealed the fact from his friends. He was fond of good fare, especially cheese, truffles, and grated radish with hemp oil; while in Paris he had eaten, so he said, baked but unwashed guts. He spoke smoothly, fluently, without hesitation, and only occasionally, for the sake of effect, permitted himself to hesitate and snap his fingers as if picking up a word. He had long ceased to believe in anything he had to say in the law courts, or perhaps he did believe in it, but attached no kind of significance to it; it had all so long been familiar, stale, ordinary. . . . He believed in nothing but what was original and unusual. A copy-book moral in an original form would move him to tears. Both his notebooks were filled with extraordinary expressions which he had read in various authors; and when he needed to look up any expression, he would search nervously in both books, and usually failed to find it. Anna Akimovna's father had in a good-humoured moment ostentatiously appointed him legal adviser in matters concerning the factory, and had assigned him a salary of twelve thousand roubles. The legal business of the factory had been confined to two or three trivial actions for recovering debts, which Lysevitch handed to his assistants.

Anna Akimovna knew that he had nothing to do at the factory, but she could not dismiss him—she had not the moral courage; and besides, she was used to him. He used to call himself her legal adviser, and his salary, which he invariably sent for on the first of the month punctually, he used to call "stern prose." Anna Akimovna knew that when, after her father's death, the timber of her forest was sold for railway sleepers, Lysevitch had made more than fifteen thousand out of the transaction, and had shared it with Nazaritch. When first she found out they had cheated her she had wept bitterly, but afterwards she had grown used to it.

Wishing her a happy Christmas, and kissing both her hands, he looked her up and down, and frowned.

"You mustn't," he said with genuine disappointment. "I have told you, my dear, you mustn't!"

"What do you mean, Viktor Nikolaitch?"

"I have told you you mustn't get fat. All your family have an unfortunate tendency to grow fat. You mustn't," he repeated in an imploring voice, and kissed her hand. "You are so handsome! You are so splendid! Here, your Excellency, let me introduce the one woman in the world whom I have ever seriously loved."

"There is nothing surprising in that. To know Anna Akimovna at your age and not to be in love with her, that would be impossible."

"I adore her," the lawyer continued with perfect sincerity, but with his usual indolent grace. "I love her, but not because I am a man and she is a woman. When I am with her I always feel as though she belongs to some third sex, and I to a fourth, and we float away together into the domain of the subtlest shades, and there we blend into the spectrum. Leconte de Lisle defines such relations better than any one. He has a superb passage, a marvellous passage. . . .

Lysevitch rummaged in one notebook, then in the other, and, not finding the quotation, subsided. They began talking of the weather, of the opera, of the arrival, expected shortly, of Duse. Anna Akimovna remembered that the year before Lysevitch and, she fancied, Krylin had dined with her, and now when they were getting ready to go away, she began with perfect sincerity pointing out to them in an imploring voice that as they had no more visits to pay, they ought to remain to dinner with her. After some hesitation the visitors agreed.

In addition to the family dinner, consisting of cabbage soup, sucking pig, goose with apples, and so on, a so-called "French" or "chef's" dinner used to be prepared in the kitchen on great holidays, in case any visitor in the upper story wanted a meal. When they heard the clatter of crockery in the dining-room, Lysevitch began to betray a noticeable excitement; he rubbed his hands, shrugged his shoulders, screwed up his eyes, and described with feeling what dinners her father and uncle used to give at one time, and a marvellous *matelote* of turbots the cook here could make: it was not a *matelote,* but a veritable revelation! He was already gloating over the dinner, already eating it in imagination and enjoying it. When Anna Akimovna took his arm and led him to the dining-room, he tossed off a glass of vodka and put a piece of salmon in his mouth; he positively purred with pleasure. He munched loudly, disgustingly, emitting sounds from his nose, while his eyes grew oily and rapacious.

The *hors d'œuvres* were superb; among other things, there were fresh white mushrooms stewed in cream, and *sauce provençale* made of fried oysters and crayfish, strongly flavoured with some bitter pickles. The dinner, consisting of elaborate holiday dishes, was excellent, and so were the wines. Mishenka waited at table with enthusiasm. When he laid some new dish on the table and lifted the shining cover, or poured out the wine, he did it with the solemnity of a professor of black magic, and, looking at his face and his movements suggesting the first figure of a quadrille, the lawyer thought several times, "What a fool!"

After the third course Lysevitch said, turning to Anna Akimovna:

"The *fin de siècle* woman—I mean when she is young, and of course wealthy—must be independent, clever, elegant, intellectual, bold, and a little depraved. Depraved within limits, a little; for excess, you know, is wearisome. You ought not to vegetate, my dear; you ought not to live like every one else, but to get the full savour of life, and a slight flavour of depravity is the sauce of life. Revel among flowers of intoxicating fragrance, breathe the perfume of musk, eat hashish, and best of all, love, love, love. . . . To begin with, in your place

I would set up seven lovers—one for each day of the week; and one I would call Monday, one Tuesday, the third Wednesday, and so on, so that each might know his day."

This conversation troubled Anna Akimovna; she ate nothing and only drank a glass of wine.

"Let me speak at last," she said. "For myself personally, I can't conceive of love without family life. I am lonely, lonely as the moon in the sky, and a waning moon, too; and whatever you may say, I am convinced, I feel that this waning can only be restored by love in its ordinary sense. It seems to me that such love would define my duties, my work, make clear my conception of life. I want from love peace of soul, tranquillity; I want the very opposite of musk, and spiritualism, and *fin de siècle* . . . in short"—she grew embarrassed —"a husband and children."

"You want to be married? Well, you can do that, too," Lysevitch assented. "You ought to have all experiences: marriage, and jealousy, and the sweetness of the first infidelity, and even children. . . . But make haste and live—make haste, my dear: time is passing; it won't wait."

"Yes, I'll go and get married!" she said, looking angrily at his well-fed, satisfied face. "I will marry in the simplest, most ordinary way and be radiant with happiness. And, would you believe it, I will marry some plain working man, some mechanic or draughtsman."

"There is no harm in that, either. The Duchess Josiana loved Gwinplin, and that was permissible for her because she was a grand duchess. Everything is permissible for you, too, because you are an exceptional woman: if, my dear, you want to love a negro or an Arab, don't scruple; send for a negro. Don't deny yourself anything. You ought to be as bold as your desires; don't fall short of them."

"Can it be so hard to understand me?" Anna Akimovna asked with amazement, and her eyes were bright with tears. "Understand, I have an immense business on my hands—two thousand workmen, for whom I must answer before God.

The men who work for me grow blind and deaf. I am afraid to go on like this; I am afraid! I am wretched, and you have the cruelty to talk to me of negroes and . . . and you smile!" Anna Akimovna brought her fist down on the table. "To go on living the life I am living now, or to marry some one as idle and incompetent as myself, would be a crime. I can't go on living like this," she said hotly, "I cannot!"

"How handsome she is!" said Lysevitch, fascinated by her. "My God, how handsome she is! But why are you angry, my dear? Perhaps I am wrong; but surely you don't imagine that if, for the sake of ideas for which I have the deepest respect, you renounce the joys of life and lead a dreary existence, your workmen will be any the better for it? Not a scrap! No, frivolity, frivolity!" he said decisively. "It's essential for you; it's your duty to be frivolous and depraved! Ponder, that, my dear, ponder it."

Anna Akimovna was glad she had spoken out, and her spirits rose. She was pleased she had spoken so well, and that her ideas were so fine and just, and she was already convinced that if Pimenov, for instance, loved her, she would marry him with pleasure.

Mishenka began to pour out champagne.

"You make me angry, Viktor Nikolaitch," she said, clinking glasses with the lawyer. "It seems to me you give advice and know nothing of life yourself. According to you, if a man be a mechanic or a draughtsman, he is bound to be a peasant and an ignoramus! But they are the cleverest people! Extraordinary people!"

"Your uncle and father . . . I knew them and respected them . . ." Krylin said, pausing for emphasis (he had been sitting upright as a post, and had been eating steadily the whole time), "were people of considerable intelligence and . . . of lofty spiritual qualities."

"Oh, to be sure, we know all about their qualities," the lawyer muttered, and asked permission to smoke.

When dinner was over Krylin was led away for a nap.

Lysevitch finished his cigar, and, staggering from repletion, followed Anna Akimovna into her study. Cosy corners with photographs and fans on the walls, and the inevitable pink or pale blue lanterns in the middle of the ceiling, he did not like, as the expression of an insipid and unoriginal character; besides, the memory of certain of his love affairs of which he was now ashamed was associated with such lanterns. Anna Akimovna's study with its bare walls and tasteless furniture pleased him exceedingly. It was snug and comfortable for him to sit on a Turkish divan and look at Anna Akimovna, who usually sat on the rug before the fire clasping her knees and looking into the fire and thinking of something; and at such moments it seemed to him that her peasant Old Believer blood was stirring within her.

Every time after dinner when coffee and liqueurs were handed, he grew livelier and began telling her various bits of literary gossip. He spoke with eloquence and inspiration, and was carried away by his own stories; and she listened to him and thought every time that for such enjoyment it was worth paying not only twelve thousand, but three times that sum, and forgave him everything she disliked in him. He sometimes told her the story of some tale or novel he had been reading, and then two or three hours passed unnoticed like a minute. Now he began rather dolefully in a failing voice with his eyes shut.

"It's ages, my dear, since I have read anything," he said when she asked him to tell her something. "Though I do sometimes read Jules Verne."

"I was expecting you to tell me something new."

"H'm! . . . new," Lysevitch muttered sleepily, and he settled himself further back in the corner of the sofa. "None of the new literature, my dear, is any use for you or me. Of course, it is bound to be such as it is, and to refuse to recognise it is to refuse to recognise—would mean refusing to recognise the natural order of things, and I do recognise it, but . . ." Lysevitch seemed to have fallen asleep. But a minute later his voice was heard again:

"All the new literature moans and howls like the autumn wind in the chimney. 'Ah, unhappy wretch! Ah, your life may be likened to a prison! Ah, how damp and dark it is in your prison! Ah, you will certainly come to ruin, and there is no chance of escape for you!' That's very fine, but I should prefer a literature that would tell us how to escape from prison. Of all contemporary writers, however, I prefer Maupassant." Lysevitch opened his eyes. "A fine writer, a perfect writer!" Lysevitch shifted in his seat. "A wonderful artist! A terrible, prodigious, supernatural artist!" Lysevitch got up from the sofa and raised his right arm. "Maupassant!" he said rapturously. "My dear, read Maupassant! one page of his gives you more than all the riches of the earth! Every line is a new horizon. The softest, tenderest impulses of the soul alternate with violent tempestuous sensations; your soul, as though under the weight of forty thousand atmospheres, is transformed into the most insignificant little bit of some great thing of an undefined rosy hue which I fancy, if one could put it on one's tongue, would yield a pungent, voluptuous taste. What a fury of transitions, of motives, of melodies! You rest peacefully on the lilies and the roses, and suddenly a thought—a terrible, splendid, irresistible thought—swoops down upon you like a locomotive, and bathes you in hot steam and deafens you with its whistle. Read Maupassant, dear girl; I insist on it."

Lysevitch waved his arms and paced from corner to corner in violent excitement.

"Yes, it is inconceivable," he pronounced, as though in despair; "his last thing overwhelmed me, intoxicated me! But I am afraid you will not care for it. To be carried away by it you must savour it, slowly suck the juice from each line, drink it in. . . . You must drink it in! . . ."

After a long introduction, containing many words such as

dæmonic sensuality, a network of the most delicate nerves, simoon, crystal, and so on, he began at last telling the story of the novel. He did not tell the story so whimsically, but told it in minute detail, quoting from memory whole descriptions and conversations; the characters of the novel fascinated him, and to describe them he threw himself into attitudes, changed the expression of his face and voice like a real actor. He laughed with delight at one moment in a deep bass, and at another, on a high shrill note, clasped his hands and clutched at his head with an expression which suggested that it was just going to burst. Anna Akimovna listened enthralled, though she had already read the novel, and it seemed to her ever so much finer and more subtle in the lawyer's version than in the book itself. He drew her attention to various subtleties, and emphasised the felicitous expressions and the profound thoughts, but she saw in it, only life, life, life and herself, as though she had been a character in the novel. Her spirits rose, and she, too, laughing and clasping her hands, thought that she could not go on living such a life, that there was no need to have a wretched life when one might have a splendid one. She remembered her words and thoughts at dinner, and was proud of them; and when Pimenov suddenly rose up in her imagination, she felt happy and longed for him to love her.

When he had finished the story, Lysevitch sat down on the sofa, exhausted.

"How splendid you are! How handsome!" he began, a little while afterwards in a faint voice as if he were ill. "I am happy near you, dear girl, but why am I forty-two instead of thirty? Your tastes and mine do not coincide: you ought to be depraved, and I have long passed that phase, and want a love as delicate and immaterial as a ray of sunshine—that is, from the point of view of a woman of your age, I am of no earthly use."

In his own words, he loved Turgenev, the singer of virginal

love and purity, of youth, and of the melancholy Russian landscape: but he loved virginal love, not from knowledge but from hearsay, as something abstract, existing outside real life. Now he assured himself that he loved Anna Akimovna platonically, ideally, though he did not know what those words meant. But he felt comfortable, snug, warm. Anna Akimovna seemed to him enchanting, original, and he imagined that the pleasant sensation that was aroused in him by these surroundings was the very thing that was called platonic love.

He laid his cheek on her hand and said in the tone commonly used in coaxing little children:

"My precious, why have you punished me?"

"How? When?"

"I have had no Christmas present from you."

Anna Akimovna had never heard before of their sending a Christmas box to the lawyer, and now she was at a loss how much to give him. But she must give him something, for he was expecting it, though he looked at her with eyes full of love.

"I suppose Nazaritch forgot it," she said, "but it is not too late to set it right."

She suddenly remembered the fifteen hundred she had received the day before, which was now lying in the toilet drawer in her bedroom. And when she brought that ungrateful money and gave it to the lawyer, and he put it in his coat pocket with indolent grace, the whole incident passed off charmingly and naturally. The sudden reminder of a Christmas box and this fifteen hundred was not unbecoming in Lysevitch.

"Merci," he said, and kissed her finger.

Krylin came in with blissful, sleepy face, but without his decorations.

Lysevitch and he stayed a little longer and drank a glass of tea each, and began to get ready to go. Anna Akimovna was a little embarrassed. . . . She had utterly forgotten in what department Krylin served, and whether she had to give him money or not; and if she had to, whether to give it now or send it afterwards in an envelope.

"Where does he serve?" she whispered to Lysevitch.

"Goodness knows," muttered Lysevitch, yawning.

She reflected that if Krylin used to visit her father and her uncle and respected them, it was probably not for nothing: apparently he had been charitable at their expense, serving in some charitable institution. As she said good-bye she slipped three hundred roubles into his hand; he seemed taken aback, and looked at her for a minute in silence with his pewtery eyes, but then seemed to understand and said:

"The receipt, honoured Anna Akimovna, you can only receive on the New Year."

Lysevitch had become utterly limp and heavy, and he staggered when Mishenka put on his overcoat.

As he went downstairs he looked like a man in the last stage of exhaustion, and it was evident that he would drop asleep as soon as he got into his sledge.

"Your Excellency," he said languidly to Krylin, stopping in the middle of the staircase, "has it ever happened to you to experience a feeling as though some unseen force were drawing you out longer and longer? You are drawn out and turn into the finest wire. Subjectively this finds expression in a curious voluptuous feeling which is impossible to compare with anything."

Anna Akimovna, standing at the top of the stairs, saw each of them give Mishenka a note.

"Good-bye! Come again!" she called to them, and ran into her bedroom.

She quickly threw off her dress, that she was weary of already, put on a dressing-gown, and ran downstairs; and as she ran downstairs she laughed and thumped with her feet like a school-boy; she had a great desire for mischief.

IV

EVENING

Auntie, in a loose print blouse, Varvarushka and two old women, were sitting in the dining-room having supper. A big piece of salt meat, a ham, and various savouries, were lying on the table before them, and clouds of steam were rising from the meat, which looked particularly fat and appetising. Wine was not served on the lower story, but they made up for it with a great number of spirits and home-made liqueurs. Agafyushka, the fat, white-skinned, well-fed cook, was standing with her arms crossed in the doorway and talking to the old women, and the dishes were being handed by the downstairs Masha, a dark girl with a crimson ribbon in her hair. The old women had had enough to eat before the morning was over, and an hour before supper had had tea and buns, and so they were now eating with effort—as it were, from a sense of duty.

"Oh, my girl!" sighed Auntie, as Anna Akimovna ran into the dining-room and sat down beside her. "You've frightened me to death!"

Every one in the house was pleased when Anna Akimovna was in good spirits and played pranks; this always reminded them that the old men were dead and that the old women had no authority in the house, and any one could do as he liked without any fear of being sharply called to account for it. Only the two old women glanced askance at Anna Akimovna with amazement: she was humming, and it was a sin to sing at table.

"Our mistress, our beauty, our picture," Agafyushka began chanting with sugary sweetness. "Our precious jewel! The people, the people that have come to-day to look at our queen. Lord have mercy upon us! Generals, and officers and gentlemen. . . . I kept looking out of window and counting and counting till I gave it up."

"I'd as soon they did not come at all," said Auntie; she looked sadly at her niece and added: "They only waste the time for my poor orphan girl."

Anna Akimovna felt hungry, as she had eaten nothing since the morning. They poured her out some very bitter liqueur; she drank it off, and tasted the salt meat with mustard, and thought it extraordinarily nice. Then the downstairs Masha brought in the turkey, the pickled apples and the gooseberries. And that pleased her, too. There was only one thing that was disagreeable: there was a draught of hot air from the tiled stove; it was stiflingly close and every one's cheeks were burning. After supper the cloth was taken off and plates of peppermint biscuits, walnuts, and raisins were brought in.

"You sit down, too . . . no need to stand there!" said Auntie to the cook.

Agafyushka sighed and sat down to the table; Masha set a wineglass of liqueur before her, too, and Anna Akimovna began to feel as though Agafyushka's white neck were giving out heat like the stove. They were all talking of how difficult it was nowadays to get married, and saying that in old days, if men did not court beauty, they paid attention to money, but now there was no making out what they wanted; and while hunchbacks and cripples used to be left old maids, nowadays men would not have even the beautiful and wealthy. Auntie began to set this down to immorality, and said that people had no fear of God, but she suddenly remembered that Ivan Ivanitch, her brother, and Varvarushka—both people of holy life—had feared God, but all the same had had children on the sly, and had sent them to the Foundling Asylum. She pulled herself up and changed the conversation, telling them about a suitor she had once had, a factory hand, and how she had loved him, but her brothers had forced her to marry a widower, an ikon-painter, who, thank God, had died two years after. The downstairs Masha sat down to the table, too, and told them with a mysterious air that for the last week some unknown man with a black moustache, in a great-coat with an astrachan collar, had made his appearance every morning in the yard, had stared at the windows of the big house, and had gone on further—to the buildings; the man was all right, nice-looking. . . .

All this conversation made Anna Akimovna suddenly long to be married—long intensely, painfully; she felt as though she would give half her life and all her fortune only to know that upstairs there was a man who was closer to her than any one in the world, that he loved her warmly and was missing her; and the thought of such closeness, ecstatic and inexpressible in words, troubled her soul. And the instinct of youth and health flattered her with lying assurances that the real poetry of life was not over but still to come, and she believed it, and leaning back in her chair (her hair fell down as she did so), she began laughing, and, looking at her, the others laughed, too. And it was a long time before this causeless laughter died down in the dining-room.

She was informed that the Stinging Beetle had come. This was a pilgrim woman called Pasha or Spiridonovna—a thin little woman of fifty, in a black dress with a white kerchief, with keen eyes, sharp nose, and a sharp chin; she had sly, viperish eyes and she looked as though she could see right through every one. Her lips were shaped like a heart. Her viperishness and hostility to every one had earned her the nickname of the Stinging Beetle.

Going into the dining-room without looking at any one, she made for the ikons and chanted in a high voice "Thy Holy Birth," then she sang "The Virgin to-day gives birth to the Son," then "Christ is born," then she turned round and bent a piercing gaze upon all of them.

"A happy Christmas," she said, and she kissed Anna Akimovna on the shoulder. "It's all I could do, all I could do to get to you, my kind friends." She kissed Auntie on the shoulder. "I should have come to you this morning, but I went in to some good people to rest on the way. 'Stay, Spiridonovna, stay,' they said, and I did not notice that evening was coming on."

As she did not eat meat, they gave her salmon and caviar. She ate looking from under her eyelids at the company, and drank three glasses of vodka. When she had finished she said a prayer and bowed down to Anna Akimovna's feet.

They began to play a game of "kings," as they had done the year before, and the year before that, and all the servants in both stories crowded in at the doors to watch the game. Anna Akimovna fancied she caught a glimpse once or twice of Mishenka, with a patronising smile on his face, among the crowd of peasant men and women. The first to be king was Stinging Beetle, and Anna Akimovna as the soldier paid her tribute; and then Auntie was king and Anna Akimovna was peasant, which excited general delight, and Agafyushka was prince, and was quite abashed with pleasure. Another game was got up at the other end of the table—played by the two Mashas, Varvarushka, and the sewing-maid Marfa Ptrovna, who was waked on purpose to play "kings," and whose face looked cross and sleepy.

While they were playing they talked of men, and of how difficult it was to get a good husband nowadays, and which state was to be preferred—that of an old maid or a widow.

"You are a handsome, healthy, sturdy lass," said Stinging Beetle to Anna Akimovna. "But I can't make out for whose sake you are holding back."

"What's to be done if nobody will have me?"

"Or maybe you have taken a vow to remain a maid?" Stinging Beetle went on, as though she did not hear. "Well, that's a good deed. . . . Remain one," she repeated, looking intently and maliciously at her cards. "All right, my dear, remain one. . . . Yes . . . only maids, these saintly maids, are not all alike." She heaved a sigh and played the king. "Oh, no, my girl, they are not all alike! Some really watch over themselves like nuns, and butter would not melt in their mouths; and if such a one does sin in an hour of weakness, she is worried to death, poor thing! so it would be a sin to condemn her. While others will go dressed in black and sew their shroud, and yet love rich old men on the sly. Yes, y-es, my canary birds, some hussies will bewitch an old man and rule over him, my doves, rule over him and turn his head; and when they've saved up money and lottery tickets enough, they will bewitch him to his death."

Varvarushka's only response to these hints was to heave a sigh and look towards the ikons. There was an expression of Christian meekness on her countenance.

"I know a maid like that, my bitterest enemy," Stinging Beetle went on, looking round at every one in triumph; "she is always sighing, too, and looking at the ikons, the she-devil. When she used to rule in a certain old man's house, if one went to her she would give one a crust, and bid one bow down to the ikons while she would sing: 'In conception Thou dost abide a Virgin . . . !' On holidays she will give one a bite, and on working days she will reproach one for it. But nowadays I will make merry over her! I will make as merry as I please, my jewel."

Varvarushka glanced at the ikons again and crossed herself.

"But no one will have me, Spiridonovna," said Anna kimovna to change the conversation. "What's to be done?"

"It's your own fault. You keep waiting for highly educated gentlemen, but you ought to marry one of your own sort, a merchant."

"We don't want a merchant," said Auntie, all in a flutter. "Queen of Heaven, preserve us! A gentleman will spend your money, but then he will be kind to you, you poor little fool. But a merchant will be so strict that you won't feel at home in your own house. You'll be wanting to fondle him and he will be counting his money, and when you sit down to meals with him, he'll grudge you every mouthful, though it's your own, the lout! . . . Marry a gentleman."

They all talked at once, loudly interrupting one another,

and Auntie tapped on the table with the nutcrackers and said, flushed and angry:

"We won't have a merchant; we won't have one! If you choose a merchant I shall go to an almshouse."

"Sh . . . Sh! . . . Hush!" cried Stinging Beetle; when all were silent she screwed up one eye and said: "Do you know what, Annushka, my birdie . . . ? There is no need for you to get married really like every one else. You're rich and free, you are your own mistress; but yet, my child, it doesn't seem the right thing for you to be an old maid. I'll find you, you know, some trumpery and simple-witted man. You'll marry him for appearances and then have your fling, bonny lass! You can hand him five thousand or ten maybe, and pack him off where he came from, and you will be mistress in your own house—you can love whom you like and no one can say anything to you. And then you can love your highly educated gentleman. You'll have a jolly time!" Stinging Beetle snapped her fingers and gave a whistle.

"It's sinful," said Auntie.

"Oh, sinful," laughed Stinging Beetle. "She is educated, she understands. To cut some one's throat or bewitch an old man—that's a sin, that's true; but to love some charming young friend is not a sin at all. And what is there in it, really? There's no sin in it at all! The old pilgrim women have invented all that to make fools of simple folk. I, too, say everywhere it's a sin; I don't know myself why it's a sin." Stinging Beetle emptied her glass and cleared her throat. "Have your fling, bonny lass," this time evidently addressing herself. "For thirty years, wenches, I have thought of nothing but sins and been afraid, but now I see I have wasted my time, I've let it slip by like a ninny! Ah, I have been a fool, a fool!" She sighed. "A woman's time is short and every day is precious. You are handsome, Annushka, and very rich; but as soon as thirty-five or forty strikes for you your time is up. Don't listen to any one, my girl; live, have your fling till you are forty, and then you will have time to pray forgiveness—there will be plenty of time to bow down and to sew your shroud. A candle to God and a poker to the devil! You can do both at once! Well, how is it to be? Will you make some little man happy?"

"I will," laughed Anna Akimovna. "I don't care now; I would marry a working man."

"Well, that would do all right! Oh, what a fine fellow you would choose then!" Stinging Beetle screwed up her eyes and shook her head. "O—o—oh!"

"I tell her myself," said Auntie, "it's no good waiting for a gentleman, so she had better marry, not a gentleman, but some one humbler; anyway we should have a man in the house to look after things. And there are lots of good men. She might have some one out of the factory. They are all sober, steady men. . . ."

"I should think so," Stinging Beetle agreed. "They are capital fellows. If you like, Aunt, I will make a match for her with Vassily Lebedinsky?"

"Oh, Vasya's legs are so long," said Auntie seriously. "He is so lanky. He has no looks."

There was laughter in the crowd by the door.

"Well, Pimenov? Would you like to marry Pimenov?" Stinging Beetle asked Anna Akimovna.

"Very good. Make a match for me with Pimenov."

"Really?"

"Yes, do!" Anna Akimovna said resolutely, and she struck her fist on the table. "On my honour, I will marry him."

"Really?"

Anna Akimovna suddenly felt ashamed that her cheeks were burning and that every one was looking at her; she flung the cards together on the table and ran out of the room. As she ran up the stairs and, reaching the upper story, sat down to the piano in the drawing-room, a murmur of sound reached her from below like the roar of the sea; most likely they were talking of her and of Pimenov, and perhaps

Stinging Beetle was taking advantage of her absence to insult Varvarushka and was putting no check on her language

The lamp in the big room was the only light burning in the upper story, and it sent a glimmer through the door into the dark drawing-room. It was between nine and ten, not later. Anna Akimovna played a waltz, then another, then a third; she went on playing without stopping. She looked into the dark corner beyond the piano, smiled, and inwardly called to it, and the idea occurred to her that she might drive off to the town to see some one, Lysevitch for instance, and tell him what was passing in her heart. She wanted to talk without ceasing, to laugh, to play the fool, but the dark corner was sullenly silent, and all round in all the rooms of the upper story it was still and desolate.

She was fond of sentimental songs, but she had a harsh, untrained voice, and so she only played the accompaniment and sang hardly audibly, just above her breath. She sang in a whisper one song after another, for the most part about love, separation, and frustrated hopes, and she imagined how she would hold out her hands to him and say with entreaty, with tears, "Pimenov, take this burden from me!" And then, just as though her sins had been forgiven, there would be joy and comfort in her soul, and perhaps a free, happy life would begin. In an anguish of anticipation she leant over the keys, with a passionate longing for the change in her life to come at once without delay, and was terrified at the thought that her old life would go on for some time longer. Then she played again and sang hardly above her breath, and all was stillness about her. There was no noise coming from downstairs now, they must have gone to bed. It had struck ten some time before. A long, solitary, wearisome night was approaching.

Anna Akimovna walked through all the rooms, lay down for a while on the sofa, and read in her study the letters that had come that evening; there were twelve letters of Christmas greetings and three anonymous letters. In one of them some workman complained in a horrible, almost illegible handwriting that Lenten oil sold in the factory shop was rancid and smelt of paraffin; in another, some one respectfully informed her that over a purchase of iron Nazaritch had lately taken a bribe of a thousand roubles from some one; in a third she was abused for her inhumanity.

The excitement of Christmas was passing off, and to keep it up Anna Akimovna sat down at the piano again and softly played one of the new waltzes, then she remembered how cleverly and creditably she had spoken at dinner to-day. She looked round at the dark windows, at the walls with the pictures, at the faint light that came from the big room, and all at once she began suddenly crying, and she felt vexed that she was so lonely, and that she had no one to talk to and consult. To cheer herself she tried to picture Pimenov in her imagination, but it was unsuccessful.

It struck twelve. Mishenka, no longer wearing his swallow-tail but in his reefer jacket, came in, and without speaking lighted two candles; then he went out and returned a minute later with a cup of tea on a tray.

"What are you laughing at?" she asked, noticing a smile on his face.

"I was downstairs and heard the jokes you were making about Pimenov . . ." he said, and put his hand before his laughing mouth. "If he were sat down to dinner to-day with Viktor Nikolaevitch and the general, he'd have died of fright." Mishenka's shoulders were shaking with laughter. "He doesn't know even how to hold his fork, I bet."

The footman's laughter and words, his reefer jacket and moustache, gave Anna Akimovna a feeling of uncleanness. She shut her eyes to avoid seeing him, and, against her own will, imagined Pimenov dining with Lysevitch and Krylin, and his timid, unintellectual figure seemed to her pitiful and helpless, and she felt repelled by it. And only now, for the first time in the whole day, she realised clearly that all she had said and thought about Pimenov and marrying a workman was nonsense, folly, and wilfulness. To convince herself of the opposite, to overcome her repulsion, she tried to recall what she had said at dinner, but now she could not see anything in it: shame at her own thoughts and actions, and the fear that she had said something improper during the day, and disgust at her own lack of spirit, overwhelmed her completely. She took up a candle and, as rapidly as if some one were pursuing her, ran downstairs, woke Spiridonovna, and began assuring her she had been joking. Then she went to her bedroom. Red-haired Masha, who was dozing in an armchair near the bed, jumped up and began shaking up the pillows. Her face was exhausted and sleepy, and her magnificent hair had fallen on one side.

"Tchalikov came again this evening," she said, yawning, "but I did not dare to announce him; he was very drunk. He says he will come again to-morrow."

"What does he want with me?" said Anna Akimovna, and she flung her comb on the floor. "I won't see him, I won't."

She made up her mind she had no one left in life but this Tchalikov, that he would never leave off persecuting her, and would remind her every day how uninteresting and absurd her life was. So all she was fit for was to help the poor. Oh, how stupid it was!

She lay down without undressing, and sobbed with shame and depression: what seemed to her most vexatious and stupid of all was that her dreams that day about Pimenov had been right, lofty, honourable, but at the same time she felt that Lysevitch and even Krylin were nearer to her than Pimenov and all the workpeople taken together. She thought that if the long day she had just spent could have been represented in a picture, all that had been bad and vulgar—as, for instance, the dinner, the lawyer's talk, the game of "kings"—would have been true, while her dreams and talk about Pimenov would have stood out from the whole as something false, as out of drawing; and she thought, too, that it was too late to dream of happiness, that everything was over for her, and it was impossible to go back to the life when she had slept under the same quilt with her mother, or to devise some new special sort of life.

Red-haired Masha was kneeling before the bed, gazing at her in mournful perplexity: then she, too, began crying, and laid her face against her mistress's arm, and without words it was clear why she was so wretched.

"We are fools!" said Anna Akimovna, laughing and crying. "We are fools! Oh, what fools we are!"

THE DOCTOR

It was still in the drawing-room, so still that a house-fly that had flown in from outside could be distinctly heard brushing against the ceiling. Olga Ivanovna, the lady of the villa, was standing by the window, looking out at the flower-beds and thinking. Dr. Tsvyetkov, who was her doctor as well as an old friend, and had been sent for to treat her son Misha, was sitting in an easy chair and swinging his hat, which he held in both hands, and he too was thinking. Except them, there was not a soul in the drawing-room or in the adjoining rooms. The sun had set, and the shades of evening began settling in the corners under the furniture and on the cornices.

The silence was broken by Olga Ivanovna.

"No misfortune more terrible can be imagined," she said, without turning from the window. "You know that life has no value for me whatever apart from the boy."

"Yes, I know that," said the doctor.

"No value whatever," said Olga Ivanovna, and her voice quivered. "He is everything to me. He is my joy, my happiness, my wealth. And if, as you say, I cease to be a mother, if he . . . dies, there will be nothing left of me but a shadow. I cannot survive it."

Wringing her hands, Olga Ivanovna walked from one window to the other and went on:

"When he was born, I wanted to send him away to the Foundling Hospital, you remember that, but, my God, how can that time be compared with now? Then I was vulgar, stupid, feather-headed, but now I am a mother, do you understand? I am a mother, and that's all I care to know. Between the present and the past there is an impassable gulf."

Silence followed again. The doctor shifted his seat from the chair to the sofa and impatiently playing with his hat, kept his eyes fixed upon Olga Ivanovna. From his face it could be seen that he wanted to speak, and was waiting for a fitting moment.

"You are silent, but still I do not give up hope," said the lady, turning round. "Why are you silent?"

"I should be as glad of any hope as you, Olga, but there is none," Tsvyetkov answered, "we must look the hideous truth in the face. The boy has a tumour on the brain, and we must try to prepare ourselves for his death, for such cases never recover."

"Nikolay, are you certain you are not mistaken?"

"Such questions lead to nothing. I am ready to answer as many as you like, but it will make it no better for us."

Olga Ivanovna pressed her face into the window curtains, and began weeping bitterly. The doctor got up and walked several times up and down the drawing-room, then went to the weeping woman, and lightly touched her arm. Judging from his uncertain movements, from the expression of his gloomy face, which looked dark in the dusk of the evening, he wanted to say something.

"Listen, Olga," he began. "Spare me a minute's attention; there is something I must ask you. You can't attend to me now, though. I'll come later, afterwards. . . ." He sat down again, and sank into thought. The bitter, imploring weeping, like the weeping of a little girl, continued. Without waiting for it to end, Tsvyetkov heaved a sigh and walked out of the drawing-room. He went into the nursery to Misha. The boy was lying on his back as before, staring at one point as though he were listening. The doctor sat down on his bed and felt his pulse.

"Misha, does your head ache?" he asked.

Misha answered, not at once: "Yes. I keep dreaming."

"What do you dream?"

"All sorts of things. . . ."

The doctor, who did not know how to talk with weeping women or with children, stroked his burning head, and muttered:

"Never mind, poor boy, never mind. . . . One can't go through life without illness. . . . Misha, who am I—do you know me?"

Misha did not answer.

"Does your head ache very badly?"

"Ve-ery. I keep dreaming."

After examining him and putting a few questions to the maid who was looking after the sick child, the doctor went slowly back to the drawing-room. There it was by now dark, and Olga Ivanovna, standing by the window, looked like a silhouette.

"Shall I light up?" asked Tsvyetkov.

No answer followed. The house-fly was still brushing against the ceiling. Not a sound floated in from outside as though the whole world, like the doctor, were thinking, and could not bring itself to speak. Olga Ivanovna was not weeping now, but as before, staring at the flower-bed in profound silence. When Tsvyetkov went up to her, and through the twilight glanced at her pale face, exhausted with grief, her expression was such as he had seen before during her attacks of acute, stupefying, sick headache.

"Nikolay Trofimitch!" she addressed him, "and what do you think about a consultation?"

"Very good; I'll arrange it to-morrow."

From the doctor's tone it could be easily seen that he put little faith in the benefit of a consultation. Olga Ivanovna would have asked him something else, but her sobs prevented her. Again she pressed her face into the window curtain. At that moment, the strains of a band playing at the club floated in distinctly. They could hear not only the wind instruments, but even the violins and the flutes.

"If he is in pain, why is he silent?" asked Olga Ivanovna. "All day long, not a sound, he never complains, and never cries. I know God will take the poor boy from us because we have not known how to prize him. Such a treasure!"

The band finished the march, and a minute later began playing a lively waltz for the opening of the ball.

"Good God, can nothing really be done?" moaned Olga Ivanovna. "Nikolay, you are a doctor and ought to know what to do! You must understand that I can't bear the loss of him! I can't survive it."

The doctor, who did not know how to talk to weeping women, heaved a sigh, and paced slowly about the drawing-room. There followed a succession of oppressive pauses interspersed with weeping and the questions which lead to nothing. The band had already played a quadrille, a polka, and another quadrille. It got quite dark. In the adjoining room, the maid lighted the lamp; and all the while the doctor kept his hat in his hands, and seemed trying to say something. Several times Olga Ivanovna went off to her son, sat by him for half an hour, and came back again into the drawing-room; she was continually breaking into tears and lamentations. The time dragged agonisingly, and it seemed as though the evening had no end.

At midnight, when the band had played the cotillion and ceased altogether, the doctor got ready to go.

"I will come again to-morrow," he said, pressing the mother's cold hand. "You go to bed."

After putting on his greatcoat in the passage and picking up his walking-stick, he stopped, thought a minute, and went back into the drawing-room.

"I'll come to-morrow, Olga," he repeated in a quivering voice. "Do you hear?"

She did not answer, and it seemed as though grief had robbed her of all power of speech. In his greatcoat and with his stick still in his hand, the doctor sat down beside her, and began in a soft, tender half-whisper, which was utterly out of keeping with his heavy, dignified figure:

"Olga! For the sake of your sorrow which I share. . . . Now, when falsehood is criminal, I beseech you to tell me the truth. You have always declared that the boy is my son. Is that the truth?"

Olga Ivanovna was silent.

"You have been the one attachment in my life," the doctor went on, "and you cannot imagine how deeply my feeling is wounded by falsehood. . . . Come, I entreat you, Olga, for once in your life, tell me the truth. . . . At these moments one cannot lie. Tell me that Misha is not my son. I am waiting."

"He is."

Olga Ivanovna's face could not be seen, but in her voice the doctor could hear hesitation. He sighed.

"Even at such moments you can bring yourself to tell a lie," he said in his ordinary voice. "There is nothing sacred to you! Do listen, do understand me. . . . You have been the one only attachment in my life. Yes, you were depraved, vulgar, but I have loved no one else but you in my life. That trivial love, now that I am growing old, is the one solitary bright spot in my memories. Why do you darken it with deception? What is it for?"

"I don't understand you."

"Oh my God!" cried Tsvyetkov. "You are lying, you understand very well!" he cried more loudly, and he began pacing about the drawing-room, angrily waving his stick. "Or have you forgotten? Then I will remind you! A father's rights to the boy are equally shared with me by Petrov and Kurovsky the lawyer, who still make you an allowance for their son's education, just as I do! Yes, indeed! I know all that quite well! I forgive your lying in the past, what does it matter? But now when you have grown older, at this moment when the boy is dying, your lying stifles me! How sorry I am that I cannot speak, how sorry I am!"

The doctor unbuttoned his overcoat, and still pacing about, said:

"Wretched woman! Even such moments have no effect on her. Even now she lies as freely as nine years ago in the Hermitage Restaurant! She is afraid if she tells me the truth I shall leave off giving her money, she thinks that if she did not lie I should not love the boy! You are lying! It's contemptible!"

The doctor rapped the floor with his stick, and cried:

"It's loathsome. Warped, corrupted creature! I must despise you, and I ought to be ashamed of my feeling. Yes! Your lying has stuck in my throat these nine years, I have endured it, but now it's too much—too much."

From the dark corner where Olga Ivanovna was sitting there came the sound of weeping. The doctor ceased speaking and cleared his throat. A silence followed. The doctor slowly buttoned up his overcoat, and began looking for his hat which he had dropped as he walked about.

"I lost my temper," he muttered, bending down to the floor. "I quite lost sight of the fact that you cannot attend to me now. . . . God knows what I have said. . . . Don't take any notice of it, Olga."

He found his hat, and went towards the dark corner.

"I have wounded you," he said in a soft, tender half-whisper, "but once more I entreat you, tell me the truth; there should not be lying between us. . . . I blurted it out, and now you know that Petrov and Kurovsky are no secret to me. So now it is easy for you to tell me the truth."

Olga Ivanovna thought a moment, and with perceptible hesitation, said:

"Nikolay, I am not lying—Misha is your child."

"My God," moaned the doctor, "then I will tell you something more: I have kept your letter to Petrov in which you call him Misha's father! Olga, I know the truth, but I want to hear it from you! Do you hear?"

Olga Ivanovna made no reply, but went on weeping. After

waiting for an answer the doctor shrugged his shoulders and went out.

"I will come to-morrow," he called from the passage.

All the way home, as he sat in his carriage, he was shrugging his shoulders and muttering.

"What a pity that I don't know how to speak! I haven't the gift of persuading and convincing. It's evident she does not understand me since she lies! It's evident! How can I make her see? How?"

A TRIFLING OCCURRENCE

Nikolay Ilyich Bieliayev, a Petersburg landlord, very fond of the racecourse, a well fed, pink young man of about thirty-two, once called towards evening on Madame Irnin—Olgo Ivanovna—with whom he had a *liaison,* or, to use his own phrase, spun out a long and tedious romance. And indeed the first pages of his romance, pages of interest and inspiration, had been read long ago; now they dragged on and on, and presented neither novelty nor interest.

Finding that Olga Ivanovna was not at home, my hero lay down a moment on the drawing-room sofa and began to wait.

"Good evening, Nikolay Ilyich," he suddenly heard a child's voice say. "Mother will be in in a moment. She's gone to the dressmaker's with Sonya."

In the same drawing-room on the sofa lay Olga Ivanovna's son, Aliosha, a boy about eight years old, well built, well looked after, dressed up like a picture in a velvet jacket and long black stockings. He lay on a satin pillow, and apparently imitating an acrobat whom he had lately seen in the circus, lifting up first one leg, then the other. When his elegant legs began to be tired, he moved his hands, or he jumped up impetuously and then went on all fours, trying to stand with his legs in the air. All this he did with a most serious face, breathing heavily, as if he himself found no happiness in God's gift of such a restless body.

"Ah, how do you do, my friend?" said Bieliayev. "Is it you? I didn't notice you. Is your mother well?"

At the moment Aliosha had just taken hold of the toe of his left foot in his right hand and got into a most awkward pose. He turned head over heels, jumped up, and glanced from under the big, fluffy lampshade at Bieliayev.

"How can I put it?" he said, shrugging his shoulders. "As a matter of plain fact Mother is never well. You see she's a woman, and women, Nikolay Ilyich, have always some pain or another."

For something to do, Bieliayev began to examine Aliosha's face. All the time he had been acquainted with Olga Ivanovna he had never once turned his attention to the boy and had completely ignored his existence. A boy is stuck in front of your eyes, but what is he doing here, what is his *rôle?*—you don't want to give a single thought to the question.

In the evening dusk Aliosha's face with a pale forehead and steady black eyes unexpectedly reminded Bieliayev of Olga Ivanovna as she was in the first pages of the romance. He had the desire to be affectionate to the boy.

"Come here, whipper-snapper," he said. "Come and let me have a good look at you, quite close."

The boy jumped off the sofa and ran to Bieliayev.

"Well?" Nikolay Ilyich began, putting his hand on the thin shoulders. "And how are things with you?"

"How shall I put it? . . . They used to be much better before."

"How?"

"Quite simple. Before, Sonya and I only had to do music and reading, and now we're given French verses to learn. You've had your hair cut lately?"

"Yes, just lately."

"That's why I noticed it. Your beard's shorter. May I touch it . . . Doesn't it hurt?"

"No, not a bit."

"Why is it that it hurts if you pull one hair and when you pull a whole lot, it doesn't hurt a bit? Ah, ah! You know it's a pity you don't have side-whiskers. You should shave here, and at the sides . . . and leave the hair just here."

The boy pressed close to Bieliayev and began to play with his watch-chain.

"When I go to the gymnasium," he said, "Mother is going to buy me a watch. I'll ask her to buy me a chain just like this. What a fine locket! Father has one just the same, but yours has stripes, here, and his has got letters . . . Inside it's Mother's picture. Father has another chain now, not in links, but like a ribbon . . ."

"How do you know? Do you see your father?"

"I? Mm . . . no . . . I . . ."

Aliosha blushed and in the violent confusion of being detected in a lie began to scratch the locket busily with his finger-nail. Bieliayev looked steadily at his face and asked:

"Do you see your father?"

"No . . . No!"

"But, be honest—on your honour. By your face I can see you're not telling me the truth. If you made a slip of the tongue by mistake, what's the use of shuffling. Tell me, do you see him? As one friend to another."

Aliosha mused.

"And you won't tell Mother?" he asked.

"What next."

"On your word of honour."

"My word of honour."

"Swear an oath."

"What a nuisance you are! What do you take me for?"

Aliosha looked round, made big eyes and began to whisper.

"Only for God's sake don't tell Mother! Never tell it to anyone at all, because it's a secret. God forbid that Mother should ever get to know; then I and Sonya and Pelagueya will pay for it . . . Listen. Sonya and I meet Father every Tuesday and Friday. When Pelagueya takes us for a walk before dinner, we go into Apfel's sweet-shop and Father's waiting for us. He always sits in a separate room, you know, where there's a splendid marble table and an ash-tray shaped like a goose without a back . . ."

"And what do you do there?"

"Nothing!—First, we welcome one another, then we sit down at a little table and Father begins to treat us to coffee and cakes. You know, Sonya eats meat-pies, and I can't bear pies with meat in them! I like them made of cabbage and eggs. We eat so much that afterwards at dinner we try to eat as much as we possibly can so that Mother shan't notice."

"What do you talk about there?"

"To Father? About anything. He kisses us and cuddles us, tells us all kinds of funny stories. You know, he says that he will take us to live with him when we are grown up. Sonya doesn't want to go, but I say 'Yes.' Of course, it'll be lonely without Mother; but I'll write letters to her. How funny: we could go to her for our holidays then—couldn't we? Besides, Father says that he'll buy me a horse. He's a splendid man. I can't understand why Mother doesn't invite him to live with her or why she says we mustn't meet him. He loves Mother very much indeed. He's always asking us how she is and what she's doing. When she was ill, he took hold of his head like this . . . and ran, ran, all the time. He is always telling us to obey and respect her. Tell me, is it true that we're unlucky?"

"H'm . . . how?"

"Father says so. He says: 'You are unlucky children.' It's quite strange to listen to him. He says: 'You are unhappy, I'm unhappy, and Mother's unhappy.' He says: 'Pray to God for yourselves and for her.' "

Aliosha's eyes rested upon the stuffed bird and he mused.

"Exactly . . ." snorted Bieliayev. "This is what you do. You arrange conferences in sweet-shops. And your mother doesn't know?"

"No—no . . . How could she know? Pelagueya won't tell for anything. The day before yesterday Father stood us pears. Sweet, like jam. I had two."

"H'm . . . well, now . . . tell me, doesn't your father speak about me?"

"About you? How shall I put it?"

Aliosha gave a searching glance to Bieliayev's face and shrugged his shoulders.

"He doesn't say anything in particular."

"What does he say, for instance?"

"You won't be offended?"

"What next? Why, does he abuse me?"

"He doesn't abuse you, but you know . . . he is cross with you. He says that it's through you that Mother's unhappy and that you . . . ruined Mother. But he is so queer! I explain to him that you are good and never shout at Mother, but he only shakes his head."

"Does he say those very words: that I ruined her?"

"Yes. Don't be offended, Nikolay Ilyich!"

Bieliayev got up, stood still a moment, and then began to walk about the drawing-room.

"This is strange, and . . . funny," he murmured, shrugging his shoulders and smiling ironically. "He is to blame all round, and now *I've* ruined her, eh? What an innocent lamb! Did he say those very words to you: that I ruined your mother?"

"Yes, but . . . you said that you wouldn't get offended."

"I'm not offended, and . . . and it's none of your business! No, it . . . it's quite funny though. I fell into the trap, yet I'm to be blamed as well."

The bell rang. The boy dashed from his place and ran out. In a minute a lady entered the room with a little girl. It was Olga Ivanovna, Aliosha's mother. After her, hopping, humming noisily, and waving his hands, followed Aliosha.

"Of course, who is there to accuse except me?" he murmured, sniffing. "He's rignt, he's the injured husband."

"What's the matter?" asked Olga Ivanovna.

"What's the matter! Listen to the kind of sermon your dear husband preaches. It appears I'm a scoundrel and a murderer, I've ruined you and the children. All of you are unhappy, and only I am awfully happy! Awfully, awfully happy!"

"I don't understand, Nikolay! What is it?"

"Just listen to this young gentleman," Bieliayev said, pointing to Aliosha.

Aliosha blushed, then became pale suddenly, and his whole face was twisted in fright.

"Nikolay Ilyich," he whispered loudly. "Shh!"

"Ask him, if you please," went on Bieliayev. "That stupid fool Pelagueya of yours, takes them to sweet-shops and arranges meetings with their dear father there. But that's not the point. The point is that the dear father is a martyr, and I'm a murderer, I'm a scoundrel, who broke the lives of both of you. . . ."

"Nikolay Ilyich!" moaned Aliosha. "You gave your word of honour!"

"Ah, let me alone!" Bieliayev waved his hand. "This is something more important than any words of honour. The hypocrisy revolts me, the lie!"

"I don't understand," muttered Olga Ivanovna, and tears began to glimmer in her eyes. "Tell me, Liolka,"—she turned to her son, "Do you see your father?"

Aliosha did not hear and looked with horror at Bieliayev.

"It's impossible," said the mother. "I'll go and ask Pelagueya."

Olga Ivanovna went out.

"But, but you gave me your word of honour," Aliosha said, trembling all over.

Bieliayev waved his hand at him and went on walking up and down. He was absorbed in his insult, and now, as before, he did not notice the presence of the boy. He, a big serious man, had nothing to do with boys. And Aliosha sat down in a corner and in terror told Sonya how he had been deceived. He trembled, stammered, wept. This was the first time in his life that he had been set, roughly, face to face with a lie. He had never known before that in this world besides sweet pears and cakes and expensive watches, there exist many other things which have no name in children's language.

THE HOLLOW

I

THE village of Ukleyevo being situated in a hollow, only the church-steeple and the chimneys of the calico factories could be seen from the high road and the railway station. When passers-by asked what village it was, they were told: "That is where the Cantor ate all the caviar at a funeral."

It seems, at the obsequies for the mill-owner Kostiukov, the elderly Cantor saw among the *hors-d'œuvres* some fresh caviar, and proceeded to gobble it up. His friends tapped him on the shoulder, they pulled him by the sleeve, but he was so literally insensible with enjoyment he felt nothing —he could only swallow. The pot had contained 4 lbs. of caviar, and he ate it all. Ten years had elapsed since then, the Cantor was dead, but everyone remembered about the caviar. Perhaps it was owing to their straitened existence, or perhaps the people were incapable of observation; however it be, this unimportant incident was the only thing related about Ukleyevo.

Fever was in perpetual abode; also a viscous mire, even in summer, particularly by the side of the palings where aged willows hanging their branches cast a shade over the road. Just about there, it always smelt of factory refuse and acetic acid, which was used in preparing the calico-print.

The factories were four in number—three calico-print ones and a tannery. They lay, not in the village, but on the outskirts, a little distance away. They were small factories, each employing about 400 workers. The residuum from the tannery frequently fouled the rivulet, the refuse infected the meadow, the peasants' cattle suffered from Siberian plague, and the tannery was ordered to close. It was considered closed, and continued to work secretly, with the assent of the commissary of police and the district doctor, to whom the proprietor paid ten rubles a month each.

There were only two decent houses in the whole village; these were built of stone, and each had a tin roof; in the one were the offices of the Volost, in the other, two-storied, just opposite the church, lived Tzybukin,—Grigory Petrov.

Grigory kept a grocery store—that was for the sake of appearances; he really dealt in vodka, cattle, leather, corn, pigs. He traded in what he required, and when, for instance, magpies were needed abroad for ladies' hats, he made 30 kopecks on each couple; he would appropriate the felling-rights of a wood, he would lend money on interest. He was, in fact, an enterprising man.

He had two sons; the elder, Anisim, served in the detective division of police, and was seldom at home. The younger son, Stepan, went into business to help his father, but, as he suffered from bad health and was deaf, they did not expect any real help from him. His wife Aksinya, a handsome svelte woman, wore a hat on holidays and carried a parasol; she rose early and went to bed late, and, with her skirts gathered up and rattling her keys, she ran about all day to the storehouse, or the cellar, or the shop. Old Tzybukin's eyes kindled with pleasure as he looked at her, and he often wished she was married to his elder son, instead of to the younger deaf one, who apparently regarded feminine beauty with indifference.

The old man was very domestic, and loved his family more than anything in the world, especially his elder son and his daughter-in-law.

Aksinya was no sooner married to her deaf husband than she revealed an unusual capacity for business, and very soon understood to whom credit could be given, and to whom not. She always kept the keys, not entrusting them even to her deaf husband; she wrestled with accounts, examined the horses by the teeth like a muzhik; was always bright or abusive; but whatever she did or said, the old man was touched and murmured: "What a daughter-in-law. Hm—yes. Matushka!"

He was a widower, but less than a year after his son's marriage he could endure his widowhood no longer, and also got married. At thirty versts from Ukleyevo they found an unmarried woman, Varvara Nikolayevna, of good family, middle-aged, and handsome. No sooner had she established herself in the house, on the second floor, than everything assumed a brighter hue, just as if new panes had been placed in all the windows. The image-lamps burned clear and undimmed. the tables were covered with cloths, or linen white as snow, red flowers appeared in the windows and in the patch in front of the house. and at dinner each had a plate given him instead of feeding out of the stewpot. When Varvara Nikolayevna smiled her pleasant kind smile, it seemed to be diffused over the whole house. And—it had never happened before—the old, the poor, the pilgrims took to coming into the yard. Through the windows were heard the sing-song voices of the Ukleyevo women, or the sickly cough of the suffering weak men discharged for drunkenness from the factories. Varvara helped them with money, bread, old clothes, and subsequently, when she got used to the place, she even drew on the grocery store for supplies. Once, the deaf one saw her carry away two-eighths of a pound of tea; this troubled him.

"Mamasha took two-eighths of a pound of tea from here," he communicated to his father—"where shall I write it down?"

The old man said nothing; stood still, reflected, knit his brows. and went upstairs to his wife.

"Varvarushka, if you require anything from the shop, take it," he said fondly. "Take anything you want—don't mind anyone."

Next day as he crossed the yard, the deaf one called to her:

"Mamasha, if you require anything—take it."

This almsgiving was something new, something bright and cheerful, like the red flowers and the image-lamps. When during carnival, or at the festival of the patron saint, which lasted three days, the peasants had such badly tainted salt-meat foisted on them that it was well-nigh impossible to stand by the barrels, and scythes, women's shawls and hats were pawned by the drunkards, and the factory-hands wallowed in the mire stupefied by bad brandy, and sin hung in the air like fog—then it all seemed somehow easier to bear, at the thought that there in the house was a quiet cleanly woman, who had nothing to do with salt-meat and brandy. Her alms acted in those dark distressful days as a safety-valve in a machine

They were always very busy in the house of Tzybukin. Before sunrise Aksinya was spluttering over her ablutions in the vestibule, the samovar was boiling in the kitchen, and hissing as if predicting something unpleasant. Old Grigory Petrov, looking neat and clean, clad in a long black frock-coat and print trousers, wearing high polished boots, walked about the room, tapping his heels like the father-in-law in a well-known song. Then the shop was opened. When it was daylight the little droshky was brought to the door, and away drove this energetic old man. As he sat there, with his cap pulled down to his ears, no one would have credited him with fifty-six years. His wife and daughter-in-law always saw him off. When he was wearing his new frock-coat, and driving his big black cob, which had cost 300 rubles, he did not like the peasants to approach him with their requests and complaints. He disliked and despised the peasants, and if he saw any peasant hanging about the gate he would shout angrily at them:

"What are you doing there? Get on with you."

And if it was a beggar he would shout:

"God will help you!"

He was on business bent. Then his wife, wearing a black apron, tidied the rooms or helped in the kitchen; Aksinya attended to work in the shop; across the yard drifted the sound of jingling bottles and money, or laughter and shouting or angry words from purchasers whom Aksinya insulted. The secret and clandestine sale of vodka was carried on in the shop at the same time. The deaf one also sat in the shop, or else, hatless, with his hands in his pockets, walked about the streets absently casting glances into the cottages or up at the sky. Tea was drunk six times a day, and four times a day they sat down to meals. In the evening the accounts were made up and inscribed, then all went to bed and slept soundly.

The three print factories were joined by the telephone to the domiciles in Ukleyevo of the mill-owners Khrymin Senior, Khrymin Junior, and Kostiukov. The telephone was also put into the offices of the Volost, but there it soon ceased to work, and bugs and cockroaches established themselves in it. The Senior of the Volost was somewhat illiterate, and wrote every word with a capital, so when the telephone broke down he said:

"It will be rather difficult for us now without the telephone."

The Senior Khrymins were always at law with the Junior Khrymins, and sometimes the Juniors fought among themselves, and brought law-suits against each other; then their factory had to close for a month, perhaps two, until peace was restored. This provided a certain amount of distraction for the inhabitants of Ukleyevo. as each row gave rise to much gossip and talk.

Kostiukov and the Junior Khrymins organised some racing for the carnival; they drove furiously through Ukleyevo slaughtering calves in their career. Aksinya, rustling in her starched petticoats, took a turn in the street by the grocery store; the Junior Khrymins caught her up, and it looked as if they had forcibly carried her off. Then out came old Tzybukin to show off his new horse, and he took with him Varvara.

In the evening, after the racing was over, and many had betaken themselves to bed, at Khrymin Junior's they made music on an expensive harmonium; if the moon was shining, it added to the sounds of joy and gaiety in Ukleyevo, which then seemed less of a hole.

II

Anisim, the eldest son, very seldom came home—only on the big festivals; on the other hand, he often sent gifts and letters to his people; the letters were written in a strange, magnificent handwriting, and each time on a sheet of paper resembling a petition. The letters were full of expressions which Anisim never used in conversation: "My dear father and mother, I send you a pound of green tea for the satisfying of your physical needs." At the end of each letter was scribbled, as if with a broken nib, "Anisim Tzybukin," and below, again in that most excellent handwriting, "Agent." The letters were read aloud several times, and the old man, touched and crimson with emotion, said: "There now, he did not want to live at home; he left to improve himself—well, quite right! Each destined for his part!"

Just before Shrove-tide there were heavy rain and sleet; the old man and Varvara go to the window to look at it, when lo! who arrives from the station in a sleigh but Anisim. They did not at all expect him. He seemed apprehensive, and uneasy from his first entering into the room, nor did this manner alter during his whole stay, although he affected a certain sprightliness. He was in no hurry to leave them again, and it rather looked as if he had been discharged from the Service. Varvara was pleased at his arrival; she observed him rather shyly, sighed and shook her head:

"Now, how is this, batushka?" she asked. "This lad is

already in his twenty-eighth year, and is still dissipating as a bachelor. Oh, fie upon it!"

Her soft, even tones did not carry into the next room. "Oh, fie upon it!" was all they heard. She began to whisper with the old man and Aksinya; their faces assumed the sly, mysterious expression of conspirators. They decided to marry Anisim.

"Oh, fie upon it! . . . your brother has been married some time," said Varvara, "while you remain without a mate, like a cock in the market-place. How is that? Get married, with God's help. Go back into the Service if you like, and your wife will stay at home to help us in the work. You lead an irregular life, my lad, and have forgotten what is order, I see. Oh! fie upon you! Shame on you townsfolk!"

When the Tzybukins married, the most beautiful brides were selected for them, as they are for the rich, so they sought for beauty for Anisim. He himself had an insignificant, uninteresting appearance, a weak, unhealthy constitution; was short, had puffy, swollen cheeks, just as if he inflated them; he never blinked, which gave him a hard, piercing expression; he had a scant carroty beard, which, when he indulged in thought, he poked into his mouth and nibbled. Added to all this, he frequently indulged in drink, which could be detected by his face and his walk. When, however, they communicated to him the fact that they had found him a bride, a very beautiful one, he said: "Oh! well, there is nothing wrong with me either. Our family of Tzybukin, one must allow, are all good-looking."

Quite close to the town was the village of Torguyevo. One half of it had, not long since, been incorporated with the town; the other half remained village. In the former lived a widow in a small house with her sister. The sister was very poor, and was hired by the day. This latter had a daughter, Lipa, who also hired by the day. Lipa's beauty was well recognised in Torguyevo, but her extreme poverty intimidated people. It was concluded, either that some middle-aged man or widower would wed her, regardless of her poverty, or he would carry her off "without more ado," and she would be able tó provide for her mother. Varvara heard of Lipa from the other marriage-promoters, and went over to Torguyevo.

Later, as is necessary, the formal interview in the aunt's house was agreed upon, with a repast of "zauski" (*hors-d'œuvre*) and wine. Lipa was attired in a new pink frock, specially made for the occasion; a crimson ribbon like a flame gleamed in her hair. She was an emaciated little being, pale and weak, with pretty soft features, and a skin tanned by exposure to the weather. The expresssions of her eyes were those of a child, trusting and inquisitive, and she always smiled in a sad timid way. She was quite young—a girl with an undeveloped figure, yet of a marriageable age. She was decidedly pleasing, except for her large masculine hands, which now hung idly by her side like two great claws.

"She has no fortune . . . we don't mind that," said the old man to the aunt. "For our son, Stepan, we also chose a wife from a poor family; now we cannot sufficiently congratulate ourselves, in the house or in the business . . . she is worth her weight in gold."

Lipa stood by the door, and seemed to say: "Do with me what you will, I trust you." But her mother, Praskovya the day-worker, was concealing herself in the kitchen, dying of fright. Once, in her youth, a merchant for whom she washed the floors, stamped on her in his rage, which so frightened her that she swooned away, and for the rest of her life fear lurked in her breast. Seated in the kitchen, she attempted to hear what the guests were saying, and all the time crossed herself, pressing her fingers to her forehead, and with her eyes fixed on the image of the saint. Anisim, slightly drunk, opened the kitchen-door, and said brightly:

"Why are you sitting here, precious mamasha? It is dull without you."

Praskovya, quailing and pressing her hand to her wasted skinny bosom, said:

"Mercy, what do you want? I am much obliged to you."

After the inspection, the wedding-day was fixed upon.

At home Anisim did nothing but walk about the rooms whistling, then, suddenly remembering something, would stand quite still, absorbed in thought, fixing his eyes on the floor as if he would like to pierce with a look far into the earth. He expressed no satisfaction at getting married, or getting married so soon—the first Monday after Quasimodo Sunday—nor a wish to see his bride-elect again; he just whistled. It was evident that he was only marrying because his father and step-mother wished it, and because in the village it was customary: sons married to provide workers in the house. He was in no hurry to leave, and behaved altogether differently to what he did on former visits. He seemed absent-minded too, and his answers were seldom to the point.

III

In the village dwelt two maiden sisters, sempstresses both. They were given the order for the new dresses for the wedding, so they often came over to fit, and stayed a long time partaking of tea. They made a cinnamon-coloured dress trimmed with black lace and jet for Varvara, and a pale green one with a yellow front and a train for Aksinya. When the toilettes were finished, Tzybukin paid the sisters in kind from the shop, and they departed from him with a heavy heart, bearing in their arms a bundle of stearine candles and some sardines which they did not at all want. When they had left the village behind them, they sat on a mound and wept.

Anisim arrived three days before the wedding in a new suit of clothes. He had new goloshes, and, instead of a tie, a red ribbon with a pattern of rings on it; he also had a new cloak, slung over his shoulder. Having solemnly addressed a prayer to God, he greeted his father, and gave him ten silver rubles and ten 50-kopeck pieces; he gave Varvara the same; and to Aksinya he gave twenty 25-kopeck pieces. The great charm of this present consisted in the fact that all the money was quite new, as if carefully selected, and gleamed in the sun. Anisim. attempting to appear staid and serious, puffed out his cheeks, twisted his face and smelt of wine—he must have jumped out at every station and run to the buffet. There was still that would-be-easy manner, something unnatural, about him. The old man and Anisim drank tea and had a bite, while Varvara turned and re-turned her new rubles in her hand, and asked questions about their fellow-countrymen living in the town.

"They are all right, thank God," answered Anisim. "There has been an event in Ivan Yegorov's family . . . he has lost his old woman, Sofya Nikiforovna, from consumption. The 'repast to her memory,' ordered at the confectioners, was two rubles and a half per head, wine included. What fellows our countrymen are! For them also it was two and a half rubles—and they ate nothing. Can a peasant appreciate good food?"

"Two and a half!" said the old man, shaking his head.

"Well, what of that? It is not the country. You enter a restaurant to take a snack, you ask for this and that, soon there is a group, you drink . . . you look up, why, it is dawn. . . . 'Excuse me, three or four rubles each to pay.' And when you are with Samarodov, he insists on coffee and cognac to end up with, and cognac is six griveniks (60 kopecks) a glass."

"It's all lies! It's all lies!" said the old man ecstatically.

"I am always with Samarodov now. It is Samarodov who writes my letters to you. He writes splendidly. And if I told you, mamasha," gaily added Anisim, turning to Varvara, "what sort of a fellow this Samarodov is, you would not believe it. We call him Muktar, for he is like an Armenian, quite black. I see through him; I know all his affairs as well as I do my own five fingers. He feels it too, mamasha, and follows me round, never leaves me, and now we are as inseparable as water. He is rather afraid of me, but cannot exist without me; where I go, he goes. I have right good eyes, mamasha; I go to a rag-fair, I see a peasant selling a shirt. 'Stay, that is a stolen shirt.' And it is true, the shirt was stolen."

"But how do you know?" asks Varvara.

"I don't know, but just my eyes are like that. I don't know what shirt is there, but only that something draws me to it: it is stolen, that's all. Among us detectives, they say now: 'Well, Anisim, go and shoot woodcock.' That means to search for stolen booty. Yes, anyone may steal, but how are they to hide it? The earth is large, but there is nowhere to conceal plunder."

"In our village, a sheep and two yearling ewes were stolen last week, at Guntoriov's," said Varvara, sighing. "And there was no one to search for them. Fie upon it!"

"Well, what of that? Search can be made—it's nothing, it's quite easy."

The wedding-day arrived; it was a cool, clear, joyous April day. From early morning troikas and pairs were being furiously driven through Ukleyevo; there was a jingle of grelots, and multi-coloured ribbons were flowing from the horses' manes and shaft-bows. The rooks were cawing among the willows, disturbed by this unusual stir and bustle, and the starlings sang unwearyingly as if rejoicing that there was a wedding at the Tzybukins'. In the house a repast was laid out consisting of long fish, hams, stuffed chickens, a variety of salt and pickled foods, and a number of bottles of vodka and wines. Added to this was a smell of smoked sausages and sour lobsters. By the table, stamping his heels and grinding one knife on another, stood the old man. Varvara was in constant request; with a harassed mien, and breathless, she ran to the kitchen, where Kostiukov's male-cook, and the neat woman-cook from Khrymin Junior, had been working since dawn. Askinya, with her hair curled, in her stays, without a dress, wearing new creaky boots, flew about the yard like a whirlwind, her bare neck and knees gleaming in the sunlight. It was all very noisy; there were high words and swearing; the passers-by paused by the wide open gate, feeling there was something unusual astir.

"They have gone for the bride," was the rumour.

The horses' bells tinkled, and the sound died far away in the distance. After two o'clock people began running; the bells were heard again: the bride is coming!

The church was full, the candelabra lit, and the choristers, according to the old man's desire, were singing from sheets of music. The glitter of lights and the bright dresses dazzled Lipa. It seemed to her that the choristers, with their loud voices, were knocking on her head with hammers. Her stays, which she was wearing for the first time in her life, and her boots, pinched her, and her impression was that of regaining consciousness after a fainting fit; she saw, and could understand nothing. Anisim in a black frock-coat, wearing a red ribbon instead of a tie, was pensive, gazing into space; and each time the choir raised their high voices he hastily crossed himself. He felt some emotion in his innermost heart, and he would have liked to have wept. The church was so familiar to him from his earliest childhood. Long ago his late mother had brought him here for communion. Long ago he had sung in the choir with the other boys. He knew so well each nook and ikon. And now they were marrying him; he must marry for propriety's sake. Then, as if he did not understand it, he forgot altogether about the wedding. Tears prevented him from seeing the ikons; he was very heavy at heart. He prayed, and asked God that the impending misfortunes which were about to engulf him, if not to-day, then to-morrow, should pass over him somehow, like the thunder-clouds during a drought pass over the country without emitting one drop of rain. And although his sins piled up in the past were many, very many, and irreparable ones, so that it seemed unavailing to pray for forgivenessness, yet he prayed, and also sobbed aloud. This nobody heeded, as they merely thought: He is drunk.

A child's plaintive voice was heard:

"Dear Nanny, take me away."

"Silence there!" called the priest.

On their return from the church the bride and bridegroom were followed by a large concourse of people. There were crowds by the shop, by the gate, in the yard, and standing by the house were some women who had come to sing pæans to the newly-married. The young couple had hardly crossed the threshold when the choristers, who were already standing in the vestibule with the music in their hands, burst loudly into song. A band, purposely hired from the town, also started to play. Frothy beverages in high beakers were brought round, then the contractor-carpenter Yelizarov, a tall spare man, with such bushy eyebrows that his eyes were almost invisible, turning to the young couple, said:

"Anisim, and you my child, love one another; be God-fearing, my children, and the Queen of Heaven will not abandon you."

He then fell on the old man's neck and wept.

"Grigory Petrov, let us weep, let us weep for joy!" he said in a shrill voice, and immediately and suddenly began to laugh, continuing in a deep bass voice: "Ho, ho, ho! And you have a good sister-in-law. She keeps everything running smooth, there is no rattling, all the machinery is in good repair and well screwed together."

Although born in the district of Yegoryev, he had worked almost since childhood in the factories of Ukleyevo and the surrounding district, and was therefore a resident in these parts. He had been known a long time as a tall and emaciated old man, and had long ago been given the name of the "Crutch." Perhaps it was because he had been occupied for upwards of forty years only on repairs in the factories, that he viewed every man and thing from the one aspect of sound or unsound: Do they want repairing? And now, before sitting down to table, he tried several chairs to see if they were sound, and he even felt the gang-fish.

After a go at the frothy beverages, every one took a seat at the tables. The guests chatted and creaked their chairs, the choristers sang in the vestibule, the band played, the peasant women in a monotone extolled the married couple; all which made such a terrifying noise and wild medley of sound that one's head felt like splitting. The Crutch twisted and turned in his chair, jostled his neighbours with his elbows, interfered with their talk, wept and laughed.

"Ah! girls, girls, girls!" he muttered quickly, "Aksinyushka, Varvarushka, we will all live in peace and good-will, my little dears."

He drank but little as a rule, and now he was drunk after one glass of "English brandy." This distasteful drink, made of no one knows what, numbed the brains of all those who drank it, just as if they were suffering from concussion.

There were priests, factory clerks with their wives, tradesmen and publicans from other villages. The Senior of the Volost and his scribe, who had served together for fourteen years, and during all that time had not signed a single paper, nor dismissed from the offices of the Volost a single person, without defrauding them or imposing on them, now sat side by side, both adipose, satiated, and looking so replete with iniquity that even the tissue of their skin had something rascally about it. The wife of the scribe, a wizen, squint-eyed woman, brought with her all her children, and, like a very bird of prey, leered at all the dishes, and seized all that came within her reach, filling her pockets for herself and her children.

Lipa sat like one paralysed, and with the same expression as she had in church. Anisim, from the time of his first acquaintance with her, had never addressed her a single word, so that he did not know, up to now, what kind of a voice she had. Sitting now by her side, he still kept silence, drinking

"English brandy," and when he had got drunk he said to his aunt, who sat opposite:

"I have a friend named Samarodov. A very special fellow. He belongs to the first guild of merchants, and so glib! But, auntie, I see through him, and he knows it. Let us drink to the health of Samarodov."

Wearied and confused. Varvara made the round of the tables, serving the guests, but was apparently satisfied that there was so much and such food that no one would be able to find fault.

The sun went down, and the supper continued. The company no longer knew what they ate or what they drank; no one could hear distinctly what was being said; only at intervals, when the music in the yard softened, some woman or other could be heard shouting:

"You have sucked our blood—devils, destruction be on you!"

In the evening there was dancing to music. The Junior Khrymins arrived with their wine, and one of them, while the quadrille was being danced, held a bottle in each hand and a glass in his mouth. This immensely added to the general hilarity. Between the quadrille they danced their squatting-dance. Green Aksinya flitted about, and her train made quite a wind; someone tore away the flounce, and the Crutch exclaimed:

"I say, children, the skirting is down!"

Aksinya had grey naïve eyes which seldom blinked, while an artless smile often lit up her face. With those unblinking eyes, a small head on the end of a long neck, and her slim figure, there was something snake-like about her. In her green dress with the yellow front, and with her peculiar smile, she resembled a viper when it looks out of the young rye in spring, stretching and drawing in its neck at the passer-by. Khrymin's behaviour with her was very free. It had long been noticed that with the elder of them she was on terms of the utmost familiarity. The deaf husband noticed nothing, never looked at her; he sat with his legs crossed, eating nuts, and made such a noise cracking them with his teeth that it sounded each time like a pistol-shot.

And now, Tzybukin himself entered the dancing circle, and waved his handkerchief as a sign that he too wished to dance. Through the house and out into the yard went the acclamation:

"Himself will dance! Himself!"

Varvara danced while the old man waved his handkerchief and tapped his heels; but the onlookers in the yard, leaning on each other and looking in at the window went into ecstasies, and for a minute forgave him all—his riches and his offences.

"Bravo! Capital fellow, Grigory Petrov!" the crowd vociferated. "Go on!—ha, ha!—you are good for a lot yet!"

All this was over late, after one o'clock. Anisim, staggering, went up to thank the musicians and singers, and presented them each with a new 50-kopeck piece. The old man, not staggering, but pausing on each foot, saw the guests off, and told each one:

"The wedding cost two thousand rubles."

When they had all dispersed, someone was discovered to have exchanged the Shikalovo publican's new "podiovka" (sleeveless coat) for an old one. Anisim at once called out excitedly:

"Wait, I'll find him at once. I know who took it! Wait!"

He ran out into the street, and chased someone. He was captured, brought home, and they shoved him, drunk, red with anger, and sweating, into the room where the aunt had already helped Lipa to bed.

IV

After the lapse of five days Anisim, about to take departure, went upstairs to Varvara to say good-bye. All the image-lamps were burning, there was a smell of incense, and

Varvara herself was seated at the window knitting stockings of red wool.

"You have stayed a very little while with us," she said; "do you find it dull? Fie upon you! We live in comfort, your wedding was celebrated in a very fitting manner. The old man says two thousand rubles were spent on it. In a word we live like tradespeople, only there it is, it's dull here. Then we defraud too many people. It makes my heart ache to cheat so. . . . Oh, my God! Whether we barter a horse, or buy anything, or hire workers, everywhere there is fraud. Fraud, and again fraud. The linseed oil in the grocery store is rancid, putrid; birch-gum would be better for people. Is it impossible, for mercy's sake, to deal in good butter?"

"Each destined for his part, mamasha!"

"But must it mean corruption? Aie, aie! If you spoke to your father . . ."

"But speak to him yourself."

"Nay, but I have, and he uses the same phrase as you do: 'Each destined for his part.' In the world beyond you will be tried for that: each destined for his part! God is a just judge."

"But of course there will be no trial," and Anisim sighed. "For you see there is no God, mamasha. Who will there be to judge?"

Varvara looked at him in astonishment, smiled, and clasped her hands. Seeing that she was so genuinely surprised at his words and regarded him as an oddity, he grew troubled:

"It may be that there is a God, but no faith," he said. "When I was married, I did not feel like myself. Look, it is like when you take an egg from under a hen and a chick chirps inside, so my conscience chirped while I was being married. I thought: There is a God. And then when I came out of the church the feeling was gone. And how should I know if there is a God or not? No one taught us about Him, the child is hardly weaned from its mother's breast before it learns: Each destined for his part. Papa, you see, does not believe in God either. You said once that Guntoriov's sheep had been stolen. . . . I found the thief; it was a peasant of Shikalovo who stole them. He stole them, and my papa has the hide. . . . There's faith for you!"

Anisim blinked his eyes and shook his head.

"And the Senior of the Volost does not believe in God," he continued, "nor the scribe either, nor the sacristan. And if they go to church and observe the fasts, it is only so that people should not speak ill of them, and in case there may indeed be some last Judgment. It is said, if the end of the world came now, it is because men have grown weak, they honour not their parents, and so forth. That's all nonsense. I, mamasha, understand that all the trouble comes from people having so little conscience. I see clearly, and understand. When a man has stolen a shirt, I can find him. The fellow is sitting in a tavern; to you it may appear that he is merely drinking tea, but I, tea or no tea, can see besides that he has no conscience. Thus you go through the whole day, and don't find a man with a conscience. The whole reason is because they do not know if there is a God or not. . . . Well, mamasha, good-bye, keep well, and bear me no ill-will."

Anisim made Varvara a low bow.

"We thank you for all you have done," he said. "You are a great benefit to our family; you are a very good woman, and I am very grateful to you."

Anisim seemed much affected, went out, then returned again and said:

"Samarodov has involved me in a business matter. Either we shall become rich or we shall be ruined. If anything should happen, you will comfort my father, won't you, mamasha?"

"Oh! come now, what are you saying? Fie upon you! . . . God is merciful. But see, Anisim, you should show a little fondness for your wife; you look at each other so crossly; if only you smiled."

"How strange she is," said Anisim, sighing. "She does not

seem to understand anything—always remains silent. She is very young, we must let her develop."

The big, sleek, white cob and tarantass were waiting at the door. Old Tzybukin sprang into it, seated himself alertly, and took the reins. Anisim embraced Varvara, Aksinya, and his brother. Lipa was also standing at the door, standing motionless, looking away, just as if she had not come to see anyone off, as if she were there without a purpose. Anisim went up to her. and touched her on the cheek ever so lightly with his lips. "Good-bye," he said. And she, without looking at him, smiled so strangely; her face quivered, and everyone, for some reason or other, felt sorry for her. Anisim also leapt into his seat, and sat with his arms akimbo as if he thought himself very elegant.

When they had climbed out of the hollow, Anisim glanced several times back at the village. It was a warm, clear day. For the first time this year the cattle were being driven out to graze, and girls and women in holiday attire were walking by the herds. A brown bull was bellowing, rejoicing in his freedom, and striking the ground with his fore-feet. The larks were singing everywhere in the air, above, below. Anisim noticed too the pretty white church—it had lately been whitewashed—and remembered how he had prayed there five days ago; he glanced at the school with its green roof, at the river where once he used to bathe and fish; and a feeling of joy possessed him—he wished a wall would suddenly rise in front of him out of the ground, and prevent him from going any further; then he would remain with only a past.

When they arrived at the station, they went to the buffet and drank a glass of sherry. The old man felt in his pocket for his purse.

"I will treat you!" said Anisim.

The old man, with a full heart, clapped him on the shoulder, and winked at the waiter as much as to say: "See what a son I have!"

"If you remain at home, Anisim, and attend to the business, you could name your price! My boy, I would gild you from head to toe!"

"It is quite impossible, papasha."

The sherry was sourish and smelt of sealing-wax, but they drank another glassful.

On his return from the station, just at first the old man hardly recognised his youngest daughter-in-law. As soon as her husband had left, Lipa underwent a change; she suddenly became quite cheerful. Barefooted, in an old worn petticoat, her sleeves turned up to the shoulder, she sang in clear, silvery tones as she scrubbed the stairs; then, as she poured the contents of the pail outside, she stood and looked at the sun, smiling so brightly that she too seemed akin to the larks.

An old worker passing by the gate shook his head, and croaked:

"That daughter-in-law of yours, Grigory Petrov, was once more sent by God," he said. "They are not women, they are angels."

V

On the 8th of July, a Friday, Yelizarov, nicknamed the Crutch, and Lipa were returning from the village of Kazanskoe, where they had been for the festival of the patron saint; the Virgin Mary of Kazan. Far behind lagged Praskovya sick and sorry and out of breath. It was towards evening.

"A-aa," said the Crutch in astonishment as he listened to Lipa. "A-aa, well?"

"I am very fond of jam, Ilya Makarych," said Lipa. "I seat myself in a corner, drink tea and eat jam. Or Varvara Nikolayevna and I drink tea together, and she tells me some pretty tale. They have a lot of jam—four pots. 'Eat, Lipa,' she says, 'don't be afraid.' "

"A-aa . . . four pots!"

"They live so well, tea and white loaves, and as much meat as they want. They live comfortably, but, Ilya Makarych, I am frightened. Oh, ee—ee, but I am frightened!"

"But what are you frightened of, my child?" asked the Crutch, glancing round to see if Praskovya was far behind.

"First, on the day of the wedding I was frightened of Anisim Grigoryich. There was nothing special—he was not rude; only when he came near me I felt cold all over me, in all my bones. And I never slept one single night; I shook all over, and prayed to God. And now, Ilya Makarych, I fear Aksinya. There's nothing wrong with her; she is always smiling, only at times she looks out of the window, and her eyes are so angry that they turn green just like those of the sheep in the shed. The Junior Khrymins be-devil her: 'Your old man, they say, has a small estate called Butiokino, 40 deciatins; on the property, they say, there is sand and water, so you, Aksinya, arrange for a brick-kiln to be erected, and we will take shares.' Bricks are now worth twenty rubles a thousand. A very profitable affair. Last evening after supper, Aksinya said to the old man: 'I want,' says she, 'to construct a brick-kiln in Butiokino: I will be superintendent.' So she says, and smiles. Grigory Petrov's face darkened; you could see it did not please him: 'So long as I live we work together.' Her eyes gleamed, and she ground her teeth. We had fritters —she never ate one."

"A-aa!" said the Crutch in astonishment. "She could not eat?"

"And I tell you, when she goes to bed, mercy!" continued Lipa. "After a short half-hour of sleep, up she jumps, walks —walks and peers about to see if a peasant is setting anything on fire, or has stolen anything. It is dreadful to be with her, Ilya Makarych. The Junior Khrymins never went to bed after the wedding; they went into town for some trial. People gossip, and say it is because of Aksinya. Two of the brothers had promised to construct the kiln, the third took offence, so the factory closed for a month, and my uncle Prokhov, out of work, was begging at the doors for crusts. 'You, uncle! begging?' says I, 'you ought to plough, or chop wood, not degrade yourself in this way.' 'I am off all honest work,' says he. 'I don't understand it, my little Lipa.' "

By a small aspen-grove they stood still to rest and await Praskovya. Yelizarov had for many years been a contractor, but as he kept no horses, he went through the whole district on foot, carrying a small sack which contained bread and onions. He strode along swinging his arms, so it was not easy to walk alongside of him. At the entrance to the grove stood a marestone; Yelizarov tried it to see if it was in good repair. Praskovya reached them panting; her wrinkled face, with its timorous expression, to-day was radiant: she had been to church like other people, and had gone to the fair, where they had drunk pear-kvass! This was so rare a treat for her, that it seemed to her that she was living in joy for the first time in her life. When they had rested, they all three proceeded on their way side by side. The sun was setting fast, its rays penetrated through the grove and threw light on the stems of the trees. There was a sound of voices in front, the Ukleyevo women had got far ahead, but had stopped in the grove, no doubt to pick mushrooms.

"Hullo! lassies!" called Yelizarov. "Hullo! beauties!"

In answer there came laughter.

"Here is the Crutch! The Crutch! Old Grizzly!"

And the echo also laughed. Soon the grove was behind them, the tops of the factory chimneys appeared, and the cross glittering on the bell-tower. This was the village, the very same village, "where the Cantor ate all the caviar at the funeral." They are very near home now; it only remains to go down into the hollow. Lipa and Praskovya, who were barefooted, sat down on the grass and put on their boots; the contractor sat down too. When you looked and saw the willows, the white church, and the river, Ukleyevo looked attractive and peaceful; it was only the roofs of the factories—painted a dark colour for economy's sake—that were unsightly. You saw the rye on the declivity on the farther side, and here and there ricks and sheaves as if strewn by a storm, and some new-mown rye lying in swaths: and the oats too were ripe, and shone in the sun like mother-of-pearl. It was harvest-time. To-day was a holiday, to-morrow was Saturday; they would gather in the rye, carry the hay, and then it was Sunday, again a holiday. Every day there was a sound of distant thunder; it was steamy, it looked like rain, and as each one glanced at the fields their thought was: May God grant us time to gather in the corn. And they were cheerful and happy, though a little uneasy.

"Mowers are expensive now," said Praskovya. "One ruble forty a day!"

People were still streaming from the fair at Kazanskoe: women, factory-hands in new caps, mendicants, children. Then a cart went by raising a cloud of dust, behind it galloped an unsold horse, as if rejoicing in the fact; then someone went by leading a stubborn cow by the horn; then again a cart, bearing drunken peasants who were hanging their legs over the side. One old woman was leading by the hand a small boy in a large cap and large high-boots. The boy was exhausted by the heat, and his heavy boots interfered with the flexion of his knees, nevertheless he continued to blow a toy trumpet with all his might. They had already reached the bottom of the hill and were turning into the street, and still the toy trumpet could be heard.

"And our factory-owners are not quite themselves," said Yelizarov. "It's unlucky! Kostiukov raged at me.—'A great number of planks went for the cornice,' he says: 'A great number!'—'As many as were required, Vasily Danilych, and no more,' I say; 'I don't eat planks with my gruel.'—'How dare you,' says he, 'speak to me like that? A blockhead like you! Don't forget I made you contractor!' he screams at me, —'What a wonder!' says I. 'Still, before I was a contractor, I drank tea every day.'—'You are all rogues,' says he. I remained silent. We may be rogues in this world, but you will be rogues in the next, I thought—ha—ha—ha! The next day he thawed. 'Don't be angry with me for what I said, Makarych

If I said more than was necessary, you see it is my privilege; I am the merchant of a more ancient guild than you—you must keep silent.'—'You are,'.I say, 'the merchant of a more ancient guild than I! I am only a carpenter, that's true. But St. Joseph was a carpenter. Our business is honourable and pleasing to God, and if you are pleased to be more ancient, then be gracious to us, Vasily Danilych.' Later I thought—that is, after this conversation—like this I thought: What is more ancient? The merchant of an ancient guild, or a carpenter? Maybe the carpenter, my children!"

The Crutch became thoughtful, then he added: "It is so, children. Whosoever suffers and labours, he is the most honourable."

The sun had set, and over the river, and around the churchyard, and from the open spaces surrounding the fabrics rose a thick mist white as milk. Then, as darkness came on apace, one by one the lights began to blink, and at times it seemed as if the mist was hovering over a bottomless abyss. It seemed to Lipa and her mother, who were born poor, and were prepared to live so to the end, ready to surrender to others all except their timid gentle souls, that, for a moment perhaps, this was some dream: a great mysterious world, and they stronger and older than anyone, standing in one of the furthest unlimited ridges of life. It was so pleasant up here; they smiled a happy smile, and forgot that it would be necessary to return below.

At last they reached home. There were mowers sitting on the ground, at the gate, and by the shop. Usually, those from Ukleyevo did not come and work for Tzybukin, so it was necessary to hire others, and it looked in the darkness as if they were people with long black beards. The shop was still open, and through the door the deaf Stepan was seen playing draughts with the servant-boy. Some of the mowers were softly singing under their breath, others were calling loudly for their wages, without obtaining them, as they were required to work again on the morrow. Old Tzybukin, in shirt-sleeves, was drinking tea with Aksinya under the birch trees by the door. A lamp was burning on the table.

"Ga—affer!" the mowers called from the gate provokingly. "Pay at least half! Ga—affer!"

Again there was a sound of laughter, then once more they started singing under their breath.

The Crutch also sat down to have some tea.

"Well, so we have been to the fair," he began. "We had an excellent walk, my dears, an excellent walk, thank the Lord. But an unpleasant incident occurred. Sasha, the farrier, buys some tobacco and gives the merchant a 50-kopeck piece. The money was false," continued the Crutch looking round. He had meant to whisper it, but spoke it in a strangulated hoarse voice that was audible to everyone. "The 50-kopeck piece turned out to be false. They ask, where did it come from? 'This,' says he, 'is what Anisim Tzybukin gave me on the occasion of his wedding. . . .' They called for the sergeant; he came. . . . Now, see, Petrovich, whatever happens there will be chatter. . . ."

"Ga—affer!" the voices provokingly called from the gate. "Ga—affer!"

There was silence.

"Ah, children, children, children," muttered the Crutch quickly, as he rose from his seat, overcome with sleep. "Thank you for the tea and sugar. It is time to rest; I am nothing but a ruin, my girders are rotting within me. Ha, ha, ha!"

And as he left he gave a sob, and said: "It must be time to die!"

Old Tzybukin did not finish his tea; he sat there buried in thought, and looked as if he was listening to the Crutch's footsteps, who was by now far down the street.

"Sashka the farrier lied, that's all," said Aksinya, guessing his thoughts.

He went into the house, and returned shortly afterwards with a packet; he opened it, and displayed the glittering new rubles. He took one, tried it on his teeth, threw it on the tray; he threw another. . . .

"Beyond doubt these rubles are false," he said incredulously to Aksinya. "Anisim brought these same ones with him; they are his wedding-present. Take them, my daughter," he whispered, thrusting the packet into her hand, "take, and throw them into the well. The devil take them! And see that there is no chatter. Whatever happens. . . . Clear away the samovar, put out the lights."

As Lipa and Praskovya sat in the shed, they saw the lights go out one by one; only upstairs in Varvara's room the blue and red image-lamp glimmered, breathing peace, contentment, and nescience. Praskovya could not get accustomed to the idea that her daughter had married into a rich family, and when she arrived she hung timidly about the vestibule, smiling apologetically. so they sent her away with some tea and sugar. Lipa could not get accustomed to it either, and after her husband had left she did not sleep in a bed, but wherever she happened to be, in the kitchen or the shed. She washed the floors, or did the ironing, which all seemed to her the same as when she was a day-worker. So now, after their return from the pilgrimage, they drank tea in the kitchen with the cook, then went out into the shed and lay against the wall between the sleighs. It was very dark, and smelt of harness. All the lights were out, the deaf one was heard closing the shop, and the mowers settling themselves in the yard for the night. Far away at the Junior Khrymins they were playing the expensive harmonium. . . . Praskovya and Lipa fell asleep.

They were awakened by some footsteps; the moon was shining brightly, and at the entrance to the shed stood Aksinya with some bedding in her arms.

"It may be cooler here," she said, and entering lay down at the very threshold with the moon shining full on her. She did not sleep, she sighed deeply, tossed and flung nearly all her clothing off; by the magic light of the moon what a beautiful, what a proud creature she looked! Some time went by, and again steps were heard; then the old man, very pale, stood in the doorway.

"Aksinya," he called, "are you here? What?"

"Well?" she answered wrathfully.

"I told you just now to throw the money into the well. Have you done it?"

"Anything else! Throw riches in the water! I paid some of the mowers. . . ."

"My God!" said the old man in astonishment and fear. "Shameless woman! Oh, my God!"

He wrung his hands and went out, and as he went he muttered to himself. A little later Aksinya sat up, heaved a deep sigh of dissatisfaction, arose, gathered up her bedding in her arms, and went out.

"Why did you marry me here, mother dear?" asked Lipa.

"Marriage is a necessity, my child, and so not in our control."

And the consciousness of an inconsolable affliction was about to overwhelm them. Then they felt as if Someone was looking down from heaven, those great blue heights from whence the stars keep watch and see all that is going on in Ukleyevo. And, however great be Evil, wondrous and peaceful is the night, and in God's kingdom Good reigns, and will ever reign peaceful and wondrous; for on earth all is waiting to emerge into right, just as the light of the moon emerges from the night.

They both felt comforted, and, leaning one against the other, they fell asleep.

VI

The news had spread some time that Anisim had been arrested for coining and circulating counterfeit money. Months went by, some six months, the long winter was over, spring had come, and the inhabitants of his home and the village had become accustomed to the idea that Anisim was sitting in prison. When anyone passed the house at night they remembered that Anisim was sitting in prison; when the church-bells tolled for some reason or other, they again remembered that Anisim was sitting in prison and awaiting his sentence.

It seemed as if a shadow lay over the place. The house darkened, the roof grew rusty, the door of the shop, once painted green and heavily bound in iron, looked, as deaf Stepan himself said, "like the disused door of a ruin." Old Tzybukin was a sorry sight, his hair and his beard grew untended, he seated himself heavily in the tarantass, he no longer shouted to the beggars: "God will help you!" His strength declined visibly; people were already less afraid of him, and the sergeant drew up an official report about the shop, but as heretofore he continued to receive the things he required. Tzybukin was summoned three times to the town, to be tried on charges of contraband dealing in wine, and each time the case was deferred on account of the non-appearance of witnesses. So the old man was worn out. He frequently went to see his son; engaged someone for something, forwarded petitions to someone or other, offered a banner somewhere. He presented to the inspector of the prison in which Anisim was detained a silver plate with the inscription in enamel, "The heart knows no measure," and a long spoon accompanied this present.

"But make a stir—is there no one to make a stir?" asked Varvara. "Oh, fie upon it! You should ask one of the gentlemen; they might write to the commander-in-chief. . . . If only they would release him till the trial. The poor lad will be ill in prison."

She was much concerned about it, but at the same time was growing stouter and paler. As heretofore, she trimmed the image-lamps, saw that the house was kept clean and tidy, regaled the guests with jam and apple-pasty. The deaf one and Aksinya attended to the business. They had started a new work, a brick-kiln at Butiokino, whither Aksinya drove every day in the tarantass. She drove herself, and on meeting any acquaintance she stretched out her neck like a viper in unripe rye, and smiled naïvely and enigmatically. Lipa was always playing with her baby, which was born just before Lent—such a small wizened piteous baby that it was even strange that he should cry, look, and be reckoned a human being, and also go by the name of Nikifor. As he lay in his cradle, Lipa would go to the door, and call out to him:

"Good-day, Nikifor Anisimych!"

Then rush headlong back and kiss him, then again go to the door, and again greet him:

"Good-day, Nikifor Anisimych!"

He would kick his little pink legs in the air, and laugh and cry at the same moment, like the carpenter Yelizarov.

At last the date of the trial was announced. The old man left five days before. Then it became known that people from the village had been called as witnesses; the old workman went too, also receiving a summons to appear. The trial was on Thursday. Sunday came, and the old man did not return, nor was there any news. On Tuesday, towards even Varvara sat at the open window listening for the old man. In the next room Lipa was playing with her baby, tossing and rocking it, and saying in a transport of joy:

"He will grow big—big. He will be a muzhik, and we will do our day's work together. We will do our day's work together!"

"Come now!" said Varvara offended. "Why do you talk of day-work, you silly? He will be a merchant."

Lipa began singing softly, but soon afterwards forgot, and again said:

"He will grow big—big, he will be a muzhik, and we will do our day-work together."

"Come now! You repeat it too often."

Lipa, with Nikifor in her arms, came to the doorway, and asked:

"Mamenka, why do I love him so? Why am I sorry for him?" she continued in a trembling voice, while tears dimmed her eyes. "Who is he? What is he? Light as a feather, a wee little thing, yet I love him, love him just like a real man. He can do nothing, say nothing, yet I understand all he wants by his little eyes."

Varvara listened: was not that the sound of the evening train arriving at the station? Was the old man coming? She no longer heard or understood what Lipa was saying, no longer knew how the time went by; she was trembling all over, not from fear but out of great curiosity. She saw a cart full of peasants dash by with a great clatter; they were the returning witnesses. As the telega drove by the shop, the old workman jumped out, and went into the yard. She heard people greeting him, and asking him about something.

"Forfeiture of his rights and estates," he said in a loud voice, "and Siberia with penal servitude for six years."

Aksinya emerged from the darkness of the shop, from whence she had just despatched some kerosene; she still held a bottle in one hand, a funnel in the other, and a piece of silver in her mouth.

"And where is papasha?" she lisped.

"At the station," answered the workman. "'When it is darker,' he said, 'I will come home.'"

When it became known in the yard that Anisim was sentenced to penal servitude, the cook, in the kitchen, set up a wailing as if someone were dead, thinking the occasion required it:

"Why did you leave us, Anisim Grigoryich, little falcon dear?"

The dogs barked anxiously; Varvara, much distressed, ran to the window, and called out with all her might to the cook:

"Enough, Stepanida, enough! Don't be in despair, for Christ's sake!"

They forgot to bring the samovar; no one could think of

anything. Lipa alone could in no way understand what was the matter, and continued to play with her baby.

When the old man arrived from the station, no one asked him any questions; he greeted them, and walked through all the rooms in silence; he had no supper.

"There was no one to plead for him," began Varvara when they were alone. "I—I told you to ask one of the gentlemen; you would not listen. . . . Perhaps a petition. . . ."

"I did petition," said the old man, with a wave of the hand. "When they read the sentence on Anisim I was with the gentleman who defended him: 'No use,' he said, 'it is too late.' And Anisim himself said, 'It is too late.' All the same, as I left the court I spoke to an advocate. I gave him earnest-money. . . . I will wait a little, a week, then I'll go again. God have mercy on us!"

The old man again wandered in silence through the rooms; when he returned to Varvara, he said:

"I can't be well. My head feels . . . in a fog My thoughts are in a muddle."

He closed the door so that Lipa should not hear, and continued in a low voice:

"My money affairs are in a bad way. You remember before the wedding, Anisim brought me some new rubles and half rubles? I hid one packet, the rest I mixed with my own. . . . Formerly, God rest his soul, when my grandfather, Dmitry Filatych, was alive he used often to go on business to Moscow or the Crimea. He had a wife: this same wife, while he was away on business, used to run riot. There were six children. Now it happened, when my grandfather was drunk, he would joke and say: 'I shall never know which are my children and which are someone else's?' A cheerful nature his! But now I can't make out which is real money and which is counterfeit, it seems to me they are all false coins."

"Well, I never! God help you!"

"When I take a ticket at the station, I hand three rubles,

then I think to myself: Are they false? And I'm frightened. I can't be well."

"They say, we are all in God's hands. . . . Oh dear! Oh dear!" said Varvara, shaking her head. "We ought to remember, too, Petrovich. . . . Times are bad, and whatever happens you are no longer a young man. You will die; then see to it that they do not wrong your grandson. Alas, I am afraid they may defraud Nikifor; they will surely. His father one may say no longer exists: his mother is young and foolish. If you left him a bit of land, say Butiokino, for the boy. Do that, Petrovich. Think about it," added Varvara, entreatingly. "He is a nice little boy; I am sorry for him. Look, go to-morrow and sign a paper. What use waiting?"

"I forgot about the grandson," said Tzybukin. "I must go and see him. So you say the boy is all right? Well, may he grow up, God grant it!"

He opened the door, and beckoned with his finger to Lipa. She came to him with the baby in her arms.

"Lipinka, if you want anything, ask for it," he said. "And whatever you have a mind for, eat; we won't complain—only keep well. . . ." He made the sign of the Cross over the child. "And take care of the grandson; though my son is not here, my grandson remains."

Tears rolled down his cheeks; he gave a sob and went out. A little while afterwards he went to bed and slept soundly, having spent seven sleepless nights.

VII

The old man went for a short visit to town. Someone told Aksinya he had been to the notary to make a will, in which he bequeathed Butiokino—that Butiokino where she had established her brick-kiln—to his grandson Nikifor. They communicated this to her one morning, as Varvara and the old man were sitting under the birch trees by the door drinking tea. She closed the door of the shop facing the street and the one into the yard; she collected all the keys she had ever had, and flung them at the old man's feet.

"I shall not work any more for you!" she screamed, suddenly beginning to sob. "I have become not a daughter-in-law but a worker! All the people jeer; 'See,' they say, 'what a good worker Tzybukin has found.' I am not in your hire! I am not poor, nor a serf, I have a father and a mother."

Leaving her tears unwiped, she turned on the old man her overflowing eyes full of spite and distorted with anger; her face and neck were crimson and all the muscles strained, as she screamed with all her might:

"I won't serve you any more! I am worn out. It's work day in day out, sitting in the shop, smuggling vodka at night, that's what I have to do, while all the benefits are for the convict's wife and her brat. She is mistress here and gentlewoman, and I am her servant! Give it all to the prisoner's wife till she stifles, I am going home. Find for yourselves another fool—damned Herods!"

The old man never once in his life had scolded or punished his children, never even entertained the thought that anyone in the family could speak rudely to him, or behave themselves in an unseemly manner: and now he was so frightened that he ran into the house and hid himself behind the cupboard. And Varvara was so panic-stricken that she could not get up from her seat, and waved both hands as if she were defending herself from bees.

"What's the meaning of this? Batiushka!" she murmured in horror. "How can she scream like that? Oh, fie upon it! The people will hear! Ai, ai! Softly, softly!"

"You have given up Butiokino to the convict's wife," Aksinya continued to scream. "Give her everything; I want nothing from you, plague you! You are all of one gang. I've seen enough of it, it will do—you rob the passer-by, the traveller, the thief, the old, the young! And who sells vodka without a license? And circulates false coins! You have filled a chest with false coins."

By the wide open gates a crowd had already assembled, and were looking into the yard.

"Let them all look!" screamed Aksinya. "I disgrace you, do I? You blush with shame for me? You are humbled by my conduct? Hie, Stepan," she called to her deaf husband. "In a moment we will be off home, I will go to my father and mother, I won't stay any longer with a convict's people. Be quick!"

The linen was hanging in the yard, she wrenched down her own skirt and camisole, which were still wet, and flung them into the deaf one's arms; throwing herself in a frenzy on the linen which was not hers, she tore it down, flung it on the ground, and trampled on it.

"Ai, ai! Batiushka! stop her," moaned Varvara. "What's all this? Let her have Butiokino, let her have it, for Christ's sake!"

"What a woman!" they said at the gate. "Wha—at a woman! She has lost her senses."

Aksinya rushed into the kitchen where the washing was being done. Lipa was washing, while the cook had gone to the brook to rinse some of the linen. The cauldron was steaming on the stove, the trough was also steaming, and the kitchen itself was full of steam. On the floor lay a heap of unwashed linen, and by it, on a seat, so that if he fell he would not hurt himself, stretching his pink legs, lay Nikifor. Just as Aksinya entered Lipa had taken her chemise out of the heap, put it in the trough, and had already stretched out her hand for the large scoop full of boiling water which stood on the table.

"Give it here," said Aksinya, looking at her with a look of hatred, and taking the chemise out of the trough. "It is not your business to touch my linen, you are a convict's wife, and it behoves you to know your place!"

Lipa looked at her panic-stricken, without understanding

what she meant, then caught the look which she threw at the child, suddenly understood, and turned into stone.

"You have taken my land—that's for you!"

Saying which, Aksinya seized the scoop with the boiling water and dashed it over Nikifor.

Then was heard a scream such as never before had been heard in Ukleyevo; no one thought a small weak creature like Lipa could have uttered such a scream. A silence fell over the yard. Askinya returned into the house without a word, smiling naïvely as heretofore. The deaf one walked about the yard for some time holding the linen in his arms, then without haste began hanging it up again. Until the cook came back from the brook, no one could make up their mind to go into the kitchen and find out what had happend.

VIII

They carried Nikifor to the local hospital, where at evening he died. Lipa did not wait till they came to fetch her, but wrapped the little dead body in a blanket, and carried it away. The hospital was quite new, having only been recently built; it had large windows, and stood on a hill; the glow of the setting sun on the glass almost gave it the appearance of being on fire. Below the hospital was a small village. Lipa came down the road before leaving the village, and sat down by its pond. Some woman or other brought a horse to drink; the horse refused to drink.

"What more do you want?" said the woman, softly and perplexed. "What is the matter with you?"

A boy in a red shirt sat by the water cleaning his father's boots. Not another soul was to be seen in the village or on the hill.

"It won't drink . . ." said Lipa, looking at the horse.

Then the woman and the boy went away, and there was no one to be seen. The sun set under a brocade of purple and gold, while long red and lilac clouds, stretching over all the sky, kept watch over him. Somewhere in the distance a bittern made a doleful and bellowing noise, just like a cow confined to its shed. The cry of this mysterious bird was heard every spring, but no one knew what kind of a bird it was, nor where it lived. Above the hospital, by the pond, in the bushes, behind the village, and all around in the fields, the nightingales were singing and trilling. The cuckoo was counting some one's age, was always getting mixed in the reckoning, and began again. The frogs, bursting with anger, were calling to one another, and you could distinctly hear the words: "e—te—takova, e—te—takova" (and you also! and you also)! What a noise there was! It seemed as if all these creatures were crying and singing on purpose, so that no one should sleep this spring night; so that everyone, even the angry frogs, should appreciate and enjoy every minute of it; for we only live once!

Lipa did not remember how long she had sat by the pond, but when she arose the silver crescent of the moon was shining in the sky, as well as a great number of stars. All in the village slept, and there was not one light anywhere. It was twelve versts home, but she did not think of her strength, nor whither she went; the moon shone sometimes in front of her, sometimes to the right, the same cuckoo cried in a hoarse-growing voice and with a seemingly derisive laugh: See, where are you going?

Lipa walked so fast that she lost her head-kerchief. She looked at the sky, and thought. Where was her little boy's soul, was it following her, or was it up above among the stars, and no longer thinking of his mother? Oh! how lonely to be in the fields at night, in the midst of these songs when you yourself could not sing, in the midst of these incessant cries of joy when you yourself could not rejoice; when the stars were watching in the skies, also lonely and indifferent as to whether it was spring or winter, as to whether people were alive or dead. When your soul is oppressed with grief, it is worse to be alone. If only her mother were with her. the Crutch, or the cook, or at least a muzhik.

"Boo—oo," cried the bittern. "Boo—oo."

Then, suddenly, a human voice it was that said distinctly: "Yoke them, Vavila."

A few paces in front. by the side of the road, a wood-fire was burning—that is to say, the red embers were glowing, there were flames. Some horses seemed to be munching; the outline of two carts could be discerned in the darkness; on one cart was a barrel, on the other some sacks, and by the carts were two men. One man was just putting a horse to, the other was standing motionless by the fire with his hands behind his back. Some dogs began to growl by the side of the carts. He who led the horse stopped, and said:

"It sounds as if someone were on the road."

"Sharik, be quiet," called the other to the dog.

By his voice you could tell the other was an old man. Lipa stayed her steps, and said: "God is our help!"

The old man went up to her, and said to her after a pause:

"Good even!"

"Your dog won't bite, gaffer?"

"No, it's all right, he won't hurt."

"I have come from the hospital," said Lipa, after a moment's silence. "My little boy died there. See, I am taking him home."

The old man must have heard this with displeasure, for he moved away, and replied hurriedly:

"That's all right. my dear. God's will be done! Lad. you are dawdling," he said. turning to his fellow-traveller. "You might hurry!"

"Can't find the shaft-bow," said the lad. "Have you seen it?"

"You arrant Vavila!"

The old man took the brand from the fire, blew on it, thus lighting up his own face; then, when they had found the shaft bow, he turned the light on Lipa. He looked at her, and his look was full of compassion and tenderness.

"You are a mother," he said—"every mother grieves for her child."

After that he sighed and shook his head. Vavila threw something on the fire, stamped it out, and darkness reigned. The visions disappeared and as a little while before there were only the fields and the star-filled sky, the sound of birds interfering with each other's sleep, and there where there had been a fire a corn-crake seemed to be twittering.

After a moment's darkness the carts, the old man, and the lanky Vavila became visible again: soon the telega started forward with a screech.

"Are you saints?" Lipa asked the old man.

"No, we are from Firsanov."

"The way you looked at me just now touched my heart. The lad too is gentle. I thought, 'they must be saints.' "

"Have you far to go?"

"To Ukleyevo."

"Seat yourself; we will take you to Kuzmenok. Then you go to the right and we go to the left."

Vavila got into the cart with the barrel, the old man and Lipa got into the other. They proceeded at a foot's pace with Vavila leading.

"My little son was in pain all day," said Lipa. "He looked at me with his little eyes and made no sound; he wanted to speak and could not. Father in Heaven have mercy on his soul! I fell to the floor in my anguish, I stood up, and fell by the bedside. Tell me, gaffer, why does a child suffer before death? When a man suffers, or a muzhik, or a woman, it is for the remittance of their sins, but a child, when it has no sin? Why?"

"Who can tell?" answered the old man.

They continued their way for half an hour in silence.

"It is impossible to know everything, the why, the wherefore," said the old man. "Birds are given two wings, not four, because it is more convenient to fly with two; so it is with man to know, not everything, but a half or even a quarter. Just so much as is necessary for him to live, that much he knows."

"Gaffer, I would find it easier to walk, for my heart feels like breaking."

"No, no, sit down."

The old man yawned and made the sign of the Cross over his mouth:

"Nichevo," he repeated, "your grief is a great grief, but life is long, and there will be more good and more bad, there will be all sorts. Great is our Mother Russia!" he said, glancing on both sides of the road. "I have been all over Russia, and see everything therein, and believe my words, my dear: there will be good and there will be bad. I have tramped through Siberia, and to the region of the Amoor, and to Altai, and settled in Siberia, tilled the ground, then grew a longing for Mother Russia, and back I came to my native village. Back I came to Russia on foot, and I remember, as we were on the ferry-boat, I, a bag of bones, in rags, barefooted, starving, sucking a crust, a passing gentleman comes on board—may God give his soul peace when he dies—and he looks at me pityingly, with tears in his eyes: 'Poor fellow,' says he, 'you eat black bread and see but dark days. . . .' I came back, without a peg to call my own: I had a wife, she stayed in Siberia, we buried her there. So I lived as best I could. Well, I tell you there was good and bad. I have no wish to die, I could live another twenty years—that means, there has been more good than bad. And great is our Mother Russia!" he said again, taking a look on both sides of the road.

"Gaffer," asked Lipa, "when a man dies, how many days after does his soul remain on earth?"

"Ah, who can tell? Here, we will ask Vavila; he has been to school. They teach them everything now. Vavila!" called the old man.

"Eh?"

"Vavila, when a man dies, how many days after does his soul remain on earth?"

Vavila stopped his horse, and answered at once:

"Nine days. My grandfather Cyril died, his soul stayed in our cottage thirteen days."

"How do you know?"

"There was a knocking in the stove for thirteen days."

"All right. Go on," said the old man; he evidently did not believe a word of it.

At Kuzmenok the carts turned on to the chaussée, and Lipa went her way. It was dawn, yet when she descended into the hollow the huts and church of Ukleyevo were hidden in mist. It was cold, and it seemed to her that the same cuckoo was calling. When Lipa reached the house everyone was still sleeping, and the cattle had not been taken out to graze. She sat on the doorstep and waited. The old man was the first to come out; he at once, at a glance, understood what had happened, and for a long while was unable to utter a word, he only moved his lips.

"Alas, Lipa," he said, "you have not kept the grandson. . . ."

They awoke Varvara, who wrung her hands, wept, and at once began to arrange the baby for burial.

"It was a nice little child. Alas, alas!" she added, "he was the only boy, and she did not keep him, dear oh dear!"

There was a requiem for him in the morning and in the evening; the next day they buried him. After the burial the guests and the clergy ate a great deal, just as if they had not eaten for a long while. Lipa served the guests, and the priest raising his fork on which he held a piece of salted orange-agaric, said to her:

"Don't fret for the child. Of such are the Kingdom of Heaven."

It was only when everyone had dispersed that Lipa realized what had happened; that Nikifor was no more, nor would be again; she understood and wept. She did not know in which room to retire and weep, as she felt now after the death of her child there was no longer any place for her in the house; she was superfluous, and the others also felt it.

"Here, what is this noise you are making?' suddenly Aksinya called out, appearing in the doorway. At the funeral she had worn new black clothes, and was powdered. "Be quiet!"

Lipa tried to stop, but being unable to she only sobbed the louder.

"Do you hear?" cried Aksinya as she stamped with rage. "To whom am I speaking? Out you go in the yard, and don't put foot inside here again, convict's wife! Off with you!"

"Now, now," rather anxiously said old Tzybukin. "Aksiuta, mutashka, be calm. . . . She is weeping, quite naturally . . . her baby has died. . . ."

"Quite naturally . . ." mocked Aksinya. "Let her stay the night, and to-morrow, may no trace of her remain. Quite naturally!" she mocked again, and with a laugh directed her steps towards the shop.

Next day, early in the morning, Lipa retired to Torguyevo to her mother.

IX

In the course of time, the roof and the door of the shop were repainted and looked like new; geraniums flowered as before in the window-sills; and all that which had happened three years ago in the house of Tzybukin was almost forgotten.

Then, and now, Grigory Petrovich is reckoned the master, but in reality everything is in the hands of Aksinya; she sells and buys, nothing is done without her consent. The brick-kiln is working well; and since the railway has required bricks, the price has gone up to twenty-four rubles a thousand; women and girls carry the bricks to the station, and load wagons, for which employment they receive a quarter ruble (25 kopecks) a day.

Aksinya has shares in the business with the Khrymins, and it is called "Khrymin Junior & Co." They opened an inn by the station; and it is there they now play the expensive harmonium. The post-master and the station-master often frequent the inn; they also are doing a bit of business. Khrymin Junior has given a gold watch to deaf Stepan, which every now and again he extracts from his pocket and puts to his ear.

In the village they say Aksinya has acquired fresh vigour; and verily if you saw her as she drives to the brick-kiln in the morning, with the usual smile on her face, looking handsome and happy, and if you saw her as she attended to business at the kiln, you would feel she had indeed a great vitality. They are all afraid of her in the house, in the village, at the kiln. When she arrives at the post-office, the postmaster jumps up and says to her:

"Pray, pray take a seat, Aksinya Abramovna."

There was one middle-aged landlord, a swell, who wore a sleeveless coat of fine cloth and high-polished boots, who sold horses to her and was so captivated by her conversation that he conceded to her all she wished, held her hand in his for quite a while, and gazing into her bright, cunning, naïve eyes, said:

"For a woman like you, Aksinya Abramovna, I am prepared to render any service. Only tell me, when can we meet alone, without interference?"

"Oh, whenever you like."

So now, the middle-aged swell comes nearly every day to the shop to drink beer. The beer is frightfully bitter, like wormwood, the landowner screws up his face but drinks it.

Old Tzybukin no longer interferes with the business. He does not even keep the money. He does not mention the fact, but he cannot be sure which is the true and which is the false coin; he speaks to no one of his failing. He has grown very forgetful, and if he is not given food he does not ask for it; they are quite accustomed to dine without him, and Varvara often says:

"Our old man went to bed again last night without food." This she says quite calmly for they are used to it. In summer or winter he walks about in a thick fur-lined pelisse. But in the very hot weather he stays at home. He usually puts on his pelisse, turns up the collar, wraps the cloak round him, and walks about the country or along the road to the station, or sits from morning to evening on the bench by the church gates. Here he sits motionless; passers-by greet him, he does not answer; as ever he dislikes the muzhik. If he is asked any question he answers quite sensibly and civilly, although briefly.

In the village gossip has it that his daughter-in-law has driven him out of his own home and does not allow him anything to eat, that he is supported by the charity of others; some people rejoice at this, others pity him.

Varvara has grown still stouter and paler and continues her good works, which Aksinya does not interfere with. There is so much jam now that they do not manage to eat it all before the fresh lot comes; it candies, and Varvara not knowing what to do with it almost weeps.

They were beginning to forget Anisim, when one day a letter came from him written in verse on a large sheet of paper looking like a petition, and in the same wonderful handwriting as before. Apparently his friend Samarodov was also wiping out his offences in prison. Below the verses, written in an ugly, hardly decipherable handwriting was one sentence: "I am ill, wretched; send help for Christ's sake."

One day—it was a bright autumn day, towards evening—old Tzybukin sat by the church gates with the collar of his pelisse turned up, so that all that was visible was his nose and the visor of his cap. At the other end of the long bench sat Yelizarov, and by his side sat the school-factotum, Yakov, an old toothless septuagenarian. The Crutch and the factotum were talking.

"Young people should support the aged; honour their father and mother." Yakov spoke irascibly. "And this here daughter-in-law has driven her father-in-law out of his own house. The old man has neither eaten nor drunk for three days. What will happen to him?"

"For three days?" said the Crutch in astonishment.

"There he sits without opening his mouth; he has grown very weak. Why remain silent? He ought to complain in court—she would not be exonerated."

"Who was exonerated in court?" asked the Crutch, not listening.

"What for?"

"The woman is all right, she is energetic; it is impossible to carry on their business without, . . . well, without fraud."

"From his own house," continued Yakov irascibly. "To make a home and then be driven out, just think what ado! Plague on it!"

Tzybukin listened without moving.

"Your own house or someone else's, it is all the same provided it is warm and the women don't get angry," said the Crutch with a smile. "When I was young I very much regretted my Nastasya; she was so gentle and it was always: 'Makarych, buy a house; Makarych, buy a horse.' And as she was dying she still said: 'Makarych, buy yourself a little droshky, so as you do not have to walk.' And the only thing I ever bought her was some gingerbread."

"The husband is deaf and stupid," continued Yakov, not listening to the Crutch. "Such a fool, that he is no better than a goose. Can he understand anything? Strike a goose on the head with a stick it won't understand either."

The Crutch arose to return to the factory, Yakov also got up, and they both left still talking. When they had gone about fifteen steps away, old Tzybukin also rose and with uncertain tread, as if he were on slippery ice, followed them.

The light of evening was descending on the village; the last rays of the sun still shone on the road above; an old woman and some children were returning from the woods carrying baskets of yellow and brown mushrooms. There were crowds of women and girls going to the station with bricks; all of them had their noses and cheeks covered in thick red brick-dust, and they sang as they went. In front walked Lipa, singing at the top of her high-pitched voice, looking up at the sky with a look of rapture and triumph, that the day, thank God, was over and they were going to rest. Her mother, Praskovya, was also in the crowd; she was carrying a small bundle and was out of breath.

"Good even, Makarych," said Lipa, catching sight of the Crutch. "Good evening, my dove!"

"Good even, Lipynka," said the Crutch, pleased to see her. "Women, girls, be fond of the rich carpenter! Ha, ha! My children, my children"—the Crutch heaved a sigh—"my little dears."

The Crutch and Yakov passed on, still talking. Then the crowd met old Tzybukin, and there was a sudden silence. Lipa and Praskovya lagged a little behind, and when the old man came in line with them Lipa bowed low to him and said:

"Good even, Petrovich."

Her mother did likewise. The old man stopped, and without answering looked at them both; his lips trembled and his eyes filled with tears. Lipa reached for a bit of porridge-paste from her mother's bundle and handed it to him. He took and ate it.

The sun had set, its rays had disappeared from the road above; it was getting dark and cold; Lipa and Praskovya passed on, and long afterwards were seen making the sign of the Cross.

AFTER THE THEATRE

Nadya Zelenina had just returned with her mother from the theatre, where they had been to see a performance of "Yevgeny Oniegin." Entering her room, she quickly threw off her dress, loosened her hair, and sat down hurriedly in her petticoat and a white blouse to write a letter in the style of Tatyana.

"I love you,"—she wrote—"but you don't love me; no, you don't!"

The moment she had written this, she smiled.

She was only sixteen years old, and so far she had not been in love. She knew that Gorny, the officer, and Gronsdev, the student, loved her; but now, after the theatre, she wanted to doubt their love. To be unloved and unhappy—how interesting. There is something beautiful, affecting, romantic in the fact that one loves deeply while the other is indifferent. Oniegin is interesting because he does not love at all, and Tatyana is delightful because she is very much in love; but if they loved each other equally and were happy, they would seem boring, instead.

"Don't go on protesting that you love me," Nadya wrote on, thinking of Gorny, the officer, "I can't believe you. You're very clever, educated, serious; you have a great talent, and perhaps, a splendid future waiting, but I am an uninteresting poor-spirited girl, and you yourself know quite well that I shall only be a drag upon your life. It's true I carried you off your feet, and you thought you had met your ideal in me, but that was a mistake. Already you are asking yourself in despair, 'Why did I meet this girl?' Only your kindness prevents you from confessing it."

Nadya pitied herself. She wept and went on.

"If it were not so difficult for me to leave mother and brother I would put on a nun's gown and go where my eyes direct me. You would then be free to love another. If I were to die!"

Through her tears she could not make out what she had written. Brief rainbows trembled on the table, on the floor and the ceiling, as though Nadya were looking through a prism. Impossible to write. She sank back in her chair and began to think of Gorny.

Oh, how fascinating, how interesting men are! Nadya remembered the beautiful expression of Gorny's face, appealing, guilty, and tender, when someone discussed music with him,—the efforts he made to prevent the passion from sounding in his voice. Passion must be concealed in a society where cold reserve and indifference are the signs of good breeding. And he does try to conceal it, but he does not succeed, and everybody knows quite well that he has a passion for music. Never-ending discussions about music, blundering pronouncements by men who do not understand—keep him in incessant tension. He is scared, timid, silent. He plays superbly, as an ardent pianist. If he were not an officer, he would be a famous musician.

The tears dried in her eyes. Nadya remembered how Gorny told her of his love at a symphony concert, and again downstairs by the cloak-room.

"I am so glad you have at last made the acquaintance of the student Gronsdev," she continued to write. "He is a very clever man, and you are sure to love him. Yesterday he was sitting with us till two o'clock in the morning. We were all so happy. I was sorry that you hadn't come to us. He said a lot of remarkable things."

Nadya laid her hands on the table and lowered her head. Her hair covered the letter. She remembered that Gronsdev also loved her, and that he had the same right to her letter as Gorny. Perhaps she had better write to Gronsdev? For no cause, a happiness began to quicken in her breast. At first it was a little one, rolling about in her breast like a rubber ball. Then it grew broader and bigger, and broke forth like a wave. Nadya had already forgotten about Gorny and Gronsdev. Her thoughts became confused. The happiness grew more and more. From her breast it ran into her arms and legs, and it seemed that a light fresh breeze blew over her head, stirring her hair. Her shoulders trembled with quiet laughter. The table and the lampglass trembled. Tears from her eyes splashed the letter. She was powerless to stop her laughter; and to convince herself that she had a reason for it, she hastened to remember something funny.

"What a funny poodle!" she cried, feeling that she was choking with laughter. "What a funny poodle!"

She remembered how Gronsdev was playing with Maksim the poodle after tea yesterday; how he told a story afterwards of a very clever poodle who was chasing a crow in the yard. The crow gave him a look and said:

"Oh, you swindler!"

The poodle did not know he had to do with a learned crow. He was terribly confused, and ran away dumfounded. Afterwards he began to bark.

"No, I'd better love Gronsdev," Nadya decided, and tore up the letter.

She began to think of the student, of his love, of her own love, with the result that the thoughts in her head swam apart and she thought about everything, about her mother, the street, the pencil, the piano. She was happy thinking, and found that everything was good, magnificent. Her happiness told her that this was not all, that a little later it would be still better. Soon it will be spring, summer. They will go with mother to Gorbiky in the country. Gorny will come for his holidays. He will walk in the orchard with her, and make love to her. Gronsdev will come too. He will play croquet with her and bowls. He will tell funny, wonderful stories. She passionately longed for the orchard, the darkness, the pure sky, the stars. Again her shoulders trembled with laughter and she seemed to awaken to a smell of wormwood in the room; and a branch was tapping at the window.

She went to her bed and sat down. She did not know what to do with her great happiness. It overwhelmed her. She stared at the crucifix which hung at the head of her bed and saying:

"Dear God, dear God, dear God."

THE RUNAWAY

It was an endless affair. Pashka and his mother, drenched with rain, tramped mile after mile, first across stubble fields, then by soft woodland paths where yellow leaves stuck to his boots, and on and on till daybreak. After that he stood two hours in a dark entrance-hall, and waited for the doors to open. In the hall, of course, it was warmer and drier than outside; but even there the piercing wind carried the rain-drops in. And as the hall slowly filled with patients, Pashka, wedging his way through the crowd, pressed his face against a sheepskin coat which smelt strongly of salted fish, and slumbered.

At last the bolt slipped, the door opened, and Pashka and his mother found themselves in the waiting-room. Yet another long delay! The patients sat on benches; no one stirred; no one opened his mouth. Pashka stared at the crowd, and likewise held his tongue, though he witnessed many ludicrous, inexplicable things. But once when a boy hopped into the room on one leg, he nudged his mother's side, grinned in his sleeve, and exclaimed—

"Look, mother—a sparrow!"

"Don't talk, child, don't talk!"

At a little window appeared the *feldscher's* sleepy face. "Come and give your names."

The waiting patients, among them the funny, hopping boy, crowded round the window. Of each the *feldscher* asked name and patronymic, age, village, dates of illness, and other questions. From his mother's answer, Pashka learnt that his name was Pavl Galaktionoff, that he was seven years old, and that he had been ill since Easter.

When the names were entered there was another short delay; and then through the waiting-room walked the doctor, in white apron, with a towel on his shoulder. As he passed the hopping boy, he shrugged his shoulders, and said in a sing-song voice—

"You're a donkey! Now aren't you a donkey? I told you Monday, and you come on Friday! Don't worry yourself so far as I'm concerned, but if you're not careful, fool, you'll lose your leg!"

The hopping boy blinked, grimaced piteously as if asking for alms, and began—

"Ivan Nikolaitch, be so kind . . ."

"None of your Ivan Nikolaitch!" said the doctor teasingly. "I told you Monday—you should obey! You're a donkey, that's all."

The reception began. The doctor sat in his room, and called for the patients in turn. Now and then from the room came shrill exclamations, the sobs of children, and the doctor's angry exclamations—

"Don't howl. I won't murder you! Sit quiet!"

At last came Pashka's turn. "Pavl Galaktionoff!" cried the doctor. Pashka's mother at first seemed dazed, as if the summons were unexpected; but she recovered herself, took Pashka's hand, and led him into the doctor's room. The doctor sat on a table, and tapped mechanically with a mallet a thick book.

"What is the matter?" he asked, without looking at his visitors.

"My boy has a boil, *batiushka,* on his elbow," answered Pashka's mother; and her expression implied that she herself was suffering from Pashka's boil.

"Take off his clothes!"

Pashka, panting, untied his neckerchief, rubbed his nose on his sleeve, and began to unbutton his coat.

"Woman! have you come to pay me a visit?" said the doctor irritably. "Why don't you hurry? Are you the only one waiting?"

Pashka hurriedly threw his coat on the floor, and, with his mother's help, took off his shirt. The doctor looked at him absent-mindedly, and slapped him on the bare stomach.

"Serious, brother Pashka," he exclaimed. "You have outgrown your corporation!" When he had said this, he sighed, and added, "Show me your elbow!"

Pashka took fright at a bowl of blood-tinged water, looked at the doctor's apron, and began to cry.

"For shame!" said the doctor mockingly. "He's big enough to get married, yet he begins to howl. For shame!"

Pashka tried to stop his tears. He looked at his mother, and his expression said, "Don't tell them at home that I cried at the hospital."

The doctor examined the elbow, pinched it, sighed, smacked his lips, and again felt the elbow.

"You ought to be whipped, woman!" he said. "Why didn't you bring him sooner? His arm is nearly gone! Look at him, idiot, can't you see that the joint is diseased?"

"It is you who know best, *batiushka!*" said Pashka's mother.

"*Batiushka!* the lad's arm is rotting off, and you with your *batiushka!* What sort of a workman will he make without arms? You'll have to nurse him all his life! If you've got a pimple on your nose you run off here for treatment, but you let your own child rot for six months! You people are all the same!"

He lighted a cigarette. While it burned away he scolded Pashka's mother, hummed a tune, shook his head rhythmically, and thought something out. Naked Pashka stood before him, listened to the tune, and watched the smoke. When the cigarette went out the doctor started, and said in a low voice—

"Listen, woman! Ointments and mixtures are no use in this case; you must leave him here."

"If it must be so, *batiushka*, so be it."

"We must have an operation. . . . And you, Pashka, you must stay," said the doctor, patting his shoulder. "We will let mother go, but you, brother, you will stay with me. It is not bad here, brother! I have raspberry bushes. You and I, Pashka, as soon as we get better, will go and catch thrushes, and I will show you a fox. We shall pay visits together. Eh? Will you stay? And mother will come for you to-morrow."

Pashka looked questioningly at his mother.

"You must stay, child," she said.

"Of course he'll stay," said the doctor merrily. "There is nothing to argue about! I'll show him a live fox. We'll drive to the fair and buy sugar-candy. Marya Denisovna, take him upstairs!"

The doctor was certainly a merry, talkative man; and Pashka was attracted, all the more because he had never been at a fair, and wanted to see a live fox. But his mother? He thought the problem out, and decided to ask the doctor to let his mother remain with him; but before he could open his mouth the nurse was leading him upstairs. With mouth wide open, he looked around. The stairs, the floors, the door-posts, all were painted a beautiful yellow; and everywhere there was a tempting smell of fast-butter. Everywhere hung lamps, everywhere lay carpets; and brass water-taps projected from every wall. But most of all Pashka was pleased by his bed with its grey, shaggy counterpane. He felt the pillows and the counterpane, and came to the conclusion that the doctor had a very nice house.

It was a little ward with only three cots. The first was vacant, the second Pashka's; and on the third sat a very old man with sour eyes, who coughed without cease, and spat into a bowl. From his bed Pashka could see through the open door part of another ward with two beds; on one lay a thin, very pallid man with a caoutchouc bladder on his head. A peasant, arms apart, with bandaged head, looking very like an old woman, sat on the other.

Having set Pashka on his bed, the nurse left him. She returned immediately with an armful of clothes. "These are for you," she said to him. "Put them on."

Pashka took off his old clothes, and, not without pleasure, arrayed himself in his new garments. After donning a shirt, a pair of trousers, and a grey dressing-gown, he looked at himself complacently, and thought how he would like to walk down the village street in his new clothes. Imagination painted his mother sending him to the kitchen garden by the river, to pluck cabbage leaves for the pig, while the village boys and girls stood round him and gaped enviously at his dressing-gown.

When next the nurse returned she brought two tin bowls, two spoons, and two slices of bread. She gave one bowl to the old man, and the other to Pashka. "Eat!" she said.

When Pashka examined the bowl he found it full of greasy soup with a piece of meat at the bottom; and again he reasoned that the doctor lived comfortably, and was not half as angry as he seemed. He dallied over the soup, licked the spoon after each mouthful, and when nothing remained but the meat, cast a sidelong glance at the old man, and felt envy. With a sigh, he began the meat, trying to make it last as long as possible. But his efforts were in vain; the meat vanished speedily. There remained only the bread. Bread without condiment is tasteless food, but there was no remedy; after weighing the problem he ate the bread also. And just as he had finished it the nurse arrived with two more bowls. This time the bowls contained roast beef and potatoes.

"Where is your bread?" she asked. Pashka did not answer, but distended his cheeks and puffed out the air.

"You've gobbled it up?" said the nurse reproachfully. "What will you eat your meat with?" She left him, and returned with more bread. Never in his life had Pashka eaten roast beef, and, trying it now, he found it very tasty. But it disappeared in a few seconds; and again only the bread was left, a bigger slice than the first. The old man, having finished his dinner, hid his bread in a drawer; and Pashka resolved to do the same, but after a moment's hesitation, he ate it up.

After dinner he set out to explore. In the next ward he found four men, in addition to those he had seen from his bed. Only one drew his attention. This was a tall, skeleton peasant, morose and hairy-faced, who sat on his bed, shook his head incessantly, and waved his arms pendulum-wise. Pashka could not tear his eyes away. At first the peasant's measured pendulum movements seemed droll, and made for the amusement of onlookers; but when Pashka looked at the peasant's face, he understood that this meant intolerable pain, and he felt sorry. In the third ward were two men with dark-red faces—red as if plastered with clay. They sat up motionless in bed, and, with their strange faces and nearly hidden features, resembled heathen gods.

"Auntie, why are they like that?" he asked the nurse.

"They are small-pox patients, laddie."

When Pashka returned to his own room he sat on his bed, and waited for the doctor to come and catch thrushes or drive to the fair. But the doctor tarried. At the door of the next ward the *feldscher* stood for a moment. He bent over the patient with the icebag, and cried—

"Mikhailo!"

But sleeping Mikhailo did not hear. The *feldscher* waved his hand, and went away. While waiting for the doctor, Pashka looked at his neighbour. The old man continued to cough, and spit into the bowl, and his cough was drawn-out and wheezy. But one thing pleased Pashka intensely. When the old man, having coughed, inhaled a breath, something whistled in his chest, and sang in different notes.

"Grandfather, what is that whistling in your inside?" asked Pashka.

The old man did not answer. Pashka waited a minute, and began again.

"Grandfather, where is the fox?"

"What fox?"

"The live one."

"Where should it be? In the wood, of course."

The hours slipped by, but no doctor came. At last the nurse brought Pashka's tea, and scolded him for having eaten the bread; the *feldscher* returned and tried to waken Mikhailo; the lamps were lighted; but still no doctor. It was already too late to drive to the fair or catch thrushes. Pashka stretched himself on his bed and began to think. He thought of the doctor's promised sugar-candy, of his mother's face and voice, of the darkness in the cabin at home, of querulous Yegorovna. And he suddenly felt tedium and grief. But remembering that his mother would come in the morning, he smiled, and fell asleep.

He was awakened by a noise. Men walked in the adjoining ward and spoke in whispers. The dim gleam of nightlights and lamps showed three figures moving near Mikhailo's bed.

"Shall we take him on the mattress, or as he is?" asked one.

"As he is. There's no room for the mattress. *Akh*, he's dead at a bad hour, heaven rest his soul!"

Then—one of the figures taking Mikhailo's shoulders, another his feet—they lifted him and the folds of his dressing-gown hung limply in the air. The third—it was the woman-like peasant—crossed himself; and all three, shuffling their feet, tripping in the folds of the dressing-gown, went out of the ward.

The sleeping man's chest whistled. and sang in different notes. Pashka heard it, looked in fright at the black windows, and jumped out of bed in panic.

"Mother!" he screamed.

And, without awaiting an answer, he rushed into the adjoining ward. The lamps and nightlights barely banished the gloom; the patients, agitated by Mikhailo's death, were sitting up in their beds. Grim, dishevelled, haunted by shades, they looked like giants; they seemed to increase in size; and far away in a dark corner sat a peasant nodding his head and swinging his pendulous hands. Without seeing the door, Pashka tore through the small-pox ward into the corridor, thence into an endless chamber full of long-haired monsters with ancient faces. He flew through the women's ward, again reached the corridor, recognised the balustrade, and rushed downstairs. And there, finding himself in the waiting-room where he had sat that morning, he looked wildly for the door.

The latch rattled, a cold wind blew, and Pashka, stumbling, sped into the yard, in his head a single thought: to flee, to flee! He did not know the road, but felt that it was enough to run without cease and that he would soon be at home with his mother. The moon shone through the clouds of an overcast sky. Pashka ran straight ahead, dashed round a shed into the shrubbery, stood a second in doubt, then rushed back to the hospital and ran around it. But there he stopped in indecision, for suddenly before his eyes rose the white crosses of a graveyard.

"Mother!" he screamed, and turned back again.

And at last, as he dashed past the black, menacing building he saw a lighted window.

In the darkness, the bright red patch breathed terror. But Pashka, mad with panic, unknowing whither to flee, turned towards it with relief. Beside the window were steps and a hall door with a white notice-board. Pashka rushed up the steps, and looked through the window. A sharp, breathless joy suddenly seized him. For there in the window at a table sat the merry, talkative doctor with a book in his hands. Pashka laughed with joy; he tried to cry out; but some irresistible force suppressed his breath, and struck him on the legs, and he staggered and fell senseless on the steps.

When he came to himself it was quite light; and the singsong voice that had promised the fair, the thrushes, and the live fox whispered in his ear—

"You're a donkey, Pashka! Now aren't you a donkey? You ought to be whipped. . . ."

VIEROCHKA

IVAN ALEXEYEVICH OGNIOV well remembers the August evening when he opened noisily the glazed hall door and went out on to the terrace. He wore a light cloak and a wide-brimmed straw hat—the very hat which now, beside his top-boots, lies in the dust underneath his bed. He remembers that he carried a heavy package of books and manuscripts, and that in his free hand was a stout stick.

In the doorway, holding up a lamp, stood his host, Kuznetzov, aged and bald-headed, with his long grey beard, and his cotton jacket, white as snow. And Kuznetzov smiled benevolently and nodded his head.

"Good-bye, old friend!" cried Ogniov.

Kuznetzov laid the lamp on the hall table, and followed Ogniov to the terrace. The narrow shadows of the two men swept down the steps, and, crossing the flower-beds, swayed, and came to a stop with the heads silhouetted against the lime-trees.

"Good-bye, and yet once more, thank you, old friend," said Ogniov. "Thanks for your heartiness, your kindness, your love. . . . Never . . . never in my whole life shall I forget your goodness. . . . You have been so kind . . . and your daughter as been so kind . . . all of you have been so kind, so gay, so hearty. . . . So good, indeed, that I cannot express my gratitude."

Under stress of feeling, under influence of the parting glass, Ogniov's voice sounded like a seminarist's, and his feeling showed not only in his words but in the nervous twitching of eyes and shoulders. And Kuznetzov, touched also by emotion and wine, bent over the young man and kissed him.

"I have grown as used to you as if I were your dog," continued Ogniov. "I have been with you day after day. I have spent the night at your house a dozen times, and drunk so much of your liqueurs that it frightens me to think of it. . . . But, most of all, Gavriil Petrovich, I thank you for your co-operation and help. Without you, I should have been worrying over my statistics till October. But I will put in my preface: 'It is my duty to express to M. Kuznetzov, President of the N. District Zemstvo Executive, my gratitude for his kind assistance.' Statistics have a brilliant future! Give my deepest regards to Vera Gavriilovna! And tell the doctors, the two magistrates, and your secretary that I shall never forget their kindness. . . . And now, old friend, let us embrace and kiss for the last time!"

Ogniov again kissed the old man. When he reached the last step, he turned his head and said—

"I wonder shall we ever meet again."

"God knows," answered Kuznetzov. "Probably never."

"I fear so. Nothing will lure you to Petersburg, and it is not likely that I shall ever return to these parts. Good-bye!"

"But leave your books," called Kuznetzov after him. "Why carry such a weight? My man will bring them to-morrow."

But Ogniov, who had not heard him, walked quickly away. Warmed with wine, his heart was full at the same time of sorrow and joy. He walked forward reflecting how often in life we meet such kindly men and women, how sad it is that they leave but memories behind. It is as on a journey. The traveller sees on the flat horizon the outline of a crane; the weak wind bears its plaintive cry; yet in a moment it is gone; and strain his eyes as he may towards the blue distance, he sees no bird, and hears no sound. So in the affairs of men, faces and voices tremble a moment before us, and slip away into the gone-before, leaving behind them nothing but the vain records of memory. Having been every day at hearty Kuznetzov's house since he arrived that spring at N., Ogniov had come to know and love as kinsmen the old man, his daughter, their servants. He knew every spot in the old house, the cosy terrace, the turns in the garden paths, the trees outlined against garden and bathing-box. And now in a few seconds when he had passed the wicket-gate, all these would be memories, void for evermore of real significance. A year—two years—would pass, and all these kindly images, dulled beyond restoring, would recur only in memory as the shapeless impressions of a dream.

"In life," thought Ogniov, as he approached the gate, "there is nothing better than men. Nothing!"

It was warm and still. The whole world smelt of heliotropes, mignonette, and tobacco-plants which had not yet shed their blooms Around shrubs and tree-trunks flowed a sea of thin, moonlight-soaked mist; and—what long remained in Ogniov's memory—wisps of vapour, white as ghosts, floated with motion imperceptibly slow across the garden path. Near the moon, shining high in heaven, swam transparent patches of cloud. The whole world, it seemed, was built of coal-black shadows and wandering wisps of white; and, to Ogniov, it seemed as if he were looking not at Nature, but at a decorated scene, as if clumsy pyrotechnists, illuminating the garden with white Bengal fire, had flooded the air with a sea of snowy smoke.

As Ogniov approached the wicket-gate a black shadow moved from the low palisade and came to meet him.

"Vera Gavriilovna," he exclaimed joyfully. "You here! After I had looked for you everywhere to say good-bye! . . . Good-bye, I am going."

"So early—it is barely eleven o'clock."

"But late for me. I have a five-verst walk, and I must pack up to-night. I leave early to-morrow. . . ."

Before Ogniov stood Kuznetzov's daughter, twenty-one-year-old Vera, whom he had seen so often, pensive and carelessly-dressed and interesting. Day-dreaming girls who spend whole days lying down in desultory reading, who suffer from tedium and melancholy, usually dress without care. But if Nature has given them taste and the instinct of beauty, this negligence in dress has often a charm of its own. And, indeed, Ogniov, recalling the vision of pretty Vera, cannot imagine her without a loose jacket, hanging in folds away from her waist, without untidy curls on her forehead, without the red, shaggy-tasselled shawl which all day long lay in the hall among the men's caps, or on the chest in the dining-room, where the old cat used it unceremoniously as bed. The shawl and the creased jacket seemed to express the easy-going indolence of a sedentary life. But perhaps it was because Ogniov liked Vera, that every button and fold exhaled to him goodness and poetry, something foreign to women insincere, void of the instinct of beauty, and cold. . . . And Vera, too, had a good figure, regular features, and pretty wavy hair. To Ogniov, who knew few women, she seemed beautiful.

"I am going away," he said again, bidding her good-bye at the wicket-gate. "Think well of me! And thanks for everything!"

And again twitching his shoulders, and speaking in the sing-song seminarist's voice which he had used to the old man, he thanked Vera for her hospitality, her kindness, her heartiness.

"I wrote about you to my mother in every letter," he said. "If all men were like you and your father, life on earth would be paradise. Every one in your house is the same. So simple, so hearty, so sincere. . . ."

"Where are you going?"

"First to my mother, in Oriol. I shall spend two days there. Then to St. Petersburg to work."

"And then?"

"Then? I shall work all winter, and in spring go somewhere in the country to collect material. Well . . . be happy, live a hundred years, and think well of me! This is the last time we meet."

Ogniov bowed his head and kissed Vierochka's hand, then in silent confusion straightened his cloak, rearranged his package of books, and said—

"What a thick mist to-night!"

"Yes. Have you not forgotten anything?"

"Nothing . . . I think."

For a moment Ogniov stood silently. Then he turned awkwardly to the gate and went out of the garden.

"Wait! Let me go with you as far as the wood," said Vera, running after him.

They followed the road. Trees no longer obscured the view, and they could see the sky, and the country far ahead. Through breaks in the veil of semi-transparent smoke, the world exposed its fairness; the white mist lay unevenly around bushes and hayricks, or wandered in tiny cloudlets, clinging to the surface as if not to cut off the view. The road could be seen all the way to the wood, and in the ditches beside it rose little bushes which trapped and hindered the vagabond mist wisps. Half a verst away rose a dark belt of forest.

"Why has she come? I shall have to see her home," Ogniov asked himself. But looking at Vera's profile, he smiled kindly, and said—

"I hate going away in weather like this. This evening is quite romantic, what with the moonlight, the silence . . . and all the honours! Do you know what, Vera Gavriilovna? I am now twenty-nine years old, yet have never had a single romance! In all my life so far, not one! So of trysts, paths of sighs, and kisses, I know only by hearsay. It is abnormal. Sitting in my own room in town, I never notice the void. But here in the open air I somehow feel it . . . strongly . . . it is almost annoying."

"But what is the cause?"

"I can't say. Perhaps it is because so far I have never

had time, perhaps simply because I have never yet met a woman who . But I have few friends, and seldom go anywhere."

They walked three hundred yards in silence. As Ogniov looked at Vera's shawl and uncovered head, he recalled the past spring and summer days, when far from his grey St. Petersburg rooms, caressed by kindly Nature and by kindly friends, pursuing his much-loved work, he had seen slip by, uncounted, sunset after dawn, day after day, nor noticed how, foreshadowing summer's end, the nightingale first, the quail, and then the corncrake ceased their songs. Time had passed unseen; and that, he supposed, meant that life had spun out pleasantly and without jar. He recalled how at the end of April he had arrived at N., a poor man, unused to society; and expected nothing but tedium, solitude, and contempt for statistics—which in his opinion took a high place among the useful sciences. He remembered the April evening of his arrival at the inn of Old-Believer Riabukhin, where for twenty kopecks a day he was given a bright, clean room, with only one restriction, that he should smoke out of doors. He remembered how he had rested a few hours, and, asking for the address of the President of the Zemstvo Executive, had set out on foot to Gavriil Petrovich's house; how he had tramped through four versts of rich meadows and young plantations; how high under a veil of cloud trembled a lark, filling the world with silver sounds, while above the green pastures, with a stolid, pompous flapping of wings, the rooks flew up and down.

"Is it possible?" Ogniov asked himself, "that they breathe this air every day, or is it perfumed only this evening in honour of me?"

He remembered how, expecting a dry, business-like reception, he had entered Kuznetzov's study timidly, with averted face, and shyly stroked his beard. And how the old man contracted his brows, and failed utterly to understand what this young man with his statistics wanted with the Zemstvo

Executive. But as he began to understand what statistics really mean, and how they are collected, Gavriil Petrovich woke up, smiled, and with infantile curiosity began to examine his visitor's note-books. . . . And on the evening of the same day, Ogniov sat at Kuznetzov's supper-table, grew tipsy on strong liqueurs, and, watching the placid faces and lazy gestures of his new acquaintances, felt spreading through his whole body that sweet, drowsy indolence of one who, wanting to continue his sleep, stretches himself and smiles. And his new-found friends looked at him lovingly, asked were his father and mother alive, how much he earned a month, and whether he often went to the theatre.

Ogniov recalled the long drives through the cantons, the picnics, the fishing parties, the trip to the convent when the Mother Superior presented each visitor with a bead-purse; he recalled the endless, heated, truly Russian arguments in which the disputants, banging their fists on the table, misunderstood and interrupted without knowing what they meant to say, wandered from the subject, and after arguing fiercely a couple of hours, exclaimed with a laugh, "The devil knows what this dispute is about. We began about health, and are now arguing about rest in the grave!"

"Do you remember when you and I rode to Shestovo with the doctor?" asked Ogniov as they drew near to the wood. "We met a lunatic. I gave him five kopecks, and he crossed himself thrice, and threw the money in my face. What hosts of impressions I carry away—if fused in a compact mass, I should have a big ingot of gold! I never understood why clever, sensitive men crowd into big cities instead of living in the country. Is there more space and truth on the Nevsky, and in the big damp houses? My house, for instance, which is packed from top to bottom with artists, students, and journalists, always seems to me to embody an absurd prejudice."

Some twenty paces from the wood the road crossed a narrow bridge with posts at the corners. During their spring walks, this bridge was a stopping place for the Kuznetzovs and their visitors. Thence they could draw echoes from the wood, and watch the road as it vanished in a black drive.

"We are at the bridge," said Ogniov. "You must return."

Vera stopped, and drew a deep breath.

"Let us sit down for a minute," she said, seating herself on a pillar. "When we say good-bye to friends we always sit down here."

Ogniov sat beside her on his parcel of books, and continued to speak. Vera breathed heavily, and looked straight into the distance, so that he could not see her face.

"Perhaps some day, in ten years' time, we'll meet somewhere again," he said. "Things will be different. You will be the honoured mother of a family, and I the author of a respectable, useless book of statistics, fat as forty albums put together. . . . To-night, the present counts, it absorbs and agitates us. But ten years hence we shall remember neither the date nor the month, nor even the year, when we sat on this bridge together for the last time. You, of course, will be changed. You will change."

"What?"

"I ask you just now. . . ."

"I did not hear."

Only now did Ogniov notice the change that had come over Vera. She was pale and breathless; her hands and lips trembled; and instead of the usual single lock of hair falling on her forehead, there were two. She did her best to mask her agitation and avoid looking him in the face; and to help in this, she first straightened her collar as if it were cutting her neck, and then drew the red shawl from one side to the other.

"You are cold, I am afraid," began Ogniov. "You must not sit in the mist. Let me see you home."

Vera did not answer.

"What is the matter?" resumed Ogniov. "You do not answer my questions. You are ill?"

Vera pressed her hand firmly to her cheek, and suddenly drew it away.

"It is too awful," she whispered, with a look of intense agony. "Too awful!"

"What is too awful?" asked Ogniov, shrugging his shoulders, and making no effort to conceal his surprise. "What is the matter?"

Still breathing heavily and twitching her shoulders, Vera turned away from him, and after looking a moment at the sky, began—

"I have to speak to you, Ivan Alekseyevich. . . ."

"I am listening."

"I know it will seem strange to you . . . you will be astonished, but I do not care. . . ."

Ogniov again shrugged his shoulders and prepared to listen.

"It is this . . . ," began Vera, averting her eyes, and twirling the shawl-tassel in her fingers. "You see, this is . . . that is what I wanted to say. . . . It will seem absurd to you . . . and stupid . . . but I cannot bear it!"

Vera's words, half smothered in incoherent stammerings, were suddenly interrupted by tears. She hid her face in the shawl, and wept bitterly. Ogniov, confused and stupefied, coughed, and, having no idea what to say or do, looked helplessly around. He was unused to tears, and Vera's breakdown seemed to make his own eyes water.

"Come, come!" he stammered helplessly. "Vera Gavriilovna? What does this mean? Are you ill? Some one has annoyed you? Tell me what it is . . . and perhaps I can help you."

And when, in a last attempt to console her, he drew her hands cautiously from her face, she smiled at him through her tears, and said—

"I . . . I love you!"

The words, simple and ordinary, were spoken in a simple

and ordinary voice. But Ogniov, covered with intense confusion, turned his face away.

His confusion was followed by fright. The atmosphere of mournfulness, warmth, and sentiment inspired by liqueurs and leave-takings, suddenly made way for a sharp, unpleasant feeling of awkwardness. Feeling that his whole soul had been turned inside out, he looked shyly at Vera; and she, having avowed her love, and cast for ever away her woman's enhancing inaccessibility, seemed smaller, simpler, meaner.

"What does it all mean?" he asked himself in terror. "And then . . . do I love her . or not?—that is the problem."

But she, now that the hardest, painfulest part was ended, breathed easily and freely. She rose from her seat, and, looking straight into Ogniov's eyes, spoke quickly, warmly, without constraint.

Those who have been overtaken by sudden terror seldom remember details, and Ogniov to-day recalls not one of Vera's words. He remembers only their import and the emotions they brought forth. He remembers her voice, which seemed to come from a strangled throat, a voice hoarse with emotion, and the magic passion and harmony in its intonations. Crying, smiling, scattering tear-drops from her eyes, she confessed that since the first days of their friendship she had been won by his originality, his intellect, his kind, clever eyes, and by the aims and aspirations of his life. That she loved him devoutly, passionately, madly; that in summer when she went from the garden into the house, and saw his coat in the hall, or heard his voice, her heart thrilled with a presage of intense joy; that his most trivial jokes had made her laugh; that every figure in his note-books exhaled to her wisdom and majesty; that even his cane standing in the hall had seemed to her lovelier than the trees

The wood, the patches of mist, even the black roadside ditches were charmed, it seemed, as they listened. But Ogniov's heart felt only estrangement and pain. Avowing her love, Vera was entrancingly fair; her words were noble and impassioned. But Ogniov felt not the pleasure or vital joy which he himself yearned for, but only sympathy with Vera, and pain that a fellow-creature should suffer so for his sake. Heaven only knows why it was so! But whether the cause was book-learned reason, or merely that impregnable objectivity which forbids some men to live as men, the ecstasy and passion of Vera seemed to him affected and unreal. Yet even while he felt this, something whispered that, in the light of Nature and personal happiness, that which he listened to then was a thousand times more vital than all his books, his statistics, his eternal verities. And he was angry, and reproached himself, though he had no idea wherein he was at fault.

What increased his confusion was that he knew he must reply. An answer was inevitable. To say to Vera plainly "I do not love you!" he had not the strength. But he could not say "I do," for with all his searchings he could not find in his heart a single spark.

And he listened silently while she said that she could know no greater happiness than to see him, to follow him, to go with him wheresoever he might go, to be his wife and helper . . . and that if he abandoned her she would die of grief.

"I cannot stay here," she exclaimed, wringing her hands. "I have come to detest this house, and this wood, and this air. I am tired of this changeless restfulness and aimless life; I can stand no longer our colourless, pale people, as like one another as two drops of water! They are genial and kind . . . because they are contented, because they have never suffered and never struggled. But I can stand it no more. . . . I want to go to the big grey houses, where people suffer, embittered by labour and need. . . ."

And all this seemed to Ogniov affected and unreal. When Vera ceased to speak he was still without an answer. But silence was impossible, and he stammered out—

"I . . . Vera Gavriilovna . . . I am very grateful to you, although I feel that I deserve no such . . . such feelings. In the second place, as an honest man, I must say that . . . happiness is based on mutuality . . . that is, when both parties . . . when they love equally."

Ogniov suddenly felt ashamed of his stammering speech, and was silent. He felt that his expression was guilty, stupid, and dull, and that his face was strained and drawn out. And Vera, it seemed, could read the truth in his looks, for she paled, looked at him with terror, and averted her eyes.

"You will forgive me," stammered Ogniov, feeling the silence past bearing. "I respect you so very, very much that . . . that I am sorry . . ."

Vera suddenly turned away, and walked rapidly towards the house. Ogniov followed her.

"No, there is no need!" she said, waving her hand. "Do not come! I will go alone. . . ."

"But still . . . I must see you home."

All that Ogniov had said, even his last words, seemed to him flat and hateful. The feeling increased with each step. He raged at himself and, clenching his fists, cursed his coldness and awkwardness with women. In a last vain effort to stir his own feelings he looked at Vera's pretty figure, at her hair, at the imprints of her little feet on the dusty road. He remembered her words and her tears. But all this filled him only with pain, and left his feelings dead.

"Yes. . . . A man cannot force himself to love!" he reasoned, and at the same time thought, "When shall I ever love except by force? I am nearly thirty. Better than Vierochka among women I have never met . . . and never shall meet. Oh, accursed old age! Old age at thirty!"

Vera walked before him, each moment quickening her step. Her face was bowed to the ground, and she did not look round once. It seemed to Ogniov that she had suddenly grown slighter and that her shoulders were narrower.

"I can imagine her feelings," he said to himself. "Shame

. . . and such pain as to make her wish for death! . . . And in her words there was life and poetry, and meaning enough to have melted a stone! But I . . . I am senseless and blind."

"Listen, Vera Gavriilovna." This cry burst from him against his will. "You must not think that I . . . that I . . ."

Ogniov hesitated and said nothing more. At the wicket-gate Vera turned, looked at him for an instant, and, wrapping her shawl tightly around her shoulders, walked quickly up the path.

Ogniov remained alone. He turned back to the wood, and walked slowly, stopping now and then and looking towards the gate. His movements expressed doubt of himself. He searched the road for the imprints of Vierochka's feet. He refused to credit that one whom he liked so much had avowed to him her love, and that he had awkwardly, boorishly scorned her. For the first time in life he realised how little one's actions depend from mere goodwill; and he felt as feels every honourable, kindly man who, despite his intentions, has caused his nearest and dearest unmeant and unmerited suffering.

His conscience stung him. When Vierochka vanished in the garden he felt that he had lost something very dear which he would never find again. With Vera, it seemed to him, a part of his youth had passed away, and he knew that the precious moments he had let slip away without profit would never return.

When he reached the bridge he stopped in thought, and sought the cause of his unnatural coldness. That it lay not outside himself, but within, he saw clearly. And he frankly confessed that this was not the rational calmness boasted by clever men, not the coldness of inflated egoism, but simply impotence of soul, dull insensibility to all that is beautiful, old age before its day—the fruit, perhaps, of his training, his grim struggle for bread, his friendless, bachelor life.

He walked slowly, as if against his own will, from the bridge to the wood. There where on a pall of impenetrable black the moonlight shone in jagged patches he remained alone with his thoughts; and he passionately longed to regain all that he had lost.

And Ogniov remembers that he returned to the house. Goading himself forward with memories of what had passed, straining his imagination to paint Vera's face, he walked quickly as far as the garden. From road and garden the mist had melted away, and a bright, newly washed moon looked down from an unflecked sky; the east alone frowned with clouds. Ogniov remembers his cautious steps, the black windows, the drowsy scent of heliotropes and mignonette. He remembers how old friend Karpo, wagging genially his tail, came up and snuffed at his hand. But no other living thing did he see. He remembers how he walked twice around the house, stood awhile before the black window of Vera's room; and abandoning his quest with a sigh returned to the road.

An hour later he was back in town; and, weary, broken, leaning his body and hot face against the gate, knocked at the inn. In the distance barked a sleepy dog; and the night watchman at the church beat an iron shield.

"Still gadding about at night!" grumbled the Old-Believer, as in a long, woman's night-dress he opened the door. "What do you gain by it? It would be better for you if you stayed at home and prayed to God!"

When he entered his room Ogniov threw himself upon the bed, and long gazed steadily at the fire. At last he rose, shook his head, and began to pack his trunk.

THE STEPPE

I

Early one July morning a springless bone-shaking britchka —one of those antediluvian ones in which only commercial travellers, drovers, and the poorer clergy drive nowadays in Russia, clattered out of N———, the chief town of the government of Z———, on to the country road. The vehicle screeched and uttered a loud scream at the slightest movement; the bucket fastened on behind sullenly chimed in. By these sounds, apart from its woefully torn leather-lining dangling on the inside of its peeling interior, you might arrive at a conclusion as to its antiquity and readiness to fall to pieces.

In the vehicle sat two inhabitants of N———: the trader, Ivan Ivanitch Kuzmitchov, a clean-shaven man wearing spectacles and a straw hat, thereby resembling some functionary rather than a tradesman, and Father Christopher Siriski, prior of the Church of St. Nicholas in N———, a long-haired little old man in a grey linen caftan, a wide-brimmed black hat, and an embroidered coloured belt. The first mentioned was absorbed in thought, and was shaking his head to keep awake; on his face the usual stern man-of-business look was struggling with the stirred feelings of a man taking leave of his native town, and who has just had a good drink. The other was looking with admiration and moist eyes at God's earth, smiling a broad smile, so broad that it seemed as if it would reach the brim of his hat; he had a red face, and it looked as if he were cold. Both of them, Kuzmitchov and Father Christopher, were going away to sell wool. As they took leave of their homestead they ate their fill of pastry and sour-cream, and, notwithstanding the early hour, had had a drink of wine, so they were both in the best of spirits.

Besides the two above-mentioned and the coachman Deniski, who unweariedly whipped his pair of fast little bay horses, there was another passenger in the vehicle, a small boy of nine, with a sun-burnt face wet with tears. This was Egorooshka, Kuzmitchov's nephew. According to the decision of his uncle, and with the blessing of Father Christopher, he was going somewhere to school. His mother, Olga Ivanovna, the widow of a collegiate-secretary and own sister to Kuzmitchov, fond of cultured people and well-bred society, implored her brother, who was going away to sell wool, to take Egorooshka with him and place him in a Gymnasium. So now, the boy, not understanding whither and why he was going, sits on the box-seat by the side of Deniski, holding on to his elbow so as not to tumble or bounce off like a teapot down a slope. They are driving so fast that his red shirt is blown out like an inflated bladder in his back, and his new waggoner's hat, with a peacock feather in it, has slipped to the back of his head. He feels he is the unhappiest of mortals, and wants to cry.

When the vehicle passes by the gaol, Egorooshka glances at the sentinel who is slowly marching by the towering white walls, at the small barred windows, at the cross glittering on the roof, and he thinks of a week ago, when, on the feast of St. Mary of Kazan, he went with his mamma to the prison church and partook of the Sacrament. And before that, at Easter, he went to the prison with the cook Ludmilla and Deniski, and took with them "Easter cakes," eggs, pasties, and roast beef; the prisoners thanked them and crossed themselves, and one of them made a present to Egorooshka of a tin shirt-button which he himself had made.

The boy observed all the well-known spots, but that hateful britchka fled past them, leaving them all behind. Beyond the gaol flashed by the black besmoked forge; and next, the snug green cemetery surrounded by a cobblestone wall. Behind the wall of the cemetery peeped the white crosses and monuments, which among the verdure of the cherry trees, and from a distance, look like white blots. He remembered when the cheery trees are in flower that these white blots blend with the cherry blossom, and it all looks like a sea of foam; and when the cherries are ripe, the white monuments and crosses are strewn with purple blood-like drops. Behind that wall and under the cherry trees sleep day and night Egorooshka's father and grandmother Zinaida Danilovna. When grandmother died, they laid her in a long narrow coffin, and placed on her eyes—because they would not close—two five-kopeck pieces. She was cheerful till the hour of her death, and always brought soft cracknels powdered with poppy from market, and now she is sleeping, sleeping. . . .

And beyond the cemetery came the smoky brick-kilns. Thick black clouds of curling smoke were issuing from beneath the long, low rush-covered roofs which were hardly above the ground, and surged slowly upwards. Above the kilns and the cemetery the sky was quite dark, and large shadows cast by the clouds of smoke crept across the field and over the road. People and horses covered in red dust were moving about in the smoke around the roof.

The town came to an end beyond the kilns, then began the open country. Egorooshka took a last look at the town, pressed his face against Deniski's elbow, and sobbed bitterly.

"That's right—not done bellowing yet!" said Kuzmitchov. "The pet again has dissolved into tears! If you don't want to go, then remain behind. Nobody is forcing you!"

"Nitchevo, never mind, sonny Egor, never mind," mumbled the voluble Father Christopher. "Never mind, sonny. . . . Say a prayer to God. . . . You are not going towards evil, but towards good. Learning, they say, is light, and ignorance is darkness—and that is so."

"Do you want to go back?" Kuzmitchov asked.

"I . . . I . . . want to," sobbed Egorooshka.

"And if you did return? It would be no use—it's going

seven versts for a spoonful of jelly (it will not requite the cost)."

"Never mind, never mind, sonny," continued Father Christopher. "Say a prayer to God. Why, Lomonossov went with fishermen, and he became a man known all over Europe. Intelligence coupled with faith produces results well-pleasing to God. What we do say in our prayers? Let us praise our Creator, be a solace to our parents, be of use to our Church and Country. . . . That is so."

"Results may vary," said Kuzmitchov, smoking a cheap cigar. "Some learn for twenty years without doing any good."

"That may happen."

"To some learning is an advantage, to others only a muddle. My sister is a woman of not much understanding; she does everything for gentility, and wants Egor to be a scholar, and does not see that I, with my business, might make Egor happy for life. I assure you if people are all going to be well born and learned, then no one will attend to trade or sow corn. They will all die of hunger."

"And if everyone attended to trade and sowing corn, there would be no one to learn."

Thinking they had both said something quite convincing and weighty, Kuzmitchov and Father Christopher each put on a serious face and coughed simultaneously. Deniski, listening to their conversation and not understanding it, shook his head, and, straightening himself, whipped both the bays. After that there was a silence.

Meanwhile, a broad limitless plain, intercepted by a chain of hills, unrolled before the eyes of the wayfarers. These hills peep and rise one behind the other until they attain an elevation which, stretching to the right of the road as far as the horizon, flows into the lilac atmosphere. You go on and on, and never can see where this horizon begins or where it ends.

The sun has already made its appearance, behind the town, and slowly, without any fuss, has begun its day's work. At first, a long way ahead, where the sky is divided from the earth near the tumuli and the windmill—which from a distance looks like a little dwarf waving his arms—a broad bright yellow streak of light crept across the earth; in a few moments the light of that streak had come a little nearer, had crept to the right and acquired possession of the hills. Something warm touched Egorooshka's back, a streak of light had come stealthily up behind, slipped past the vehicle and the horses, rose to meet the other streak, and suddenly all the wide steppe cast aside the penumbra of dawn, smiled, and began to sparkle with dew. The reaped corn, the high grass, the wart-wort, the wild hemp, all a rusty brown and half dead from the summer heat, now bathed in dew and caressed by the sun, revived, ready to flower again. An arctic petrel flew across the road with a cheerful cry, the Siberian marmots called to each other in the grass; far away to the left somewhere, a peewit wailed; a covey of partridges, startled by the britchka, rose up, and with their soft "trrr" flew away to the hills; grasshoppers, crickets, field-mice and mole-rats struck up their squeaking monotonous music in the grass.

But after a short lapse of time the dew evaporated, the air lost its freshness and the misguided steppe reassumed its languishing July appearance. The grass drooped, and the sounds of life died away. The brown-green, sunburned hills, the lilac distance with its tints as restful as shade, the plain with its misty limits, and the inverted-looking sky—for in the steppes, where there are no forests or high mountains, the sky seems fearfully deep and pellucid—at this moment appeared limitless and torpid with grief.

How suffocating and depressing! The britchka speeds along, and Egorooshka sees all the while the same thing: sky, plain, hills. The sounds in the grass have subsided, the petrel has flown away, there are no partridges to be seen. Tired of doing nothing, the rooks fly over the withered grass;

they all resemble one another, and render the steppe even more uniform.

A kite with a flowing movement of his wings floats in the air, then suddenly stops, as if it recollected the nuisance of existing, then, shaking his wings, darts off like an arrow across the steppe, and no one knows why he is flying, nor what he wants. In the distance the windmill is waving its fans.

To make a little variety, a white bit of bark or cobblestone gleams in the long grass; or a grey stone-pile or a dried white-willow, with a blue crow sitting in its topmost branch. up-rises for a minute: a marmot runs across the road; then once more you settle down to the long steppe-grass, hills and rooks. But now, thank God, a cart laden with sheaves of corn is coming towards them. A girl is lying on the top of the load. Sleepy and overcome by the heat, she just raises her head to look at the travellers. Deniski gaped at her, the horses put out their heads towards the corn, the britchka gave a piercing scream as it saluted the cart, and a shower of spiky ears of corn settle wreathlike round the brim of Father Christopher's black hat.

"Don't run over people, fat-face!" Deniski calls to her. "What's the matter with your face, has a bee stung you?"

The girl smiles sleepily, moves her lips, and lies down again. . . . And now, behind a hill, a solitary poplar appears; who put it there, and why it is there, God alone knows! One can hardly take one's eye off its symmetrical form and green attire. Is this handsome stripling happy? In summer the heat, in winter the cold and the blizzards, in the autumn the awful nights when there is only fog to be seen and there is no sound except that of the wanton angry raging wind, and worst of all, being alone, alone, all one's life. . . . Beyond the poplar is a bright yellow carpet. Great stretches of wheat reach from the summit of the hills to the edge of the road; on the hillocks the wheat is cut and gathered into sheaves, at their base the corn is still standing. . . . There are six mowers in a line swinging their scythes: the scythes flash brightly and rhythmically, and all together make the same sound: "vjjji, vjjji." From the way the women tie up the sheaves, from the faces of the mowers, by the glint on the scythes, it is not difficult to see how oppressive and suffocating the heat is. A black dog with his tongue hanging out runs from the mowers towards the britchka, no doubt with the intention of barking, but stops halfway and looks with indifference at Deniski threatening him with the whip; it's too hot to bark! One woman, standing up and holding her aching back with both hands, follows with her eyes Egorooshka's red fustian shirt. Is it that the colour pleases her, or is she thinking of her own children? Anyhow she stands a long time looking at the wayfarers without moving.

And now the wheat has vanished, the burnt expanse of plain appears again, the scorched hillocks, the blazing sky, and once more the kite is floating in the air. Far away, as before, the windmill is waving its fans, and looks like a little dwarf waving its arms. It is tiresome to look at, for it seems as if one would never reach it, and as if it were running away from the vehicle.

Father Christopher and Kuzmitchov remain silent, Deniski whipped the bays and shouted, Egorooshka was no longer crying, and looked at the landscape with indifference—the heat and the tediousness of the steppe had exhausted him. It seemed to him that they had been bumping and driving, and that the sun had been baking his back, for a very long while. They had not gone ten versts yet, and he was already thinking: "It is time we rested!" The look of benevolence on his uncle's face gradually wore off, leaving only the stern business look; this stern look on his clean-shaven gaunt face, particularly in spectacles and when his nose and temples were covered in dust, added something implacable and inquisitorial to his expression. Father Christopher continued to look with admiration at God's world, and smiled: he was silently thinking of something innocent and pleasant, and a kind benign smile coagulated on his face; it seemed also as if the innocent and pleasant thought had coagulated in his brain from the heat.

"Well, Deniski, do you think we shall overtake the train of waggons?" Kuzmitchov asked.

Deniski looked at the sky, sat up, whipped the horses, and subsequently answered:

"At night-fall, God grant it, we may overtake them. . . ."

Then there was a sound of dogs barking, and six enormous sheep-dogs of the steppes sprang out as from an ambush, and rushed with savage howlings at the vehicle They were all six of them unusually vicious, with very hairy pointed muzzles and wrathful red eyes. They surrounded the britchka, and with much jealous emulating of each other yelled hoarsely; their hatred was so great that it looked as if they were prepared to tear to pieces horses, vehicle, and people. Deniski, who loved scolding and whipping, rejoiced at this opportunity, so, with a malevolent expression on his face, he leant over and lashed at the dogs. The dogs' howling grew hoarser and more furious, and the horses bolted. Egorooshka, hardly able to maintain himself on his seat, seeing the eyes and teeth of these dogs, understood that if he fell off he would be torn to bits in a moment, but he felt no fear and looked just as malignant as Deniski, and was only sorry that he, too, had not a whip in his hands.

The britchka drew alongside a flock of sheep.

"Stop!" cried Kuzmitchov. "Wait! Tprrri!"

Deniski, lying right back, reined in the horses, and the vehicle came to a standstill.

"Come here!" Kuzmitchov called to the shepherd. "Stop those damned dogs!"

The old shepherd, ragged and barefooted, wearing a thick cap, with a dirty sack slung over his hip, and holding in his hand a staff with a crook to it—quite an Old Testament figure—quieted the dogs, and, removing his cap from his head, walked up to the britchka. A similar Old Testament figure stood without moving at the side of the flock, and looked unconcernedly at the travellers.

"Whose flock is this?" asked Kuzmitchov.

"Varlamov's," loudly answered the old man.

"Varlamov's," repeated the shepherd standing at the far side of the flock.

"Oh! Did Varlamov go past here last night or not?"

"Not at all. . . . His steward went by, that's all. . . ."

"Go on."

The vehicle moved on, and the shepherds and their vicious dogs remained behind. Egorooshka involuntarily looked ahead into the lilac distance, he began to think that the windmill with its waving fans was getting nearer. It was growing larger and larger and one could get quite a precise idea of its fans: one was old and patched, the other had been recently made with new wood and looked quite polished in the sun.

The britchka went to the right, and the windmill began to move somewhat to the left; they went on and on, and it moved always to the left without disappearing from sight.

"What a splendid windmill Boltva's son put up!" Deniski remarked.

"Isn't his farm in sight?"

"It's over there, in the valley."

Soon Boltva's farm appeared in sight, and still the windmill was not left behind, but continued to watch Egorooshka, waving its polished fan. What a wizard!

II

About mid-day the britchka turned off the road to the right, went a little distance at a foot's pace, and then came to a standstill. Egorooshka heard a soft, very soothing murmur, and felt something cool and velvety on his face like some other kind of air. From a hillock, made by nature cementing some immense and monstrous stones together, ran a narrow stream of water through a pipe of hemlock, placed there by some unknown benefactor. The stream was clear, playfully splashed to the ground, glistened in the sun, and, roaring gently as if it imagined itself a strong and boisterous brook, flowed swiftly somewhere to the left. Not far from the hillock the stream crept down into a little pool; the burning rays and the parched soil thirstily drank it up and bereft it of its strength; but a little farther on it seemingly flowed into another such streamlet, for along its course, a hundred steps or so from the hillock, grew some green thick luxuriant reed-grass, out of which, when the vehicle went by, flew three snipe with a cry.

The wayfarers disposed themselves to rest by the stream and feed their horses. Kuzmitchov, Father Christopher, and Egorooshka sat on a felt mat spread in the scant shade afforded by the vehicle and the unharnessed horses, and took a little food. The innocent and pleasant thought which had coagulated from the heat in Father Christopher's brain, after he had had a drink of water and eaten a boiled egg, evinced itself outwardly. He looked fondly at Egorooshka, munched a little, and began:

"I too studied, sonny. From my earliest youth God had endowed with me sense and understanding, so that I cannot serve as an example to others, for even when I was only as old as you I cheered my parents and instructors by my intelligence. When not yet fifteen I could recite and compose Latin verses just as easily as Russian. I remember I was crosier-bearer to the Most Eminent Christopher. Once, after mass—I remember it as if it were now, it was on the names-day of the Most Pious Emperor Alexander Pavlitch, of blessed memory—he was putting off his vestments in the sanctuary; he looked kindly at me, and asked: 'Puer bone, quam appelaris?' and I answered: 'Christophorus sum,' and he: 'Ergo connominati sumus,' that is to say, 'We are name-sakes. . . .' Then he asked me in Latin 'Who are you?' and I again answered in Latin that I was the son of the Cantor Siriski of the village of Lebedinsko. Pleased with my precocity and the directness of my answers, the Most Eminent gave me his blessing and said: 'Write to your father that I will not forget him, and that I will keep my eye on you.' The archpriest and the priest who were in the sanctuary, hearing a Latin disputation, were not a little surprised, and both of them expressed their satisfaction by praising me. When I was still without a moustache, sonny, I could read Latin, Greek, French. I had learnt philosophy, mathematics, civil law, and all the sciences. God had given me a surprising good memory. If I read a thing through twice I knew it by heart. My instructors and benefactors were astonished, and prophesied that I would become the most learned of men, a luminary of the Church. I myself thought of going to Kieff to continue my studies, but my parents did not consent. 'You will be learning your whole life,' said my father, 'when shall we ever see *its* use?' On hearing such remarks I threw up my studies and took up my duties. Of course I did not become a man of learning, but, as against that, I was not undutiful to my parents; I comforted them in their old age, and buried them with honour. Obedience is more than fasting or prayers!"

"You must have forgotten all your learning now," Kuzmitchov remarked.

"How could I help forgetting it? Thank God, I have passed the eighth decade! I still remember something of philosophy and rhetoric, but languages and mathematics I have entirely forgotten."

Father Christopher screwed up his eyes, thought a little, then said in an undertone:

"What is a being? That which is self-existent and not requiring aught else for its completion."

He turned away his head, and smiled a little with emotion. "Spiritual food!" he said. "Of a truth, matter feeds the flesh and spirtual food the soul!"

"That is the lesson of lessons," sighed Kuzmitchov; "and if we don't overtake Varlamov it will be a lesson to us!"

"A man is not a needle—we shall find him! He is 'circling' somewhere in these parts."

Over the reed-grass flew the three afore-mentioned snipe, by their piping they expressed their agitation and annoyance at being driven from their stream. The horses gravely browsed and snorted; Deniski moved about near them, and, wishing to show his complete indifference towards the cucumbers, pies, and eggs which the masters were eating, was absorbed in killing the gadflies and flies which were settling on the horses' stomachs and backs. He struck apathetically at his victims, uttering some rather peculiar and spiteful sound in his throat if successful, or in the case of failure croaking with vexation and following with his eyes each lucky fly who escaped death.

"Deniski, what are you doing there? Come and eat," said Kuzmitchov with a deep sigh, meaning thereby that he had eaten enough.

Deniski shyly approached the felt mat, and chose for himself five large yellow cucumbers known as "saffronated" (he scrupled to choose smaller or fresher ones), he took two boiled eggs which were dirty and cracked, then undecidedly, as if he feared he might get a rap on his outstretched hand, touched a patty with the tips of his fingers.

"Take it, take it," Kuzmitchov hastened to reassure him.

Deniski took the patty resolutely, and, moving well away to one side, sat on the ground with his back to the britchka; immediately after was heard such a loud munching that even the horses turned round and looked suspiciously at Deniski.

Having eaten all he wanted, Kuzmitchov took some sort of a bag out of the vehicle, and said to Egorooshka:

"I am going to sleep, just you watch that no one takes this bag from under my head."

Father Christopher took off his cassock, his belt and caftan. Egorooshka, who was watching him, nearly died of surprise. He never supposed that priests wore trousers, but Father Christopher disclosed proper linen trousers in addition to his high boots; he also wore a short jacket of striped linen. Egorooshka thought in this costume, so incongruous to his position, and with his long hair and beard, that he looked very like Robinson Crusoe. Having undressed, Father Christopher and Kuzmitchov lay down in the shade of the britchka, face to face, and closed their eyes. Deniski, having finished chewing, stretched himself out in the blazing sun face upwards, and also closed his eyes.

"Just see that no one takes the horses," he said to Egorooshka, and immediately fell asleep.

Then, no more sound of voices: one heard the horses munching and snorting, and the snoring of the sleepers; somewhere quite far away one heard the cry of a peewit; and now and again was heard the piping of the three snipe who had flown back to see if the unwelcome guests had not gone; softly whirring, babbled the brook; but all these sounds did not break the silence, they did not stir the stagnant air—on the contrary, they lulled it to sleep.

Egorooshka, oppressed by the heat, which was particularly observable after eating, ran towards the reed-grass and surveyed the locality from there. He saw exactly the same as that which he had seen till noon—the plain, the hillocks, the sky, the lilac distance: the only thing was, the hillocks were nearer, and there was no windmill—it had remained far behind. Beyond the rocky hillock, in which the stream had its source, rose another hillock, smoother and wider; to it clung a little village of five or six houses. There was no life to be seen near the cottages, nor trees, nor shade, just as if the little village had been overcome by the burning rays and had pined away. As he had nothing to do, Egorooshka caught a "fiddler" in the grass, held it in the palm of his hand to his ear, and listened to it for a long time playing on its fiddle. When the music bored him, he began to chase a number of yellow butterflies fluttering about the reed-grass, and did not notice that he was approaching the vehicle again. His uncle and Father Christopher were sleeping soundly; their sleep would probably last two or three hours, till the horses were rested. How was he to kill that long time, and where was he to go to escape the heat? Rather a difficult problem. . . . Mechanically Egorooshka put his mouth to the trickle flowing from the pipe; the water was cold and smelt of hemlock; at first he drank from thirst, but afterwards immoderately, till the pungent cold in his mouth had overrun his whole body, and until his shirt was soaked. Then he walked back to the vehicle, and took a look at the sleepers. His uncle's face still wore that stern business look. Being a fanatic in his affairs, Kuzmitchov even in his sleep, or during prayers in church, when they were singing "Hail, cherubim," &c., was thinking of his business; he could not forget it for a moment, and now probably he was dreaming of bales of wool, horses and carts, prices, Varlamov And Father Christopher, a gentle heedless person, always disposed to laugh, never once in his life had understood any business which could, like a boa-constrictor, stifle his soul. All the various concerns which he had undertaken during his life-time had tempted him not so much for themselves as by reason of the fuss and the intercourse with people which necessarily follows any undertaking. As, for instance, in the present trip, it was not so much the wool, Varlamov, and prices, which interested him, as much as the long journey, the conversations *en route*, the sleeping in the shade of the vehicle, eating at irregular hours. . . . And now, judging by his face, he was dreaming undoubtedly of the Most Eminent Christopher, the Latin disputation, his popess, the puffs with sour-cream, and all that about which Kuzmitchov was unable to dream.

While Egorooshka looked at the sleeping faces he suddenly heard a low singing. Somewhere quite far away a woman was singing, but where exactly, and on which side, it would have been difficult to say. The song was tender and melancholy, more resembling weeping, scarcely audible; it sounded now to the right, now to the left, now in the air, now on the ground, just as if some unseen spirit were floating about the steppe and singing. Egorooshka looked round, and could not understand where this strange singing came from; afterwards, when he had listened attentively, he began to think that it was the grass singing. In her song without words she, half dead and passed away, plaintively and simply, was persuading someone that she was in no way to blame, that the sun had scorched her unjustly; she affirmed that she passionately desired to live, that she was still young and would be pretty if it were not for the heat and the drought; it was no one's fault, but she begged someone's forgiveness, averring it was unbearably painful, sad, and a pity for her.

Egorooshka listened a little while, then began to think that owing to the plaintive tender song the air was becoming stuffier, hotter, and stiller. So as to drown the singing he hummed, tapped with his feet, and ran back to the reed-grass. From thence he looked on all sides, and discovered what was singing. By the nearest cottage of the little village stood a woman. She wore short small-clothes, was long-footed and long-legged like a heron, and her hair was turning a little grey. From beneath her sieve some white dust lazily trailed down the hill-side. It was evident now that she it was who was singing. About two and a half yards away from her stood a little boy, hatless, and wearing only a shirt; he stood quite still as if fascinated by the song, and was gazing at something below, probably at Egorooshka's red fustian shirt.

The song ceased. Egorooshka went slowly back to the vehicle; having nothing to do, he again played with the trickle of water. The plaintive song began again; that same long-legged woman was singing in the little village on the hillock. Then suddenly Egorooshka's feeling of weariness returned; he left the pipe alone, and looked up. What he now saw was so unexpected that he was rather frightened. Above his head, on one of the large misshapen rocks, stood a small puffy-faced boy with a prominent stomach, thin little legs, and wearing nothing but a shirt; it was the same little boy who had been standing by the woman. In dumb astonishment, not unmixed with fear, as if he saw a spirit from the world beyond, he stared with wide-open mouth at Egorooshka's red fustian shirt, and at the vehicle. The colour of the shirt allured and tempted him, and the vehicle with the sleeping people beneath it aroused his curiosity. It may be that he himself was not aware how pleasant the red colour was, and it was curiosity that drew him away from the little village; very likely he was surprised now at his temerity. Egorooshka looked at him a long while, and he at Egorooshka; they both remained silent and felt a certain awkwardness. After a protracted silence, Egorooshka asked:

"What's your name?"

The cheeks of the stranger grew puffier, he pressed closer to the rock, opened his eyes very wide, made a movement of his lips, and answered in a hoarse low voice:

"Tit."

The boys said not one word more to each other. Still keeping silence and without taking his eyes off Egorooshka, the mysterious Tit drew up a leg, felt for a projection with his heel, and clambered up the rock. From thence he moved backwards, keeping his eye on Egorooshka as if he were afraid this latter might strike him in the back; he climbed over the next rock, and so on till he disappeared from sight over the summit of the hillock.

Having followed him with his eyes, Egorooshka sat down, doubled himself up and hugged his knees. The glowing rays of the sun scorched his head, neck, and back; the plaintive song at times died down, then again broke on the stagnant air; the stream murmured monotonously, the horses went on browsing, and the hours seemed never ending, just as if they too had coagulated and stood still. It seemed as if a hundred years had gone by since the morning. . . . Was it not God's desire that Egorooshka, the britchka, and horses should die in this atmosphere, turn to stone like the hillocks, and so remain in this place for evermore?

Egorooshka raised his head, and with dim-grown eyes

looked straight in front of him. The lilac distance, which had remained motionless till now, began to rock, and together with the sky move somewhere farther away; some noiseless power was drawing it, and the heat and that wearisome song started in pursuit of them. Egorooshka's head dropped forward and his eyes closed. . . .

The first to awake was Deniski; something must have stung him, for he jumped up hastily, scratched his shoulder, and muttered:

"Anathema, the demons! Destruction be upon them!"

Then he went towards the stream, drank some water and washed himself for a long time. His snuffling and splashing awoke Egorooshka from his slumbers. The boy looked at the drops and large freckles on the man's wet face, and thought it very much resembled marble. He asked:

"Are we going soon?"

Deniski looked to see how high the sun stood, and answered:

"Sure to, soon."

He wiped himself on the end of his shirt, then, looking very serious, stood on one leg.

"Come along, who'll get to the reed-grass first!" he said.

Egorooshka was exhausted from the heat, and was still half-asleep, but all the same he raced after him. Deniski was already nearly twenty years old: he acted as coachman, and was about to get married, but he was none the less of a boy. He was very fond of letting fly at a snake, chasing pigeons, playing at knuckle-bones, running races, and was always mixed up in the children's games and quarrels. It was only necessary for the masters to go out or to go to sleep, for him at once to start doing some such thing as hopping or throwing pebbles. All the grown-ups, at the sight of the unaffected enthusiasm which he exhibited in the company of the little ones, found it difficult to refrain from saying: "What a dotty fellow!" But the children did not see anything strange in the invasion of the big coachman into their domain: let him play, provided he did not fight them! Just in the same way, small dogs see nothing strange in some big light-hearted dog thrusting himself upon them and joining in their games.

Deniski out-hopped Egorooshka, which apparently pleased him very much. He winked an eye, and, so as to show that he could hop any distance you liked, he proposed to Egorooshka that they should both hop as far as the road and back to the vehicle without resting. Egorooshka rejected this proposal, as he was very out of breath and felt languid.

Suddenly Deniski, looking very serious—a thing which did not happen even when Kuzmitchov was giving him a scolding and waving his stick over him—listened attentively and went down on one knee, while on his face appeared an expression of awe and fear, such as you notice on the faces of people hearing some heresy. He fixed his eyes on one spot, slowly raised a tuft of grass with one hand, and, arching the other, fell suddenly forward on the ground, clapping his hand over something in the grass.

"It is!" he said in hoarse triumphant tones, and as he got up he placed a large grasshopper before Egorooshka's eyes.

Imagining the grasshopper liked it, Egorooshka and Deniski stroked its wide green back, and touched its feelers; then Deniski caught a fat fly tipsy with blood and presented it to the grasshopper; this latter quite calmly, and as if he had known Deniski all his life, extended his large maxillaries, which resembled a visor, and ate the fly's stomach. Then they released him; he flashed the pink lining of his wings and fluttered into the grass, at once croaking his little song. They also let the fly go; it spread its wings, and stomachless flew to the horses.

There was the sound of a deep sigh behind the vehicle; it was Kuzmitchov waking up. He quickly raised his head, and looked anxiously in the distance; by that look, which disregarded Egorooshka and Deniski, it was evident that on awaking he had only thought of wool and Varlamov.

"Father Christopher, get up, it's time," he said in alarm.

"You'd sleep on and miss all your business! Deniski, harness quick!"

Father Christopher awoke with the same smile with which he had gone to sleep; his face looked wrinkled and creased, and seemed to have shrunk to half its size. Having washed and dressed himself, he drew a small greasy psalter from his pocket, then standing with his face to the East, began to whisper and cross himself.

"Father Christopher!" said Kuzmitchov reproachfully. "It's time to start, the horses are ready, and you, for God's sake. . . ."

"Yes, yes, at once . . ." murmured Father Christopher. "I must read the Cathisma. . . . I have not done so yet."

"You can do your Cathismas afterwards."

"Ivan Ivanitch, each day, it is my rule. . . . No, it is impossible. . . ."

"God will not call you to account."

Father Christopher stood a whole quarter of an hour with his face to the East moving his lips, while Kuzmitchov looked at him almost with hatred, and shrugged his shoulders impatiently; it made him particularly angry when Father Christopher, after each "Gloria," drew in his breath, crossed himself quickly, and purposely, so that the others should cross themselves, said aloud three times:

"Alleluia, Alleluia, Alleluia, praise be to God!"

At last he smiled, looked up at the sky, replaced his psalter in his pocket, and said:

"Fini!"

The next minute the britchka had started on its way. It seemed as if the travellers were going back instead of forward. The landscape was the same as it had been at noon. The hillocks faded into the lilac distance—one saw not the end of them; the steppe-grass, the pebble-stones flashed by, the bands of reaped corn rushed past, and there were all those same rooks and the kite sedately flapping their wings flying over the steppe. The air had become even more stagnant from the heat and stillness; submissive nature grew torpid in silence; there was not a breath of wind, nor a cheering cool sound, nor a cloud. But now, at last, when the sun was about to descend towards the west, the steppe, the hills and the air could no longer bear the pressure; jaded and their patience worn out, they made an attempt to throw off the restraint. Beyond the hills unexpectedly appeared an ash-grey curly cloud. It exchanged a glance with the steppe—well, I'm ready—and looked threatening. Immediately there was a rift in the stagnant air, the wind sprang up, and with a clamour and a whistling whirled about the steppe. The grass and the steppe-grass at once began to whisper, a spiral cloud of dust got up from the road, and fled over the steppe, drawing after it bits of straw, dragon-flies, and feathers, and the dark twirling column rose towards the sky, darkening the sun. The rolling-flax fluttered and tripped about the steppe, and one of them got caught in the whirlwind, twisted like a bird, flew up towards the sky and, transforming itself into a black dot, disappeared from sight. Then another one got caught, then a third, and Egorooshka saw two rolling-flaxes hurtling themselves in the azure heights and clinging to each other as if engaged in a duel.

A bustard took wing from the sides of the road; as it flashed its wings and tail in the sun's glare it resembled some tin-bait for fish, or some pool's butterfly whose wings as it flits over the water blend with its antennae, with the result that antennae seem to grow in front, behind, at the side; . . . quivering in the air like an insect, with a shimmer of speckled colours, the bustard rose upwards in a straight line, then, probably frightened by the cloud of dust, it shifted away to one side, though for a long while the flash of its wings was to be seen. . . .

Next, alarmed by the whirlwind, and not understanding what was the matter, a corn-crake rose out of the grass. It flew with the wind, and not against it as most birds, consequently his feathers were disarranged; he seemed to swell to the size of a partridge, and he looked very angry and important. Only the rooks who had grown up in the steppe, and were used to the steppe disturbances, calmy floated above the grass, or placidly, without heeding anything else, prodded the hard ground with their beaks.

Beyond the hillocks came a distant sound of thunder, followed by a little breath of fresh air. Deniski gave a cheerful whistle and whipped up his horses. Father Christopher and Kuzmitchov held on to their hats, and strained their eyes in the direction of the hillocks. . . . How nice if there were to be a drop of rain! Just one more little effort, so it seemed, one spurt, and the steppe would have the upper hand. But an invisible tyrannical power little by little fettered the wind and the air, laid the dust, and once more, as if nothing had happened, silence reigned. The cloud went and hid itself, the sun-burned hillocks grew wrinkled, the air submissively stagnated; only some startled peewits puled and complained of their fate. . . . Shortly afterwards the daylight crept away.

III

Through the dusk appeared a large one-storied house with a rusty iron roof and unlit windows. This house called itself a tavern, and consequently professed to have a yard—but there was no such thing, as it stood unsurrounded in the middle of the steppe. Somewhat to one side a woeful little cherry garden was discernible; besides which, by the windows, stood some somnolent sunflowers hanging their heavy heads. In the little garden a tiny mill was rattling so as to frighten the hares away with its noise. Otherwise, nothing else was to be seen or heard near the house except the steppe.

Hardly had the vehicle drawn up to the little perron with its pent-roof, than there was a sound of glad voices from the house—one was a man's, the other a woman's voice; a swing-door gave a squeak, and in another moment a full-grown tall spare figure stood by the britchka waving his arms and the folds of his coat. This was the taverner. Moses Mosevitch, a middle-aged man, with a very pale face and a handsome beard black as Indian ink. He wore a worn black frock-coat, which dangled from his narrow shoulders as from a clothes-peg, and the folds flapped like wings each time Moses Mosevitch clasped his hands with joy or fear. Besides the frock-coat, this taverner wore wide white trousers, and a velvet waistcoat with a pattern of reddish flowers rather resembling gigantic bugs. Moses Mosevitch, when he recognised the arrivals, at first nearly died in the fulness of his joy, then clasped his hands and moaned. The folds of his frock-coat flapped, he bowed till his back was bent double, and his face became distorted with such a smile that it seemed as if the sight of the britchka was not only pleasant but also too painful-sweet.

"Ach! Oh God, oh God!" he began saying in a high sing-song voice, breathless, fussing, and with his many gestures preventing the wayfarers from climbing out of the vehicle. "How fortunate a day this is for me! Ach, and what now shall I do? Ivan Ivanitch! Father Christopher! And what a dear little gentleman is sitting on the box-seat, God bless me! Ah! What am I doing standing here and not inviting the guests in? Come in, I most humbly beg . . . welcome, welcome! Give me all your things. . . . Ach, oh God!"

Moses Mosevitch fumbling in the britchka and helping the arrivals to climb out, suddenly made a half-turn back and called in an odd choked voice, just as if he were drowning and calling for help:

"Solomon! Solomon!"

"Solomon! Solomon!" a woman's voice repeated in the house.

The swing-door squeaked, and on the threshold appeared a shortish young Jew with a large beaky nose, coarse curly carroty hair and a bald place on top; he wore a short very shabby jacket with rounded folds and abbreviated sleeves, so, with his short woven trousers as well, he presented the appearance of a tailless fledgling. This was Solomon, brother of Moses Mosevitch. Silently, without bestowing any greeting, merely smiling strangely, he went up to the vehicle.

"Ivan Ivanitch and Father Christopher have come," Moses Mosevitch said to him, in the tone of one who was afraid he might be disbelieved. "Aye, aye, a wonderful thing such good people arriving without warning! Here, Solomon, take the things. Pray come in, welcome guests!"

Shortly afterwards, Kuzmitchov, Father Christopher, and Egorooshka were seated in a large sombre and empty room at an old oak table. The table was quite lonesome, for in this large room besides itself, a wide divan upholstered in an oil-cloth full of holes, and three chairs, there was no other furniture whatever. Moreover, it is not everyone who would have decided to call them chairs. They were something which had a kind of pitiful resemblance to furniture, assisted by oil-cloth which had outlived its century, and backs curved so unnaturally far outward that the chairs were really more similar to children's sleighs. It was difficult to grasp what convenience the unknown joiner had in view when he so unmercifullly bent those backs, and one was rather inclined to think that, in this instance, it was not the joiner who was to blame, but some passing athlete, who, desirous of exhibiting his strength, bent the backs of the chairs, then attempted to straighten them, and bent them yet more. It was a gloomy room. The walls were grey, the ceiling and cornice blackened with smoke. in the floor were lengthened crevices and gaping holes of inconceivable origin (one might imagine that same athlete had broken them through with his heels). Altogether, it seemed as if even if one hung half a score of lamps in the room it would not be otherwise than gloomy. Neither on the walls nor in the windows was anything resembling adornment. However, on one wall was hung in a grey wooden frame some kind of precept with a double-headed eagle, and on another, in the same kind of frame, an engraving with the inscription, "The indifference of men." Towards what men were indifferent it was impossible to gather, as the engraving was very much dimmed by age and liberally fly-blown. The room, too, had a musty noisome smell.

As he led his guests into the room Moses Mosevitch continued to bow and clasp his hands, hesitate, and utter exclamations of joy: he considered it necessary to go through all this to appear unusually pleasant and civil.

"When did our waggons go by?" Kuzmitchov asked him.

"One lot went by this forenoon, Ivan Ivanitch, and the other rested here for dinner and moved on before evening."

"Ah! . . Has Varlamov gone by or not?"

"No, Ivan Ivanitch. Yesterday forenoon his agent, Gregory Egoritch, passed, and said most likely by now he would be at the Milkite's farm-house."

"Excellent; therefore we shall soon overtake the train of waggons, and then go on to the 'Milkite.' "

"God have mercy on us, Ivan Ivanitch!" said Moses Mosevitch in alarm and clasping his hands. "Where will you get to at night? No, sup and spend the night, and to-morrow, God be willing, you leave in the forenoon and overtake whom you like!"

"No, no, . . . excuse me, Moses Mosevitch, some other time, not now. We will remain a quarter of an hour and then go on, and perhaps spend the night at the Milkite's."

"A quarter of an hour!" with a piercing scream said Moses Mosevitch. "Have the fear of God, Ivan Ivanitch! You almost compel me to hide your hats and double-lock the doors! At least have a bite of something and drink some tea!"

"There's no time for tea and sugar!" said Kuzmitchov.

Moses Mosevitch inclined his head to one side, bent his knees, and stretching out the palms of his hands as if defending himself from a blow, and with the pained-sweet smile, began imploring:

. "Ivan Ivanitch! Father Christopher! Do be so kind as to take tea with me! Am I indeed such an unworthy person that you cannot even drink tea with me? Ivan Ivanitch!"

"Oh, well, we might have a little tea," Father Christopher sighed feelingly. "That won't keep us."

"Oh, very well!" assented Kuzmitchov.

Moses Mosevitch jumped up with a sigh of relief, and hesitatingly, as if he had only just come out of the cold water into the warmth, ran to the door and called in the odd choked voice with which he had previously called to Solomon:

"Rosa! Rosa! Bring the samovar!"

A moment later the door opened, and Solomon entered carrying a large tray. Having placed the tray on the table, he looked away derisively and, as before, smiled a strange smile. By the present light of the lamp it became possible to examine that smile. It was very complex, and expressed much feeling, but that which predominated was—unfeigned scorn He seemed to be thinking of something humorous and foolish, of some one whom he disliked and despised, of something which pleased him, and he was only watching for the suitable moment to sting with ridicule, and burst out laughing. His long nose, fleshy lips, cunning mouth, and his protruding eyes, seemed strained with suppressed laughter. As Kuzmitchov glanced at his face he smiled quizzically, and asked:

"Solomon, why did you not come to our Fair in N——— this summer and give us a Jewish recitation?"

Egorooshka very well remembered that two years ago Solomon at the N———ski Fair had related scenes out of Jewish life in one of the booths, and had had a great success. The remembrance of this made no impression whatever on Solomon. Without giving an answer he left the room, and shortly afterwards returned with the samovar.

Having performed his duties at the table he stepped to one side, crossed his arms, stood with one foot in advance of the other, and stared derisively at Father Christopher. There was something defiant, arrogant, and scornful in his attitude; at the same time it was in the highest degree pitiful and comic, because the more imposing his attitude became the more conspicuous became his short trousers, his short-tailed coat, caricature of a nose, and fledgling-like appearance.

Moses Mosevitch brought a stool from another room, and sat down at some distance from the table.

"A good appetite to you! Tea and sugar!" he began by way of amusing the guests. "Drink to your healths! Such rare guests, so very rare; and Father Christopher I have not seen for five years. And no one seems to want to tell me to whom this dear little man belongs!" he enquired, looking tenderly at Egorooshka.

"He is the son of my sister Olga Ivanovna," answered Kuzmitchov

"And where is he going to?"

"To be educated. We are taking him to the Gymnasium."

Moses Mosevitch out of politeness evinced an air of surprise, and significantly nodded his head.

"Oh, that's right!" he said menacing the samovar with a finger. "That's right!" You will come away from the Gymnasium such a gentleman that we shall all take our hats off to you. You will be learned, rich, ambitious, and your mamma will be glad. Oh, that's right!"

He was silent for a little, rubbed his knees, and then continued in a tone of deferential raillery:

"You will forgive me, Father Christopher, if I write a letter to the Prelate saying that you are deflecting the traders' living! I shall write on stamped paper, and say that evidently Father Christopher has such a small pittance he is obliged to take to trade, and is selling wool."

"Yes, this entered his head in his old age," said Father Christopher laughing. "Instead of pope I am now inscribed as trader. Instead of sitting at home, and praying to God, I race along like a Pharaoh in a chariot. . How vainglorious!"

"Still, groats will accumulate!"

"Oh! no! Pears come more my way than groats. The goods are not mine but my son-in-law Michael's."

"Why has he not come himself?"

"Oh, because. . . . Well, his mother's milk is not dry on his lips yet! He does not know what wool to buy or how to sell it, he is too young. He squandered all his money wanting to prosper and fling up a dust, he hurried hither and thither, and no one would attend to him or his prices. The youth lived from hand to mouth for a year, then came to me: 'Papa, be so kind as to sell the wool! I understand nothing in these matters!' That's how it was. And as it was then so it may be the same with papa as it formerly was without him! When he purchased he stopped to ask no questions, and in a like hurry am I. If it were not for Ivan Ivanitch, papa would have done nothing at all! Bother take them all!"

"Yes, children are troublesome, I tell you!" sighed Moses Mosevitch. "I myself have six of them. One has to be educated, another doctored, the third has to be made a fuss of, and when they grow up there is even more bother. It is not only nowadays—in Holy Scriptures it was just the same. When Jacob had young children he wept, and when they grew up he wept even more."

"M—yes," agreed Father Christopher thoughtfully looking at his glass. "For myself, I have no grudge against God. I have fulfilled the term of my life, as may God grant to others. . . . My daughters are settled, my sons made their way in the world—they are now independent, have their business, although they are scattered far and wide. I live quietly with my popess, I have enough to eat and drink, I can sleep, I have my grandchildren, I pray to God, and I have no need of anything further. I ride like cheese on butter, and mind nothing or no one. From my youth upwards I have had no sorrows, and supposing now the Tsar were to say: 'What would you like? What do you want?'—why, I want nothing! I have everything I could wish, thank God! There is no happier man than I in the town. Only, I am a sinful man; but then, after all, God alone is without sin. Is not that true?"

"It is so."

"Of course, I have no teeth, my back is rheumatic—it goes without saying I have asthma and such like. . . . I fall ill, the body is weakly, but then there is no denying, I am a good age! I am in my eighth decade! One cannot last for ever, we must not ask for too much."

Father Christopher suddenly remembered something, laughed in his glass, and choked. Moses Mosevitch, for decorum's sake, also laughed and choked.

"Such a joke!" said Father Christopher waving his hand. "My eldest son Gavrila came to pay me a visit. He is in the medical profession, and is a country doctor in the government of Tchernigov. Very well. . . . I said to him: 'See here, I have asthma, you are a doctor, cure your father!' At once he stripped me, sounded me, listened, various tricks of that sort . . . kneaded my stomach; at last he said: 'Papa, what you want is a compressed air-cure.'"

Father Christopher went into convulsions of laughter, wept, and got up.

"And I said to him: 'To the deuce with the compressed air!'"—he articulated through his laughter, and waving both hands, "'to the deuce with the compressed air!'"

Moses Mosevitch also got up, and, holding his stomach, laughed a shrill laugh, resembling the bark of a lapdog.

"To the deuce with the compressed air!" Father Christopher repeated, still laughing.

Moses Mosevitch went two notes higher, and laughed so convulsively that he could hardly stand on his feet.

"Oh, good Lord! . . ." he groaned in his laughter. "Give one time to draw breath . . . I have laughed so, that . . . och! . . . it'll be my death. . . ."

He spoke and laughed, all the time casting suspicious and timid glances at Solomon. The latter was standing in the same attitude as before, still smiling. Judging by the look in his eyes and his smile, he despised and hated them in sober earnest, yet his expression appeared to correspond so little with his fledgling appearance, that it seemed to Egorooshka as if the defiant attitude and sarcastic scornful smile were adopted on purpose, like the play-acting of a facetious person, and to amuse favoured guests.

Having drunk six glasses of tea in silence, Kuzmitchov cleared a space in front of him on the table, took out his bag, the very same which while he slept by the vehicle he had laid under his head, untied the slender cord, and shook it out Out of the bag fluttered whole packets of paper-money.

"Now that we have time, come on, we'll count, Father Christopher," said Kuzmitchov.

At the sight of the money Moses Mosevitch was put out of countenance; he got up again from his seat, and, like a tactful person afraid of prying into other people's secrets, left the room on tiptoe, swaying his arms. Solomon remained where he was.

"In how many shall I do the rouble-packets?" inquired Father Christopher.

"By fifties. . . . The three-rouble ones by nineties. . . . The quarter and hundred-roubles put together in thousand packets. Count out seven thousand eight hundred for Varlamov, and I will count the same for Gussevitch. And see that you don't make a mistake. . . ."

Never in his life had Egorooshka seen such a heap of money as now lay on the table. There must in fact have been a lot of money, for the packet of seven thousand eight hundred roubles which Father Christopher put aside for Varlamov, in comparison with the entire lot, looked quite small. At any other time perhaps such a quantity of money would have astounded Egorooshka, and tempted him to speculate how many piles of Easter-cakes, knuckle-bones, poppy-seed cakes one could buy with it. He looked at it now, however, unmoved, and was only aware of a loathsome smell of rotten apples and kerosene which emanated from the pile. He was worn-out by the jolting drive in the britchka, and longed to drop asleep. His head was growing very heavy, his eyes would close and his thoughts get mixed like tangled threads. If it had been possible he would so gladly have dropped his head on the table, have closed his eyes so as not to see the lamp and the fingers moving over the packets of money, and would have permitted his drowsy sluggish thoughts to confuse themselves altogether. When he strove to overcome his sleepiness the flame of the lamp, the glasses, the fingers all seemed doubled; the samovar rocked, and the smell of the rotten apples became even more sour and loathsome.

"Ah, money, money!" sighed Father Christopher with a smile. "Woe to you! No doubt, now, my Michael is sleeping, and sees that I am bringing him this pile."

"Your Michael Timothevitch is an incompetent person," said Kuzmitchov in an undertone. "He does not look after his affairs, but you have understanding and judgment. If you gave up your wool to me, as I have said, and you yourself go back, and I gave you—as I have already consented—half a rouble more than my price, and that, only out of consideration . . ."

"No, Ivan Ivanitch," sighed Father Christopher. "I thank you for your kindness. . . . Naturally, if it were mine I would not have any discussion about it, but, as you well know, the goods are not mine. . . ."

Moses Mosevitch entered on tiptoe. With a tactful effort not to look at the piles of money, he stole up to Egorooshka and tugged him by the back of the shirt.

"Here, come with me, little man," he said in an undertone. "I have such a mole-rat to show you! Such a fearful angry one! Ugh!"

Sleepy Egorooshka got up, and lazily dragged himself after Moses Mosevitch to look at the mole-rat. He entered a small room, the noisome musty smell of which caught his breath before he ever saw the inside of the room. The smell was much worse here than in the large room, and probably it was from here that it spread over the whole house. One half of the room was occupied by a large bed covered with a filthy counterpane, the other half by a chest of drawers and a high mountain of every conceivable kind of rag, beginning with a stiffly starched petticoat and finishing with children's braces and trousers. On the drawers burned a tallow dip.

Instead of the promised mole-rat, Egorooshka saw a large very fat Jewess with flowing hair wearing a red spotted black flannel costume. She was with difficulty squeezing through the narrow passage between the bed and the chest of drawers, heaving the while long-drawn moaning sighs just as if she had a toothache. When she saw Egorooshka she screwed up her face, drew a deep breath, and before he had time to look round she had shoved into his mouth a slice of bread spread over with honey.

"Eat, childie, eat!" she said. "You are here without your mammy, and nobody has given you anything to eat. Eat!"

Egorooshka ate, although, after the barley-sugar and the poppy-seed cakes which he had every day at home, he did not find anything specially good in the honey, half of it being composed of wax and bees' wings. He ate, and Moses Mosevitch and his wife looked and sighed.

"Where are you going to, childie?" asked the Jewess.

"To school," answered Egorooshka.

"How many children has your mammy?"

"Only me; there are no others."

"Ah!—oh!" with a sigh said the Jewess and casting her eyes upwards. "Poor mammy, poor mammy! How lonely she will be, how she will cry! In a year we shall be sending our Neomi to his studies! Oh, ho!"

"Ah, Neomi, Neomi!" sighed Moses Mosevitch, while his white face twitched nervously. "And he is so sickly."

The filthy counterpane heaved, and from beneath it appeared a child's curly head, a very thick neck, and two shining black eyes which looked inquisitively at Egorooshka. Moses Mosevitch and his wife, not ceasing to sigh, went to the chest of drawers and began to speak in Hebrew about something. Moses Mosevitch spoke in a deep bass undertone and altogether his Hebrew conversation sounded like an incessant: "Gaul—gaul—gaul—gaul . . ." and his wife answered him in a high turkey-hen voice, and it sounded something like: "Too—too—too—too. . . ." While they were consulting by the tallow-dip, another curly head looked out from under the filthy counterpane, then a third, then a fourth. . . . Had Egorooshka possessed a fertile imagination he might have thought that a hundred-headed hydra lay beneath that counterpane.

"Gaul—gaul—gaul—gaul . . ." said Moses Mosevitch.

"Too—too—too—too . . ." answered the Jewess.

The conference ended by the Jewess diving into the chest of drawers, unwrapping a green rag and procuring from thence a large heart-shaped rye-gingerbread.

"Here, childie," she said, handing the gingerbread to Egorooshka. "Your mammy is not here, and there is no one to give you presents."

Egorooshka thrust the gingerbread into his pocket and directed his steps towards the door, as he could no longer breathe in the musty noisome atmosphere in which these people lived. Returning to the larger room, he settled himself as comfortably as he could on the divan, and did not trouble any further to control his thoughts.

Kuzmitchov had just finished counting his money and was putting it back into the bag. He was not treating it with such regard, piling it into the dirty bag without any care whatever, and with as much indifference as if instead of money it was nothing but paper rubbish.

Father Christopher was talking to Solomon.

"Well, now, Solomon the Wise?" he said yawning and making a cross over his mouth, "how is business?"

"Of what business are you speaking?" asked Solomon as spitefully as if he had been detected in some crime.

"In general. . . . What are you doing?"

"What am I doing?" repeated Solomon shrugging his shoulders. "Why, the same as others. . . . You can see for yourself: I am a servant, I serve my brother, my brother is a servant to the passers-by, the passers-by are servants to Varlamov, and had I ten millions Varlamov would be a servant to me."

"What do you mean? How would he be your servant?"

"How? Because there is no gentleman or millionaire who will not shake hands with a miserly Jew if only he has a superfluity of kopecks. I, at present, am a miserly and indigent Jew, and everyone treats me like a dog, but if I had money, then Varlamov would make as great a fool of himself before me as Moses does before you."

Father Christopher and Kuzmitchov glanced at one another. Neither of them understood Solomon; Kuzmitchov looked at him sharply and sternly, and said:

"How does a fool like you dare to compare himself to Varlamov?"

"I am not yet such a fool as to compare myself to Varlamov," Solomon answered, looking sarcastically at his interlocutors. "Although a Russian, Varlamov is at heart a miserly Jew; the whole interest of his life is in money and profits, whereas I burnt my money in the stove. I do not require money, nor land, nor sheep, nor people to be afraid of me or take off their hats when I pass; which means I am wiser than your Varlamov, and am more human."

Shortly afterwards Egorooshka through his dreams heard Solomon speaking in a hollow hoarse voice about the Jews, choking with hatred, and with a thick hurried pronunciation. At first he had spoken in correct Russian, afterwards he relapsed into the manner of a narrator of Jewish life, and began to speak as he did that time in the booth with an egregiously Jewish accent.

"Stay," Father Christopher interrupted him. "If you are dissatisfied with your faith, change it, but it is wicked to make fun of it. He who scoffs at his faith is the most despicable of creatures."

"You don't understand anything," rudely retorted Solomon. "I am speaking of one thing and you of another. . . ."

"One can see at once that you are a stupid fellow," sighed Father Christopher. "I am teaching you what I know, and you get angry. I do it gently like an old man, while turkey-like you go 'bla—bla—bla!' In truth, you are very odd. . . ."

Moses Mosevitch came in. He looked anxiously at Solomon and at his guests, and again his face twitched nervously. Egorooshka raised his head and looked round. He caught a glimpse of Solomon's face just at the moment when it was three-quarters turned towards him, and with the shadow of his long nose lying across his left cheek. The contemptuous smile, combined with the shadow, the gleaming sarcastic eyes, arrogant expression and plucked appearance, flashing across Egorooshka twice as vividly as before, now gave him no longer the resemblance to a buffoon, but rather to some evil spirit one might dream about.

"Someone in your house is possessed, Moses Mosevitch. God be with him!" said Father Christopher with a smile. "You ought to make some provision for him, or marry him, or something. . . . He is unlike a human being. . . ."

Kuzmitchov frowned angrily. Moses Mosevitch again looken anxiously and searchingly at his brother and at his guests.

"Solomon, leave the room!" he said sternly. "Go!" and he added something in Hebrew.

Solomon gave a short laugh, and went out.

"What is the matter?" Moses Mosevitch anxiously asked Father Christopher.

"He forgets himself," answered Kuzmitchov. "He is rude and thinks too much of himself."

"I knew it!" said Moses Mosevitch in horror and wringing his hands. "Oh God! oh God!" he muttered to himself. "But you will be so good as to forgive, and not be angry. Oh, what a man, what a man! Oh God! oh God! He is my own brother, and he has caused me nothing but sorrow. For you know, he . . ."

Moses Mosevitch tapped his forehead with his fingers and continued:

"He is not right in the head . . . he is a ruined man. And what I am to do with him I don't know. He is fond of no one, respects no one, is afraid of no one. . . . Do you know, he laughs at everyone, talks nonsense, thees-and-thous everyone to their face. You would scarce believe it, Varlamov came here once, and Solomon said such things to him that he beat him with a whip, and me too. . . . Now why beat me? Is it my fault? God deprived him of reason, it was therefore His Will, but is it my fault?"

Ten minutes went by, and Moses Mosevitch was still grumbling in a low voice and sighing.

"He doesn't sleep at night, but thinks and thinks and thinks; and what does he think about? God alone knows! If you go to him at night he gets angry and laughs at you. He does not like me. . . . And he does not want anything! Papa when he died left us each six thousand roubles. I bought myself a tavern, married, and have got children. He burnt all his money in the stove. What a shame, what a shame! Wherefore burn it? You don't want it; well, give it to me, but why burn it?"

Suddenly the swing-door squeaked, and the floor shook with someone's footsteps. A light breeze blew over Egorooshka, and it seemed to him that some large black bird poised just above his face and waved its wings. He opened his eyes. . . . His uncle, with his bag in his hand ready to set forth, was standing by the divan. Father Christopher holding his black hat in his hand, was bowing to someone, and smiling, not softly and tenderly as he usually did, but deferentially and stiffly, which did not at all suit his style of face. And Moses Mosevitch, exactly as if his body had been broken into three parts, was swaying and doing his utmost not to overbalance. Solomon alone, as if nothing was happening, stood in a corner with his arms crossed, and as before smiling contemptuously.

"Pray forgive us, your Excellency, it is not very clean here!" stuttered Moses Mosevitch with his pained-sweet smile, no longer taking any notice of Kuzmitchov or Father Christopher, merely swaying with his whole body so as not to overbalance. "We are simple folk, your Excellency!"

Egorooshka opened his eyes. There in the room no doubt stood Her Excellency, in the person of a young, very pretty and plump lady in a black dress and a straw hat. Before Egorooshka had time to look at her features, somehow the tall lonely poplar which he had seen that day by the hillock came into his mind.

"Has Varlamov passed here to-day?" asked a woman's voice.

"No, your Excellency," answered Moses Mosevitch.

"If you see him to-morrow, ask him to come and see me for a minute."

Suddenly, quite unexpectedly, half a yard away from his face, Egorooshka saw a pair of dark velvety brows, large brown eyes, soft dimpled cheeks, and a smile which like the rays of the sun was diffused over the whole face—someone who smelt quite deliciously.

"What a dear little boy!" said the lady. "Who does he belong to? Kasimir Michaelitch, look what a darling! Oh God! He is asleep! Dear little chubby child! . . ."

The lady gave Egorooshka two good kisses on either cheek; he smiled and, thinking he was dreaming, closed his eyes. The swing-door squeaked—and he heard some hasty footsteps—somebody came in and went out.

"Egorooshka! Egorooshka!" came the sound of two deep voices in a whisper. "Get up; we must go!"

Someone, probably Deniski, placed Egorooshka on his feet and led him by the hand. On the way he half-opened his eyes, and once more he saw the lovely lady in the black dress who had kissed him. She was standing in the middle of the room, and smiled as she watched him go out, and gave him a friendly nod. When he got to the door he saw a handsome stout dark man in a bowler hat and gaiters. Evidently he was the lady's escort.

"Tprrr!" sounded in the yard.

Egorooshka saw a new luxurious-looking carriage and a pair of black horses standing by the door. On the box-seat sat a man in livery with a long whip in his hand.

Solomon was the only one who accompanied them to the door. His face wore a strained expression of suppressed laughter; he looked as if he were waiting in the greatest impatience for the departure of the guests in order to indulge in a good laugh at them.

"The Countess Dranitska," whispered Father Christopher, getting into the vehicle.

"Yes, Countess Dranitska," repeated Kuzmitchov, also in a whisper.

The impression created by the arrival of the Countess was evidently very great, for even Deniski spoke in a whisper, and he only made up his mind to whip his bays and shout at them when they had driven a quarter of a verst away, and when far behind, instead of the tavern, nothing but a dim light was to be seen.

IV

But who, finally, is this elusive mysterious Varlamov, of whom everyone is speaking, whom Solomon despises, and who is wanted even by the beautiful Countess? As he sat by Deniski on the box-seat this very man was the object of sleepy Egorooshka's thoughts. He had never seen him, but had often heard of him, and not infrequently pictured him to himself. He knew that Varlamov owned several tens of thousands of acres of land, nearly a hundred thousand sheep, and a very great deal of money. Of his mode of life and occupations Egorooshka only knew that he always "circled about these parts," and that everyone was always looking for him.

At home Egorooshka had also heard a lot about the Countess Dranitska. She too owned several tens of thousands of acres, large numbers of sheep, a stud, and lots of money; but she did not "circle," she lived on her own rich property, about which Ivan Ivanitch and others, who had several times been to visit the Countess on business, reported wonderful things. Thus, so they said, in the Countess's drawing-room, where hung portraits of all the Polish kings, was a large table-clock in the shape of a rock, on the rock stood a rearing gold horse with eyes of brilliants, and on the horse sat a gold rider, who, every time the clock struck, waved his hat to the right and to the left. They also said that the Countess gave a ball twice a year to which she invited all the nobles and functionaries in the district, and to which Varlamov also went. All the guests had tea from silver samovars, were given the most unexpected things to eat—for instance, in winter, at Christmas-time, raspberries and strawberries were served to them—and they danced to a band which played day and night. . . .

"And how pretty she is!" thought Egorooshka remembering her face and smile.

Kuzmitchov was evidently also thinking of the Countess, for when the vehicle had gone about two versts, he said:

"He swindles her well that Kasimir Michaelitch! Three years ago, do you remember, when I bought some wool from her, he made a profit of three thousand over one of my purchases."

"It is useless to expect anything else from a Pole," said Father Christopher.

"And she does not care much. As they say, young and foolish. There is nothing but air in her head!"

For some reason or other Egorooshka felt inclined to think only of Varlamov and the Countess, particularly this latter. His drowsy brain utterly refused to think the usual things; it was befogged, and managed to get hold of nothing but improbable and fantastic forms, which, however, have the one convenience, that they somehow arise in the brain of themselves without any effort on the part of the thinker, and it only becomes necessary to shake one's head when they disappear and leave no trace. None of the surroundings either adapted themselves to the wonted thoughts. To the right were the dark shadows of the hillocks, looking as if they were hiding something unknown and fearful; to the left, all over the horizon, the sky was flushed incarnadine, and it was difficult to ascertain whether it was owing to some conflagration or whether it was the moon preparing to rise. The horizon was as visible as in the day-time, but its soft lilac tints had disappeared in the black night-mist; the whole steppe was hid in the mist, like Moses Mosevitch's children under the counterpane.

At dusk, and in the night-time in July, quails and corncrakes no longer utter their call-notes, nor does the nightingale sing in the woody swamps; there is no scent of flowers, yet the steppe is still beautiful and full of life. No sooner has the sun set and a mist enwrapped the earth, than the woes of the day are forgotten and forgiven, and the steppe breathes evenly and deeply. Owing perhaps to the fact that the state of the grass is invisible in the dusk, there arises the sound of a cheerful youthful buzz, which does not occur in the day-time; there are buzzings, whistlings, scratchings; steppe-basses, tenors, and trebles all mingle in one incessant monotonous sound, to the accompaniment of which it is pleasant to think and be melancholy. The monotonous crackling lulls one to sleep like a cradle-song. You drive along aware that you are dozing, when suddenly, from somewhere comes the short alarmed cry of some unsleeping bird, or there echoes an undefinable sound resembling some human voice saying an astonished "A-ah," then slumber again closes your eyes. Then you may perchance drive by the edge of a swamp, where bushes grow, and you hear a bird which the dwellers of the steppe call "spluker" for it calls to someone "Splu, splu, splu"; sometimes it goes "Ha, ha, ha," or indulges in hysterical weeping—it is an owl. Who it calls to, and who listens to it in this plain, God alone knows, but its cry has something sad and plaintive. . . . There is a smell of hay, dried-up grass, and belated flowers; it is a heavy, stale, sweet, and delicate smell.

Everything is visible through the mist, but it is difficult to make out the colour and features of the objects. Things look different from what they are. You drive along, and suddenly you see standing before you by the side of the road a silhouette resembling that of a monk; it stands motionless, waiting, and holding something in its hand. . . . Is he a cut-throat? The figure approaches, gets taller, it is now on a line with the vehicle, and you discover it is not a human being but a lonely bush or a bit of rock. Similar motionless expectant forms are dotted about the hillock, hide behind the tumuli, peep out of the steppe-grass; they all have a resemblance to human beings and fill one with suspicious fears.

When the moon rises, the night grows pale and dim. The mist seems to disappear, the atmosphere becomes clear, light and warm, everything becomes more distinct, and by the road-side you can even distinguish the separate stalks of the steppe-grass. In the far distance you can discern bits of bark and stones. The suspicious-looking figures resembling monks, against the pale background of the night, look blacker and sterner. Often and often amid the monotonous buzzing, that someone's "A-ah" of astonishment resounds in the silent air, or the cry of a wakeful or delirious bird is heard. Broad shadows pass over the plain like clouds in the sky, and in the far inconceivable distance, if you keep your eyes on them, you see dark and fantastic shapes issuing and grouping themselves one after the other. . . . It is rather frightening. If you glance up at the pale green star-sprinkled sky, where there is not a cloud or a blot, you understand why the warm air is so still, why nature is on the watch and afraid to stir: she is sorry and afraid of misapplying even one instant of life. It is only possible to conceive how immense and limitless is the sky, either at sea or in the steppe at night when the moon is shining. It is fearful, beautiful, inviting, looks languid, beckons to one till one turns giddy with its blandishments.

On you drive for another hour. . . . By the road-side you come across some silent time-honoured tumulus, or a stone-pile, put there by God knows whom, and when some night-bird flies noiselessly over the ground, little by little there come into your mind those legends of the steppes, wayfarers' stories, old steppe folk-tales, and all those things which you yourself can imagine and apprehend in your soul. And then in the buzz of the insects, in the suspicious figures and tumuli, in the azure sky, in the light of the moon, in the flight of night-birds, in all that which you see and hear, is discernible a great beauty, youth, revival of strength and passionate thirst for life. The soul responds to lovely stern nature, and is desirous of flying over the steppe together with the night-birds. But in its solemn beauty and its excess of joy you are aware of tension and grief, as if the steppe acknowledges she is lovely, that her richness and inspiration perishes for the universe in vain, her praises celebrated by no one, she is needed by no one, and amid her joyous accents you detect the melancholy, hopeless call for: "A bard! a bard!"

"Tprrr! How are you, Panteli? All well?"

"Yes, praise be to God, Ivan Ivanitch!"

"Have you seen Varlamov, my lad?"

"No, I have not seen him."

Egorooshka woke and opened his eyes. The vehicle was standing still. On the right of the road stretched a long train of waggons, alongside of which people were moving to and fro. All the waggons, owing to the fact that they were piled up with large bales of wool, looked inflated and high, while the horses looked very small and short-legged.

"That being the case we will go on to Milkite!" said Kuzmitchov in a loud voice. "The Jew said that Varlamov would spend the night at the Milkite's. So then, good-bye, mates! God speed you!"

"Good-bye, Ivan Ivanitch," answered several voices.

"Here, I'll tell you what, my lads," said Kuzmitchov briskly, "you'll take my little boy with you! What is the good of his bumping along with us? Panteli, seat him on your bales of wool and let him come along leisurely, we must hurry. Get down, Egor, go on, it's all right! . . ."

Egorooshka clambered off the box-seat. Several pairs of hands caught hold of him, raised him somewhere in the air, and he sank on to something large and soft and slightly moist with dew. It seemed to him now, that the sky was quite close and the earth far off.

"Hie, take his coat!" Deniski shouted from somewhere far below.

The coat and his little bundle were thrown from below and fell close to Egorooshka. Not wishing to stop and ask himself questions he quickly laid his head on his bundle, wrapped himself in his coat, and stretching himself at full length, with a little shudder at the dew, he smiled with satisfaction as he thought: "Sleep, sleep, sleep. . . ."

"See here, you fellows, don't you forget him!" Deniski was heard saying below.

"Good-bye, mates! God speed you!" shouted Kuzmitchov. "I trust to you."

"Don't worry, Ivan Ivanitch!"

Deniski shouted to his horses, the vehicle gave a piercing scream and moved on, but not by the road, somewhere away to one side. There was silence for two minutes, just as if the train of waggons had fallen asleep, the only sound being the gradually dying screech of the bucket fastened on at the back of the britchka, then suddenly someone in the forefront of the waggons shouted:

"Kiruha! Move on!"

The first waggon creaked. Then another, then a third; Egorooshka felt the waggon on which he was lying rock, and heard it also creak: the train of waggons was on the move. Egorooshka held firmly on to the rope by which the bales were fastened, again smiled with satisfaction, adjusted the ginger in his pocket, and began to doze just as he usually dozed in his bed at home.

When he awoke the sun had risen. Concealed by a tumulus it was striving to shed its light on the earth, its beams were radiating on all sides and flooding a golden light on the horizon. It seemed to Egorooshka that the sun was not in its proper place, for yesterday it rose behind him whereas to-day it was very much to his left . . . but besides none of the surroundings were like yesterday's. There were no hillocks, and wherever you looked was a brown cheerless plain without any end to it. Small tumuli rose here and there, and yesterday's rooks were flying about. Far ahead shone a steeple and the cottages of some village. It being a Sunday the "Topknots" were sitting at home baking and boiling, as was evident by the smoke issuing from all the chimneys and a grey-blue transparent cloud hanging over the village. In the space between the church and the cottages shimmered the blue line of a river, and beyond it was a hazy distance. But nothing bore so little resemblance to the things of yesterday as the road. Instead of a road, a kind of track very unusually wide, bold and imposing extended over the steppe. It was a grey strip much driven over and covered with dust like all roads, but several tens of yards in width. Its width aroused Egorooshka's curiosity and turned his thoughts to legendary tales. Who drives along such roads? For whom is such width necessary? It is inconceivable and strange One might really think that those enormous seven-league-stepping people, like Ilia Murometz and Solovia the Robber, had not yet disappeared from Russia, and that the heroes' horses were not yet extinct. Egorooshka gazed at the road, and pictured to himself six large racing chariots in a row like those he had seen in drawings in Holy Scriptures; six wild and frenzied horses were harnessed to them; the wheels would raise a cloud of dust up to the skies, and the horses were being driven by people such as one might dream of, or who appear in legendary tales. And how these figures would correspond to the steppe and the road if only they existed!

On the right-hand side, the whole length of the road, were telegraph poles with two wires. They grew smaller and smaller, and disappeared altogether in the village behind the cottages, then came in view again in the lilac distance as small thin sticks similar to pencils popped into the ground. Hawks, merlins and crows sat on the wires, and looked calmly at the moving train of waggons.

Egorooshka was lying on the very last waggon, and therefore had a view of the whole length of the train of them. There were about twenty waggons in all and there was one driver to each three waggons. By the last waggon where lay Egorooshka walked an old man with a grey beard. He was as thin and small as Father Christopher, but the expression on his sunburnt face was stern and thoughtful. It was more than likely that this old man was neither stern nor thoughtful, but his red eye-lashes and long pointed nose, lent his face a hard cold expression which is found among people who are accustomed to think very seriously, and in solitude. Like Father Christopher he wore a wide-brimmed black hat, and he was barefooted. Probably from a habit acquired in the winter months, when more than once it happened to him to freeze as he tramped along by the side of the waggon, he slapped his thighs and stamped his feet as he walked. Having noticed that Egorooshka was awake, he looked at him for a bit, then with a shrug as if he were cold, said:

"Ah! you've woken up, laddie. Is it son you are to Ivan Ivanitch?"

"No, his nephew."

"To Ivan Ivanitch? You see I have taken off my boots and hop along barefooted. My feet hurt, pester me; without boots one walks freer . . . freer, laddie. . . . That is to say, without boots . . . So then, you're his nephew? He is a good fellow, nitchevo . . . God give him health! Nitchevo.

. . . About Ivan Ivanitch . . . he went to Milkite's. . . . Oh, Lord have mercy on us!"

The old man spoke as if it were very cold weather, pausing continually and hardly opening his mouth; he pronounced the lip consonants badly, stammering over them as if his lips were frost-bitten. His expression was stern and he never once smiled as he looked at Egorooshka.

Further on a man in a long rusty-brown coat, wearing a cap and high-boots, with very crumpled boot-legs, and a whip in his hand, came out from between two carts. He was not an old man,—about forty. When he turned round, Egorooshka saw he had a red face with a scanty goat's-beard, and a spungious lump beneath his right eye. Besides this very ugly lump he had another characteristic which struck one; he held his whip in the left hand and waved his right hand about as if he were conducting some invisible choir; occasionally he held his whip under his arm and conducted with both hands, humming at the same time.

The driver next to him was a long rectilinear figure with very sloping shoulders and a back as flat as a board. He looked as if he were marching or had swallowed a poker, his arms did not swing but hung stiffly by his side, and he stepped along in as wooden a manner as a toy-soldier, scarcely bending his knees and striving to make his step as long as possible; whilst the old man or the owner of the spungious lump took two steps, he succeeded in taking only one, wherefore it seemed as if he were walking slower than anyone else and would be left behind. His face was bound round with a rag, and on his head was something in the shape of a monk's skull-cap; he wore a short Little Russian coat, all patched, blue loose trousers and bast shoes.

Egorooshka did not look to see what the other drivers were like. He lay on his stomach, picked a hole in the bale, and having nothing to do began to twine the threads of wool. The old man walking along below turned out to be less stern than one might guess from his face. Having once started the conversation he did not want to discontinue it.

"Where are you going to?" he asked as he stumped along.

"To school," answered Egorooshka.

"To study? Aha! . . . Well, the Queen of Heaven help you! So. Two brains are better than one. To one man God gives one brain, to another two, to another three . . . to another three, that's quite true. . . . We are born with one, the second comes with education, and the third with a good life. So you see, little mate, it is good if a man has three brains. It is not only easier to live, but to die—yes, to die. . . . But we die all the same."

The old man scratched his forehead, looked with red eyes up at Egorooshka, and continued:

"Maxim Nicolaitch, a gentleman from Slavianoserbska, also took his little boy last year to school. I can't say how he is with regard to the sciences, but the boy was all right, quite right. . . . God give him health! A fine gentleman . . . yes, also sent him away to study. In Slavianoserbska, there is no institution certainly, to teach you the sciences, there isn't . . . but the town is all right, quite all right. . . . There is the usual school for plain folk, but as regards deeper studies there isn't . . . there isn't, that's true. What's your name?"

"Egorooshka."

"Consequently, Egor. . . . The holy and great martyr, Egor the Victorious, whose date is twenty-third of April. My saint's name is Panteli . . . Panteli Zaharov Holodov. . . . We are Holodovs. I am a native of Tim Government of Koursk, maybe you've heard? My brothers worked themselves up to be citizens and are in some trade in the town, but I am a moujik . . . I remained a peasant. Seven years back I drove thither . . . that is to say, home. . . . I have been in the country and in the town. . . . I mean I have been to Tim. They were all alive and well then, thank God, but now, I don't know . . . maybe some have died. . . . It is time too they died, for they are all old, some of them are older than I am. Death is all right, quite all right, only of course, one must not die impenitent. There is nothing worse than a shameless death. A shameless death is the Devil's joy. And if you want to die penitent, that is, so that God's gates will not be shut against you, pray to Varvara, Greater Martyr. She is mediatrix. She is, that's true. . . . Because God appointed her such a task in Heaven, so that everyone therefore should have full right through her to pray for penitence."

Panteli mumbled on and apparently did not worry whether Egorooshka listened to him or not. He spoke in a drowsy, droning voice, neither raising nor lowering his tone, yet managed to say a great deal in a short while. What he said was in fragments having very little connection with each other, and quite uninteresting to Egorooshka. It may be that he was only talking, because having spent the night in silence now that it was morning he wanted to articulate aloud his thought: whether they all were well at home? Having finished about penitence he again spoke of that certain Maxim Nicolaitch of Slavianoserbska.

"Yes, he took his little boy. . . . He took him, that's so. . . ."

One of the drivers who was walking far ahead left his place, ran to one side, and began thrashing the ground with his whip. He was a tall broad-shouldered man of about thirty, with flaxen curly hair, and evidently very strong and healthy; judging by his activity with the whip, and his eagerness characterised by his attitude, he was beating some live beast. Another driver, a short thick-set man with a bushy black beard, wearing a waistcoat and an embroidered shirt; ran towards him. He burst into a deep hoarse laugh and shouted:

"Mates, Dimov has killed a snake! As true as God!"

There are people whose minds can be ascertained by their voice and their laugh. The black-bearded man happened to belong to that fortunate class: one heard how insurmountable was his stupidity by his voice and his laugh. When he had finished thrashing, flaxen-haired Dimov raised his whip and laughingly hurled something resembling a rope at the waggons.

"It's not a snake, it's an adder," shouted someone.

The man of the wooden walk and bound-up face, walked quickly up to the dead snake, looked at it, and wrung his stick-like fingers.

"You galley-slave!" he called in a hollow whimpering voice. "What did you kill an adder for? What had it done to you, wretch? To kill an adder!"

"He ought not to have killed it, that's true . . ." calmly mumbled Panteli, "ought not. It is not venomous. Although it looks like a snake it is a gentle harmless beast. . . . Likes people . . . adders do. . . ."

Dimov and the black-bearded man evidently felt guilty, for they laughed loudly, and without heeding the grumblings lazily went back to their waggons. When the last waggon reached the place where lay the dead adder, he with the bound-up face standing by the adder, turned to Panteli and asked him in a whimpering voice:

"But, dad, what did he kill an adder for?"

His eyes, as Egorooshka now saw, were small and lustreless, his face was grey, unhealthy, and also looked as it were lustreless, and his chin looked very swollen and red.

"Dad, why did he kill it?" he repeated walking alongside of Panteli.

"A stupid fellow whose fingers itch, he must kill something," answered the old man. "But he oughtn't to kill an adder, that's true. . . . Dimov is a devil-may-care, as everyone knows, and kills anything within his reach, and Kiruha did not prevent it. He ought to have stopped it, instead he went—'ha, ha, ha,' then 'ho, ho, ho. . . .' But you, Vassia, don't be angry. . . . Why be angry? It's dead, well, God have mercy on them . . . devil-may-care Dimov, and Kiruha the shallow-brained. . . . It's all right. . . . They are stupid folk, dull of understanding, well, God have mercy on them! Emilian there, never harms anything he shouldn't . . . never. That's true. . . . He is educated, and they are stupid. . . . Emilian there . . . he does no harm."

The driver in the rusty brown coat, with the spungious lump, and who conducted an invisible choir, hearing his name stopped, and waiting till Panteli and Vassia came alongside of him joined them.

"What's the talk about?" he asked in a hoarse strangled voice.

"Vassia here is angry," said Panteli. "I have told him some things so that he should not be angry, that is . . . oh! my feet hurt, they are a pest! Oh! Oh! Hurting extra for Sunday, God's holy day!"

"It's from walking," observed Vassia.

"No, boy, no . . . it's not from walking. When I walk it's really better, when I lie down they burn—it's death to me. Walking is easier."

Emilian in the rusty brown coat was between Panteli and Vassia, and waved his hand as if these others were preparing to sing. Having waved a while he dropped his hand and croaked hopelessly.

"I have no voice!" he said. "It's a real disaster! All night and all the morning I have tried to get that triad of the 'Lord have mercy on us,' which we sung at the nuptial benediction of the Marinovski. It's in my head and my throat so to speak, but I cannot sing it! I have no voice."

He was silent for a moment while he thought of something, then continued:

"I was in the choir for fifteen years, in all the Luganski works there was no one with such a voice. Then, like a fool three years ago I bathed in the Donets, and since then I cannot sing a true note. I took cold in my throat. And without a voice I am no better than a workman without hands."

"That's true," agreed Panteli.

"I reckon now that I am a ruined man and nothing more."

At this moment Vassia suddenly caught sight of Egorooshka. His eyes glittered and grew smaller.

"A little sir is driving with us!" he said, covering his nose with his sleeve as if he were blushing. "What an important driver! If he remain with us, he'll drive the waggons and trade in wool!"

The incongruity of the idea of one and the same person being gentleman and driver, evidently seemed to him very odd and witty for he laughed heartily and continued to develop the idea. Emilian also looked up at Egorooshka, cursorily and coldly. He was busy with his own thoughts, and had it not been for Vassia he would not have noticed the presence of Egorooshka. Five minutes had hardly gone by before he again waved his hand about, then again described to his fellow-travellers the beauty of the nuptial benediction of "Lord have mercy on us" which he had remembered during the night, placed his whip under his arm, and flourished both arms.

About a verst from the village the train of waggons stopped by a well with a crane. When he lowered his bucket into the well the black-bearded Kiruha lay belly-down on the framework, and thrust his woolly head, his shoulders, and part of his body into the dark hole, so that all Egorooshka could see of him were his short legs which could hardly touch the ground. When he saw the reflection of his head at the bottom of the well, he was so pleased that he gave vent to his deep foolish laugh, and the well's echo answered likewise; when he got up from the side of the well he was as red as a lobster. The first one to run and get a drink was Dimov. He drank and laughed, often interrupting to tell Kiruha something funny, then he turned round and loudly, so that the whole steppe could hear, he uttered five very bad words. Egorooshka did not understand what such words meant, but that they were bad he was very well aware. He knew the dislike which his relatives and friends silently maintained towards them, and he himself for some unknown reason shared that feeling and was accustomed to think that only drunkards and evil-doers indulged in the privilege of using these words out loud. He recollected the murder of the adder, listened to Dimov's laugh, and felt something like hatred for this man. As if by design Dimov at this juncture caught sight of Egorooshka, who having clambered down from his waggon was going towards the well; he laughed loudly and called out:

"Mates, the old man has given birth to a son in the night!"

Kiruha choked with laughter. Someone else also laughed, and Egorooshka, blushing all over, finally decided that Dimov was a very bad man.

Flaxen-haired and curly Dimov, hatless and with his shirt unfastened, looked handsome and of great strength; in all his movements one detected the athletic and devil-may-care very well aware of his merits. He had a swing of the shoulders, held his arms akimbo, spoke and laughed louder than anyone else, and looked as if he were on the point of performing some feat whereby he would astonish the world. He threw a foolish mocking look on the road, on the train of waggons and on the sky, it settled nowhere and seemed to be seeking out of idleness something to kill and something to laugh at. He evidently feared no one, was ashamed of nothing, and very likely was not at all interested in Egorooshka's opinion. But Egorooshka, already hating with his whole soul his flaxen-hair, clean face, and strength, listened to his laugh with disgust and horror and tried to think of some bad words to retort to him.

Panteli also approached the bucket. He pulled a green image-lamp from his pocket, wiped it with a rag, dipped it into the bucket, drank from it, dipped it in once more, then wrapping it in the rag placed it back in his pocket.

"Dad, why do you drink out of a little lamp?" asked Egorooshka in surprise.

"Some drink out of a bucket and some out of little lamps," answered the old man evasively. "Each to his taste . . . you drink out of a bucket, well, drink, and be well."

"My pet, fond mother mine!" suddenly said Vassia in a wheedling, whimpering voice, "my little pet!"

His eyes were fixed on something in the distance, they glistened and smiled, and his face assumed the expression it had earlier when he espied Egorooshka.

"What's the matter with you?" asked Kiruha.

"A dear little fox . . . lying on its back and playing just like a dog. . . ."

They all looked into the distance and searched for the fox with their eyes, but could discover nothing. Vassia alone saw something with those troubled grey little eyes of his, and was in ecstasies. His sight, as Egorooshka afterwards learnt, was astonishingly penetrating. His sight was so good that the brown empty steppe for him was always full of life and matter. He had only to look into the distance to see a fox, or a hare, or a bustard, or some other living creature holding itself aloof from mankind. The wonder was, not to see the running hare or the flying bustard, for anyone driving over the steppe can do that,—but it is not given to everyone to see these creatures in their free daily life when they are not running or hiding or looking about in alarm. Vassia saw foxes and hares playing, washing their faces with their paws, great-bustards smoothing their wings, or little-bustards sitting on their "points." Thanks to his keen-sightedness, besides the world which everyone could see Vassia had another world, his own, accessible to no one, and most likely a very pleasant one, for when he looked and grew enraptured it was difficult not to envy him.

When the train of waggons moved on the bells from the church were ringing for Mass.

V

The train of waggons set out from the village along the banks of the river. The sun was as scorching as on the previous day, the air was as stagnant and suffocating. There were several willows along the banks of the river, but their shade fell not on the road but over the water, where it was useless, and in the shade of the carts it was so stuffy and tiresome. The water was very blue as the sky was reflected in it, and it looked madly inviting.

The driver, Stepka, on whom Egorooshka's attention only now fell, an eighteen-year-old Little Russian youth, wearing a long shirt without a belt, and wide trousers fluttering about in his walk like a flag, quickly threw off his clothes, ran down the steep bank and flung himself into the water. He dived under the water three times, then swam on his back and blissfully closed his eyes. He smiled and knit his brows as if it tickled, hurt, and amused him.

On those hot days when there is no refuge from the sultry and stifling heat, the splash of water and loud breathing of a man bathing acts on the ear like wonderful music. As Dimov and Kiruha looked at Stepka they quickly threw off their clothes, and one after the other with a loud laugh, anticipating enjoyment, fell into the water. And the quiet modest stream resounded with snufflings and splashings and shouts. Kiruha choked and laughed and screamed as if they were trying to drown him, and Dimov chased him, trying to catch him by the foot.

"Eh, eh, eh!" he screamed, "catch him, stop him!"

Kiruha went "ho, ho, ho," and enjoyed himself, but the look on his face was the same as on dry land, stupid and stunned. just as if someone had crept up unnoticed to him from behind and dealt him a blow on the head with the butt-end of an axe. Egorooshka also undressed, but instead of sliding down the bank he took a run and a leap and dived into the water; he plunged pretty deep but did not reach the bottom for some cold pleasant power gropingly caught hold of him and brought him up to the surface. He spluttered and snuffled, blew bubbles and opened his eyes, and found the sun was shining on the river almost exactly in his face. At first there were blinding sparks, then rainbows and black spots dancing before his eyes; he hastened to dive once more, opened his eyes in the water, and saw something muddy-green similar to the sky on moonlit nights. Once again that power prevented him from touching the bottom and tarrying where it was cool, it brought him to the surface, where he spluttered and breathed so deeply that he felt refreshed and comfortable even down to his stomach. Then, so as to make the most of the water, he indulged in every luxury: he lay and floated on his back, splashed himself, turned somersaults, swam on his stomach, on one side, on his back and standing up, just as he felt inclined, and until he was tired. The further bank turning gold from the sun, was thickly overgrown with reeds whose flowers were bending over the water in lovely tufts. In one place the reeds shook, their flowers bowed low, there was a dry cracking sound. Stepka and Kiruha were in pursuit of cray-fish.

"A cray-fish—look, mates, a cray-fish!" triumphantly shouted Kiruha as he displayed one.

Egorooshka swam to the reeds, dived in and searched among the roots of the rushes. As he rummaged in the fluid mud he felt something sharp and nasty, maybe it was a cray-fish, but at this moment someone seized him by the leg and drew him to the surface. Coughing and choking Egorooshka opened his eyes, and saw before him the wet mocking face of the impudent Dimov. He was breathing heavily and judging by his expression he was inclined to continue his tricks. He held Egorooshka firmly by the leg and was already raising his hand to take him by the neck, when Egorooshka with fear and loathing, as if he apprehended that the athlete might drown him, broke away from him saying:

"Fool! I'll hit you in the face!"

Feeling that this was insufficient to express his hatred, he thought a moment, and added:

"Villain! Son of a slut!"

But Dimov, as if nothing was the matter, took no further notice of Egorooshka and swam off towards Kiruha, shouting:

"Hie! Hie! Hie! Let us catch fish! Boys, let's have some fish!"

"Why not?" Kiruha agreed. "There must be a lot of fish about here."

"Stepka, run over to the village and ask the moujiks for a casting-net."

"They won't give it."

"They will. Ask them. Say, for the sake of Christ as we are travellers."

"That's true."

Stepka emerged from the water, quickly put on his clothes, and ran hatless towards the village. After his encounter with Dimov the water lost all its attraction for Egorooshka; he therefore came out of it and put his clothes on again. Panteli and Vassia were sitting on the steep bank dangling their legs and watching the bathers. Emilian was standing naked in water up to his knees close to the bank, he held the grass with one hand so as not to fall in and stroked his body with the other. He presented a very funny appearance with his long shoulder-blades, spungious lump under his eye, doubling himself up and evidently shrinking from the water. He was very seriously and resentfully looking at the water, as if making up his mind to chide it for having given him a cold that time in the Donets, and so deprived him of his voice.

"Why don't you bathe?" Egorooshka asked Vassia.

"Oh! . . . so . . . don't like it . . ." answered Vassia.

"Why is that swelling on your chin?"

"It hurts. . . . You see, little sir, I worked in a match-factory . . . the doctor said it was from that my jaw tumefied. The atmosphere is unwholesome. Besides myself three children had swollen jaws, one of them rotted away altogether."

Soon Stepka returned with the casting-net. Dimov and

Kiruha were getting quite violet and ochreous from staying so long in the water, but they set about catching fish with great zest. First they went to a deep place by the reeds. Dimov was up to his neck in the water and squat Kiruha up to his chin, he choked and blew bubbles, while Dimov stumbling on the spinous roots fell and got mixed in the casting-net. They both floundered about and made so much noise that their fishing turned into a frolic.

"It's so deep," said Kiruha in a hoarse voice, "you can't catch anything."

"Don't pull, you devil!" shouted Dimov, striving to lay the casting-net. "Hold it with your hands!"

"You won't catch any there!" Panteli shouted to them from the bank. "Only bad ones— Try to the left. It is shallower."

Once a large fish appeared over the casting-net; everyone held their breath, but Dimov with a look of annoyance hit with his fist on the place where it had disappeared.

"Eh!" croaked Panteli, stamping his feet. "They have let him slip. It's gone!"

Moving more leftwards, Dimov and Kiruha little by little made a cast for small fish, and began to fish more seriously. They floundered on about three hundred feet farther; one could see them choosing the deepest parts nearest the reeds, dragging the net after them, beating on the water with their hands, and shaking the reeds to drive the fish into the net. From the reeds they got on to the farther bank, and dragged up their net; then, with a very disenchanted look on their faces, they went back to the reeds. They were talking about something; what it was no one could hear. Meanwhile the sun was scorching their backs, the flies were stinging, and their flesh had now turned purple instead of violet. Behind them walked Stepka with a bucket in his hands, and with his shirt tucked up under his arms and held in his teeth. After each lucky haul, he raised in the air some kind of fish which glittered in the sun, and shouted:

"Just look—what a catch! We have five like that!"

Each time they dragged up the net, Dimov, Kiruha, and Stepka rummaged a long time in the mud, put some things in the bucket, and threw away others. Occasionally something found in the net was passed from hand to hand; they each looked at it with curiosity, then it also was thrown away.

"What have you got?" they shouted from the bank.

Stepka answered something, but it was difficult to hear what.

And now he emerged from the water holding the bucket in both hands, and, forgetting to let down his shirt, ran towards the waggons.

"It's already full!" he cried, panting. "Give us another!"

Egorooshka looked into the bucket; it was quite full. A young pike's ugly nose was sticking out of the water: there were also cray-fish and other small fish stirring about. Egorooshka put his hand to the bottom, and stirred up the water; the pike disappeared under the cray-fish, and in its place a perch and a tench swam to the surface. Vassia looked into the bucket. His eyes glistened, and his expression softened as it did when he saw the fox. He picked something out of the bucket, carried it to his mouth, and there was a sound of crunching.

"Mates," said Stepka in surprise. "Vassia is eating live minnow! Ugh!"

"It is not a minnow, it's bean-pod," calmly answered Vassia, and he continued to crunch.

He pulled a fish's tail out of his mouth, looked sweetly at it, and put it back. As he chewed and crunched, it seemed to Egorooshka it was not a man he saw standing before him; Vassia's swollen chin, lustreless eyes, unusual keen-sightedness, the fish's tail in his mouth and the relish with which he ate the minnow. gave him more the resemblance to a wild animal.

Egorooshka was bored in his company—besides the fishing was over, so he walked past the waggons, and, not feeling amused, wandered towards the village.

A few moments later he was standing in the church close to someone who smelt of hemp, and listening to the singing. Mass was nearly over. Egorooshka understood nothing about church-singing, and felt quite indifferent towards it. He listened for a little while, yawned, and began to examine the backs and napes of the people. He recognised one nape which was ruddy and wet from recent bathing—it was Emilian's His hair was shaved so close that his ears stood out like lop-ears on either side, and seemed to feel out of place. As he studied the back of his head and his ears, Egorooshka somehow realised what a very unhappy person Emilian was. He thought of his conducting, his hoarse voice, timid glances when he was bathing, and felt an immense pity for him. He wanted to say something kind.

"I am here too," he said, gently pulling his sleeve.

People who have sung in the choir, either as bass or as tenor, and especially those who have conducted, even if only once in their lives, are accustomed to look at little boys in a severe and unfriendly manner. They do not give up this habit even after they have ceased to be in the choir. Emilian, half turning round and looking at Egorooshka over his shoulder, said:

"Don't chatter in church!"

So then Egorooshka made his way up closer to the ikonstase. Here he saw some quite interesting people. Right in the forefront, on a carpet to the right, he saw a gentleman and a lady. The gentleman, in a well-pressed blue suit, was standing stiffly, like a soldier saluting, and was holding his dark clean-shaven chin well in the air. By his stand-up collar, his well-poised chin, his slight baldness, and his walking-stick, you felt he was a person of great merit. From the excess of his merit did his neck and chin strain upwards with such vigour that his head seemed ready any minute to make away and fly aloft. The lady, who was plump and middle-aged, was wearing a white silk shawl, and, holding her head on one side, she looked as if she had just conferred a favour on someone, and was about to say, "Oh! don't bother to thank me, I don't like it." All around the carpet stood a thick wall of "topknots."

Egorooshka went up to the ikonstase, and began kissing the ikons thereon. Before each image he slowly made a low bow to the ground, and without rising looked back at the people, then rose and kissed the image. The contact of the cold floor with his forehead was very pleasant. When the warden came from behind the altar with a long pair of snuffers to put out the candles, Egorooshka quickly rose from the ground and went towards him.

"Have they given the wafers?" he asked.

"Aren't any—aren't any," gruffly mumbled the old man; "no use looking. . . ."

The Mass was over. Egorooshka slowly left the church, and started to wander round the open squares. In his time he had seen not a few villages and squares and moujiks, and all the things which now came under his notice did not at all interest him. Having nothing to do, and so as to kill time somehow, he went up to a shop over the doors of which hung a broad red fustian stripe. The shop consisted of two spacious and badly lit halves; in the one half they sold red wares and grocery, and in the other half stood barrels of tar, and it was hung with horse-collars up to the roof. In both halves there was a good smell of leather and tar. The floor of the shop had been watered, and he who had watered it was evidently a great fantast and free-thinker, for it was all covered with patterns and cabalistic signs. Behind the counter, and leaning on it, was a fat shopman with a broad face and a rounded beard; he was probably a Great Russian. He was drinking tea and eating a bit of sugar with it, and after each gulp breathed a deep sigh. His expression was one of complete indifference, but every sigh seemed to say, "Just wait, I'll give it you!"

"Give me a kopeck's worth of dry sunflower seeds," Egorooshka said, addressing him.

The shopman raised his eyebrows, came from behind the counter, and poured a kopeck-worth of sunflower seeds into Egorooshka's pocket—the scales, by the way, were being used by an empty pot of pomade. Egorooshka had no wish to leave. He looked for a long time at the boxes with the ginger-bread, thought a bit, and asked as he pointed to some small gingers, which owing to the great lapse of time were thick with mildew:

"How much are those ginger-breads?"

"Two a kopeck."

Egorooshka fetched out of his pocket the ginger-bread given him by the Jewess, and asked:

"And these kind of ginger-breads, how much?"

The shopman took the ginger-bread in his hand, looked at it on every side, and raised an eyebrow.

"These?" he asked.

Then he raised the other eyebrow, thought a moment, and answered:

"Two for three kopecks."

There was a silence.

"Who are you?" asked the shopman, pouring himself out some tea from a red copper teapot.

"The nephew of Ivan Ivanitch."

"There are several Ivan Ivanitches," sighed the shopman; he looked past Egorooshka's head through the door, was silent a moment, then asked: "Don't you want any tea?"

"Please. . . ." Egorooshka assented somewhat unwillingly, although he felt a great longing for his morning tea.

The shopman poured him out a glass, and handed it him, together with a gnawed bit of sugar. Egorooshka sat on the folding-stool, and began to drink. He was about to inquire how much a pound of sugared almonds cost when a buyer entered, so the shopman, setting his glass on one side, attended to other business. He led the buyer into the half of the shop which smelt of tar, and spoke to him a long time about some affair or other. The buyer was evidently a very obstinate man and a cunning blade, for he shook his head perpetually in the negative and then went towards the door. The shopman assured him of something, and began pouring oats into a large sack.

"Such oats!" ruefully said the buyer. "They are only half oats, they'd make a chicken laugh. . . . Oh! well, I'll go to Bondarenka!"

When Egorooshka returned to the river-side he saw the smoke of a small wood-pile. The drivers were cooking their dinners. Stepka was standing in the midst of the smoke, and was stirring in a pot with a jagged spoon. A few steps away, Kiruha and Vassia, with eyes reddened by smoke, were sitting cleaning the fish. In front of them lay the casting-net covered in mud and weeds, wherein also lay dead fish and some cray-fish crawled.

Emilian, who had not long since returned from the church, was sitting with Panteli waving his hands, and, in a scarcely audible hoarse voice, was humming: "To Thee we sing." Dimov was wandering among the horses.

Having finished cleaning the fish. Kirhua and Vassia gathered up the fish and the live cray-fish into the bucket, rinsed them, then poured them all into the boiling water.

"Did you put in any fat?" Stepka asked, removing the scum with his spoon.

"What for? Fish are full of it," answered Kiruha.

Before removing the pot from the fire, Stepka strewed in three handfuls of millet-meal and a spoonful of salt; finally he tried it, smacked his lips, licked the spoon, and croaked in a very self-satisfied way—that meant the gruel was ready.

All except Panteli sat round the pot, and set to work with their spoons.

"Oh! You! Give the little sir a spoon," sternly remarked Panteli. "Does he not want to eat too?"

"Ours is moujik's food . . ." sighed Kiruha.

"And very good too, if he is hungry."

They gave Egorooshka a spoon. He ate his food without sitting down, standing by the pot and looking down into it as into a deep pit. The gruel smelt of raw fish, and in fact there were fishes' scales mixed with the millet. It was quite impossible to catch the cray-fish with the spoon, so the eaters had to take them out of the pot with their hands. Vassia, in particular, made very little ceremony about it—he even dipped his sleeves as well as his hands into the gruel. All the same, the gruel tasted excellent, and it reminded Egorooshka of the cray-fish soup which his mamma made at home on fast-days. Panteli sat apart from them, and munched bread.

"Dad, why aren't you eating with us?" Emilian asked him.

"I don't eat cray-fish. The devil take them!" said the old man, turning away with disgust.

During the meal there was general conversation. From this conversation, Egorooshka gathered that all his new acquaintances, regardless of their differences in age and character, were alike in one particular: they all of them had had a wonderful past, and the present was very bad. They all spoke of their past with ecstasy and treated the present almost with contempt. A Russian loves to reminisce but dislikes the act of living. Egorooshka did not yet know this, so before the gruel was all eaten, he profoundly believed that around the cauldron sat people who had been insulted and wronged by fate. Panteli told of days past when there were no railroads, when he walked with his waggons to Moscow and to Nijni, when he worked such a lot he did not know where to put all his money. And what merchants there were in those days, what fish, how cheap everything was! Nowadays their routes were shorter, merchants were meaner, the people poorer, bread dearer, everything had diminished and dwindled to a minimum. Emilian told how formerly he had worked in the mill in Lougansk, and sung in the choir. He had had a remarkable voice, and could read music quite well, now he had relapsed into being a peasant, and living on the charity of others who sent him with their horses and so took half his earnings. Vassia had worked in a match-factory, Kiruha had been coachman with some very good people, and been reckoned as the best driver of a troika in the neighbourhood. Dimov was the son of a well-to-do moujik, lived in comfort and idleness, and had not a care. He had hardly attained his twentieth year when his stern, cruel father, wishing to instruct him in business and fearing lest he should get spoiled at home, sent him off as driver, just like any landless peasant or worker. Stepka alone remained silent, but by his beardless face one could tell that he had seen much better days than the present ones.

Dimov, as he thought of his father, frowned and ceased to eat. He looked at his companions out of the corner of his eye, and his glance rested on Egorooshka.

"You heathen, take off your hat!" he said rudely. "Does anyone eat in a hat? Not even a bairn!"

Egorooshka took off his hat without saying a word, but the gruel had lost its flavour, nor did he hear that Panteli and Vassia were taking his part. His bosom heaved with anger against that impudent fellow, and he made up his mind that come what might he would have his revenge.

After their dinner they all wandered off to the waggons, and stretched themselves in the shade.

"Dad, are we soon going on?" Egorooshka asked Panteli.

"When God wills we shall go on. . . . We shan't go now, it's too hot. . . . Oh! Lord, Thy will. . . . Holy Virgin. Lie down, little sir!"

Soon the sound of snoring was heard from beneath the waggons. Egorooshka would have liked to have gone back to the village, but he thought it over, yawned, and laid himself down near the old man.

VI

All day the waggons remained by the river, and only left their place when the sun went down.

Once more Egorooshka lay on the bale of wool while the waggon softly creaked and rocked; below walked Panteli, stamping his feet, slapping his thighs, and mumbling; and like on the previous day the air hummed with the steppe music.

Egorooshka lay on his back with his hands behind his head, looking up at the sky. He saw it on fire with the redness of dusk, and then he saw the light go out; the guardian angels drew their golden wings over the horizon and disposed themselves for their night's rest; the day had been successful, the soft blissful night was beginning, and they might sit quietly at home in heaven. . . . Egorooshka saw the sky grow dim, the mist descending over the ground, and the stars light up one after the other.

If you keep your eyes fixed for a long while on the vast sky, somehow your thoughts and your soul acquire the consciousness of solitude. You begin to feel yourself irrevocably lonely; all which you had considered previously as close to you and related to you becomes illimitably distant and of no value. The stars which have been looking from the skies for thousands of years, and the incomprehensible sky itself, and the mist, unconcerned as they all are with man's short life, oppress you by their silence when you stand face to face with them and strive to fathom their thoughts. The thought comes into one's mind of that loneliness which awaits each one of us by the grave, and the barrenness of life seems something despairing and dreadful. . . .

Egorooshka thought of his grandmother, now sleeping in the cemetery under the cherry trees: he remembered her lying in her coffin with the five-kopeck pieces on her eyes, how they afterwards closed her in and put her in the grave; he remembered the dull thuds of the clods of earth on the lid. . . . He represented to himself his grandmother in her dark narrow coffin, helpless and by all forsaken. His imagination drew his grandmother as suddenly awakening and not understanding where she was, knocking on the lid, calling for help, and in the end fainting away with fright and dying over again. He pictured to himself as dead, his mother, Father Christopher, Countess Dranitska, Solomon. But, try as he would, he could not picture himself in a dark grave, far from home, abandoned, helpless, dead—it would not come; for himself personally he could not admit the possibility of death, and felt he would never die. . . . And Panteli, whose time it was to die, walked below calling over the roll of his thoughts:

"Nitchevo . . . nice gentleman . . ." he mumbled—"took the little sir to study, and how he does there, never heard about that. . . . In Slavianoserbska, they say, there is no institution to lead to much learning. . . . There isn't, that's true. . . . The little sir was all right, nitchevo . . . when he grows up he will help his father. Egor, you are young still, but when you are a big man you'll support your father and mother. It is so ordained by God. . . . Honour your father and mother. . . I my own self had some children; they were burnt . . . my wife was burnt, and the children. . . . That's true . . . on Christmas night our cottage was burnt. It was not my house, I had gone to Orel. In Orel . . . Mary ran out into the street, then remembered that the children were asleep in the cottage, ran back, and was burnt with the children. . . . Yes. . . . The next day we found only the bones."

Towards midnight, the drivers and Egorooshka were again assembled around a fire. While the steppe-grass was kindling, Kiruha and Vassia went somewhere to a marsh for water; they disappeared in the darkness, but the clank of their buckets and their voices could be heard all the time, therefore the marsh could not be very far away. The light of the fire cast a large flickering halo on the ground; although the moon was shining, the things outside the red halo looked impenetrable and dark. The drivers were partly dazzled by this light, and they could only see a portion of the great road; the waggons with the bales, and the horses were hardly noticeable in the gloom except in the semblance of a mountain of undefined outline. Some twenty steps from the fire, by the edge of the road, stood a wooden grave-cross leaning over to one side. Egorooshka, before the fire was aflame and it was possible to see some distance away, had noticed that just another such a leaning cross stood on the other side of the great highway.

When Kiruha and Vassia returned with water, they filled up the cauldron and fixed it over the fire. Stepka, with the jagged spoon in his hand, took up his post in the smoke by the cauldron, and, looking thoughtfully into the water, waited for the first signs of scum bubbles. Panteli and Emilian sat side by side in silence, deep in thought; Dimov lay belly downwards, resting his head in his hands and looking into the fire; Stepka's shadow danced over him, and at times it hid and at times it revealed his handsome face. . . . Kiruha and Vassia wandered some little distance away gathering grass and birchbark for the fire. Egorooshka, with his hands in his pockets, stood by Panteli and watched how the flames devoured the grass.

Everyone was resting, thinking, looking casually at the grass over which danced the red light. There is something very melancholy, dreamy, and in the highest degree poetic in a lonely grave . . . You hear its silence, and in this silence you feel the presence of the soul of the unknown being who lives beneath that cross. How do their souls like the steppe? Do they not feel sad on moonlit nights? And the steppe around a grave seems sorrowful, dismal, museful, the grass more afflicted, and it would seem as if even the grasshoppers' cry were in some measure subdued. There is no passer-by who would not mention that soul in his prayers, and look back at that grave until it remained far behind veiled in mist.

"Dad, why is that cross there?" asked Egorooshka.

Panteli looked at the cross, then at Dimov, and asked:

"Mike, this must be the place where the mowers murdered the traders?"

Dimov reluctantly turned over on his elbow, looked at the road, and answered:

"The very same. . . ."

There was a silence. Kiruha broke up and kneaded the dry grass, then shoved it under the cauldron; the fire flared up, Stepka was enveloped in the black smoke, and in the gloom on the road among the waggons flickered the shadow of the cross.

"Aye, murdered . . ." Dimov said reluctantly. "The traders, a father and son, were on their way to sell a picture. They stopped at a tavern not far from here, kept now by Ignatius Thomin. The old man drank to excess, and began to boast that he had a lot of money with him. Traders are a boastful lot if ever there were. . . . He could not refrain from showing off before our friend. At this time some mowers were spending the night at the tavern, whereupon, hearing how this merchant boasted, they took counsel together. . . ."

"Oh, Lord. . . . Holy Virgin!" sighed Panteli.

"The next day, when it was scarce light," Dimov continued, "the traders prepared to continue their journey, and the mowers attached themselves to them: 'Let us go, your Honour, together. It is merrier, and the peril will be lessened, as not far from here is a dark spot.' The traders drove at a foot's pace so as not to break the picture, and this quite suited the mowers. . . ."

Dimov knelt up and stretched himself.

"Yes," he continued with a yawn. "It was no good; as soon as the traders reached that spot, they set on them with their scythes. The son, brave fellow, snatched a scythe from one of them and went for them. . . . But of course they were overpowered—there were eight of them. They hacked the traders so that there was not a sound place left on their bodies. When they had finished, they dragged them off the road, the father to one side, the son to the other. . . . If it is whole, I don't know. . . . Can't see from here."

"It is whole," said Kiruha.

"They say there was very little money."

"Very little," Panteli affirmed. "A hundred roubles."

"Yes; and three of them died, for the young trader, had also hacked well with his scythe. . . . Died of loss of blood. He caught one on the arm, and he ran, so they say, four versts without his hand; they found him on a mound at Kurikovo; he was squatting with his head on his knees as if he were thinking, they looked—there was no breath in him —he was dead."

"They found him by the bloody trail," said Panteli.

Everyone looked at the cross in silence. Somewhere, probably from the marsh, came the mournful note of a bird: "Splu, splu, splu. . . ."

"There are many wicked people in the world," remarked Emilian.

"Many, many!" affirmed Panteli, and drew nearer the fire, just as if he had grown apprehensive. "Many," he continued in an undertone. "In my time I have seen life inside and out. . . . Ah, yes, wicked people. . . . Saintly and righteous have I seen many, and sinful more than I can count. . . . Save and have mercy, Heavenly Virgin! . . . I remember once, thirteen years ago, and maybe more, I was taking a merchant out of Morchanska, an estimable merchant both in himself and with his money, that merchant was . . . a good fellow, nitchevo. . . . So, therefore, we drove and stopped to spend the night at a tavern. In Greater Russia the taverns are not like what they are in these parts. There the yarsa are roofed like foundations, or let us say sheds, on the big farms—only the sheds are higher. Well, we stopped and all went well—my merchant to his room and I to the horses, all as it should be. And now, mates, with a prayer to God, so as consequently to sleep, I took a walk around the yard. The night was dark—couldn't see a thing however you tried. I walked on a bit, and when beyond the waggons I see the dim light of a fire. What is that? Methought the taverner had long ago gone to bed, and except myself and the merchant there were no other inmates. What was the meaning of that fire? A doubt seized me. I crept up closer . . . to that fire

. . . Lord have mercy and save us! Holy Virgin! I look; a little window near the ground with iron bars . . . in the house. . . . I lay on the ground to see in—as I look a shiver runs through my body. . . ."

Kiruha, trying not to make a noise, shoves a bundle of grass into the fire. Waiting till the steppe-grass has finished crackling and hissing, the old man then went on:

"I see there a cellar, not very large, and dark as pitch. . . . On a barrel burns a little lantern. In the centre of that cellar stand ten men in red shirts with turned-up sleeves and sharpening their long knives. . . . Ho—hè! So then we have fallen among a gang of thieves! What was to be done? I ran to the merchant, gently woke him up, and said to him: 'Merchant, don't you be frightened, but this is a nasty business . . . we have fallen into a robber's nest.' His face dropped, and he asked: 'And what now, Panteli, shall we do? I have so much orphans' money with me. As for my soul, it is in the hands of God. I have no fear of death, but,' says he, 'it is very grievous that orphans' money should go astray.' . . . What could we do? The gates were locked, no possible means of escape. . . . If there had been a fence one could have climbed over it, but that yard was roofed! . . . 'Well,' says I, 'merchant, be not afraid, but pray to God. Maybe the Lord has no wish to wrong orphans. You remain here, and do not lose courage. I in the interval may think of something.' Agreed. . . . I prayed, and God put a thought in my mind. . . . I climbed into our carriage, and gently, very gently, so that no one should hear, I began pulling the straw from the thatching, made a hole and clambered out—yes, out. . . . Then I jumped down from the roof, and fled along the road as if there were an evil spirit after me. I ran and ran, exhausting myself to death. . . . I must have run five versts without drawing breath, if not more. . . . Then, thank God, I saw a village. I ran to a cottage, and knocked at the window. 'Oh! Orthodox, if such you be, let not a Christian soul perish.' . . . They all awoke—the moujiks assembled and followed me . . . some with ropes . . . some with cudgels, some with pitchforks. . . . We beat down the gates of the tavern-yard and so into the cellar. . . . The robbers had just finished sharpening their knives, and were preparing to slay the merchant. The moujiks seized every one of them, bound them, and led them to the authorities. The merchant in his joy offered them three hundred roubles, and to me five golden coins and engraved my name in his memory. They say, that in the cellar were afterwards found untold numbers of human bones. . . . Those bones signified that folk were plundered, and afterwards buried so that no trace should remain. . . . Well, so then, the robbers were taken to Morchanska and handed over to the executioner."

Panteli, having finished his story, glanced at his listeners. They all were silent, with their eyes fixed on him. The water was boiling, and Stepka removed the scum.

"Is the fat ready?" Kiruha asked him in a whisper.

"Wait another bit . . . soon."

Stepka without taking his eyes off Panteli, as if afraid he would begin some story without him, ran towards the waggons, and quickly returned from thence with a small wooden cup, in which he began to bray some pig's fat.

"I went another time also with a merchant," continued Panteli, as before in an undertone and without blinking. "He was called, as I remember, Peter Gregoritch. He was a goodly fellow . . . that merchant was. . . . We stopped in the same manner as before at a tavern. . . . He to his room, I to my horses. . . . The taverner and his wife seemed goodly, kindly folk, the workers seemed quite all right, but, mates, I could not sleep, my mind was not at ease—just not at ease. The gates were open, plenty of people around, but all the same there was something fearful—not as it should be. Everyone had long ago fallen asleep, it was altogether night, and soon we should have to get up, and I alone, lying in the carriage, had my eyes wide open, just as if I were a brown owl. But, mates, something I hear: 'Tup, tup, tup!' Someone is creeping up to the carriage. I raise my head, I look—a woman in nothing but a chemise, barelegged, stands there. . . . 'What is it, woman?' say I. She, all of a tremble and scared out of her wits, says, 'Good fellow, get up! Disaster. . . . The master and mistress have imagined evil . . they intend to slay your merchant. I myself heard the master whispering to the mistress'. . . . So it was not for nothing my mind was uneasy! 'But you, who are you?' I ask. 'I,' says she, 'am their cook. . . .' Agreed. . . . I climb out of the carriage and go to the merchant; I awake him and say: 'There is, Peter Gregoritch, rather a dirty business. . . . May your Honour have had sleep enough, and now, while there is time, dress and with a whole skin escape from evil. . . .' He had no sooner started putting on his clothes when the door opened, and—God bless you, I see—Holy Mother! into the room walk the taverner and his wife and three labourers; that is, they had told the labourers: 'The merchant has a lot of money, so you see we'll divide.' . . . All five had long knives in their hands. . . . Each a knife . . . the master locks the door and says: 'Pray, travellers, to God. . . . But should you be disposed to scream we shall not give you time to pray before you die.' . . . Where was he who could scream? Our throats were choked by fear, and there was no scream in us. . . . The merchant sobbed, and said: 'Oh! Orthodox, you have resolved to kill me because you are covetous of my money. So be it. I am not the first and I am not the last; many others of my brother-merchants have been slain, in these taverns. But wherefore,' said he, 'my brothers-Orthodox, kill my driver? Why inflict that pain on him in order to take my money?' So compassionately he said this. And the master answered: 'Yet if we leave him among the living then will he be chief witness against us. It's all the same,' said he, 'if we kill one or two. To seven wrongs the same end. . . . Pray to God, and have done with it—talking is no good!' The merchant and I knelt down side by side, wept, and said our prayer to God. He thought of his children; at that time I was a youth and wanted to live. . . . We look at the picture of the saint; we pray, and so piteously that tears still flow. . . . The mistress looked at us and said: 'You,' says she, 'are good people; do not bear us a grudge for this, and do not pray God to visit this upon us, for we are doing this out of necessity.' We prayed, we prayed, we wept, we wept, and God heard us. He was moved to pity, that is. . . . At the very moment when the taverner seized the merchant by the beard to cut his throat there was a knock outside on the window! We all nearly sat down, and the knife fell out of the taverner's hand. . . . Someone was knocking at the window, and seemed to call out: 'Peter Gregoritch, are you there? Get ready, let us go!' That taverner and his wife seeing someone had come to fetch the merchant, were scared and took to their heels. . . . We were in the yard double quick, put the horses to, and away like a vision. . . ."

"Who was it rapped at the window?" asked Dimov.

"At the window? Must have been a saint or an angel, for there was no one about. . . . When we got outside there was not a human being anywhere . the work of God!"

Panteli told other stories, and in all of them alike the "long knives" played a rôle, and all alike had the same note of unreality. Had he heard these tales from someone, or had he himself invented them in the far away past, and later, when his memory failed, mixed his experiences with fiction and ceased to be able to distinguish the one from the other? Anything may be true, but one thing was strange that this time and during the whole journey, when he happened to tell a story, he ostensibly gave the preference to fiction and never spoke of what he had experienced. At the moment Egorooshka accepted this all as pure gold and believed every word; subsequently it seemed to him odd, that a man who in the course of his life had been all over Russia, who knew and who had seen so much, a man whose wife and children had been burnt, should so undervalue the richness of his life as each time, sitting by the fire, or remaining silent or talking, to dwell on that which had never been.

They all ate their gruel in silence thinking over what they had heard. Life is so fearful and wonderful that, however fearful is the story you tell in Russia, and however you set it off with robbers' dens, long knives and wonders, it always evokes in the mind of the listener that which has been, and it is only he who is deeply tinctured with learning who looks askance and grows taciturn. The crosses by the road, the dark bales, the wide steppe, and the fates of the people gathered around the fire were in themselves so wonderful and fearful, that the fantastic unreal paled and mingled with the real.

They all ate out of the cauldron except Panteli, who sat a little apart and ate his gruel out of a wooden cup. His spoon was not like those of the others, but of cypress wood, with a little cross. Egorooshka looked at him, and, remembering the little lamp-glass, whispered to Stepka:

"Why does the old dad sit apart?"

"He belongs to the Old Faith," answered Stepka and Vassia in a whisper, and as they said it they conveyed the impression of having mentioned some failing or secret vice.

They all remained silently occupied with their own thoughts. After the terrible tales no one felt inclined to talk of the usual things. Suddenly, amid the stillness, Vassia sat bolt upright, pricked up his ears, and strained his eyes at some invisible object.

"What is it?" Dimov inquired of him.

"There is somebody walking," answered Vassia.

"Where do you see him?"

"Over there . . . you can hardly see him."

There, where Vassia was looking, was nothing to be seen except the darkness; they all listened, but they could hear no footsteps.

"Is he coming down the road?" asked Dimov.

"Nay, over the grass . . . he is coming here."

A minute went by in silence.

"Maybe it is the merchant whom they buried here haunting the steppe," said Dimov.

They all cast furtive glances at the cross, then looked at each other, and finally burst out laughing: they were ashamed of their timidity.

"Why should he walk?" said Panteli. "It is only those whom the ground will not keep who walk at night. But the merchant was all right . . . he received the crown of martyrdom."

But now they heard footsteps; someone was approaching in haste.

"He is carrying something," said Vassia.

One could hear the rustle of the grass and the crackling of the steppe-grass, but beyond the light of the fire there was nothing to be seen. At last the footsteps sounded quite close, and someone coughed; the flickering light seemed to withdraw, and, as if a veil had fallen from their eyes, the drivers suddenly saw before them the figure of a man.

Either it was that the fire gleamed brightly, or that they were all so anxious primarily to see this man's face, that what they saw of him first of all was not his face nor his clothes but his smile. It was a most unusually kind, broad, gentle smile, like that of a waking child, one of those infectious smiles to which it is difficult not to respond with a smile. The stranger, when they had taken him in, appeared to be a man of about thirty, not good-looking or with anything very characteristic. He was a tall "Top-knot," long-legged, long-armed, and long-nosed; in fact everything about him was long except his neck, which was so short that he might have been considered hump-backed. He wore a clean white shirt with an embroidered collar, wide white trousers and new boots, and in comparison to the drivers was quite a dandy. He was carrying in his arms something large and white and queer; and over his shoulder peeped the barrel of a gun, which was also long.

As he entered the bright circle out of the darkness, he stood as if rooted to the spot, and for a full half minute looked at the drivers as if he meant to say: "Just look what a smile I have!" Then he walked up to the fire, smiling even more radiantly, and said:

"Good cheer, mates!"

"Be welcome!" Panteli answered for them all.

The stranger put down by the fire that which he had been carrying—it was a great bustard—and again gave them a greeting.

They all went to have a look at the bustard.

"A fine bird! What did you get him with?" Dimov asked.

"A bullet . . . shot would be no good, wouldn't reach him. . . . Buy him, mates! I will give him up to you for twenty kopecks."

"And what should we do with it? Roasted it is all right, but boiled it would be tough and tasteless."

"Oh bother! If I take it to the people at the farm they will give me fifty kopecks, but it is a long way, fifteen versts!"

The new-comer sat down, and laid his gun by his side; he seemed sleepy and languid, smiled, blinked at the fire, and apparently was thinking of something pleasant. They gave him a spoon, and he began to eat.

"Who are you?" Dimov asked him.

The stranger did not hear the question; he returned no answer, and did not even look at Dimov. Apparently this smiling individual did not notice the taste of the gruel, for he munched as it were mechanically, lazily putting the spoon to his mouth—at one time very full, at another quite empty. He was not drunk, but there was something crazy at work in his brain.

"I am asking you who you are," repeated Dimov.

"Who, I?" said the unknown, with a start. "Constantine Zvonik of Rovno. Four versts from here."

Then, anxious to make it clear from the very first that he was not a peasant as were the others, but better than they, Constantine hastened to add:

"We keep bees and pigs."

"Do you live with your father or by yourself?"

"No, by myself. We parted. This month, after the St. Peter, I was married. I am a husband now! . . . This is the eighteenth day since I was law-bound."

"Excellent business," said Panteli. "A good wife . . . God's blessing. . . ."

"The young woman is sleeping at home while he wanders over the steppe," Kiruha joked. "Queer fellow!"

Constantine gave a start as if he had been touched to the quick, laughed and flushed.

"But Lord, she is not at home!" he said quickly, withdrawing his spoon from his mouth, and giving them all a look of joy and surprise. "She is not! She has gone to her mother for two days! God to witness she went and I am as it were unmarried. . . ."

Constantine flourished his hand and shook his head; he wanted to continue his thoughs, but his felicity was too great. Just as if he were uncomfortable sitting down, he changed his attitude, laughed, and again flourished his hand. He felt a certain compunction at yielding his pleasant thought to strangers, but at the same time he had an overwhelming desire to let them share his joy.

"She went to Demidovo to her mother!" he said, blushing, and removing his gun from one place to another. "To-morrow she comes back. She said she would be back to dinner."

"Are you bored?" asked Dimov.

"But Lord, what do you think? Married such a little while, then for her to go away. . . . Eh? But it's the worst, spare me, God! She is so sweet, so precious, so mirthful, so full of song, it's all the purest enchantment. With her your head goes whirling round, and without her you are lost; see, here I tramp about the steppe like a fool. I have walked since dinner hardly heeding where I go."

Constantine rubbed his eyes, looked at the fire, and smiled.

"You are in love, that is," said Panteli.

"She is so sweet, so precious," repeated Constantine, not listening, "such a little housewife, so sensible, so very sensible, there is no other like her in the entire district. She left; she finds it wearisome, I know! I know, little magpie! She said she would return for dinner to-morrow. . . . But then, what a muddle it is!" almost screamed Constantine, suddenly going a tone higher and changing his position—"now she is in love and bored, and also she did not want to marry me!"

"Yes, but eat," said Kiruha.

"She did not want to marry me!" continued Constantine not listening. "I was at her for three years! I saw her at the fair at Kalatchika, I fell madly in love—hurtling head over heels. But I to Rovno, she to Demidovo, friend divided from friend by twenty-five versts, and nothing I could do. I despatched a marriage-promoter, and she answers: 'I will not!' Oh! you little magpie. So I try this and the other, earrings, ginger-breads, and honey: 'I will not!' Well, I must go myself. She no doubt considers I am no match for her. She is young, pretty, all sunbeams, and I am old, shall soon be thirty, and so handsome, a bushy beard—all ends, a clean face—all over pimples! What comparison was there with her? If we had even lived very comfortably; but then they too, the Vahremenki, live in comfort—they have three pairs of oxen and two labourers. I fell in love, mates, and grew muddle-brained. . . . Could not sleep, could not eat, and in my head, the Lord have mercy, thoughts like a prickly bush! . . . I want to see her, and she is in Demidovo. . . So what do you think? Spare me, God, I am not raving. Three times in a week I went there on foot, just to have a look at her. I chucked my work. So eclipsed became my reason that I thought of hiring myself as a labourer in Demidovo, so as to be nearer to her. I was in torment! My mother spoke of a witch, my father took ten times to beating me. Well, I suffered three years, then I resolved: be thrice anathema, but I'll to the town and be a droshky-driver. . . . Yet I was not!

On a Saint's day, I went to Demidovo for one last look at her. . . ."

Constantine threw back his head and broke into a soft merry laugh, as if he had that moment very cunningly taken someone in.

"I see her. she is by the stream with her washing," he continued. "Malice spoke to me. . . . I called her to one side, and for the space of an hour I talked. . . . She fell in love! Three years she had not loved me, and fell in love at my words! . . ."

"And what words?" inquired Dimov.

"Words? I don't remember. . . . Would you remember? Then, they flowed without respite like water from a spout and now I cannot utter a single one. . . . Well, she came to me. . . . And the little magpie has now gone to her mother, so I without her roam the steppe. I cannot stay at home—it is more than I can bear!"

Constantine clumsily freed his foot from underneath him, stretched himself out on the ground, rested his head on his hands, then raised himself again into a sitting posture. They all thoroughly understood that the man was very enamoured and happy—almost painfully so; his smile, his eyes, and every gesture expressed a languid bliss. He could not rest, did not know what pose to take or what to do not to succumb to the superabundance of pleasant thoughts. Having poured out his soul to the others, he was able, at last, to sit quietly looking at the fire and think.

At the sight of this happy man they all felt vexed, each desiring happiness too. They became very thoughtful. Dimov rose from his place and walked around the fire; by his walk and the movement of his shoulders, it was evident that he felt languid and bored; he stood still, looked at Constantine, and sat down again.

The fire was going out; it no longer flared, and the red halo had shrunk and grown dim. . . . And the faster the fire went out, the clearer became the moonlit night. Already the road in all its great width was visible, the bales of wool, the waggon-thills, and the browsing horses. On the far side the dim outline of the other cross could be seen.

Dimov rested his cheek in his hand, and softly sang some plaintive ditty. Constantine sleepily smiled, and accompanied him in a faint voice; they sang for half a minute, then stopped. Emilian gave a start, his elbows began to move, and his fingers to become restless.

"Mates," said he in a supplicating voice, "let us sing some sacred song!"

The tears sprang to his eyes.

"Mates," he repeated, pressing his hand to his heart, "let us sing sacred music!"

"I don't know how to," said Constantine.

They all refused, so then Emilian sang alone. He began to wave both hands about, to nod his head; he opened his mouth, but from his throat only proceeded a hoarse hollow gasp. He sang with his hands, his head, his eyes, and even with the lump; he sang passionately and with longing, and the more he strained his chest to extract from it but one note, the more hollow grew his breathing. . . .

Egorooshka, as were they all, was overcome by weariness; he walked to his waggon, clambered up on to the bales, and lay down. He gazed up at the sky, and thought of happy Constantine and his wife. "Why do people marry? Why are there women in the world?" Egorooshka asked himself these obscure questions, and decided that men were surely always happy when a fond, cheerful, pretty woman lived beside them. For some reason he thought of the Countess Dranitska, and reflected that it was probably very pleasant to live with a woman like that; he would have been very glad, if you like, to marry her if it had not been so wicked. He remembered her eyebrows, her distended pupils, her carriage, the clock with the horseman. . . . The silent warm night came down to him and whispered something in his ear, and it seemed to him that it was a lovely woman bending over him and smiling, and that she was about to kiss him. . . .

Two little red eyes, ever growing smaller and smaller, were all that remained of the fire; the drivers and Constantine, black and motionless figures, sat beside it, and it seemed as if their number had increased. Both crosses were likewise visible, and far, far away, somewhere by the highway, burned a little fire; very likely other people were cooking gruel.

"Our mother Russia is head of all the world!" suddenly sang Kiruha in a loud voice, then choked and was silent. The steppe-echo caught up the sound, and those senseless words rolled away, borne on heavy wheels over the steppe.

"It is time to move on," said Panteli. "Get up, boys!"

While they put the horses to, Constantine walked around the waggons talking in transports about his wife.

"Good-bye, mates!" he shouted when the waggons moved on. "Thank you for your good cheer! I shall walk on to that fire. I can't bear it!"

He soon vanished in the gloom, and for a long while his steps were heard receding in the direction of the fire, where he would disclose his happiness to other strangers.

When Egorooshka awoke the next morning it was very early, the sun had not risen. The waggons were standing still. Some man in a white foraging-cap and wearing a costume of cheap grey material, and riding a Cossack cob, was by the foremost waggon talking with Dimov and Kiruha. About two versts ahead of the waggons was the outline of some long low store-houses, and cottages with tiled roofs; there were neither yards not trees around the cottages.

"Dad, what is that village?" asked Egorooshka.

"That, my lad, is an Armenian farm," answered Panteli. "Armenians live there. A goodly people. . . . Armenians are."

The man in grey, having finished speaking with Dimov and Kiruha, reined back his horse and turned to look at the farm.

"What an affair, just think!" sighed Panteli, also looking at the farm, and hugging himself, chilled by the early morning air. "He sent a man to the farm for some papers, and he has not come back. He ought to have sent Stepka."

"Who is that, dad?" inquired Egorooshka.

"Varlamov."

"My God!" Egorooshka sprang up on to his knees and looked at the white forage-cap. In that small grey-clad man, with high boots, sitting on a seedy little horse, conversing with moujiks at that hour, when all righteous people are asleep, it was hard to recognise the mysterious elusive Varlamov, whom everyone is looking for, who is always "circling," and has a great deal more money than the Countess Dranitska.

"Nitchevo, a goodly person . . ." said Panteli, gazing towards the farm. "God give him health, a fine gentleman . . . is Varlamov, Simon Alexandritch. The earth is supported by such people, mate, that's the truth. . . . The cocks have not yet crowed, and he is afoot. . . . Another would be sleeping, or sitting at home with guests tari-bari rasta-bari talking, but he the day-long circles about the steppe. . . . He does not let his affairs lie . . . he doesn't. He is a fine fellow."

Varlamov did not take his eyes off the farm, and continued to talk; the cob impatiently lifted one foot after the other.

"Simon Alexandritch," shouted Panteli taking his hat off, "allow us to send Stepka! Emilian, shout to him, that we will send Stepka!"

But at last a rider was seen coming from the farm. He slanted over to one side and the other, flourished his short leather whip above his head as if he were a Kïang, and wanted to astonish everyone with his dashing horsemanship, and came towards the waggons with the swiftness of a bird.

"That must be his patrol," said Panteli. "He has them . . . those patrols, perhaps a hundred of them or more."

When he reached the first waggon the rider reined in his horse, took off his hat, and handed Varlamov some kind of little book. Varlamov took several sheets of paper out of the booklet, read them, and exclaimed:

"But where is Ivanushka's entry?"

The rider took the booklet, looked at the papers, and shrugged his shoulders; he began saying something, probably justifying himself, and asking to be allowed to return to the farm. The cob suddenly became restive as if Varlamov had grown heavier. Varlamov was also moving about.

"Begone!" he shouted angrily, swinging his whip over the rider.

He then turned his horse back, and, still studying the booklet, passed along the waggons at a foot's pace, and as he came alongside the last waggon Egorooshka strained forward to have the best look he could at him. Varlamov was no longer young: he had a small grey beard, an honest Russian sunburnt face, which at the moment was red, wet with dew, and covered with little blue veins; his expression was just as stern and business-like as Ivan Ivanitch's, just that same fanaticism for business. Still, one felt what a difference existed between him and Ivan Ivanitch! With uncle Kuzmitchov, besides his hard man-of-business expression, there was always mingled fuss and fear that he would not find Varlamov, would be late, lose some good bargain. Nothing similar—peculiar to inferior and dependent people—was noticeable either in Varlamov's expression or in his person. This man himself made the prices; he was searching for no one, nor was he dependent on anything else. Not only was there absence of subordination in his exterior, but even in his way of holding his whip there was the consciousness of his strength and the exercise of power over the steppe.

As he went by he never even looked at Egorooshka. The cob alone honoured him with his attention, by looking at him with his large stupid eyes, and it did that much very unconcernedly. Panteli bowed low to Varlamov, which this latter noticed without taking his eyes off the slips of paper, and said:

"Good-day, old fellow."

Varlamov's dialogue with the rider and his swing of the whip evidently produced a depressing effect on all the waggoners—they all looked very serious.

The rider, discouraged by the anger of his powerful master, sat in silence with his hat off and with loosened rein by the foremost waggon, finding it hard to believe that the day should have begun so badly for him.

"A harsh old man . . ." murmured Panteli. "It's said that he is so harsh, but he is all right, a goodly person. His anger is just . . . nitchevo. . . ."

Having studied the sheets of paper, Varlamov put them into his pocket; the cob, divining his intention, did not wait for a sign, but started off at a gallop down the road.

VII

On the following night the drivers were making a halt and boiling their gruel. This time from the very first they all felt a kind of indefinable melancholy. The air was heavy; they all drank a good deal, and could not succeed in quenching their thirst. The rising moon was a deep purple, looked gloomy and indisposed; the stars were also downcast, the mist was very dense, and the distance very hazy. Nature was apprehensive and languid.

Yesterday's animation and conversation were absent around to-night's fire; everyone was weary, and spoke drowsily and unwillingly. Panteli only sighed, complained of his feet, and in fact brought the conversation round to impenitent death. Dimov lay belly-down munching bits of straw in silence; he had an expression of loathing on his face, rather as if the straw had a bad smell, looked weary and evilly-disposed. Vassia complained that his jaw was aching, and predicted bad weather; Emilian was not waving his arms, but sat in glum silence looking at the fire. Egorooshka was also depressed; walking tired him, and his head was aching from the day's heat.

When the gruel was cooked, Dimov, out of sheer boredom. sought to pick a quarrel with his companions.

"Lumpy sits the longest, and is always in first with his spoon," he said, looking spitefully at Emilian. "Such greed—always watches his chance and gets first to the gruel-pot! Was in the choir, so thinks he is—a barin! There are a lot of those choristers about the highways asking for alms."

"Well, what are you so close for?" asked Emilian, also looking spiteful.

"Just to see that you don't dip into the pot first. That's not difficult to understand."

"Fool, that's all you are!" hoarsely said Emilian.

Knowing by experience how such discourse usually ended, Panteli and Vassia intervened and tried to persuade Dimov not to quarrel about nothing.

"A chorister! . . ." not heeding them, continued the devil-may-care, smiling contemptuously. "Anyone can sing like that, seat themselves in the church by the porch, and whine: 'Give alms for the sake of Christ!' Ugh!"

Emilian remained silent. This exasperated Dimov to the utmost; he cast a look of hatred at the erstwhile singer, and said:

"He won't have anything to do with me, or I would show him what to think of himself!"

"Here now, what do you want with me, Mazeppa?" burst out Emilian. "What harm am I doing you?"

"What did you call me?" asked Dimov, straightening himself up and with blood-red eyes. "What? I, Mazeppa? Was that it? There's for you! go and look for it!"

Dimov seized the spoon out of Emilian's hand, and flung it away to one side. Kiruha, Vassia, and Stepka jumped up and went to search for it; Emilian stared pleadingly and questioningly at Panteli, then his face suddenly seemed to grow smaller and wrinkled; he blinked several times, and finally the erstwhile chorister burst into tears like a child.

Egorooshka, whose hatred of Dimov was of long-standing,

now felt that the atmosphere had become unendurably stifling and scorched his face like the flames of the grass fire; he thought of escaping to the waggons and the darkness, but that devil-may-care's angry tired eyes courted him instead. Passionately longing to say something in the highest degree offensive, he stepped up to Dimov and articulated breathlessly:

"You are the worst of the lot! I can't bear you!"

After that it would have been advisable to have run for the waggons, but he could not move from where he was, and continued:

"In the next world you'll burn in Hell! I'll complain to Ivan Ivanitch! You are *not* to insult Emilian!"

"Also say, if you please," said Dimov, grinning at him,—"All little pigs before the milk is dry on their lips squeak ukases!"

Egorooshka felt he was choking, and—a thing which had never happened to him before—he shook all over, stamped his feet, and in a shrill voice screamed:

"Beat him! Beat him!"

The tears welled in his eyes, of which he was so ashamed that he turned and ran to the waggons. He did not see what impression his scream had made. He lay on a bale sobbing, and thumping with his hands and feet, while he called:

"Mamma! Mamma!"

The people, the shadows around the fire, the black bales of wool, the distant lightning flashing every minute on the horizon, all now seemed to him unearthly and grim. He was frightened, and in his despair asked himself how and why he had arrived in these unknown parts in the company of dreadful moujiks? Where now were his uncle, Father Christopher, and Deniski? Why are they so long away? Have they forgotten him? At the idea that he was forgotten and abandoned to the buffetings of fate he shuddered, and such dread fell on him that several times he had almost resolved to jump off the bales, and run back along the road without once turning round; but the thought of the dark gloomy crosses, which he would surely encounter on his way, and the distant flashes of lightning deterred him. It was only when he whispered "Mamma, Mamma," that he felt a little better.

Dread must also have fallen on the drivers, for after Egorooshka had escaped from the side of the fire, they remained a long while silent; then in undertones they alluded to something that was coming, and that they must make all haste to depart and go away from it. . . . They supped in a hurry, put out the fire, and put the horses to in silence. By the bustle and their discontented phrases, it was evident that they foresaw some misfortune.

Before they started on their way, Dimov went up to Panteli and asked softly:

"What is his name?"

"Egor . . ." answered Panteli.

Dimov placed one foot on the wheel, and raised himself by a rope which was bound round a bale, and Egorooshka caught sight of a face and a curly head. Dimov was pale, looked tired and grave, but no longer spiteful.

"Era!" he called softly. "Go on, beat me!"

Egorooshka looked at him in surprise; at that moment there was a flash of lightning.

"Nitchevo, beat me," repeated Dimov.

But, not waiting for Egorooshka either to beat him or speak to him, he jumped down, saying:

"Ugh! It's wearisome!"

Then rolling and swinging his shoulders, he lazily dragged himself along the line of waggons, repeating as he went, in a semi-wailing, semi-vexed voice:

"It's wearisome! Oh, Lord! But don't be offended, Emilian," he said as he passed Emilian. "Ours is a cruel damned life!"

There was a flash of lightning on the right, and exactly as if there had been a reflection in a mirror it was repeated in the far distance.

"Egor, here take this!" shouted Panteli, throwing him up something large and black.

"What is it?" asked Egorooshka.

"A mat to cover you when the rain comes."

Egorooshka raised himself and took a look round. The horizon was growing visibly blacker, and already a pale light blinked as frequently as if it had eyes. The blackness, just as if it were overweighted, was bending to the right.

"Dad, is there going to be thunder?" inquired Egorooshka.

"Oh! my poor feet—they pester me!" drawled Panteli, not listening to him and treading painfully along.

To the left someone seemed to strike a match in the sky—a pale phosphorescent streak gleamed and went out. There was a very distant sound as of someone walking over an iron roof; very likely that someone was barefooted, for the iron gave a hollow rumble.

"It's all around," cried Kiruha.

Betwixt the distance and the right of the horizon the lightning flashed so brightly that it illumined part of the steppe, and the spot where the clear sky bordered on the dark. A tremendous cloud, with large black tatters hanging along its edge, slowly moved in one compact mass; similar tatters, pressing one over the other, were gathering on the right and the left horizon. This ragged and tatter-demalion condition of the clouds gave them a kind of drunken, devil-may-care appearance. Sharply, and no longer dully, sounded the thunder. Egorooshka crossed himself, and quickly put on his coat.

"It's wearisome!" came Dimov's cry from the foremost waggon, and by the tone of his voice one might conclude that he was getting angry again. "Wearisome!"

Suddenly a wind got up, and with such violence that it nearly carried away Egorooshka's bundle and mat; the mat sprang up, straining on all sides and flapping the bales, and in Egorooshka's face. The wind whistled and tore over the steppe, whirled about frantically, and raised such a noise in the grass that it deadened the sound of the thunder and the screech of the wheels. It blew from the black cloud, bearing with it tomes of dust, and a smell of rain and damp earth. The light of the moon grew dim, or as it were dirtier, the stars became more overcast, and one saw the fog of dust and its shadow rolling hurriedly back along the side of the road. By now, in all probability, the whirlwind, in its evolutions having drawn up the dust, the dry grass, and feathers from the ground, has reached the sky itself; probably by that very dark cloud that rolling-flax are flying, and surely how frightened they must be! But through the dust which stopped up one's eyes nothing was to be seen except the flashes of lightning.

Egorooshka, thinking every minute that the rain would come, knelt up and covered himself in the mat.

"Pantel-li," cried someone in front; ". . . a . . . re . . . !"

"Can't hear!" loudly and hoarsely answered Panteli.

"A . . . a . . . re! Fa—ar!"

The thunder rolled over the sky from right to left, then back, demising somewhere near the foremost waggon.

"Holy, holy, holy Lord God of Sabaoth," whispered Egorooshka, crossing himself, "Heaven and earth are full of Thy praise. . . ."

The lurid sky opened its mouth and breathed out white fire, immediately the thunder roared; hardly had it ceased when there flamed such a brilliant flash of lightning that through the rents in the mat Egorooshka saw for an instant the whole wide road to its farthest end, all the drivers, and even Kiruha's waiscoat. The black tatters on the left were ascending, and one of them, a scraggy ugly one, like a paw with outspread toes, was approaching the moon. Egorooshka decided to close his eyes, to take no further notice, and wait till it was all over.

The rain, for some reason, was very long in coming. Egorooshka, in the hope that the cloud had passed away, looked out from the mat. It was terribly dark. Egorooshka could not see Panteli, nor the bales, nor himself. He glanced at the place where lately the moon had been; as deep a gloom reigned there as over the waggons, while in the dark the flashes of lightning seemed so frequent and blinding that they hurt one's eyes.

"Panteli!" called Egorooshka.

There came no answer. But now, finally, one last time the wind harried the mat and fled some whither away. Then was heard an even calm noise. A large cold drop fell on to Egorooshka's knee, another crept on to his hand. He noticed that his knees were not covered up, and thought of arranging the mat: but at that moment there was a pelting and a tapping on the road, on the horses, and the bales. The rain had come. It and the mat seemed to understand each other. They spoke of something hurriedly, gaily and disputatiously like two magpies.

Egorooshka knelt up, or rather sat back on his heels. When the rain pattered on to the mat, he leant forward with his body to protect his knees, but on the other hand, in less than a minute, he felt an uncomfortable dampness behind, in the lower part of his back and in the calves. He returned to his former position, left his knees to the rain, and thought over what was to be done to adjust the invisible mat in the dark. His hands were wet and his sleeves. Water was trickling down his collar, and he was chilly about the shoulders; so he decided to do nothing but sit still and wait till it was all over.

"Holy, holy, holy . . ." he murmured.

Suddenly, with a fearful deafening din, the skies were smashed just above his head; he crouched and held his breath, waiting for the fragments to rattle down on his head and back. He involuntarily opened his eyes, and saw a blinding bright light as it were bursting and gleaming five times at the tips of his fingers, along his wet sleeves, and down the trickles flowing over the mat, the bales, and down on to the ground. There was another clap of thunder louder and more alarming than ever. It was no longer a rattle and a rumble overhead, but a crisp crackling noise like the dry crackle of a falling tree.

"Trrrach! Tach! Tach! Tach!" clearly rapped out the thunder, rolling about the sky, stumbling somewhere over the foremost waggon, or else somewhere far behind gave it up with a last spiteful exclamation of "Trra!"

At first the lightning had only been alarming, now with this thunder it was fraught with malice. Its magic light transpierced one's closed eyelids, and sent a cold shiver through one's body. What was to be done not to see it?

Egorooshka decided to turn and face the other way. Very carefully, as if afraid that he was being watched, he stood on all fours, and pressing the palms of his hands on the wet bale of wool, he turned himself round.

"Trrrach! Tach! Tach!" again sounded over his head, fell by the waggon, and died away with a "Rrr!"

Again Egorooshka involuntarily opened his eyes, and saw a new danger this time: behind the waggons walked three enormous giants with pikes! The lightning darted about the points of their pikes and clearly admitted their forms to be descried. They were of immense size, with invisible faces, bowed heads, and a ponderous tread. They seemed to be sad and low-spirited, absorbed in deep meditation. Very likely they were not marching behind the waggons to do them any harm, yet their presence was fearsome.

Egorooshka quickly turned the other way, and, trembling all over, called out:

"Panteli! Dad!"

"Trrach! Tach! Tach!" answered the heavens.

He looked to see if the drivers were there: the lightning flashed on both sides, and lit up the highway to its farthest end, all the train of waggons and the drivers. Alongside the road there were flowing streams all over bubbles. Panteli was tramping along by the waggon; he had covered his head and shoulders with a small mat, he evinced no alarm or uneasiness, no more than if he had been deaf to the thunder and blind to the lightning.

"Dad! The giants!" Egorooshka called to him, sobbing.

But the old dad did not hear. Farther on walked Emilian; he was covered in a large mat from head to foot, and formed an exact triangle. Vassia had no covering, and was stepping along as woodenly as ever, raising each foot very high and not bending his knees. At each flash of lightning it looked as if the train of waggons was at a standstill, as if the drivers had congealed and Vassia's leg was numbed. . . . Egorooshka again called the old man. Receiving no answer, he sat there motionless, no longer expecting it all to be over. He was convinced that the thunder would kill him the very next minute, that his eyes would open unexpectedly and he would see the dreadful giants. He no longer crossed himself, nor called the old dad, nor thought of his mother; he simply grew torpid with cold and the conviction that the thunderstorm would never end.

Suddenly there was the sound of a voice.

"Egor—ho there! Are you asleep?" shouted Panteli from below. "Come down! Are you deaf, little fool?"

"That *was* a storm!" said an unknown deep voice, as husky as if the owner had but just swallowed an excellent glass of vodka.

Egorooshka opened his eyes. Below stood Panteli, the triangular Emilian, and the giants. These latter were now of much smaller stature, and when he examined them Egorooshka saw they were ordinary moujiks, carrying on their shoulders not pikes but the usual pitchforks. In the space between Panteli and Emilian shone the light from the window of a low little cottage. Evidently the waggons were standing in a village. Egorooshka threw off the mat, picked up his bundle, and hurried off the waggon. Now that people were talking quite close to him and there was the light of a window, he was no longer afraid, although the thunder was crackling as before and the lightning was streaking the skies.

"It was a fine thunderstorm, nitchevo," mumbled Panteli. "Thank God . . . my feet are a little better from the bit of rain—they're all right. . . . You coming, Egor? So, go into the cottage! . . . Nitchevo . . ."

"Holy, holy, holy . . ." said Emilian hoarsely. "It must have struck somewhere. . . . Are you of this place?" he asked the giants

"Nay, from Glinov. . . . We are Glinovskis. We work for the master Platerov."

"Threshing, eh?"

"Various things; at present we are wheat-gathering. And the lightning—eh, the lightning! It's a long time since there's been such a storm. . . ."

Egorooshka went into the cottage; he was met by a lean hump-backed old woman with a pointed chin. She held in her hand a tallow candle, screwed up her eyes, and breathed heavily.

"Such a storm God sent us!" she said. "Our folk are in the steppe for the night, a bit rough, poor dears. Undress, batushka, undress. . . ."

Trembling with cold and with a squeamish hesitancy. Egorooshka discarded his soaking coat, and stood for a long while without moving, with his legs apart and his arms held far from his body. The smallest movement recalled to him the unpleasantness of being cold and wet. The sleeves and back of his shirt were wet, his trousers clave to his legs, water was dripping from his head. . . .

"How now, laddie. what do you make bandy-legs for?" said the old woman. "Come and sit down."

Keeping his legs well apart, Egorooshka walked up to the table, and sat down on a bench close to someone's head. The head moved, heaved a deep breath through its nose, chewed a bit, and then was quiet. There was a mound stretching away from the head covered in a sheep-skin coat. It was some sleeping woman.

The old woman sighed, went out, and soon returned with a water-melon and a melon.

"Eat, batushka, there's nothing else . . ." she said yawning, then fumbling on the table she produced from there a long sharp knife, very similar to those wherewith robbers cut merchants' throats in taverns. "Eat, dear sir!"

Egorooshka, trembling as if he had fever on him, ate a slice of melon with some black bread. Then a slice of water-melon; after that he felt even colder.

"Our folk are in the steppe for the night . . ." sighed the old woman whilst he was eating. "Our Saviour's Passion! . . . I'd light the little lamp before the image, but I don't know where Stepanida has put it. Eat, batushka, eat. . . ."

The old woman yawned, and, bending her right arm, scratched her left shoulder.

"Must be two o'clock by now," she said. "Soon time to get up. Our folk are in the steppe. . . . They'll all be wet. . . ."

"Batushka," said Egorooshka, "I'm sleepy."

"Lie down, batushka, lie down . . ." sighed the old woman with a yawn. "Lord Jesus Christ! Myself I was sleeping, and heard as 'twere a knocking. I awoke and said 'It's God's own storm.' . . . I'd light the little lamp, but can't find it."

Talking to herself, she took from the bench some kind of rags—probably her bed, unhooked two sheep-skins from a nail by the stove, and spread them out for Egorooshka.

"That storm does not abate," she mumbled on. "Howbeit till now nothing's burnt. Our folks too are in the steppe. Lie down, batushka; go to sleep. . . . Christ be with you, childie. . . . I'll leave the melon, perhaps you'll eat some more."

The sighs and yawns of the old woman, the continuous breathing of the woman asleep, the crepuscular light of the cottage, the patter of rain on the window, all conduced to slumber. Egorooshka was shy of undressing before the old woman, so he only took off his boots, then lay down and covered himself with the sheep-skins.

"The little lad has lain down?" in a few moments came a whisper from Panteli.

"He has lain down," answered the old woman in a whisper. "Our Saviour, our Saviour's Passion! It is thundering, thundering—when will it end? . . ."

"It'll be over soon," hoarsely whispered Panteli, seating himself. "It's got quieter. . . . The boys have gone into the cottages, and two have stayed with the horses . . . the boys have. . . . They must . . . or the horses'd be stolen. . . . I'll sit a bit, then I'll take a shift. . . . We must, they'd be stolen. . . ."

Panteli and the old woman sat side by side at Egorooshka's feet speaking in sibilant whispers, interrupting their talk with sighs and yawns. Meanwhile, Egorooshka could not get warm; he had over him that thick heavy sheep's coat, but all the same he was shivering, and he had cramp in his hands and feet. . . . He undressed himself beneath his sheep's covering, but that did not help. His feeling of cold grew worse and worse.

Panteli went out to take his shift, and then returned, and still Egorooshka could not sleep and was shivering all over. Something was pressing on his head and chest, and he did not know what it was—whether it was the old people murmuring, or the oppressive smell of the sheep-skins; also the slices of melon and water-melon had left an unpleasant metallic taste in his mouth; to add to it all, he was being bitten by fleas.

"Dad, I'm cold," he said, and hardly recognised his own voice.

"Go to sleep, childie, go to sleep," sighed the old woman.

The thin-legged little Tit approached the bed, waved his arms, then grew up to the ceiling and became the windmill. Father Christopher, not as he was when he sat in the vehicle, but in full priestly vestments, with the aspergill in his hand, walked around the windmill, sprinkling it well with holy water, whereupon it ceased to wave its fans. Egorooshka, realising this was delirium, opened his eyes.

"Dad," he called, "give me some water."

No one answered. Egorooshka was finding it unbearably stuffy, and very uncomfortable lying down. He got up, put on his clothes, and went outside the cottage. The dawn was rising, the sky was overcast, but it was no longer raining. Shivering and wrapping himself up in his wet coat, Egorooshka walked across the muddy yard, listening to the silence; he caught sight of a little shed with a grass mat over its half-open doorway. He peeped into the shed, walked in, and sat on a perch in a dark corner.

His head was aching, his thoughts were getting mixed, and his mouth was dry and unpleasant from the metallic taste. He gazed at his hat, straightened the peacock's feather and remembered how he had gone with his mother to buy that hat. He put his hand in his pocket, and extracted thence a clod of brown sticky mastic. However did that mastic get into his pocket? He reflected, smelt it: it smelt of honey. Ah-ha, it was the Jewess's ginger-bread! How soft the poor thing had become!

Egorooshka looked at his coat. His coat was grey, with large bone buttons arranged like those of an overcoat. Being a new and expensive article, it hung at home not in the vestibule but in the bedroom alongside of his mother's clothes, and he was only allowed to wear it on festivals and holidays. Egorooshka, as he looked at it now, felt sorry for it; he recollected that he and the coat were both abandoned to the buffetings of fate, that he would never go back home, and he sobbed so that he nearly fell off his perch.

A large white dog drenched by the rain, with tufts of hair on his face somewhat resembling curling-papers, entered the shed and stared very inquisitively at Egorooshka. It evidently was wondering if it should bark. Having decided not to bark, it went carefully up to Egorooshka, ate the mastic, and went out again.

"It's Varlamov's!" cried someone from the road.

When he had cried himself out, Egorooshka came out of the shed, skirted a large puddle, and slowly went towards the street. Exactly by the gates on the road stood the train of waggons. The wet drivers, with muddy boots, looking as sleepy as autumn flies, were hanging round or sitting on the thills of the waggons. Egorooshka looked at them, and thought, "How tiresome and uncomfortable to be a moujik!" He went up to Panteli, and sat by his side on a thill.

"Dad, I'm cold!" he said, shivering and pulling his sleeves down over his hands.

"It's all right, we'll soon be moving," yawned Panteli. "It doesn't matter—you'll soon be warm."

The waggons moved on early, as it was not too warm. Egorooshka lay on the bale of wool, trembling with cold, although the sun soon appeared in the skies and dried his clothes, the bales and the ground. Each time he closed his eyes he saw Tit and the windmill. Conscious of a languor and heaviness creeping over him, he exerted all his strength to drive away those figures, but they had hardly disappeared when the devil-may-care Dimov flung himself at Egorooshka with a shout, blood-shot eyes and upraised fists, and he heard him complaining, "It's wearisome!" Varlamov on his Cossack cob went by, and the happy Constantine walked past with his smile and his bustard. How heavy, unbearable, and irksome these people were!

Then—this was towards evening—he raised his head to ask for something to drink. The waggons were standing by a large bridge spanning a wide river. There was a smoke over the river, and through the smoke was a steamer with a barge in tow. Over the river in front was a high hill dotted with houses and churches; at the foot of the hill, by some goods vans, there was a locomotive moving about.

Never before had Egorooshka seen steamers or locomotives, or wide rivers Gazing upon them now he felt neither fear nor astonishment, not even the faintest resemblance to curiosity was depicted on his face. He only felt giddy, and hastened to lie downwards on the edge of the bales, and was sick. Panteli, noticing this, turned round, and exclaimed:

"Our little laddie is taken ill. It must be a chill . . . the laddie has. . . . Away from home. . . . Bad affair!"

VIII

The waggons halted not far from the wharf of a large commercial inn. As he slid down from the waggon, Egorooshka recognised a very well-known voice. Someone was helping him to descend, and saying:

"But we arrived last evening. We have waited a whole day for you. They thought to overtake you last night, but it didn't work, they took another road. Eh, but how you've crumpled your coat! You'll catch it from your uncle!"

Egorooshka looked at the marble face of him who was addressing him, and recognised Deniski.

"Your uncle and Father Christopher are in their rooms," continued Deniski, "drinking tea. Come alone!"

He led Egorooshka into a large two-storied building, dark and gloomy and similar to the charitable institution in N——. They crossed the vestibule, passed up a dark staircase and through a long narrow passage, and entered a small room in which there indeed sat Ivan Ivanitch and Father Christopher drinking tea. When they saw the boy both the old fellows expressed much joy and surprise.

"Ah, Egor Nicola-aitch," half sang Father Christopher—"Mr. Lomonossov!"

"Ah, noble young man," said Kuzmitchov, "be welcome!"

Egorooshka took off his coat, kissed his uncle's hand and Father Christopher's, then sat down at the table.

"Well, how has *puer bone* fared?" Father Christopher began, overwhelming him with questions, pouring him out some tea, and, as usual, with a radiant smile on his face. "I'm afraid he was bored. God forbid travelling on waggons or bullocks! You go on and on—the Lord forgive me—you look ahead, and the steppe is just the same vast stretch as before: you can't even see the beginning of the end! It's no progression, it's a scandal! What—you won't drink tea? Drink it! While you were crawling along with the waggons, we have satisfactorily settled our business, thank God! Sold the work to Tcherepahin, and God grant the like to everyone. . . . We did very well."

When he first rejoined his own again, Egorooshka's almost irresistible inclination was to complain. He did not listen to Father Christopher, but cogitated how he should begin and of what he should complain: then Father Christopher's voice sounded so unpleasant and harsh that it prevented him from concentrating his thoughts, and confused them instead. He had hardly sat five minutes at the table when he got up, went to the sofa, and lay down.

"Well, now!" exclaimed Father Christopher. "And what about your tea?"

Still cogitating what he could say, Egorooshka hid his face against the back of the sofa, and burst out crying.

"Well, now!" repeated Father Christopher, getting up and going to the sofa. "Egorie, what's the matter with you? Why are you crying?"

"I . . . I am ill," sobbed Egorooshka.

"Ill?" said Father Christopher anxiously. "But that's very wrong, lad. How do you get ill on the way? Aie, aie,—lad, what do you feel, eh?"

He lay his hand on Egorooshka's forehead, stroked his cheek, and said:

"Yea, your head is burning. . . . You must have got a chill, or eaten something. . . . Say a prayer to God."

"Give him some quinine," said Ivan Ivanitch, rather worried.

"Nay, better give him something hot. . . . Egorie, will you take a little soup? Eh?"

"Don't . . . don't want any," answered Egorooshka.

"Did you get cold—what?"

"Before I was cold, now . . . now I'm hot. I've pain everywhere."

Ivan Ivanitch went up to the sofa, touched Egorooshka lightly on the head, gave a troubled cough, and returned to the table.

"Come now, you'll undress and go to bed," said Father Christopher; "it's sleep you want."

He helped Egorooshka to undress, gave him a pillow, covered him up, and put Ivan Ivanitch's coat over him as well, then moved away on tiptoe, and sat at the table. Egorooshka closed his eyes, and at once began to feel that he was not in the room at all, but on the highway by the fire. Emilian was waving his hands, and Dimov, red-eyed, was lying belly-down, looking derisively at Egorooshka.

"Beat him! Beat him!" screamed Egorooshka.

"He is delirious," said Father Christopher in an undertone.

"What a nuisance!" sighed Ivanitch.

"We ought to rub him with oil and vinegar. God grant he be better to-morrow."

So as to shake off his heavy dreamings, Egorooshka opened his eyes, and looked into the fire. Father Christopher and Ivan Ivanitch had finished their tea, and were whispering together. The former was smiling happily, and apparently could not at all forget the good prices they had got for the wool: it was not so much the thought of the profit which cheered him, as the idea that when he got back he would collect all his large family, slily wink and laugh, at first mislead them all, and say that the wool was sold below its price, then hand to his son-in-law Michael a fat roll of papers, saying to him: "There, take it: that's the way to do business!" Kubmitchov did not seem satisfied; his face wore the same stern worried man-of-business expression as usual.

"How could one know Tcherepahin would give those prices?" he said in an undertone. "I would not have sold those three hundred pouds at home to Makarov. How vexatious! But who could know prices would have gone up here?"

A man in a white shirt carried away the samovar and lit the little image-lamp in the corner. Father Christopher whispered something in his ear, he put on a face of mystery like a conspirator—I quite understand—left the room, and returned shortly after bringing the required article. Ivan Ivanitch made himself a bed on the floor, yawned several times, lazily said some prayers, then lay down.

"I'm thinking of going to the Cathedral to-morrow morning," said Father Christopher. "There is a sacristan there I know. I must go to his Eminence after Mass, but they say he is ill."

He yawned, and put out the lamp; the only light that remained was the little image-lamp.

"They say he won't receive anyone," continued Father Christopher disrobing. "But I'll go even if he doesn't see me."

He removed his caftan, and Egorooshka saw before him Robinson Crusoe. Robinson mixed something in a saucer, went up to Egorooshka, and whispered to him:

"Lomonossov, you asleep? Get up a bit; I'll rub you with oil and vinegar. It'll do you good, say only a prayer to God."

Egorooshka quickly sat himself up. Father Christopher took off his shirt, and, breathing jerkily as if it was he who was being tickled, set about rubbing Egorooshka's chest.

"In the Name of the Father, the Son, and the Holy Ghost . . ." he murmured. "Lie with your back up—that's it—you'll be quite well to-morrow, but don't do it in future. You are like a fire, you are so hot. I'm afraid you had a storm on the way?"

"We had."

"That's enough to make you fall ill! In the Name of the Father, Son, and Holy Ghost. . . . That's quite enough!"

Having rubbed Egorooshka, Father Christopher put his shirt on, covered him up, made the Sign of the Cross, and left him. Egorooshka then saw him say his prayers. Very likely the old man knew a great number of prayers by heart, for he stood a long time whispering before the image. When he had finished he made the Sign of the Cross to the window, the door, Egorooshka, Ivan Ivanitch; lay on a little sofa without a pillow, and covered himself over with his caftan. In the corridor the clock struck ten Egorooshka, remembering how many hours there would be before morning, in anguish pressed his forehead against the back of the sofa, and no longer made any attempt to rid himself of the hazy troublesome delirium. And morning came sooner than he expected.

He seemed to have been quite a short while with his forehead against the sofa's back, yet when he unclosed his eyes there was a streak of sunlight streaming on the floor from both windows of their room. Father Christopher and Ivan Ivanitch were not there. The room was tidy, light and comfortable, and smelt of Father Christopher, who always exuded a smell of cypress and cornflower (at home he always made the aspergill and ornaments for the image-cases of cornflowers, so that he was permeated with the scent of them). Egorooshka took a look at his pillow, at the oblique sun-rays, at his boots, which had now been cleaned and had been placed by the side of the sofa—and smiled. It seemed to him odd not to be on the bales of wool, that everything around him should be dry, and that there was no thunder or lightning in the ceiling.

He sprang off the sofa, and started dressing. He felt extremely well: nothing remained of yesterday's illness except a slight weakness in the legs, and a little pain in the neck. Evidently the oil and vinegar had been very effectual. He remembered the steamer, the locomotive, the broad river, which he had indistinctly seen the previous day, and now hurried through his dressing so as to turn down to the wharf and look at them. When he had washed, and was putting on his red fustian shirt, there was a rattle at the lock of the door, and on the threshold appeared Father Christopher in his wide-brimmed hat, his staff in his hand, and wearing his brown silk cassock over the linen caftan. Smiling and beaming (old men who have just returned from the church always beam), he laid his wafer and some kind of parcel on the table, and with a prayer asked:

"God be with us! Well, how are you?"

"I'm all right now," answered Egorooshka, kissing his hand.

"Thank God! . . . I've just come from Mass. . . . I went and saw the sacristan I knew. He invited me to come and have some tea; I did not go. I don't like being a guest so early. God be with them!"

He took off his cassock, stroked his chest, and without haste undid his parcel, whereupon Egorooshka saw a small tin of soft caviar, a bit of dried sturgeon, and some French roll.

"There, I went past a fish-shop and bought this," said Father Christopher. "One can't live sumptuously every work and week-day, was my thought, and at home nothing like it, so it is as it were excusable. It's good caviar too—it's sturgeon."

The man in the white shirt brought in the samovar and some plates on a tray.

"Here, eat," said Father Christopher, spreading some caviar on a slice of bread and handing it to Egorooshka; "but then go for a walk—the time for your studies is drawing near. Now see, learn carefully and diligently, that there be some result. If it is learning by heart, learn by heart, and if it is to express thoughts in your own words, no matter the form, use your own words. But strive to learn all there is to be learnt. Some know mathematics very well, and never heard of Peter the Hermit: others have heard of Peter the Hermit, and cannot explain the moon. That won't do; try to learn so that you understand it all! Learn Latin, French, German, Geography of course—History, Theology, Philosophy, Mathematics. . . . And when you have learnt it all, not with undue haste, but with prayers and with zeal, then enter the service. When you know everything, any career is easy to you. Only study; acquire these blessings, and God will show you what you are to do—whether it is doctor or judge or engineer or what. . . ." Father Christopher spread a little caviar on a small slice of bread, placed it in his mouth, and said:

"The Apostle Paul says: 'Strive not after strange and diverse learnings.' Of course, should it be black magic, idle talk of calling-up spirits from the world beyond, like Saul, or such like sciences, no use in themselves or to people, then it is better not to learn. It is necessary to discriminate what is favourable unto God. Do like this. . . . The holy Apostles spoke in all languages, therefore you learn languages. Vassili the Great taught mathematics and philosophy, therefore learn these; Saint Nestor wrote history, therefore learn and write history. Do as the saints did."

Father Christopher sipped out of his saucer, wiped his lips, and slowly turned his head.

"Good!" he said "Formerly I learnt a lot. I've forgotten a good deal, yet all the same I live differently from the rest—one can't even make a comparison. For instance, if in company after dinner, or at some assembly or other, someone quotes in Latin, or speaks of history or philosophy, people like it, and I too like it . . . or even when the District Judge comes round, and they have to swear in, all the other priests are embarrassed, but I am hail-fellow with the judge and the procurators and the attorneys; I can talk learnedly with them, I have tea with them, we joke, I tell them things they don't know . . . and they like it. So there it is, lad. Learning is light, and ignorance darkness. Study! It is hard, of course. At the present time it is difficult to dispense with learning. . . . Your mamma is a widow, lives on a pension, and you see besides . . ."

Father Christopher looked apprehensively towards the door, and continued in a low tone:

"Ivan Ivanitch will help. He won't forsake you. He has no children of his own, and he will help you—don't worry!"

He looked very grave, and pursued, in a still lower tone:

"Only look, Egorie, God forbid that you should forget your mother and Ivan Ivanitch. Honour your mother is one of the Ten Commandments, and Ivan Ivanitch is your benefactor and takes the place of your father; for if you really become learned, God forfend that you should be annoyed or set people at naught by reason of their being stupider than you, for then woe, woe to you!" Father Christopher raised his hand aloft, and repeated in a shrill voice:

"Woe! Woe to you!"

Father Christopher, having got into his talking mood, was quite wound up, and would not have finished till dinner-time had not the door opened, and Ivan Ivanitch walked in. Uncle hastily greeted them, sat down at the table, and quickly began gulping down his tea.

"Well, all the business is done," he said. "We ought to go back home to-day, but then there is more bother with Egor. We must settle him. My sister said that some friend of hers, Nastasia Petrovna, lives somewhere here, and maybe will have him and look after him."

He fumbled among his papers, and produced a crumpled letter and read:

" 'Malaya Nijnaya Street, Nastasia Petrovna Toskunova, her own house.' We must go and look for it at once. What a bother!"

Directly they had finished their tea, Ivan Ivanitch and Egorooshka left the commercial inn.

"What a bother!" mumbled the uncle. "You've fastened on to me like a burdock—to God with you! You want education and nobility, and I only have worries with you. . . ."

When they crossed the yard, there were no longer any waggons or drivers—they had all left the wharf early in the morning. In the farthest corner of the yard stood the familiar britchka; by it were the bays eating some oats.

"Good-bye, britchka!" thought Egorooshka.

They first had a long climb up a hill along the boulevard, then they crossed a large market-place: here Ivan Ivanitch inquired of a constable where the Malaya Nijnaya was.

"Ugh!" smiled the constable. "It's a long way, over by the pasture."

On the way they met several little open cabs, but such a weakness as to drive in a cab uncle did not allow himself, save on very exceptional occasions, or on very high holidays. He and Egorooshka walked a long way through paved streets, and streets where there was only a footpath and no paved road, and finally they reached a street where there was neither footpath nor paved roadway. When, by means of their legs and their tongues, they had reached the Malaya Nijnaya Street, they were both crimson, and removed their hats to mop their perspiring foreheads.

"Tell me, if you please," Ivan Ivanitch accosted an old man sitting by the door of his shop, "which is the house of Nastasia Petrovna Toskunova?"

"There is no Toskunova here," answered the old man after a little reflection. "Perhaps it is Timoshenko?"

"No, it is Toskunova."

"Excuse me, there is no Toskunova."

Ivan Ivanitch shrugged his shoulders, and walked slowly on.

"It's no good looking!" shouted the old man. "I tell you there isn't, and that means there isn't."

"Listen, auntie," said Ivan Ivanitch, addressing an old woman at a corner by a fruit-stand selling dried sunflower seeds and pears, "which is the house of Nastasia Petrovna Toskunova?"

The old woman looked at him in surprise, and laughed.

"Ay, but Nastasia Petrovna doesn't live in her own house now," she said. "Lord, it's eight years since she married her daughter and left the house to her son-in-law. Her son-in-law is there now."

With her eyes she was clearly saying: "How could you, silly folk, not know that simple fact?"

"And where is she now living?" asked Ivan Ivanitch.

"Oh, Lord!" in surprise, and clasping her hands, said the old woman. "She has been in lodgings a long time. Since eight years, when she left the house to her son-in-law. Eh, you!"

She very likely expected Ivan Ivanitch also to be surprised and exclaimed: "No, not possible!" but he very quietly inquired:

"And where is her lodging?"

The vendor turned up a sleeve, and, pointing in the direction with her bare arm, said in a piercing shrill voice.

"Go on quite straight, straight, straight . . . till you pass a little red house, and there will be a little alley on your left. Go by this little alley, and look for the third gate on the right. . . ."

Ivan Ivanitch and Egorooshka went to the little red house, turned to the left into the alley, and directed their steps towards the third gateway on the right. A grey wooden fence, with very wide rifts in it, extended on either side of these grey and very old gates; the right half of the fence inclined very far forward and threatened to fall down altogether, the left inclined back into the yard; the gates stood upright, and seemed to be choosing which would be the most comfortable way to lie down, forwards or backwards. Ivan Ivanitch undid the latch, and together with Egorooshka saw a large yard overgrown with steppe-grass and burrs. A hundred steps from the gates stood a small house with a red roof and green window-shutters. A plump woman with tucked-up sleeves, holding up the corner of her apron and strewing something on the ground, was standing in the middle of the yard, and screaming in as piercing shrill a voice as the vendswoman:

"Chick! . . . Chick! . . . Chick!"

Behind her sat a chestnut-coloured dog with pointed ears. When it saw the visitors, it ran towards the gates and barked in a tenor voice (all chestnut-coloured dogs bark in a tenor voice).

"What do you want?" shouted the woman, shielding her eyes from the sun with her hand.

"Good-day!" also shouted Ivan Ivanitch, warding off the chestnut-coloured dog with his stick. "Tell me, if you please, does Nastasia Petrovna Toskunova live here?"

"She does—and what do you want?"

Ivan Ivanitch and Egorooshka went up to her; she looked at them suspiciously, and repeated:

"What do you want with her?"

"Oh, maybe you are Nastasia Petrovna?"

"Well, I am!"

"Very pleased . . . you see, your very old friend Olga Ivanovna Kniazeva greets you. This is her son. And I, maybe you remember, am her brother Ivan Ivanitch. . . . For you are from N——; you were brought up with us, and married from there. . . ."

There was a silence. The plump woman stared idiotically at Ivan Ivanitch, as if she did not believe or understand; then it flashed on her, she clasped her hands, the oats fell out of her apron, and tears welled in her eyes.

"Olga Ivanovna!" she screamed, breathing heavily with emotion. "My very own dear! Ah, batushka, what am I doing standing here like an idiot? And you little angel mine. . . ." She threw her arms round him, bedewed his cheeks with tears, and wept heartily.

"Lord!" she said wringing her hands. "Little Olga's son! What a love! Just like his mother! Exactly like her! But what are you standing here for? Pray come in!"

Crying and breathless, and talking as she went, she hurried into the house, the guests following her slowly.

"Nothing is tidy here," she said, ushering her guests into a small stuffy room, all adorned with pictures and flower-pots. "Ah! Mother of God's Vassilissa open at least the window-shutters! Angel mine! Beauty ineffable! And I did not know that Olga had such a dear little son!"

When she was quieter, and had got accustomed to her guests, Ivan Ivanitch begged to speak to her alone. Egorooshka went into the next room; there he found a sewing-machine, in the window a bird-cage with a lark in it, and as great a number of pictures and flowers as in the other room. A little girl with flushed and puffy cheeks like Tit's, and wearing a clean print dress, sat motionless by the sewing-machine. She stared at Egorooshka, and apparently felt very shy. Egorooshka looked at her in silence for a little while, then asked:

"What's your name?"

The girl moved her lips, looked ready to cry, and answered softly:

" 'Atka. . . ."

That meant: Katka.

"He will live with you," whispered Ivan Ivanitch in the other room, "if you will be so kind, and we will pay you ten roubles a month for him. He is not a spoiled little boy—very quiet. . . ."

"I don't know what to say, Ivan Ivanitch!" with a whimper sighed Nastasia Petrovna. "Ten roubles is a lot of money, but someone else's child is a dreadful responsibility, suppose he suddenly falls ill or something."

When they called Egorooshka back into the parlour, Ivan Ivanitch was standing with his hat in his hand taking his leave.

"So, then, it means for the present he can stay with you?" he said. "Good-bye! You'll stop, Egor . . ." he said, turning towards his nephew. "Don't give trouble, and obey Nastasia Petrovna. . . . Good-bye! I'll come again to-morrow."

He went out, Nastasia Petrovna once more gave Egorooshka a hug, called him an angel, and, still shedding tears of joy, began to arrange for the dinner. Not long afterwards, Egorooshka was sitting at the table by her side, answering her endless questions, and eating greasy hot sour cabbage-soup.

That evening he sat again at that same table with his head in his hand listening to Nastasia Petrovna. She, between laughing and crying, was telling him about his mother's youth; about her own marriage, her children. . . . A cricket chirped by the stove and the lamp-burner droned in an inaudible way. The woman spoke in a low voice, and every now and again dropped her thimble in her emotion; each time her grandchild Katka slid under the table after it, and spent a long time there, probably looking at Egorooshka's feet. Egorooshka sat and listened, musing and gazing at the old woman's face, her wart and its several hairs, and at her tearstains. And he felt sad, very sad! They allowed him the coffer to sleep on, and informed him if he felt hungry in the night, that he was to get up and go himself into the passage, and take some chicken from a covered plate in the window.

The next morning early, Ivan Ivanitch and Father Christopher came to say good-bye. Nastasia Petrovna was overjoyed, and was preparing to bring in the samovar, but Ivan Ivanitch, in a great hurry, waved his hand and said:

"Some other time we'll have tea and sugar with you! We are starting at once."

Before saying farewell, they all sat down a moment and remained silent. Nastasia Petrovna heaved a deep sigh, and looked with tearful eyes at the image.

"Well," began Ivan Ivanitch, rising, "so then you'll remain. . . ."

The stern business-look disappeared from his face, he flushed a little, laughed sadly, and said:

"Mind now, you study. . . . Don't forget your mother, and listen to Nastasia Petrovna. If you are a good boy, Egor, and study well, I won't forsake you."

He drew his purse from his pocket, turned his back to Egorooshka, fumbled a long time among his small change, then finding a ten-kopeck piece, handed it to Egorooshka.

Father Christopher sighed, and slowly gave his blessing to Egorooshka. "In the Name of the Father, Son, and Holy Ghost . . . study," he said. "Try hard, lad. . . . If I die, say a prayer for me. And here is a grivenik (ten-kopeck) also from me."

Egorooshka kissed his hand, and cried a little. Something whispered to him that he would never see the old man again.

"I have already, Nastasia Petrovna, forwarded the petition to the Gymnasium," said Ivan Ivanitch in a voice as if there was a corpse in the room. "You'll take him for his examination on the 7th of August. . . . Well, good-bye. God be with you! Good-bye, Egor!"

"If only you'd wait for some tea!" sobbed Nastasia Petrovna.

His eyes were so full of tears that Egorooshka did not see his uncle and Father Christopher leave the room. When he rushed to the window, they had already left the yard, and the chestnut-coloured dog was running back from the gates with the air of having fulfilled his duty of barking at someone. Egorooshka himself, not knowing why, tore from the window and fled from the room. When he got to the gates, Ivan Ivanitch and Father Christopher, the one waving his crooked stick, and the other his staff, were vanishing round the corner. Egorooshka felt that when these two people went, all that phase of life which he had known up to now was gone for ever, like smoke. . . . In sheer impotency he returned to the house, greeting with bitter tears the new unknown life which was now beginning for him. . . . What will that life be?

ROTHSCHILD'S FIDDLE

The town was small—no better than a village—and it was inhabited almost entirely by old people who died so seldom that it was positively painful. In the hospital, and even in the prison, coffins were required very seldom. In one word, business was bad. If Yakov Ivanov had been coffin-maker in the government town, he would probably have owned his own house, and called himself Yakov Matveyich; but, as it was, he was known only by the name of Yakov, with the street nickname of "Bronza" given for some obscure reason; and he lived as poorly as a simple muzhik in a little, ancient cabin with only one room; and in this room lived he, Marfa, the stove, a double bed, the coffins, a joiner's bench, and all the domestic utensils.

Yet Yakov made admirable coffins, durable and good. For muzhiks and petty tradespeople he made them all of one size, taking himself as model; and this method never failed him, for though he was seventy years of age, there was not a taller or stouter man in the town, not even in the prison. For women and for men of good birth he made his coffins to measure, using for this purpose an iron yardwand. Orders for children's coffins he accepted very unwillingly, made them without measurement, as if in contempt, and every time when paid for his work exclaimed:

"Thanks. But I confess I don't care much for wasting time on trifles."

In addition to coffin-making Yakov drew a small income from his skill with the fiddle. At weddings in the town there usually played a Jewish orchestra, the conductor of which was the tinsmith Moses Ilyich Shakhkes, who kept more than half the takings for himself. As Yakov played very well upon the fiddle, being particularly skillful with Russian songs, Shakhkes sometimes employed him in the orchestra, paying him fifty kopecks a day, exclusive of gifts from the guests. When Bronza sat in the orchestra he perspired and his face grew purple; it was always hot, the smell of garlic was suffocating; the fiddle whined, at his right ear snored the double-bass, at his left wept the flute, played by a lanky, red-haired Jew with a whole network of red and blue veins upon his face, who bore the same surname as the famous millionaire Rothschild. And even the merriest tunes this accursed Jew managed to play sadly. Without any tangible cause Yakov had become slowly penetrated with hatred and contempt for Jews, and especially for Rothschild; he began with irritation, then swore at him, and once even was about to hit him; but Rothschild flared up, and, looking at him furiously, said:

"If it were not that I respect you for your talents, I should send you flying out of the window."

Then he began to cry. So Bronza was employed in the orchestra very seldom, and only in cases of extreme need when one of the Jews was absent.

Yakov had never been in a good humour. He was always overwhelmed by the sense of the losses which he suffered. For instance, on Sundays and saints' days it was a sin to work, Monday was a tiresome day—and so on; so that in one way or another, there were about two hundred days in the year when he was compelled to sit with his hands idle. That was one loss. If anyone in town got married without music, or if Shakhkes did not employ Yakov, that was another loss. The Inspector of Police was ill for two years, and Yakov waited with impatience for his death, yet in the end the Inspector transferred himself to the government town for the purpose of treatment, where he got worse and died. There was another loss, a loss at the very least of ten rubles, as the Inspector's coffin would have been an expensive one lined with brocade. Regrets for his losses generally overtook Yakov at night; he lay in bed with the fiddle beside him, and, with his head full of such speculations, would take the bow, the fiddle giving out through the darkness a melancholy sound which made Yakov feel better.

On the sixth of May last year Marfa was suddenly taken ill. She breathed heavily, drank much water and staggered. Yet next morning she lighted the stove, and even went for water. Towards evening she lay down. All day Yakov had played on the fiddle, and when it grew dark he took the book in which every day he inscribed his losses, and from want of something better to do, began to add them up. The total amounted to more than a thousand rubles. The thought of such losses so horrified him that he threw the book on the floor and stamped his feet. Then he took up the book, snapped his fingers, and sighed heavily. His face was purple, and wet with perspiration. He reflected that if this thousand rubles had been lodged in the bank the interest per annum would have amounted to at least forty rubles. That meant that the forty rubles were also a loss. In one word, wherever you turn everywhere you meet with loss, and profits none.

"Yakov," cried Marfa unexpectedly, "I am dying."

He glanced at his wife. Her face was red from fever and unusually clear and joyful; and Bronza, who was accustomed to see her pale, timid, and unhappy-looking, felt confused. It seemed as if she were indeed dying, and were happy in the knowledge that she was leaving for ever the cabin, the coffins, and Yakov. And now she looked at the ceiling and twitched her lips, as if she had seen Death her deliverer, and were whispering with him.

Morning came; through the window might be seen the rising of the sun. Looking at his old wife, Yakov somehow remembered that all his life he had never treated her kindly, never caressed her, never pitied her, never thought of buying her a kerchief for her head, never carried away from the weddings a piece of tasty food, but only roared at her, abused her for his losses, and rushed at her with shut fists. True, he had never beaten her, but he had often frightened her out of her life and left her rooted to the ground with terror. Yes, and he had forbidden her to drink tea, as the losses without that were great enough; so she drank always hot water. And now, beginning to understand why she had such a strange, enraptured face, he felt uncomfortable.

When the sun had risen high he borrowed a cart from a neighbour, and brought Marfa to the hospital. There were not many patients there, and he had to wait only three hours. To his joy he was received not by the doctor but by the feldscher, Maksim Nikolaïch, an old man of whom it was said that, although he was drunken and quarrelsome, he knew more than the doctor.

"May your health be good!" said Yakov, leading the old woman into the dispensary. "Forgive me, Maksim Nikolaïch, for troubling you with my empty affairs. But there, you can see for yourself my object is ill. The companion of my life, as they say, excuse the expression . . ."

Contracting his grey brows and smoothing his whiskers, the feldscher began to examine the old woman, who sat on the tabouret, bent, skinny, sharp-nosed, and with open mouth so that she resembled a bird that is about to drink.

"So . . ." said the feldscher slowly, and then sighed. "Influenza and may be a bit of a fever. There is typhus now in the town . . . What can I do? She is an old woman, glory be to God. . . . How old?"

"Sixty-nine years, Maksim Nikolaïch."

"An old woman. It's high time for her."

"Of course! Your remark is very just," said Yakov, smiling out of politeness. "And I am sincerely grateful for your kindness; but allow me to make one remark; every insect is fond of life."

The feldscher replied in a tone which implied that upon him alone depended her life or death. "I will tell you what you'll do, friend; put on her head a cold compress, and give her these powders twice a day. And good-bye to you."

By the expression of the feldscher's face, Yakov saw that it was a bad business, and that no powders would make it any better; it was quite plain to him that Marfa was beyond repair, and would assuredly die, if not to-day, then to-morrow. He touched the feldscher on the arm, blinked his eyes, and said in a whisper:

"Yes, Maksim Nikolaïch, but you will let her blood."

"I have no time, no time, friend. Take your old woman, and God be with you!"

"Do me this one kindness!" implored Yakov. "You yourself know that if she merely had her stomach out of order, or some internal organ wrong, then powders and mixtures would cure; but she has caught cold. In cases of cold the first thing is to bleed the patient."

But the feldscher had already called for the next patient, and into the dispensary came a peasant woman with a little boy.

"Be off!" he said to Yakov, with a frown.

"At least try the effect of leeches. I will pray God eternally for you."

The feldscher lost his temper, and roared:

"Not another word."

Yakov also lost his temper, and grew purple in the face; but he said nothing more and took Marfa under his arm and led her out of the room. As soon as he had got her into the cart, he looked angrily and contemptuously at the hospital and said:

"What an artist! He will let the blood of a rich man, but for a poor man grudges even a leech. Herod!"

When they arrived home, and entered the cabin, Marfa stood for a moment holding on to the stove. She was afraid that if she were to lie down Yakov would begin to complain about his losses, and abuse her for lying in bed and doing no work. And Yakov looked at her with tedium in his soul and remembered that to-morrow was John the Baptist, and the day after Nikolay the Miracle-worker, and then came Sunday, and after that Monday—another idle day. For four days no work could be done, and Marfa would be sure to die on one of these days. Her coffin must be made to-day. He took the iron yardwand, went up to the old woman and took her measure. After that she lay down, and Yakov crossed himself, and began to make a coffin.

When the work was finished, Bronza put on his spectacles and wrote in his book of losses:

"Marfa Ivanovna's coffin—2 rubles, 40 kopecks."

And he sighed. All the time Marfa had lain silently with her eyes closed. Towards evening, when it was growing dark, she called her husband:

"Rememberest, Yakov?" she said, looking at him joyfully. "Rememberest, fifty years ago God gave us a baby with yellow hair. Thou and I then sat every day by the river . . . under the willow . . . and sang songs." And laughing bitterly she added: "The child died."

"That is all imagination," said Yakov.

Later on came the priest, administered to Marfa the Sacrament and extreme unction. Marfa began to mutter something incomprehensible, and towards morning, died.

The old-women neighbours washed her, wrapped her in her winding sheet, and laid her out. To avoid having to pay the deacon's fee, Yakov himself read the psalms; and escaped a fee also at the graveyard, as the watchman there was his godfather. Four peasants carried the coffin free, out of respect for the deceased. After the coffin walked a procession of old women, beggars, and two cripples. The peasants on the road crossed themselves piously. And Yakov was very satisfied that everything passed off in honour, order, and cheapness, without offence to anyone. When saying good-bye for the last time to Marfa, he tapped the coffin with his fingers, and thought "An excellent piece of work."

But while he was returning from the graveyard he was overcome with extreme weariness. He felt unwell, he breathed feverishly and heavily, he could hardly stand on his feet. His brain was full of unaccustomed thoughts. He remembered again that he had never taken pity on Marfa and never caressed her. The fifty-two years during which they had lived in the same cabin stretched back to eternity, yet in the whole of that eternity he had never thought of her, never paid any attention to her, but treated her as if she were a cat or a dog. Yet every day she had lighted the stove, boiled and baked, fetched water, chopped wood, slept with him on the same bed; and when he returned drunk from weddings, she had taken his fiddle respectfully, and hung it on the wall, and put him to bed—all this silently with a timid, worried expression on her face And now he felt that he could take pity on her, and would like to buy her a present, but it was too late. . . .

Towards Yakov, smiling and bowing, came Rothschild.

"I was looking for you, uncle," he said. "Moses Ilyich sends his compliments, and asks you to come across to him at once."

Yakov felt inclined to cry.

"Begone!" he shouted, and continued his path.

"You can't mean that," cried Rothschild in alarm, running after him. "Moses Ilyich will take offence! He wants you at once."

The way in which the Jew puffed and blinked, and the multitude of his red freckles awoke in Yakov disgust. He felt disgust, too, for his green frock-coat, with its black patches, and his whole fragile, delicate figure.

"What do you mean by coming after me, garlic?" he shouted. "Keep off!"

The Jew also grew angry, and cried:

"If you don't take care to be a little politer I will send you flying over the fence."

"Out of my sight!" roared Yakov, rushing on him with clenched fists. "Out of my sight, abortion, or I will beat the soul out of your cursed body! I have no peace with Jews."

Rothschild was frozen with terror; he squatted down and

waved his arms above his head, as if warding off blows, and then jumped up and ran for his life. While running he hopped, and flourished his hands; and the twitching of his long, fleshless spine could plainly be seen. The boys in the street were delighted with the incident, and rushed after him, crying, "Jew! Jew!" The dogs pursued him with loud barks. Someone laughed, then someone whistled, and the dogs barked louder and louder. Then, it must have been, a dog bit Rothschild, for there rang out a sickly, despairing cry.

Yakov walked past the common, and then along the outskirts of the town; and the street boys cried, "Bronza! Bronza!" With a piping note snipe flew around him, and ducks quacked. The sun baked everything, and from the water came scintillations so bright that it was painful to look at. Yakov walked along the path by the side of the river, and watched a stout, red-cheeked lady come out of the bathing-place. Not far from the bathing-place sat a group of boys catching crabs with meat; and seeing him they cried maliciously, "Bronza! Bronza!" And at this moment before him rose a thick old willow with an immense hollow in it, and on it a raven's nest. . . . And suddenly in Yakov's mind awoke the memory of the child with the yellow hair of whom Marfa had spoken. . . . Yes, it was the same willow, green, silent, sad. . . . How it had aged, poor thing!

He sat underneath it, and began to remember. On the other bank, where was now a flooded meadow, there then stood a great birch forest, and farther away, where the now bare hill glimmered on the horizon, was an old pine wood. Up and down the river went barges. But now everything was flat and smooth; on the opposite bank stood only a single birch, young and shapely, like a girl; and on the river were only ducks and geese where once had floated barges. It seemed that since those days even the geese had become smaller. Yakov closed his eyes, and in imagination saw flying towards him an immense flock of white geese.

He began to wonder how it was that in the last forty or

fifty years of his life he had never been near the river, or if he had, had never noticed it. Yet it was a respectable river, and by no means contemptible; it would have been possible to fish in it, and the fish might have been sold to tradesmen, officials, and the attendant at the railway station buffet, and the money could have been lodged in the bank; he might have used it for rowing from country-house to country-house and playing on the fiddle, and everyone would have paid him money; he might even have tried to act as bargee—it would have been better than making coffins; he might have kept geese, killed them and sent them to Moscow in the winter-time—from the feathers alone he would have made as much as ten rubles a year. But he had yawned away his life, and done nothing. What losses! Akh, what losses! and if he had done all together—caught fish, played on the fiddle, acted as bargee, and kept geese—what a sum he would have amassed! But he had never even dreamed of this; life had passed without profits, without any satisfaction; everything had passed away unnoticed; before him nothing remained. But look backward—nothing but losses, such losses that to think of them it makes the blood run cold. And why cannot a man live without these losses? Why had the birch wood and the pine forest both been cut down? Why is the common pasture unused? Why do people do exactly what they ought not to do? Why did he all his life scream, roar, clench his fists, insult his wife? For what imaginable purpose did he frighten and insult the Jew? Why, indeed, do people prevent one another living in peace? All these are also losses! Terrible losses! If it were not for hatred and malice people would draw from one another incalculable profits.

Evening and night, twinkled in Yakov's brain the willow, the fish, the dead geese, Marfa with her profile like that of a bird about to drink, the pale, pitiable face of Rothschild, and an army of snouts thrusting themselves out of the darkness and muttering about losses. He shifted from side to side, and five times in the night rose from his bed and played on the fiddle.

In the morning he rose with an effort and went to the hospital. The same Maksim Nikolaïch ordered him to bind his head with a cold compress, and gave him powders; and by the expression of his face, and by his tone Yakov saw that it was a bad business, and that no powders would make it any better. But upon his way home he reflected that from death at least there would be one profit; it would no longer be necessary to eat, to drink, to pay taxes, or to injure others; and as a man lies in his grave not one year, but hundreds and thousands of years, the profit was enormous. The life of man was, in short, a loss, and only his death a profit. Yet this consideration, though entirely just, was offensive and bitter; for why in this world is it so ordered that life, which is given to a man only once, passes by without profit?

He did not regret dying, but as soon as he arrived home and saw his fiddle, his heart fell, and he felt sorry. The fiddle could not be taken to the grave; it must remain an orphan, and the same thing would happen with it as had happened with the birchwood and the pine forest. Everything in this world decayed, and would decay! Yakov went to the door of the hut and sat upon the threshold stone, pressing his fiddle to his shoulder. Still thinking of life, full of decay and full of losses, he began to play, and as the tune poured out plaintively and touchingly, the tears flowed down his cheeks. And the harder he thought, the sadder was the song of the fiddle.

The latch creaked twice, and in the wicket door appeared Rothschild. The first half of the yard he crossed boldly, but seeing Yakov, he stopped short, shrivelled up, and apparently from fright began to make signs as if he wished to tell the time with his fingers.

"Come on, don't be afraid," said Yakov kindly, beckoning him. "Come!"

With a look of distrust and terror Rothschild drew near and stopped about two yards away.

"Don't beat me, Yakov, it is not my fault!" he said, with a bow. "Moses Ilyich has sent me again. 'Don't be afraid!' he said, 'go to Yakov again and tell him that without him we cannot possibly get on.' The wedding is on Wednesday. Shapovalov's daughter is marrying a wealthy man. . . . It will be a first-class wedding," added the Jew, blinking one eye.

"I cannot go," answered Yakov, breathing heavily. "I am ill, brother."

And again he took his bow, and the tears burst from his eyes and fell upon the fiddle. Rothschild listened attentively, standing by his side with arms folded upon his chest. The distrustful, terrified expression upon his face little by little changed into a look of suffering and grief, he rolled his eyes as if in ecstasy of torment, and ejaculated "Wachchch!" And the tears slowly rolled down his cheeks and made little black patches on his green frock-coat.

All day long Yakov lay in bed and worried. With evening came the priest, and, confessing him, asked whether he had any particular sin which he would like to confess; and Yakov exerted his fading memory, and remembering Marfa's unhappy face, and the Jew's despairing cry when he was bitten by the dog, said in a hardly audible voice:

"Give the fiddle to Rothschild."

And now in the town everyone asks: Where did Rothschild get such an excellent fiddle? Did he buy it or steal it . . . or did he get it in pledge? Long ago he abandoned his flute, and now plays on the fiddle only. From beneath his bow issue the same mournful sounds as formerly came from the flute; but when he tries to repeat the tune that Yakov played when he sat on the threshold stone, the fiddle emits sounds so passionately sad and full of grief that the listeners weep; and he himself rolls his eyes and ejaculates "Wachchch!" . . . But this new song so pleases everyone in the town that wealthy traders and officials never fail to engage Rothschild for their social gatherings, and even force him to play it as many as ten times.

CPSIA information can be obtained at www.ICGtesting.com
Printed in the USA
LVOW12s1627030814

397311LV00001B/142/A